THE Swallow TALES

D0726215

www.randomhousechildrens.co.uk

Also by K. M. Peyton:

PENNINGTON'S SEVENTEENTH SUMMER
THE BEETHOVEN MEDAL
PENNINGTON'S HEIR

FLAMBARDS
THE EDGE OF THE CLOUD
FLAMBARDS IN SUMMER
FLAMBARDS DIVIDED

A PATTERN OF ROSES
THE RIGHT-HAND MAN
DEAR FRED
DOWNHILL ALL THE WAY
DARKLING
POOR BADGER
THE BOY WHO WASN'T THERE
THE WILD BOY AND QUEEN MOON
WINDY WEBLEY
UNQUIET SPIRITS
FIREHEAD
THE PARADISE PONY
THE SCRUFFY PONY
PONY IN THE DARK
STEALAWAY
SMALL GAINS
GREATER GAINS
BLUE SKIES AND GUNFIRE

THE *Swallow* TALES

K. M. PEYTON

With an introduction by Meg Rosoff

CORGI BOOKS

THE SWALLOW TALES
A CORGI BOOK 978 0 552 56692 6

THE SWALLOW TALE
First published in Great Britain in 1995 by Doubleday,
an imprint of Random House Children's Publishers UK
A Random House Group Company
Copyright © K. M. Peyton, 1995

THE SWALLOW SUMMER
First published in Great Britain in 1995 by Doubleday,
an imprint of Random House Children's Publishers UK
A Random House Group Company
Copyright © K. M. Peyton, 1995

SWALLOW, THE STAR
First published in Great Britain in 1998 by Corgi,
an imprint of Random House Children's Publishers UK
A Random House Group Company
Copyright © K. M. Peyton, 1998

This collection first published as THE SWALLOW TALES by Corgi,
an imprint of Random House Children's Publishers UK
A Random House Group Company

This edition published 2012

5 7 9 10 8 6

Copyright © K. M Peyton, 2012

Penguin Random House is committed to a sustainable future for
our business, our readers and our planet. This book is made from
Forest Stewardship Council® certified paper.

MIX
Paper from
responsible sources
FSC® C018179

Set in Goudy

RANDOM HOUSE CHILDREN'S PUBLISHERS UK
61–63 Uxbridge Road, London W5 5SA

www.randomhousechildrens.co.uk
www.totallyrandombooks.co.uk
www.randomhouse.co.uk

Addresses for companies within The Random House Group Limited can be found at:
www.randomhouse.co.uk/offices.htm

THE RANDOM HOUSE GROUP Limited Reg. No. 954009

A CIP catalogue record for this book is available from the British Library.

Printed and bound in Great Britain by Clays Ltd, St Ives plc

CONTENTS

Introduction

Like many readers of my generation, I first discovered K. M. Peyton via the extraordinarily evocative *Flambards*, a book overflowing with glorious heroes and villains, affairs of the heart and history – and horses. For me, it was love at first paragraph.

It was nearly thirty years later that a wise bookseller put me onto more of Peyton's books – *Fly-by-Night*, *The Team* and, of course, the delightful *Swallow* series – and turned me into a bona fide Peyton groupie. I devoured book after book with the joy of a twelve-year-old pony-lover and the critic faculties of a hard-to-please middle-aged writer and reviewer. Neither version of myself was ever disappointed, except in the realization that so many of her books were ones I wished I'd written.

We were obviously destined to meet.

Ever the shameless American, I tracked her down and discovered not some doddery old *grande dame*, but a brilliant, sparkling writer, wit and horse-lover who had only recently given up riding following the death of her beloved mare, Essie.

'That mare would jump anything,' she told me on our first meeting, and it struck me that the same was true of the eighty-one-year-old Kathleen. Her own life has been an extraordinary tale of sailing, hiking and mountain climbing with her husband, tearing cross country on horseback, while putting dinner on the table and bringing up two daughters. What more do we ask of a true adventure heroine?

It's no surprise, then, that the details I most love in Kathleen's books are the ones she swears are true – the abandoned ponies and hopeful owners, the crashing falls and soaring jumps, the plots to save one horse or buy another, while all the time learning to ride and saving up for a bale of hay or a pair of jodhpurs without holes in the knees.

Pick up any of her novels and you enter a world of triumphs and disappointments, of young life and young love, all rendered with perfect emotional insight and subtlety. I have fallen in love with her heroes, identified with her heroines and ridden her ponies in my dreams.

Meg Rosoff

THE *Swallow* TALE

For Primrose

Chapter One

Rowan was silent, sitting in the car beside her father as they came over the brow of the hill above Long Bottom. Her father was in a bad mood, she could tell. He usually was when he came home, after the hassle of commuting from London. He wasn't a country man at all and Rowan suspected that he was regretting their move out of suburbia and into the country. Last year she had dreaded leaving London, but now she would dread moving back even more.

He drove too fast, fresh off the motorway. It was going dusk. The hedges were high and the early sloe blossom made a blurred wall, shutting out the view.

'What?'

The brakes screamed. Rowan was flung violently forward into her seat belt as the car skidded sideways and slammed up against the left-hand bank. Soft earth rained on the windows and sparks spun across the road ahead. Sparks? Rowan could not think, shocked rigid. A black shape like a flying witch's cloak filled the windscreen then disappeared into the sloe hedge. There was a crashing sound and what sounded like an animal scream mixed with the awful noise of her father swearing. His new BMW was his most darling possession.

John Watkins leaped out of the car to see the damage and Rowan followed warily. There was glass over the road, plain and coloured.

'My headlight! And the indicator! God in heaven – just what I need! Look at it!'

Rowan looked. On the bent metal frame of the headlight blood and fur were imbedded.

'It was an animal! Look! You've injured it!'

'Injured it! Pity I didn't break its ruddy neck!'

'You can't leave it. It might have a broken leg!'

Rowan ran to the hedge, standing on tiptoe to peer over. She was small for her eleven years and had difficulty making anything out. The black animal had blended into the dusk. It had gone through the hedge – she could see the broken twigs – and into the grass field, but the field was large, stretching right down to the back gardens of the village houses below and she could see nothing moving.

She helped her father kick the glass into the ditch. The front light still worked but shone crookedly sideways.

'That's a garage job! But I can claim insurance – animals are the owner's responsibility—'

'We can't just leave it,' Rowan said. 'You hit it. It's hurt.'

'Serves it right – bally animal—'

Rowan thought her father was ridiculous. Her mind was full of the black shape and the scream . . . whinny? It was a pony! The sparks had been its shoes on the road, skidding. A pony—

'I know! It's the pony Charlie was talking about! He saw it – loose on the down last week! They tried to catch it but couldn't. He said a few people had tried to catch it. No one knows where it's come from.'

'It's a disgrace! Animals roaming loose! We might have been killed!'

Sometimes her father was very childish. It wouldn't be wise to tell him he had been going too fast. Best to wait until he cooled down. No way could they leave that pony injured, but he didn't seem to realize that. They drove down through the village to their house, called Home Farm, in the middle. What had once been the farm's barns had been converted into smart houses behind it. The burglar lights came on as the car swung into the drive.

Rowan waited until her father had huffed and puffed about the accident to his wife, and then she stated that it was their duty to follow up the wounded animal.

'If you think I'm going to go out chasing the damned thing in the dark—'

'Charlie will catch it. Just run me up to the farm and I'll tell them what's happened – or I'll go on my bike – we'll do it—'

'It's dark. Daddy will run you, won't you, darling? I do think Rowan's right, dear. But won't you have your tea first?'

'No. It's urgent. I can go on my bike, Dad, honest.'

'Don't be silly,' he said.

Why did parents think there were murderers lurking all over the place? Rowan liked the village darkness with just the house windows showing golden lamps and flickering television, but her father was already agitating for street lighting. When they had had their accident he had been driving her home from her piano lesson, which she could easily have gone to on her bike (save it was a bit hilly).

'Come on, then. Jump in.'

With one headlamp doused, he drove her up the

hill. The farm where Charlie lived, High Hawes, was half a mile up on the right, a scrambling old farm whose barns had been turned not into houses but into stables. John Watkins was impressed by the fact that the family that lived there was called Hawes as well as the house, but this was actually a coincidence, not a sign of ancient family bloodlines. Certainly the family had lived there for many years – they didn't count as 'incomers' like the Watkins – but they were not real farmers like Mr Flint and Mr Bailey down in the valley – they hadn't enough land for that, only fifty acres. Mr Hawes was said to live on his wits, although he called himself a horse dealer. He had five children who were all into horses, and an absent-minded wife called Joan who was a brilliant cook.

Mr Watkins pulled up in the entrance to the yard and let Rowan out.

'Don't be all night, now. Ring me if you want a lift back.'

'No. I'll be all right.' Did he think she had no legs?

To her relief he backed out and drove away. Rowan walked up the slope into the main yard where the lights were shining. There were looseboxes all round and eager heads looked over doors at the sounds coming from the feed shed. Rowan had discovered her own paradise on earth here since coming to Long Bottom and haunted this place, doing lowly chores to earn her acceptance.

'Charlie?'

She went towards the feed shed and Charlie came out, hearing the car drive away. Charlie was seventeen, the second eldest of the Hawes children after his sister Josephine. Josephine never spoke to Rowan, but Charlie was easy-going and friendly.

'What's up?'

Rowan told him.

'Several people have seen that pony,' he said. 'I've seen it up on the downs above us. But no one can catch it. It's been down by our fences several times but every time you go near it it runs off.'

'It's in Mr Bailey's big cow field now.'

'It jumps like a stag. If we go after it, it'll jump out.'

'But it's hurt. We gave it a real crack, bashed in the headlight.'

'Fair enough. I'll come down with you. We can't leave it if it's injured. I'll just finish feeding and we'll go down in the Land Rover.'

Charlie was tall and gangly, long-legged. He looked fantastic on a horse. The Hawes children all rode brilliantly, from cool Josephine down to Shrimp the nine-year-old. Rowan had first met them – the younger ones – on the school bus. She got on well with the two middle ones, Lizzie and Hugh (she had been put in the same class as Hugh), but Charlie was her darling. He had a gypsyish look, with thick black curls, very dark eyes and spare, hollow cheeks. The others were all fair or mousy and quite ordinary in looks. Rowan was slightly nervous of Charlie, liking him so much. She would never have presumed to ask him favours ordinarily, but an injured pony – one was bound to seek help.

He told his parents where he was going – Hugh and Shrimp wanted to come too but were not allowed – and Rowan scrambled into the Land Rover beside him. She was so excited she could feel her heart bumping. If they caught the pony . . . no one knew who it belonged to . . . finders-keepers? Would her father agree? She longed to have her own pony.

'It's not a scruff,' Charlie said. 'It's nice – a Welshman by the look of him.'

They drove down the hill and turned right when they came to the village street. Rowan had a glimpse through the windows of her father getting himself a gin and tonic from the sideboard, to calm his nerves. He would be in a dreadful temper over the car. The Hawes parents didn't fuss at all and never drank gin and tonic. Rowan sighed. Life as lived by the Hawes had been a revelation to her. They all worked incredibly hard, and yet there was no coercion. The ponies and horses were a full-time job and they enjoyed it and accepted it, on top of working hard at school. The three of them at school were bright, and never took days off, in spite of all they had to do at home.

They drove up the street to the Baileys' farm, which was the last building. It was called Low Bottom. There was a house further up called, amazingly, High Bottom, and just below it one called Middle Bottom, and in the village street there was a Bottoms Up, which Rowan thought was great but her parents thought vulgar.

'I'll just call and tell Ted Bailey what we're up to. Don't want him to think he's got rustlers in the field.'

They got out of the Land Rover and Rowan walked on past the stockyards to where the gate let into the field. It was going dark and a mist lay across the bottom of the hill, out of which Ted Bailey's Friesian cows loomed menacingly. Their breath made clouds around their monotonously revolving jaws and their sad eyes stared at her. Rowan, a London girl, wasn't sure about cows.

'What you doin'?'

Rowan jumped. She turned and saw the farmer's daughter behind her, a square girl called Barbara. The Hawes family called her Babar the Elephant, which she didn't seem to mind.

'There's a pony . . .' Rowan explained what had happened.

'Aar, I saw 'um. 'E's there.'

Babar talked like a simpleton, but got one hundred per cent in maths. She had a straight no-nonsense fringe, very direct currant-bun eyes in a puddingy face, and always wore a brown anorak and gumboots. She had a pony which she adored; it was a very odd shape – 'a Fell pony gone wrong, frightened by the thoroughbred weed' according to Fred Hawes. Its name was Black Diamond.

('Sounds like a beer,' Hugh said. His pony was called Cascade.

'Like washing-up liquid,' said Shrimp. Hugh threw his dirty sponge at her and she hit him with a sweat-scraper. They fought a lot, the Hawes.)

'I think he's hurt. He ran across in front of our car and we hit him.'

'We'll need to catch 'um then.'

Charlie came back, carrying a head collar, and said,

'You got a few nuts in a bucket, Babar, that we can rattle at him?'

Babar plodded off in her gumboots and fetched the bait, and they opened the gate and went in amongst the cows. It was all right with the others, Rowan found; she was terrified of being a fool in front of these calm country people. But she could still feel her heart lurching with excitement.

A black pony was hard to see in the mist-heavy dusk, but it gave itself away by a nervous snort up the hillside. They moved towards the snort, but Charlie told the girls to hang back and went on with the bucket, talking softly into the mist. Shortly the pony came whirling down towards the gate, swerving past Charlie and skittering to a stop when it saw the girls. Rowan had a dazzled look at it, the head held high and wild, forelock on end, eyes shining, before it did an about turn and went to join the cows.

'Oh, he's gorgeous!'

Babar said, 'Darned contrary. He'll never be caught, that one.'

Charlie came back. 'He's dead lame. He needs looking at.' Rowan had never noticed. 'We'll block off the drive out to the road, open the gate, drive off the cows and see if we can tempt him into the stockyard.

Tie your pony up out in the yard, Babar, and that might attract him.'

He went and manoeuvred his Land Rover so that it was across the drive, blocking off the road, and Babar fetched her pony from his stable and tied him up outside. Rowan saw why the Hawes tribe derided him, for he was a strange-looking beast, like an old-fashioned cab horse, with large knees, a slightly swayed back, a hogged mane and a sad expression. He was a clipped-out black, a dull mousey colour, and looked as if he would have very hairy heels were they not clipped. His tail looked as if the cows had been nibbling it.

'Darling Diamond,' Babar said, kissing him on the nose. Rowan was touched. Babar came back and went off to chase the cows away from the gate and Charlie told Rowan to stand just clear of the gate and try and deflect the pony in if he came her way.

'Wave your arms at him.'

Rowan was terrified she would mess up the whole operation, being so unsure of these large and uncooperative animals, but Charlie knew what he was doing and was able to catch the pony's attention with the rattling nuts in the bucket. Having attracted it, he walked slowly back towards the gate, shaking the bucket, and the pony followed hesitantly. Charlie walked into the stockyard and started feeding the nuts to Black Diamond, who made eager, starving noises as he dived his head into the bucket. This attracted the black pony and, as Rowan shrank back to make herself invisible, he walked through the gate and into the stockyard. Rowan nipped up and shut the gate into the field, and then the stockyard gate, and the pony was caught.

'Well done!' called Charlie.

He put the bucket down and managed to get the head collar on without any difficulty. Black Diamond stood with tragic eyes, watching his feed disappearing down the other pony's throat.

'Great. Good work. That could have taken all night. We were lucky,' Charlie said.

'Clever,' said Babar admiringly.

'It's nice. Worth the bother. Finders keepers, eh, Rowan?' Charlie winked at Rowan, and Rowan felt the heart-bumping excitement come back, suffocating her. If only! To have this pony for her own . . . it was a wish that felt like madness. And as if in appeal, the pony lifted his head out of the empty bucket, looked straight at her and let out a deafening whinny.

The pony, even to her ignorant eyes, looked a beauty, as elegant and classy as Black Diamond was ill bred. He was very dark brown or black, with a small snip of white between his nostrils and a star on his forehead. He stood about fourteen hands, and was strongly built, but with a fine neck and shoulders and a very pretty head.

'A Welshman,' Charlie said. 'With a dash of thoroughbred, I'd say.' He was looking at the pony's legs to find the damage. 'Hold him for me, will you?'

Rowan took the head-collar rope. She had never held a pony before. She could smell his hot, nervous breath on her hand and see the glint in his eye. He looked wild, but stood quietly, trembling.

There was a gash on his off foreleg just above the knee, and the knee was swollen, but nothing terrible.

'He'll be stiff for a day or two. Have you got a stable for him down here, Babar? It wouldn't do him a lot of good to take him up to Hawes.'

'He can go next to Diamond, where my tack is. I'll clear it out.'

The stables were old, with worn hollows in the brick floors where once the carthorses had stood, and long wooden mangers along the back wall. Babar moved her tack and Charlie threw in a couple of bales of straw to make a bed. Rowan led the pony behind Black Diamond into his new quarters. A wooden partition with iron railings separated the two. The wild pony seemed to want to stay with Diamond, which was what Charlie had reckoned on. Babar fetched him an armful of hay and a bucket of water, with which Charlie cleaned the injury, then Babar refilled it for the pony to drink. Charlie was so quick and practised that the whole operation only took a short time. He went off to tell Ted Bailey what had happened. Rowan waited for him, leaning over the stable door, unable to remove her eyes from this magic pony. He had leaped into her arms, she thought. He was hers by right.

''E's bin loose for a while,' Babar said. 'We seen 'um a few times. Will you keep 'um?'

'We'll have to tell the police.'

'They won't want to know,' Babar said. 'No one's lookin' for 'um, not that we've 'eard.'

'How do you know? Are you sure?'

'No one's bin round the market. That's where they come lookin'.'

'I would love to have him! But my father—' Her voice failed her. Her father was not an animal-lover. Especially of the animal that had damaged his beastly car. They had no field or stable, in spite of living in a house called Home Farm.

'You could keep 'um 'ere. Company for Diamond like.'

16

But Rowan knew she would prefer to keep him at High Hawes – should the luck ever come her way to own him.

Charlie came back and thanked Babar for her help. 'I'll come down and sort him out in the morning. Meanwhile he'll be safe shut way here. Good on yer, Babar.'

'Ta ra,' said Babar.

Charlie got back in the Land Rover and Rowan climbed in beside him. She was boiling hot, still stirred up with excitement. The pony was magnificent!

'Do we have to tell the police?'

Charlie laughed. 'It's the drill, yes. You fancy him, then?'

'Oh yes!'

'He's very nice. Not a beginner's pony by the look of him, though.' Rowan knew she was a beginner but Charlie's condescension deflated her. Everybody could ride around here; even Babar the Elephant was an expert compared with herself. She was deluding herself, she knew, if she harboured dreams of owning that lovely pony.

'What we'll do,' Charlie said, as they drove back into the village, 'is, tomorrow morning I'll bring Hugh's camera down – it spits the films out straight away – you know the sort – and we'll take a couple of shots in to the police in town. I've got to go in anyway, to Arnold's dump – I've got an old engine he wants. You can come with me if you like and we'll find out if he's been reported missing.'

'Babar says he hasn't. Not on the market, at least.'

'They generally know up there.'

'What if no one claims him?'

'I suppose he's yours, then.' Charlie grinned at her in the dark. He pulled up outside her house and leaned across to open her door. 'You never know your luck!'

Rowan hopped out. 'Thank you very much for – for what you did.'

'See you in the morning, then. I'll pick you up. Say nine-ish.'

'Yes. I'll be ready.'

The Land Rover turned the corner and went away up the hill. Rowan went in round the back. She could feel herself trembling with excitement and tried to steel herself against her father's bad temper. What if the police let her take the pony and her father wouldn't allow it? She was terrified of the muddle and disappointment that seemed likely to erupt from her evening's adventure. But Charlie – she trusted in Charlie. Utterly. He would see everything came right.

Chapter Two

Charlie came the next morning on the dot of nine. John Watkins had already set off for the garage to see about his damage, so Rowan did not have to explain to him. Her mother was sympathetic, but not very hopeful about Rowan owning a pony.

'It all costs money, Rowan, and we've taken on a big mortgage for this house. Your father won't want it, I know.'

'But if I get him *free?*'

'Oh, come on – pigs might fly! If it's as lovely as you say, someone must be looking for it.'

'Oh, Mum – if – *please*—'

'Let's wait and see what happens.'

Rowan knew she was jumping the gun and getting all tizzed up for something that wasn't going to happen. Concentrate on lovely Charlie – that was joy enough for one day, to be going out with Charlie.

She fetched her anorak and ran out as the Land Rover rattled to a halt outside her house.

Charlie had the camera.

'We'll see what we've got in the daylight,' he said. He grinned at her, his gypsy-dark eyes full of the joy of living. Rowan had never seen Charlie down, even when his father was nagging him. The Land Rover was loaded with what looked like half a car.

'You won't mind if I stop off and do a bit of wheeler-dealing at Arnold's? Someone told me he's got some lights that might do for my MG, and I've got an engine he might buy off me which I got for next to nothing at a farm clear-out.'

Charlie was a mechanical whizz and had scraped his own living at mending cars and tractors since leaving school. At school apparently he had been useless, while Josephine had sailed through everything with top marks. Rowan had learned all this from Lizzie. 'What he can do, like ride and mend the horsebox – he can do without, somehow, learning it – it's instinct with him. Josephine – she's a great rider, but she's really worked at it – had high-powered lessons and everything, and yet when it comes to the push, it's Charlie who can get a horse to do almost anything, more than Josephine. She doesn't say anything, but it makes her mad. Charlie's not interested in competing – Dad makes him, to show off the horses he wants to sell – but really, although he can do it so well, he's not bound up in it like Josephine. I think he wouldn't really bother with horses at all if it wasn't the thing at home. Dad's living, I mean.'

Perhaps Charlie could have mended her father's BMW. They pulled up outside the Baileys' farm and walked up the drive into the stockyard. Babar was there, mucking out. Rowan felt her heart banging with excitement again, and tried to pull herself together.

'I've fed 'um,' Babar said. 'E's settled good enough.'

'Great,' said Charlie.

They went into the stable and Rowan peered over the old-fashioned rails of the loosebox. The pony was snatching at a hay net, and looked round at them nervously. Charlie had the camera with him.

'We'll have to have him outside for the photo.' He explained to Babar what he was doing, and Babar fetched a head collar. They led the pony out into the yard. Babar held him while Charlie focused the camera. Rowan just stood and stared.

The pony was glorious to her eyes. He was a very dark brown, blue-black across the quarters, like a swallow. Looking at him, Rowan thought suddenly that he must be called Swallow. Swallow for flight, for freedom, for acrobatics, for agility. The pony flung up his head and whinnied loudly, as he had last night, looking in Rowan's direction. He's mine, she thought. Her knees were trembling.

'I bathed his leg,' Babar said. 'It's not bad.'

Charlie examined it. 'It's fine.'

'You think we should let 'um out?'

'No. We'll never catch him again. Keep him in today, till we come back from the police station. We'll call in on the way back.'

Rowan could sense Charlie's meaning: with luck we'll be shot of the problem. He took four photos, and then wrote down the pony's description on a bit of paper, including what Rowan thought were odd characteristics, like the placings of his whorls, where the hair of his coat made little whirlpools here and there, lying in different directions.

'Like his fingerprints, really,' Charlie said. 'They're different on all horses. Mind you, not many people have a note of them anyway, so it doesn't count for much. Freeze-marking's the best security, or nowadays a microchip.'

Rowan thought freeze-marking was branding with a number on the horse's back, but didn't like to ask. She was so ignorant. But she had noticed that Lizzie's pony had a number on her back, under where the saddle went. Swallow wasn't freeze-marked.

'I think he ought to be called Swallow,' she said, as they took him back into the loosebox.

'Why not?' said Charlie. 'Short and sweet.'

They said goodbye to Babar and drove off up the village street.

'She's a good kid, Babar,' Charlie remarked. 'Pity about her awful pony. But she only hacks about, and it's OK for that, I suppose. They all make fun of her in the Pony Club, and yet she knows more than most of 'em put together. She'd make a good vet.'

'A vet?' Rowan's smart school in London had said you had to be super-powered to get into veterinary school.

Charlie said, 'It's not only brain you need for a vet. You need to have an instinct for an animal, especially a horse. Babar thinks horse.'

Rowan thought, I think horse. But she didn't know anything at all.

'What's the Pony Club?'

Perhaps that was where you learned.

'Oh, it's a lark for the kiddies. Earnest ladies have you trotting around in circles watching your diagonals.

I hated it but Josephine loved it, so do Lizzie and Hugh and them. Lots of competitions and you go to camp and have midnight feasts. That bit's all right.'

'Can anybody go?'

'If you join, and have a pony to ride, yes.'

What bliss, Rowan thought! If she had Swallow . . .

They climbed up out of the valley and past the spot where the pony had appeared out of the blue. Rowan saw the headlamp glass glinting in the verge. She could not think about anything except the pony. It was as if he had bewitched her.

'Is he valuable, do you think?'

'He's the sort – by the look of him – who would be a real winner with a tough rider. But not many kids can handle a strong pony like that. Most people want quiet, safe ponies for their kiddy-winkies, not tearaways. But if he is well-mannered and doesn't tank off, then, yes, I'd say he was worth a bit. He's very well made. And only six.'

'Someone's bound to be looking for him!'

'You'd think so.'

But when they got into town and found the right officer in the police station, it appeared there was no record of a missing pony.

'We know about him, mind you. He's been reported

as a danger to traffic several times, once on the motorway. It's a wonder he hasn't caused a bad accident, or got himself killed by now. Have you got the facilities to keep him for the time being, while we make enquiries?'

'Yes.' Charlie produced his paper with drawings of the pony's white markings and the distribution of his whorls. He wrote Rowan's name and address on the bottom.

'She found him.' He gave her a wink. 'He's hers, if no one claims him.'

'I think we'll probably place him. We'll be in touch with the Horse Watch people, and put the description out. Mind you, some people abandon ponies, like they do dogs and cats, but they're generally poor clapped-out things they can't sell.'

'Oh, he's not like that,' Rowan said quickly.

'No, he's a decent animal,' Charlie said. 'Been well cared for, by the look of him.'

'We'll be in touch. Quite soon if we're lucky.'

They took their leave and went back to the Land Rover.

'That's that done. We'll go to Arnold's now and see if I can sell him this junk. I've got a living to make.'

Rowan went into a dream of owning Swallow and

riding him in competitions against Hugh and Lizzie. Life was going to be unbearable, waiting to hear from the police station.

'You might hear by tonight. They've got it all on computer these days,' Charlie said, scotching her dreams.

He drove quite fast, but carefully in the country lanes, in case someone was riding a horse round the next bend. 'Could be me,' he grinned. 'Josephine got shunted up the rear a couple of years ago, and the horse had to be put down.'

Suppose they had hit Swallow really hard and killed him, Rowan thought! And he'd been on the motorway . . .

'Traffic and horses don't mix any more. When I was little, I rode everywhere and it was perfectly safe, but now–' Charlie shrugged. 'Now a driver will give you the V sign. You give it him back and he sees it in his mirror and he'll stop and get out and come up to you. I've had that.'

'What did you do?'

'I just rode at him. He fell in the ditch. I took his number, in case. They don't understand.'

Rowan thought, secretly, her father might do that. He was always in a hurry and quick-tempered. It made them edgy at home. Her mother was a worrier and tried to keep the peace. She was always saying, 'Your father works so hard, he can't help it.' Charlie's father worked hard too and he was fairly bad-tempered. He shouted, but the next minute he was laughing, so it wasn't too bad.

Arnold's dump was an eyesore tacked onto the edge of a pretty village. There were some decrepit barns and a field full of nettles and ragwort where a thin horse grazed, with a strand of barbed wire keeping it away from Arnold's impressive collection of broken-down cars. Charlie drove in and hooted.

'Sorry about this, it shouldn't take too long.'

Charlie hopped out and went to meet a young man who came out of the barn to meet him.

Rowan sat in the cab, waiting. She watched the thin horse cropping the weedy grass and thought how poorly it compared with her gorgeous Swallow. She was impatient to get home and go back to Babar's and see how he was getting on. The thin horse looked like the sort the policeman said people abandoned. It was a chestnut with a white streak down its nose. As she watched it Rowan noticed that it had some dreadful cuts on its back legs, some of which were oozing pus and blood. It needed Babar. Charlie had glanced at the horse, before going to the back of the Land Rover to unload his junk. Arnold came to help him. Rowan could hear them haggling. Then Arnold said he would go and fetch his price book, whatever that was. When he had disappeared Charlie went over to the wire fence and stood looking at the horse. It came over to him and he took hold of its nose and looked at its teeth.

Rowan got out of the cab. 'What are you doing?'

'I know this horse,' Charlie said. 'I'm looking at its teeth – see how old it is.'

'It's a terrible old horse.'

'She was a good horse once. Fedora. She's only nine.'

She looked like a knacker's horse. When Arnold came back he said she was for the knacker's. Waiting for the lorry to come.

Charlie said, 'You can have this engine in exchange for the horse.'

Arnold did not blink. 'Done,' he said.

They set about transferring the engine out of the Land Rover and onto a fork-lift truck. Rowan sat, pop-eyed at the transaction. So casual. The mare was still cropping the grass, unaware that she had been saved from the jaws of death. She was tall and skinny, with her ribs showing, yet her belly underneath was fat. She was a bright chestnut, with a raggedy red mane and tail. She had dull eyes, and a resigned demeanour, as if used to hard times.

Charlie came back and they drove off. The Land Rover felt light and bouncy, having been delivered of its burden.

'Have you got a bargain?' Rowan asked.

'You never know, with a horse.'

'It doesn't look worth much to me.'

'No. She's starving and full of worms. But she's in foal, by the look of her. And she had a good owner a year ago, a man with sense enough to send her to a good stallion. So it could be a good foal. But he died, and his horses were sold.'

'And she fell on bad days?'

'Yes, and got hung up in a barbed-wire fence. The new owner's an ignorant fool who bought a nice thoroughbred and ruined it. She was a racehorse, and ex-racehorses don't often make quiet hacks for ignorant people.'

'I want Swallow to be a good hack for an ignorant person.'

Charlie laughed.

'Good, class horses are rare, believe me.'

But Rowan could see that, inside, Charlie was

excited by his sudden deal, although he was trying not
to show it. She sensed that he was a bit like her with
Swallow. On to a dream . . . what might be.

'What will you do with her?'

'Point-to-point her, with luck. She's fast.' Then he
added, 'Dad won't be pleased.'

Like hers. 'Why not?'

'He wants me to ride the yard horses – the ones for
sale. Get them mannered. If I've got my own, I haven't
as much time for his.'

'Does he pay you? Employ you, sort of?'

'You must be joking! Employ me, yes. Pay me, no.
That's why I muck about with machinery.'

So Charlie had parent problems too. It made Rowan
happy to think she had a bond with Charlie. She
wriggled with excitement. All the things to think
of . . .

They stopped at the Baileys' farm.

'Will you tell Babar what happened? I want to get
the trailer and go back to fetch that mare. If the
knacker lorry gets there first it'll take her, I'm
sure.'

'Yes, of course.'

Rowan hopped out and Charlie roared off. Rowan
went into the stockyard. There was a crashing noise

coming from the stable. A loud and unmistakable whinny rent the air. Rowan hurried anxiously into the stable.

There was no sign of Babar, and Black Diamond's box was empty. But Swallow was rampaging round his box, dripping with sweat, and letting fly with his heels at the walls.

'Whatever's the matter?' Rowan was shocked at the pony's distress.

When he saw her he came to the door, letting out his wild whinnies. He kicked the door with his front feet. His bad knee was swollen up again and he had hollows in his flanks. His coat was wet all over.

Rowan could see that something was wrong but had no idea what. She wished Charlie had come in. He would know. Or Babar. Perhaps Babar was in the house. She decided to go and find her. But as she went out of the yard she met Ted Bailey coming in on his tractor. She waited while he parked it. He got down and smiled at her.

'That little beggar'll 'ave my stable down. 'Ark at 'im!' He didn't seem to mind.

'What's wrong with him?'

''E'll be all right when Barbara comes back. She's gone for a ride, and 'e's missing the other pony, like.'

Was that all? Rowan was amazed.

'Did the police know anything about 'um?' (So that's where Babar got the 'um from.)

'No. But they're going to find out.'

'Ah well. I daresay they'll come up with sommat.'

'Is it all right, him being here with you?' What if he threw Swallow out for attacking his stable?

But Ted Bailey was a patient, affable man, nothing like John Watkins and Fred Hawes. 'Oh, aye, 'e's no trouble. 'E can bide 'ere till they find 'is owner.'

'That's very kind of you.'

He went off towards the cowshed and Rowan was left with a panic that perhaps, because he was looking after him, Mr Bailey might claim the pony if the police didn't come up with an owner. He might want him for Babar! Anyone with any sense would prefer Swallow to Black Diamond. While she stood there worrying, Babar rode into the yard. She wore her brown anorak and green gumboots for riding, just the same as for everything, but she had added a hard hat, without bothering to cover its uncompromisingly grey surface with the usual jolly silk. As soon as Swallow saw Black Diamond he stood still and stopped whinnying.

'I know 'e was upset, but 'e's got to learn, same as all,' Babar said. 'I can't not ride, 'cause of 'um.'

She lumbered down from the saddle and led Diamond into his box. Swallow was now all happy little whickering noises, his kicking forgotten. Rowan was amazed.

'What did the police say?' Babar asked, as she unsaddled Diamond.

Rowan told her. 'Do you think they'll find the owner?'

'Likely.'

Babar took off the bridle and kissed Diamond several times on the nose. He stood with his eyes shut, breathing heavily. He had long, lop ears, which tended to fall out sideways, and his neck was concave along the top instead of convex.

Rowan, unable to bear the anxiety of perhaps Ted Bailey claiming him, said, 'I hope they don't! I would love to keep him.'

Babar lifted her large round face from Diamond's nose and looked at her with surprise.

'Keep 'um? You?'

'Yes!'

'You don't know . . . you never . . .' She stopped.

'Would you want him?' Rowan blurted out.

'Me?' Babar laughed. 'What would I want 'um for, when I got my darling 'ere?'

The great weight lifted from Rowan and she laughed too. 'Oh, I would so love to have him! More than anything I can think of! I would so love to have a pony.'

'A pony, yes. But this one? You don't know nothin'.' This was spoken quite kindly, as a fact, not with scorn.

'I could learn!'

'You got to learn with a pony as'll teach you.'

Rowan thought people taught, not ponies. She was out of her depth. She did not want to show any more of her ignorance and knew it was time to go home for lunch, or her parents would be worrying. She looked at her watch.

'I must go. Shall I come back and help you look after Swallow later?'

'Swallow?'

'I've called him Swallow.'

'Oh aye. Well, 'e's mucked out for today. You could come up in the morning and do 'im if you want.'

'What time?'

'Six-thirty, say.'

Rowan flinched. What would her mother say? 'Yes, all right. And thank you – thank you for looking after him.'

Babar gave her a puzzled look, from which Rowan

surmised that people like the Baileys always looked after an animal if it was there, under their noses, and it was not something to be thanked for. Babar made her feel incredibly suburban. Babar came with her out of the stockyard carrying her saddle and bridle. As they did so there was a clatter of hooves on the lane outside and a girl about their own age rode past on a gleaming bay pony. The girl wore bright cross-country clothes with a matching silk and the pony had bandages and boots to match. The pair were as unlike the Bailey turnout as it was possible to be.

'Who's that?' Rowan asked, as the girl passed on – having glanced in with stony eyes and made no greeting.

'That's Matty Prebble. She lives at High Bottom.' And then, in a tone of ineffable scorn – 'Show-jumper.'

Chapter Three

'So, did you find out who owned that pony?'

Rowan scrambled home just in time for lunch and her mother asked the leading question.

'No. But the police will ring here if they find the owner.'

'So whose is it at the moment?' her father asked.

'Mine.' Rowan heard her own voice quiver with defiance. Her mother darted her an anxious look.

'And you are paying for its food and keep?'

'Well, Mr Bailey hasn't said anything about that. He doesn't mind having him there.'

'They're a hard bunch when it comes to money, these farmers.' As far as Rowan was aware her father didn't know any farmers. He certainly had made no steps to be friendly with Mr Bailey and Mr Flint. Mr Bailey hadn't struck Rowan as hard. Soft, she would have said, to the point of squelchiness.

'Mr Bailey's not hard. He said I could keep him there. Or I could keep him at High Hawes.'

'The question doesn't arise, save for a day or two until the police find the owner.'

'But if they don't—'

'They must have an arrangement for disposing of such animals.'

'Charlie said they just want to get shot of them. I could have him, Charlie said. For my own.'

'That's out of the question.'

'He would be *free*,' Rowan cried, picking on the most likely attraction for her father. 'And he's valuable. Charlie said so. Only six and very nicely made. We'd get a valuable pony for nothing.'

'Hmm. If it's that valuable, someone is bound to be looking for it.'

But he didn't exactly say she couldn't have Swallow. Rowan was clever enough to change the subject at this point.

'I saw a girl called Matty Prebble who lives at High Bottom. She's a show-jumper.'

Although Babar had sounded so scornful, Rowan had been impressed with her glimpse of Matty Prebble. She hoped she would grow up more like Matty than Babar.

Her mother said, 'Oh, I've met Mrs Prebble. She's very smart. Outspoken. Her husband's in a merchant bank.'

When Rowan went up to High Hawes after lunch and mentioned Matty Prebble to Hugh, he crossed his eyes and made being-sick noises.

'Yuk!'

'What's that mean?'

'She thinks she's so wonderful! They spend thousands on her show-jumpers. All she has to do is ride them. Any fool could do that.'

Hugh was in the stable saddling up his pony Cascade. Cascade was a tough-looking flea-bitten grey of about fourteen hands, rather the same build as Swallow, but not so pretty. Cascade had cost almost nothing, being considered unrideable by the poor disillusioned children who had struggled with him during his chequered former career. Most of the Hawes children's ponies were cast-outs picked up for a song by their father. The Hawes's combined expertise nearly always reformed them, and then they were sold on for a lot of money. But Cascade, according to Hugh, was not for sale. He adored Cascade.

'I bet *she* couldn't get this one round a set of

show jumps,' he said scathingly. 'For all she thinks she's so marvellous.'

'Can you?'

'Of course.'

Rowan wished she hadn't asked. Unlike Charlie, Hugh was a bit prickly at times, no doubt by having to keep his end up amongst his siblings and handicapped by being nearly the youngest. He had a competitive nature, and was very strong for his age (eleven) and could unload hay bales like a grown man. He was fair, a scalped blond, with light blue eyes, finely chiselled features and a naturally worried expression. Rowan liked him and rather admired him. He was in the same class as her at school and was quite clever.

'Charlie says you've got yourself a pony,' he remarked, pulling up Cascade's girth. He kept his elbow well out to fend off as the pony turned round to bite him. 'He says he's nice.'

'Only until he's claimed.'

'He might not be. If he's trouble, someone might rather have the insurance money.'

'Charlie says he looks valuable.'

'Charlie's potty. That horse he got this morning – Dad's furious. It's rubbish. Dad says he won't have it in his yard.'

'Why not?'

'He doesn't like Charlie acting off his own bat. He wants Charlie to work on the yard horses, not have one of his own. He's mad now, but he'll cool down later. He's like that.'

What a liability parents were! Rowan thought.

'What will Charlie do if he can't bring the mare back here?'

'He's going to put her in with Bailey's cows for the time being.'

Rowan decided to go down to the Baileys' again to see the homecoming. Charlie had gone off in the horsebox an hour ago and it was to meet him coming back with his mare that she had come up to High Hawes. She was in the wrong place.

Hugh led Cascade out of his loosebox and hopped on without using the stirrup. They made a good pair, Rowan thought – two of a kind – strong and bossy and handsome. She fetched her bike and they rode out of the yard together. Above the farm the lane led up into some woods and above that to the open down where one could ride for miles. On the other side were racehorse gallops and in the next valley several racing stables. Hugh went uphill and Rowan went down. She whizzed down to the village, thinking how lucky she was to have High Hawes so close, and all its interesting, warring factions. She braked as she came to the village street, turned right past her own house (her father was mowing the lawn and did not look up) and pedalled furiously up to the Baileys'. The High Hawes horsebox was in the drive and Charlie was just getting out of the cab.

'Hi, trouble,' he said. 'My dad's furious with you.'

'Whatever for?' Rowan was startled.

'Not stopping me buying this mare. Anyone with any sense, he said, would have pointed out what a stupid idea it was. He's refused to let me bring her home.'

'Yes. Hugh just told me.'

Charlie laughed. 'All for the best. I thought we could turn 'em out together – yours and mine. A mare for a companion should keep your little beast happy. Stop him jumping out.'

He let down the back ramp and pulled down the slatted doors. The chestnut mare looked at them with her resigned expression.

'No, it's not the knacker's. Lucky old you,' Charlie said to her. He led her down the ramp and into the stockyard and tied her up outside the stables. From inside Swallow let out one of his loud whinnies.

Rowan was drawn to the door, to see his bright flashing eyes regarding her through the rails of his loosebox. If only he were really hers! She would look as happy as Charlie. It was obvious that his father's wrath was not deterring him.

Babar came out and admired the mare, and fetched some hot water from the kitchen, a basin and cotton-wool to bathe the mare's legs. She and Charlie crouched down, heads touching, to examine the cuts, and Rowan knew she was only a spectator. She wandered back to the stable and stood absorbing the atmosphere, sniffing the pleasant smell of horse and fresh hay. She had fallen in love with this world, she realized. Even before Swallow, she had been drawn to High Hawes by its peculiar dedication to the routine imposed by a stableful of horses: it gave a sense of purpose and stability and absorbed the frustrations that Rowan had become familiar with in her old suburban life – what to do, where to go . . . there was no time to be bored. It was very physical and outdoor, and yet there were intriguing problems, she had noticed, which required brain and cunning and the innate horse-sense which she recognized in Charlie and Babar and Hugh, and which she guessed she would never learn, however hard she tried. Horse-sense – it was a description that had transcended the horse world and was used in everyday life. She wished dearly that she had it.

Black Diamond, covered with his old jute rug, stood munching hay in his corner, not looking up, while Swallow paced round his box, excited by the goings-on outside. Rowan stroked him, but he would not respond to her fondling, but jerked away and whinnied again.

'What's wrong with him?' she asked Charlie.

'Nothing.'

'Your horses don't all whinny and stamp about.'

'They would if they'd been running wild for a couple of weeks, been out on the motorway, hit by a car, lost their own home and friends and been shut up in a strange place all of a sudden.'

Rowan digested this. It made sense.

'It takes time,' Charlie said. 'Horses are creatures of habit. They like their routine. The same every day. Otherwise they get upset. Your pony is upset, that's all. Nothing is wrong.'

'Not like this 'un,' said Babar darkly. 'Them legs—' She shrugged.

'They will heal.'

'Knackers next week instead o' this,' said Babar.

'Oh, come on!' Charlie looked uneasy. 'She'll win. Everything's oozing beautifully.'

'Poison.'

'I want to put her out. I believe in nature. It's cleaner out.'

'Dad said you can use the Thin Acre.'

'Good. That'll suit her fine. I thought Rowan's pony could go out with her, might settle him.'

'Yeah, good idea.'

'Suppose he jumps out again?' Rowan asked anxiously.

'He won't,' they both said together.

How did they know? Rowan wondered.

Babar fetched a head-collar and led Swallow out. He came with a rush, ears pricked, hooves skidding. His coat almost glittered in the pale spring sunshine, the blue cast on his back giving way to brownish lights round his eyes and mouth. Charlie's poor mare lifted up her head and pricked her ears with interest, her nostrils rippling. Swallow let out one of his loud neighs.

'Give over!' said Babar. Then to Rowan, with a sly smile, 'D'you want 'im? 'E's yours.'

Charlie looked worried. 'Hang on, whatever you do.'

Rowan took the rope from Babar, very nervous.

Charlie said to her, 'You take the mare.'

He handed her the mare's lead rope and took Swallow, without asking her. Rowan was relieved, rather than upset.

The Thin Acre was up the road about a hundred yards, on the opposite side from the farm. The field lay alongside the lane, long and thin as its name implied, sloping down to a stream on the far side. It was surrounded with high, rampant hedges and trees and the grass was long and sweet. Babar, going ahead, opened the gate and Rowan led the mare through first. She put her head down before she was half through the opening and started to tear at the good grass. Charlie barged past, half dragged by Swallow, and Babar, shoving Fedora's quarters out of the way, closed the gate.

'Let her go. Leave the head collar on,' Charlie said.

Rowan unclipped the rope. The mare made no move to explore but just stood cropping greedily, while Swallow, released, galloped up to the top of the field. Rowan was petrified he would go through the hedge, but it was thick and high and he stopped with a great tearing of hooves in the turf, flung himself round and galloped back right down to the bottom end. They all stood watching.

'Cor, he can move!' Charlie said.

Infected by the pony's exuberance, Fedora suddenly put up her old head with a toss of the raggedy mane and cantered a few paces after him, before the wounds in her hind legs suggested it would be better to desist – just enough to show the lovely smooth action of the good thoroughbred. For a moment, she looked beautiful. Even Rowan, tearing her gaze from Swallow, could see it.

'She's not a bad 'un, moving,' Babar said stolidly.

'I tell you, she's a really good mare. I remember her winning at Newbury. Dad wouldn't believe me.'

They leaned on the gate in a row, watching the two animals. Swallow settled down quite quickly and started to graze, keeping very close to the mare. Rowan thought of her, destined for the knacker's, being waylaid in the nick of time and turned out into what she obviously thought was paradise, and tears came into her eyes. And Swallow – finding this good home and a friend . . . it wasn't just herself who found the sight satisfying, for Charlie was in no hurry to go home.

'Babar said, 'You needn't keep coming down. I'll see to her legs – tonight, like, and in the morning.'

'I'll come down if I can. But knowing Dad, he'll find me plenty to do.'

Rowan wasn't sure if she had to do anything. She didn't know if horses just stayed out, or whether you had to feed them or anything. She didn't like to ask. She noticed that on the far side of the stream the field sloped up to the house of the Prebbles: High Bottom. Where the ground levelled out at the top there was an enclosure full of show jumps where no doubt Matty Prebble did her practising. Matty Prebble would have horse-sense, like Babar and Charlie.

'A good day's work,' Charlie said, as they walked back up the road. He closed up the back of the horse-box and climbed up into the cab. Babar saw the lorry out into the road and Charlie drove away. Rowan had no excuse to linger, although she wondered if she should offer to clean out Swallow's stable again. She offered, and Babar said it didn't matter, so Rowan fetched her bike and rode home.

Having Swallow out in the field just down the road made it very easy for her to visit. She went down with titbits the moment she got home from school and both horses would come to the gate and nuzzle at her as she groped in her pockets. Fedora's legs started to heal nicely. Swallow stopped whinnying and galloping about and worrying, and started to look the model of a quiet, safe pony. Every day Rowan expected her mother to say she had heard from the police, but nothing happened. Monday, Tuesday, Wednesday, Thursday . . . Rowan became more and more optimistic.

Friday.

She burst into the kitchen, throwing off her school blazer and scrimmaging in the bread bin for crusts. Her mother came through from the dining room and said, 'Oh, a man rang this afternoon. He said the police had given him our number. That pony you found – he thinks it's his. He's coming over in the morning.'

Chapter Four

Rowan's father decided to accompany Rowan to meet the man who thought Swallow was his. The man had arranged to call at the farm at eleven o'clock. Rowan had wished Charlie would come, and thought perhaps Mr Bailey might take an interest, but on Saturday morning there was only Babar in the yard when she went down.

She told Babar what had happened. She had come down an hour ahead of her father, to talk to Swallow before he might disappear. She could not stop a few tears falling out when she told Babar; but Babar, for all she was commonsensical, was not scornful.

'You got fond of 'um. It's a shame.'

Rowan tried to cheer herself up by picturing a lovely family arriving and falling on Swallow with exclamations of delight, and Swallow whinnying back to them with love and affection. But why had they taken so long? Perhaps they had been on holiday. But it was a bit early for holiday time.

'Will you come and meet them, at eleven o'clock?'

She was nervous of catching Swallow by herself, and revealing how awkward she was with ponies in front of her father. But perhaps when Swallow caught sight of his erstwhile owners he would canter over and plunge his nose into their hands full of titbits.

It was a cold, miserable day. Rowan had a feeling everything was going to go wrong. She hated the idea of her father coming down and saying all the wrong things to these people. He had no idea. The man was called Mr Harvey, the police said. He was able to describe the pony exactly, right down to a wire scar on the off hind fetlock. Rowan had never noticed this herself and nor had Charlie.

Babar finished grooming Black Diamond and they went down to the field together. The two animals were grazing down by the stream. When he saw them Swallow lifted his head, ears pricked, and started to walk over, and Charlie's mare followed, but more slowly. Watching them, Rowan was choked with disappointment. She told herself she had only known Swallow a week, and not to be so stupid. But when he came close his nostrils rippled a greeting and he came to her like an old friend. Rowan howled.

'Your dad's coming,' Babar said anxiously.

The BMW was pulling up on the verge. Rowan blew her nose hastily. Her father got out and came marching up.

'So this is the fellow?' He put out a hand and pulled it back hastily as Swallow reached towards it, thinking it held something nice. 'It's very good of your father to take it in,' he said to Babar.

Babar looked at him with disdain, obviously wondering what else he would have done. Shooed it off down the road? She did not reply.

John Watkins looked at his watch. 'I hope he's not going to keep us waiting. I've got work to do.'

Rowan was used to her father's impatience. He didn't really have any work to do, save clean the car and mow the lawn, as far as she knew, not like Mr Bailey who had a hundred and twenty cows to milk twice a day, as well as make hay and grow corn. Yet Mr Bailey was never impatient. Rowan knew her father charged his clients an enormous sum by the hour. If Ted Bailey charged by the hour he would be a millionaire. But he had no one to charge. Life was very unfair.

But before her father had time to get cross, a car

came down the road from the top, pulling a horse trailer. Rowan was shocked by seeing the trailer. This man must be quite sure! The car slowed down by the gate and the driver put his head out of the window. He was quite young, wore a tweed cap, and had a rather ferrety face. There was no doting family with him; he was alone.

'Are you—?'

'Watkins. John Watkins. Got your pony, I believe?' Rowan's father sprang forward. Rowan thought he sounded as if he couldn't wait to get Swallow loaded up.

'So I understand. Can I park somewhere?'

'In the drive.' Babar gestured down the road towards the farm.

He drove on and into the farmyard, and came back on foot, carrying a head collar. He wore jodhpurs and was rather bandy, like a jockey. He did not look like a kind father looking for his darling daughter's lost pony, which was rather what Rowan had been expecting.

He introduced himself. 'Ken Harvey. The police tell me that our fellow's been here a week or so now. I've been away, I'm afraid. Only heard last night.'

'This is the one. I take it he's yours?'

Ken Harvey took a cursory glance at Swallow and

said, 'That's the fellow. Cornhill Amethyst – my daughter's show pony.'

His eyes flickered quickly over Swallow. He went up to him and put his head collar on, but Swallow did not nuzzle him happily as Rowan had been expecting. In fact, he stepped away and put back his ears. But Ken Harvey was obviously experienced at handling ponies and brooked no nonsense.

John Watkins, perhaps sensing that it was all too easy, said, 'I take it you can identify him in some way?'

'Yes, of course. I think you'll find he's got a small scar on his hind fetlock, near side. Shaped like a star. Want to have a look? Six years old – have you looked in his mouth? And, if you look under his mane, off side, there are some white hairs in his coat, just a few.'

Rowan had never noticed. She lifted up the mane and looked. It was true. There were. She felt bitterly disappointed. She felt the tears rising up again and turned away. Babar opened the gate and Ken Harvey led the pony out. Fedora came to the gate and looked sadly after them, and gave a soft whinny. Swallow turned his head and bellowed in reply. Ken Harvey chucked at his head.

'What do I owe you, for his keep for a week?'

'Nothing,' said Babar. 'It's only grass.'

Rowan's father said, 'There will be an insurance claim, I'm afraid, for damage to my car. Your animal jumped out of a hedge in front of me and my headlight was broken. Perhaps you'll give me the particulars of your insurance, and your address?'

'Certainly. We'll box him up and I'll give you my card. I'll sort it out with the insurance.'

Babar let down the ramp of the trailer and Harvey led Swallow in. Rowan went to the front and went in by the groom's door to Swallow's front end; she let herself cry in the soft gloom while the two men talked outside. Swallow licked her hands and she kissed the softness of his muzzle.

'I don't like your Mr Harvey,' she said. She had wanted a jolly father and a nice girl with loving eyes and a white-toothed smile, who would write her letters later on, and invite her home for weekends. Not a bandy-legged jockey with a ferrety face.

'Come on, Rowan,' her father called.

She retreated. It was awful. She didn't care who saw her crying now. She ran away from them and got into her father's car and sobbed. She heard her father directing the man out into the village street, and then the acceleration as the car drove away, and thought she heard a last faint whinny. Her father came back to the car.

'Bit of luck, that. Looks as if I shall get my insurance claim.'

Rowan was so angry at her father's callous remark that she jumped out of the car and ran back to Babar's stable. Babar understood, at least. She was going to go for a ride but she stopped tacking up when she saw Rowan and stood there looking sympathetic.

'He was horrible!' Rowan cried out.

'Aye.'

'And my father's horrible too! All he's bothered about is his beastly insurance money!'

'Aye.'

'I did want to keep Swallow. I really wanted to!'

'Perhaps your dad would let you have a pony, all the same, if you want one.'

'I only want Swallow!'

Rowan knew she was behaving like a child but she couldn't help herself. It was all right with Babar. If Charlie had been there she would have tried to be more sensible.

'I'm sorry,' she mumbled. 'I know I'm being stupid. It's just that he was such a horrid man.'

Babar said, 'He was just that. Jus' took it for granted. No thanks.'

'No. He never said thank you at all! Or even looked pleased.'

'An' the pony didn't know him, like.'

'What do you mean?'

'Looked like it to me, when he put the head collar on – the pony seemed like he thought 'e was a stranger.'

'Yes, he did!' Rowan was alarmed at what Babar was hinting. 'You think he – he—'

'I wouldna' trust 'um myself. Not farther than I could throw 'um. But 'e knew the pony's marks, 'is age and everything . . .' She shrugged.

'My father's got his card, his address. I don't see how he could cheat us.'

'No. Right. 'E just smelled like a wrong 'un.'

'Yes, he did.'

Rowan could see that Babar wanted to be off on her ride so she retreated and walked slowly home. Babar's remarks had set her thinking. She asked her father if she could see the card the man had given her, and he said it was on the mantelpiece, why?

'I just want to see where he lives. If it's near.'

She copied down the address. It was the same county

but she had no idea where it was. She wrote down the telephone number. She wanted to talk to Charlie. After lunch she got her bike and cycled up to High Hawes. The yard was empty, so she knocked at the kitchen door.

'Come in!' someone yelled.

The Hawes family were sitting down to lunch in the kitchen. Joan Hawes was lobbing hot cheese rarebits out of the grill, apparently ready to go on until nobody wanted any more, and eating one herself as she worked. Rowan was embarrassed, having thought lunch time would be over, but nobody minded and Joan Hawes did one for her too. Lizzie and Hugh budged up at the table and let her in, without seeming cross about it, and Charlie grinned at her from across the table.

'Someone came for Swallow. He says he's his and has taken him away.'

Charlie's grin vanished. 'Oh, bad luck!'

'Wow, that's quick,' Hugh said.

'The police rang last night. And he came with a trailer this morning.'

'What, just like that? How did he know, without looking first?'

'He knew all his marks, scars and things. He was

horrid. Really horrid.' She was afraid she might burst into tears again and picked up her cheesy toast.

'Who was he? Anyone we know?'

'Ken Harvey.'

'Rings no bells.'

'I knew a Ken Harvey, years ago,' Fred Hawes said. 'A jockey. Crook. Got banned.'

'He looked like a jockey. He looked like a ferret.'

'Yeah, like a ferret.'

None of this was at all cheering to Rowan. Only Charlie guessed how she felt and he, being practical, was concerned for Fedora, left on her own.

'She'll be better off up here. I'll fetch her this afternoon.' He looked cautiously at his father, who shrugged and said, 'She'll have to go out with the youngsters. If they run her round . . . it's up to you.'

'She'll be OK. She's not flighty.'

Fred shook his head, but did not argue. He was a thickset, tough-looking man with a lined face but surprisingly gentle eyes. Horses would do anything for him, Babar had told Rowan. The magic had rubbed off on Charlie. But Fred found humans difficult to handle and was not as successful as he should have been. High Hawes was not in debt, but there was no spare cash for a new horsebox or a good eventer for the ambitious

Josephine. Josephine was going to have to make her own eventer out of one of the bargain youngsters bought on a trip to Ireland. It was her job, and Charlie's, to break them in. Josephine was nothing like Charlie, being very quiet and cold by nature. She kept herself very much to herself, but missed nothing with her clear, blue-grey eyes. If she had done anything to enhance her looks she would have been strikingly beautiful, Rowan thought, in awe of her. She was working for her Pony Club. A test, which Rowan understood from Hugh and Lizzie was phenomenally difficult to pass.

After lunch Rowan went out into the yard with Hugh and Lizzie who were going for a ride.

She was so transparently miserable that Lizzie said, 'If we had something quiet to ride, you could have a go. But we haven't. When we come back you could ride Cascade up the lane, I suppose. If Hugh leads him.'

'I don't mind,' said Hugh obligingly.

'It doesn't matter,' Rowan said. It really didn't, just then. She didn't want to ride another pony. Only Swallow.

She went with Lizzie to tack up Lizzie's pony Birdie. Birdie was a bay, almost thoroughbred, of fourteen and a half hands, a lean and beautiful mare with a wilful nature. Her proper name was Bird in the Wilderness. She had been christened by a woman called Mrs Brundle who had 'rescued' her. Mrs Brundle had given her to Lizzie. The Hawes called Mrs Brundle Mrs Bundle, because she looked like one, her terrible old clothes tied around the middle with a piece of binder twine. She lived alone in an ancient house at the opposite end of the village from the Baileys and was thought to be eccentric but harmless, a collector of unwanted dogs, cats, goats, donkeys and ponies and injured hedgehogs, owls, orphan fox cubs and one-winged pheasants. She was elderly and said to be an Honourable something, but looked like a bag lady. The Hawes said she was all right. Batty but all right.

Lizzie was never convinced that being given Birdie was a good thing. Her father said it was, naturally, but Birdie was very hard to get on with.

'Charlie schools her for me when I get desperate. She's all right with him.'

'Desperate?' Rowan was surprised.

Lizzie had her head down, groping under the pony's belly for her girth. She mumbled, 'She can be awfully silly, you can't imagine. She was spoilt as a youngster and doesn't understand obvious things, like obedience.

Nobody taught her. I'm having to do it, about three years too late.'

'Is it hard work?'

Lizzie's head popped up over the saddle and her blue eyes looked sharply at Rowan.

'It's not very easy, no. It's all right for the others – Charlie and Hugh – and even Shrimp – she's only nine but she's got no nerves at all – but I'm not as good as the rest of them. Hugh's better than I am and he's two years younger. I hate not being as good as him, you can't imagine.'

Rowan was surprised at the sudden misery in Lizzie's voice. Lizzie was small and thin with rather wild curly hair which sprang out spectacularly when she took her riding hat off. She was rather scatty and impulsive by nature, unlike Charlie and Hugh. Perhaps horses preferred calm natures, Rowan thought; it seemed logical. If Birdie was scatty too, it might not be a good mix.

'Why can't your father sell her and let you have something easier?'

'He's going to. She's got a fabulous jump and the idea is to sell her to Matty Prebble. Mrs Prebble wants her, but Dad's holding out. He likes annoying Mrs Prebble. And I'm supposed to be improving Birdie, so he can get more money.'

'Mrs Brundle won't mind?'

'Not as long as she goes to a good home. Dad's already discussed it with her. I suppose he'll give her some of the money.'

Lizzie led the pony out into the yard and Rowan followed. How complicated this pony business seemed to be! Rowan was impressed by Lizzie's confidences, reassured by finding that she wasn't the only one with problems. Being an only child, she had never considered how competitive it must be having four brothers and sisters to be compared with.

'I'll muck out while you're away,' she said, to be helpful.

'You haven't got to. You could fetch Fedora with Charlie.'

So Rowan mucked out their empty looseboxes and when Charlie came out she walked down with him to fetch Fedora. He too was sympathetic, but had seen so many loved horses whipped from under him to be sold by his father that he took it as a fact of life. 'Someone was bound to turn up for a little cracker like him.'

Fedora was standing by the gate looking as bereft as Rowan.

'Lost your mate, old girl?' Charlie gave her a friendly

pat and put the head collar on. 'She's in foal. I had the
vet look at her. He thinks it's due around June. Could
be something nice, if we're lucky. I'll try and find out
when it's born – what stallion she was sent to – so I can
get it registered. She looks better already, doesn't she –
a week on good grass?'

Certainly the mare had lost her hang-dog look, and
her cuts were healing nicely.

'I can feed her when I get her home. I knew Dad
would give in.'

They walked back up the hill with the mare between
them, and Charlie turned her out with some shaggy
two-year-olds. By then Lizzie and Hugh had returned
and were unsaddling their ponies.

Lizzie said to Rowan, 'Hugh had an idea. He said
that man who took your pony – he might have
pinched it – you know, just said it was his.'

'But he knew his markings, his scar and that.'

'Hugh said, if you could be bothered, you could
come one night and find his markings, when nobody
was about. If you heard that a pony had been found,
you see, and asked the police where it was. Hugh said
it would be easy.'

'Lots of people knew about him. Babar's father asked
around at the market on Wednesday, Babar said.'

'Well, your Mr Harvey could have heard.'

'But he gave us his card. His address and phone number. He can't be a thief.'

'It might be false. People do that.'

'We could ring him up and see!'

'Yes. If it's right and he answers, we can pretend to be those people who want to sell you double glazing.'

'Yes!'

'Another thing, what did you say he said the pony's name was? Cornhill Amethyst?'

'Yes.'

'Because we know a lot of show ponies and we've never heard of the prefix Cornhill.'

'He made it up!'

Rowan's hunch that Ken Harvey was all wrong was being substantiated. She felt herself filling with excitement. If her father had been swindled, he would be as keen to get the pony back as she was. Such was his nature, he could not bear to be bettered.

'We'll ring him,' Hugh said. 'You've got the number? Come on.'

They shut the stable doors and ran across the yard to the house. It was a cold day, and a lovely warmth hit them as they burst into the kitchen. Joan Hawes was rolling out pastry on the kitchen table and Shrimp was painting a picture of a horse, her tongue sticking out as she concentrated. She was a volatile, very independent child, like Lizzie in looks, small for her age and with an elfin face. Her ears stuck out and she anchored her hair firmly behind the useful holders. Charlie had taught her to ride when she was two and she was phenomenally gifted, even for a Hawes, and was much in demand by owners of small show ponies to show them in the ring. Her photo, hair tightly plaited and tied with red bows, was often in 'Horse and Hound' sitting on a pony decorated with championship ribbons. Delighted owners rewarded her with presents and she had become conceited, according to Lizzie, and revolting. The rest of the family derided showing, unless it involved jumping. Shrimp had so many rides she didn't want a pony of her own – 'All that horrid work – no thank you!'

Hugh looked at her painting and said, 'What's that, a giraffe?' Shrimp kicked him and Hugh pulled her hair out from behind her ears so that she couldn't see him.

'Hugh,' said his mother, quite quietly, and he stopped teasing immediately and said, 'Can we use the phone?'

'What for?'

He explained. Joan Hawes was quite interested and said yes, but be tactful.

Rowan found her heart was pulsing with excitement. 'Do you want to do it?' Hugh asked.

'No!'

'I will,' said Lizzie, and snatched up the receiver. Rowan held out the paper with the number on and Lizzie dialled it.

After a few moments she said, 'It's not ringing. Just making a burring noise.'

'Ring the operator!' Hugh shouted.

Lizzie rang the operator and was told it was a discontinued number. She put the receiver down and they all stared at each other in triumph.

'There, he's a fraud!'

'What about the address?' Hugh snatched the paper.

The address was a farm in a village about twenty miles away.

'I bet it doesn't exist,' Hugh said.

'We know someone in that village,' Lizzie said. 'That girl with the show jumper called Jiminy Cricket. She lives there. What's her name?'

'Rachel Potterton.'

'Yes. That's it. We could ring her and ask about this

farm. Elder's End. If Ken Harvey does live there, she's bound to know him.'

They looked up Potterton in the phone book and found the number. Lizzie rang again. Rachel answered the phone. Lizzie said they were trying to trace someone called Ken Harvey at Elder's End but his phone didn't work. Then she was silent while Rachel apparently chattered away. Then she said, 'No wonder we couldn't get an answer! Thank you very much,' and put the phone down.

'There!' She turned triumphantly to Rowan. 'Elder's End is derelict and no one has lived there for years. And Rachel's never heard of Ken Harvey. So he is a thief!'

Rowan's mind whirled. 'But where's Swallow now? Where's he taken him?'

'He'll sell him on the market. That's what horse thieves do. For cats' meat!'

Chapter Five

Rowan wept again and Mrs Hawes gave her a biscuit straight out of the oven. Hugh said they should all have a day off school on Monday to go round the markets. Charlie came in and said to Rowan, 'Of course he won't go for cats' meat, he's too classy,' and they sat round the table arguing about what was to be done.

Fred Hawes came in and said if he saw Ken Harvey again he'd come heavy with him. The only market on Monday was over Porchester way and that was very likely where the pony would turn up, unless Mr Harvey had private customers.

'He's in a strong position, because the real owners seem to have gone missing.'

'Rowan's the real owner,' Hugh said.

'No. Morally, perhaps, but not in law. If Ken Harvey sells this pony on the market, there's no one to prosecute him if the real owners don't turn up. You could go and explain what's happened to the police on Monday morning but I doubt if they'll bother to go into it. See it from their point of view. It's not worth their trouble.'

'So what shall we do?'

'Go to market and see if we can see him before he goes in the ring,' said Charlie. 'Then, if Mr Harvey's any sense, he'll melt quietly away and you'll get your pony back.'

'But it's school tomorrow!' Rowan wailed.

'Perhaps your father will go?'

Angry as he might be, Rowan's father was not the sort, Rowan thought, to want to go round a cattle market hassling dubious characters. It wasn't his scene at all. Hassling them in a smart office, in his dark suit and club tie, was a different matter.

'Can't you go?' she whispered to Charlie. 'Ken Harvey'd be frightened of you.'

She wouldn't have dared to have asked him, only it mattered so much. He looked dubious, and glanced at his father.

'I could skip school,' Rowan said. 'I'm sure my father would let me, for this.'

She had not underestimated her father's reaction.

He was furious when he heard of the spurious address and non-existent telephone number. Rowan knew it was because he wouldn't get paid for the damage to his car, not really because he had been cheated out of the pony.

'You didn't want the pony anyway,' his wife reminded him.

'I didn't want the pony but I don't like being cheated. The man's a rogue. A real rogue.'

But he refused to take a day off from the office to go and chase him at the market.

'Ask those horsey friends of yours to go. We're laying no claim to the pony. If they catch the fellow, they can keep it, as far as I'm concerned.'

'Would you let me off school to go with them?' Rowan asked.

'Well, this once, I might.'

Rowan rang Charlie and told him what her father had said. 'If we find him, you can have the pony, Dad says.'

'He's not his to give.'

'No. But he thinks he is,' Rowan explained.

'Well, it's worth a throw, I suppose. We keep him and if no one claims him for long enough, he'd be ours. I'll ask Dad.'

Fred Hawes said it was up to Charlie, if he wanted to go cavorting round the country on a wild-goose chase. Charlie told Rowan he'd go, and she could come with him. Rowan was certain Charlie only said it to comfort her, because he was so nice. He didn't want to go, she was sure. She felt humbled and warm, because he was so kind, and rather guilty about taking up his time.

But the next morning, when the school bus went off without her, she was excited about the prospect ahead of her, and raced up to High Hawes on her bike. It was a cold but sunny day, and Josephine was already out schooling in the home-built manège that they had tried hard to make horizontal on the side of the hill. (Charlie had dug it out with a borrowed JCB when he was only fifteen, and most of the spoil had been turned into a splendid bank and drop-jump exercise at the far end of the schooling field.) Josephine had a young horse which her father had obtained as part exchange in a deal, and which he would not sell on – 'I've a reputation to maintain.' It looked perfectly all right to Rowan. She did not know about these things. Josephine rode with total concentration, her pale face expressionless beneath the hard grey hat. Her slender body and long, long legs looked brilliant on the thoroughbred. But Rowan remembered with a little leap of joy that Charlie was better – Lizzie had said so. She found herself blushing as Charlie appeared out of the tack shed and gave her his cheerful smile. She could not help it.

'Glutton for punishment – that's you! Or do you just want a day off school?'

'I want Swallow.'

'Seriously, don't expect too much. It's only an outside chance that he'll be there.'

'I know. You don't really mind coming, do you?'

'No. I like a day out occasionally.'

'Mum gave me money for the petrol, and said to buy you lunch.'

'But not the pony?' Charlie laughed. Then he said, 'Sorry,' because he saw the look on Rowan's face. 'Cheer up. We'll sort it out, one way or another.'

They climbed into the Land Rover.

'It's a rough old market, this. Anything turns up there, mostly grot. But if you're very lucky, you can get a bargain.'

'Was Fedora a bargain?'

'I think so. Especially if she has a nice foal. When she's had it I want her to go back to racing. She was really good in her day.'

Rowan, hearing the optimism in his voice, wished

desperately that she could have a pony, join this fascinating world. If they got Swallow back, would she be able to persuade her father to come to an agreement with Mr Hawes that she might ride him? Perhaps it was in her favour that her father, having been swindled, now wanted the pony back. Her father wasn't very understanding. He would let her have any amount of money if it was for things like school trips, the best trainers or her own computer, but he seemed to think the horse world was unladylike and rough. Babar in her old anorak and gumboots hadn't impressed him. He ought to see Josephine, so elegant and beautiful, riding her tall bay . . . Rowan went into a dream of her father falling for Josephine (only slightly, not enough to leave his wife) and taking her, Rowan, up to High Hawes every evening so that Josephine could give her riding lessons. Then he would buy a trailer and take her to horse shows so that he could watch Josephine compete—

'Damn,' Charlie said suddenly.

'What's the matter?'

'Our electrics are on the blink.' A red light was flashing on the dashboard. 'I'll have to pull in and find out what's wrong. Sorry about this.'

It took ages. The fan belt was broken. Charlie said

there was a spare somewhere amongst the junk in the back. When he found it, the spanner didn't fit . . . He sweated and swore, attacking the uncooperative bolts. Rowan glanced at her watch. It was gone twelve o'clock and she knew the sale started at ten.

'Hell, I'm sorry,' Charlie said, as he climbed back into the driving seat. 'But we can still trace him, if he went through the ring.'

He zoomed down onto the motorway and drove as fast as the old machine could manage. Rowan, bitterly disappointed, told herself they were on a wild-goose chase anyway, but by the time they turned off and made for the small town where the sale was being held, she was in a bad state of nervous excitement. She had to force herself to keep cool, and not embarrass poor Charlie with her daftness. She bit her tongue to stop it wagging, and got down in the market yard without saying a word.

Charlie seemed to know a lot of people, nodding hellos as he threaded his way through the crowd. In the ring a cow was being sold, the auctioneer chanting on his rostrum in unintelligible fashion, and pens of heifers were waiting to go through the ring. All the horses in sight were tied up to railings or being loaded into lorries, obviously having taken their turn and been sold. Some of the lorries were already driving away – Rowan looked around desperately, aching for a sight of that eager head and the pricked ears, listening for that bellowing whinny.

'We'll go in the office and ask for a look at the books,' Charlie said. 'Norm knows us – he'll tell us if the pony was here.'

Having a dealer for a father made the task considerably easier. Norm in the office was sympathetic.

'Dark bay fourteen-hand gelding? There was a clapped-out twenty-year-old . . . six, you say? Perky beast? Yes, there was one. Looked like a Welshman, very pretty. Not very well-behaved.'

'Was it sold?'

'Yes. Five hundred quid. Its manners put them off.'

'Who to?'

'A Miss Laura Griffiths. She runs a riding school out Arminster way. We know her.'

'Did she pay cash?'

'Aye. It's gone through. Fellow collected it in the office here.'

'The pony's stolen.'

'Bit late to tell us that, Charlie. You should have got here earlier.'

'Yeah. We broke down.'

'You'd better go and see Miss Griffiths about it, Charlie.' Norm looked worried. 'We sold it in good faith. Don't want any trouble.'

'No, it's not your fault.'

Charlie sighed and gave Rowan a wry look. 'Sorry, I've messed it up good and proper. We'll go and see if we can find this woman. You got her address, Norm?'

Norm scribbled it down on the back of an envelope. 'She's probably still around. Pale blue trailer, blue Land Rover with a white stripe on the side. Go and look in the parking.'

'What's she look like?'

'Young. Early twenties. Pale. Frizzled blonde hair. Worried looking.'

'OK.'

They left the office and Charlie started to make his way towards the back of the yard where the lorries and trailers were parked.

'At least we've traced him. I doubt if we'll get him back though. We haven't really got right on our side, have we?'

Rowan managed to choke back her tears. If only they'd been in time! Ken Harvey would have handed him over once he was challenged, she was sure. They would only have had to tell Norm the pony was stolen, and he wouldn't have put it through the ring. She followed Charlie nervously, trying to picture Miss Laura Griffiths. Was she a gentle, loving soul, or a harpy? Worried looking. What was she worried about? She would have plenty when she found she had bought a stolen pony.

'There's her trailer,' Charlie said suddenly.

It stood between two cattle flats, apparently deserted. It was rather a broken-down-looking combination. On the door of the Land Rover was written *Half Moon Riding Stables*.

'Let's have a look.'

Charlie went round to the trailer, opened the groom's door and laughed. 'Here's your chap!'

The eager, familiar face stared out from the gloom and gave a throaty, welcoming nicker. Rowan climbed in and flung her arms round his neck.

'Oh, you darling!' By a terrific feat of self-control she did not burst into tears. She was telling herself at least he was found: if she tried hard enough she knew where he was to buy him back. If she saved all her money, and went out to work (what? where?) and cajoled her father . . . it was all possible. While she had her nose buried in Swallow's thick mane, Miss Laura Griffiths arrived, holding a hot dog to her face and looked understandably surprised.

'Hey—'

Rowan left the explaining to Charlie. She knew Charlie wasn't going to pretend that they legitimately owned the pony; he explained the situation as it was.

'We were going to take it back off this Harvey guy before he got into the sale ring, but as it turned out—' Charlie shrugged.

The undeniably pale Laura Griffiths turned a shade paler at the news and looked horrified.

'I can't be that unlucky! I can't lose my five hundred quid – I'm nearly down the drain as it is! I'm desperate for a pony this size and this market was my only chance. I know most of them are bad 'uns, but I thought this one might turn out OK if he got enough work to stop his nonsense. Which he'll get at my place. I was actually thinking I might have got a bargain. I might have known!'

She looked as if she, like Rowan, could easily burst into tears. Charlie looked worried, surrounded by hysterical females. He gave Rowan a rather frantic look and she, understanding, said hastily, 'It's all right. We're not going to take him back!'

As she spoke these desperate words it was all she could do not to wail aloud. They had missed their chance because of the wretched breakdown and there was no mending the situation.

'He's not ours to take back. Honestly. We know he's not gone to the meat man, that he's going to a good home. That's all that matters,' she lied.

'Except I've bought a stolen animal!'

'In good faith,' Charlie said. 'You can't get into trouble.'

'If the real owners turn up, they can claim him back.'

'Well, if they were going to turn up, I reckon they'd have done so by now. They've had their chance.'

'If they do, you needn't given them my name and address?' Miss Griffiths appealed bleakly.

Charlie shrugged. 'Only if they agreed to buy him back, then we might,' he said.

'I could stand that. But I can't stand losing five hundred quid – no way. Please don't let me in for that!'

'No. Promise. We've all done our best.'

He was obviously anxious to depart, Rowan could see. She took the address of the riding school, went and gave Swallow a final hug and a kiss, and then followed Charlie back to the Land Rover. She didn't cry, but it took all her resolution not to. They drove away in silence.

About five miles later Charlie said, 'Hell, I'm really sorry about that.'

And the episode of Swallow was over.

Chapter Six

'It's a really daft thing – we've got twenty-five horses in our yard, and Rowan wants to learn to ride and we haven't anything suitable to put her on.'

Charlie, having a bad conscience and wanting to comfort Rowan on the way home, had rashly promised that between them, up at High Hawes, they would teach her to ride. Having announced this at the supper table he was met with, 'Who on?'

Hugh jeered, 'Fedora will do. She can hardly put one leg in front of the other.'

'Ha, ha. If you'd taught Cascade manners by now, which any half-decent rider would have done, we could use him.'

'If I had a decent pony instead of Birdie, I could teach her,' Lizzie said.

'She'd do best to ask Babar,' Joan Hawes said. 'You all laugh at her pony, but at least she's safe.'

'We're a dealing yard, not a riding school,' Fred pointed out.

'Yes, well, with two children having left school and wanting to stay at home, I think setting up a riding-school department might make us a bit of money.'

The whole family stared at their mother, who was not given to making pronouncements on lifestyle. Even Fred looked up sharply from his salt beef and dumplings.

Joan went on, 'To diversify is very sensible. We deal chiefly in hunters, and hunting is becoming more threatened every year. If it's not saboteurs, it's local councils or meddling politicians. You should be facing facts, not sticking your head in the sand. Nearly every day the phone rings with some mother asking whether her daughter could come up here for riding lessons, or if not, where could she go? There's absolutely nothing round here. And I just turn away all this good business, because you have Josephine and Charlie schooling hunters all day, instead of teaching little girls.'

The whole family looked at her aghast.

'Teaching little girls!' Charlie's jaw dropped.

'You offered to teach Rowan, I thought.'

'Only Rowan! And only because I owe it to her,

making such a boob of getting that pony back.'

'There are dozens of Rowans wanting to be taught. Josephine could make a fortune teaching, with the name she's made for herself at shows.'

Josephine went a shade paler than normal.

'Teaching *beginners?*'

'There's a demand. I'm only stating what's completely obvious. You needn't all look as if I've gone round the bend, for heaven's sake. It's exactly what Charlie just said – twenty-five horses and not one safe for a beginner. Madness.'

Everyone went on eating, silent, digesting. Lizzie exchanged a glance with Hugh and Hugh raised his eyebrows, but kept his head down. When their mother said something, it was always important. She never wasted words. Her expression was not indignant or heated. Just calm, as ever. Hugh had never wondered about his mother, taking her completely for granted, as one did, but now he wondered a bit that she never complained or seemed discontented. Rowan's mother, for example, had a cleaning lady for a house that was never dirtied, and did absolutely nothing all day as far as he could see. His mother washed and cleaned and cooked and made clothes and never got hurried or more than mildly cross, and was always there to talk to if you wanted. Not that he did, often, because there wasn't anything to get worried about, really. Of course, if the bottom dropped out of their business, there might be. Rowan said she couldn't ever speak to either of her parents about anything that mattered, because they just didn't understand. Hugh had taken it for granted that his mother understood.

'You're suggesting we run a riding school?' Fred asked.

'You're always saying Josephine's entry fees cost a fortune. She might earn them, if just in the evenings, after school. A class of six, say, three times a week . . . people keep asking. Start with Rowan.'

'What on?'

'Exactly. Back to square one.'

No more was said at the time, but Joan's words were not forgotten. Josephine supposed she ought to see about passing her British Horse Society teachers' thing – even if she never did actually get round to teaching, it might come in useful when she left home and wanted to find a job; Fred told himself he would look round for a few decent children's ponies, and Lizzie and Hugh decided they would give Rowan a lesson on Cascade and see what happened.

'As long as we don't let go of him—'

'Couldn't we put him on the lunge?'

'He might buck.'

'Well, she's got to learn to fall off. It's all part of it.'

'Not in her first lesson.'

They announced the news to Rowan, that she was to come up for her first ride.

'Who's going to teach me?' Her eyes glowed, thinking Charlie.

'We are,' said Hugh. 'Lizzie and me.'

Rowan went quiet. Hugh was so bossy, a real bighead. But Lizzie, who was (Rowan knew) afraid of Birdie, would know how she felt. If she was there it would be all right.

'We'll lend you a hat and things.' Lizzie guessed that Mrs Watkins was likely to rush out and buy a black showing jacket and £100 jods if she heard the news. 'You might hate it, you never know.'

Rowan could not believe that. 'Tonight?'

'Tonight? Oh well, why not?' Hugh's enthusiasm was dying off quite quickly.

After school, before Rowan came, he rode Cascade out and tried to make him tired, but Cascade was so fit he didn't get tired, only excited, which Hugh realized (too late) was a mistake. He tried to cool him down, riding him round the manège, but it was so *boring*.

'I'm not cut out to be a teacher,' he said to Lizzie.

'Bad luck,' she said. 'She's here.'

Mr Watkins had brought Rowan up in the car. Lizzie and Hugh were terrified he was going to stay and watch. The Watkins had insisted on paying for the lesson, which was very worrying. If Cascade bucked her off, Hugh decided, they would give the money back.

But, thank goodness, Mr Watkins drove away, and Rowan came out to the manège with Lizzie, fastening up her borrowed helmet.

'First, you must learn to mount,' Lizzie said. 'Hugh will demonstrate.'

Hugh demonstrated. Then he got off and showed how he could vault on, and after two vaults, he showed Rowan how he could run up from behind and jump up astride Cascade's rump.

'If I took the saddle off, I'd land in the right place,' he said. 'Like a cowboy robbing a bank.'

'Look,' Lizzie said. 'This is a riding lesson, to learn to do it properly. Not a circus audition.'

'Cascade's brilliant at gymkhana,' said Hugh. He wanted to add, *So am I*, but thought it was rather too boastful, so said instead, 'We're in the Prince Philip team.'

'What's the Prince Philip team?'

'The mounted games team, for the Pony Club. You know, the finalists do it on television. We've been in the final, me and Cascade.'

'Oh, do shut up, Hugh,' Lizzie said. 'You didn't win. This is supposed to be a riding lesson. Come and hold Cascade and I'll show Rowan how to mount.'

Rowan managed to get on the proper way and Lizzie showed her how to hold the reins. After that Lizzie and Hugh supposed you just walked round. They couldn't think of anything else, except keep your heels down, elbows in and squeeze a sponge with your hands. That only took a minute and there still were fifty minutes to go. Pressing with her heels to move on was quite unnecessary, as Cascade was champing to go faster.

'He feels very joggy,' Rowan said rather anxiously.

'He'll settle down when he realizes it's not jumping,' Lizzie said.

Cascade had never walked round the manège without being asked to do anything. He got nervous, stopping and starting, wondering at the strange feel in his saddle. Nobody but Hugh had ridden him for years.

'He might go better on the lunge,' Hugh decided. 'He knows what's wanted, on the lunge.'

Lizzie was undecided, but Hugh went off to the tack

room and came back with the long lunging rein and head collar. He put it on and said to Lizzie, 'You can do it.'

The idea was that the pony went round Lizzie in large circles, on the end of the rein, obeying her voice, while Rowan got the feel of things. Hugh sat on the fence looking bored, thinking how quite extraordinary it was that a person couldn't ride. What was so difficult about it? He just couldn't see. Yet Rowan couldn't even walk without lurching about and looking terrified.

'Relax,' Lizzie said.

Clever idea, Hugh thought. Perhaps Lizzie was a born teacher and would make the Hawes a fortune. People who can, do; people who couldn't, taught; he remembered the saying. It was true that some of the best riding teachers he knew of (he had never had a lesson, as such, only been shouted at by his father) had never been seen on a horse themselves.

Suddenly there was a loud scream and Rowan came flying through the air in his direction, to land on the edge of the manège with a terrific flump. She hit her head on the wooden fence with a crack that shook the whole rail and lay still. Hugh felt his jaw fall open with amazement. Lizzie dropped the rein and ran towards Rowan, and Cascade took to his heels and went tearing round the manège bucking and fly-kicking.

'Catch your stupid pony!' Lizzie screamed at him.

'What happened?' Hugh hadn't taken it in at all.

'He let out an enormous buck. He's really *stupid*! Just like his owner!' She was jibbering with fury.

Hugh looked at Rowan, feeling a bit sick. Lizzie dropped down beside her. Rowan lay face down with her nose in the peat and appeared to be quite unconscious.

'What shall we do?'

'She'll come round in a minute. We don't want Mum and Dad to know, for goodness sake! Rowan!' Lizzie hissed in Rowan's ear.

'Is she breathing?' Hugh asked. 'You're supposed to put a mirror up to their nostrils and it mists over if they're still alive.'

'Oh, do shut up, if you can't say anything more intelligent! She's saying something. Her lips are moving. She's coming round. Rowan!'

Lizzie gave Rowan a little shake and moved her head to the side.

'You shouldn't move her in case she's broken her neck.'

'*Shut up!* Rowan, can you hear me?'

Rowan groaned and her eyes opened.

'Hooray,' said Hugh. 'It's nothing.' But he knew how she must be feeling.

'Rowan! It's me, Lizzie. Can you see me? Are you all right?'

Hugh left them to it and went to catch Cascade, who was now standing by the gate, obviously not wanting to be a riding-school pony. He looked anxiously at Hugh, aware of his disobedience. But Hugh was on his side. He took off the lunging rein and said, 'It's all right, mate.' They went back to the stable yard, and Hugh put Cascade away and hung up the tack. There was no one around save Charlie, who was starting evening feeds.

'That was a very short lesson,' Charlie said.

Hugh hesitated. He looked out of the back window of the feed room and saw that Rowan was still lying down, although she seemed to be talking.

'He bucked her off,' Hugh said.

'Jeez, you're hopeless,' Charlie said. 'Can't you control that pony at all?'

'She got knocked out.'

Charlie, shocked, dropped the feed-bin lid. 'You idiots!'

He hurried out to the school and Rowan was able to focus her blurred vision on lovely Charlie, his gypsy eyes staring with great concern into her own. After ascertaining that there was nothing seriously wrong, Charlie picked her up and carried her back to the tack room. Rowan, in Charlie's arms, felt it was worth being bucked off for. She felt fuzzy but secure, initiated into this glorious life. He laid her tenderly in the dog-hairy armchair beneath the rows of saddles and said, 'I'll get Mum to ring yours, and she can take you to the surgery. Concussion can be dangerous.'

With one breath, Rowan, Lizzie and Hugh exclaimed, 'No!'

'I'm not concussed,' Rowan said quickly. 'Honestly.'

'Don't tell them,' Hugh said crossly. 'It'll spoil everything.'

'We'll get into awful trouble,' Lizzie said.

'You mustn't,' Rowan said. 'You know what my parents are like! They'll fuss terribly, and not let me come here any more.'

Charlie frowned, knowing they were right.

'Nobody saw. I'll be quite all right in ten minutes,' Rowan said. 'Honestly.'

The threat of her parents knowing terrified her. Her father would kick up a terrible furore and talk about suing. And they would never, ever let her have a riding lesson again.

Charlie, thank goodness, realized the danger.

'No, well. I can see what you mean.'

But he was worried about being in collusion, responsible enough to know the seriousness of it.

'You wouldn't have known if I hadn't told you,' Hugh very reasonably pointed out. 'Go back to feeding and pretend you don't know anything. You'll spoil everything if you tell.'

'Please!' Rowan said. 'I'm fine, really,' she lied.

'OK.' He was dubious, but departed.

'Thank goodness for that!' Lizzie said. 'I'll make you a cup of tea, Rowan. That's good for shock.'

There was a kettle and tea things in the tack room. Lizzie made the tea and Rowan sat in the armchair convincing herself that she felt all right. She tried standing up, but had to hastily sit down again, as the room tipped from side to side like they were at sea. Her head ached hideously.

'You're sort of green,' Hugh said, not very helpfully.

'She'll be all right in half an hour,' Lizzie snapped.

'I feel a bit sick,' Rowan admitted.

'Don't worry,' said Lizzie. 'We've all done it. Charlie

broke a vertebra when he was fourteen, and Hugh was out for four hours once.'

'Five,' Hugh said.

'Don't swank.'

'Lucky it was right at the beginning of the lesson,' Hugh said. 'You've still got three-quarters of an hour to get better. Is your father coming back for you?'

'I told him not to, but he said he would.'

By the time the hour was up Rowan could walk in a straight line, although she felt terrible. They waited in an anxious row as Mr Watkins drove into the yard. Luckily it was going dusk and he didn't notice Rowan's pallor.

'How was it?' He was in a good mood for once. 'Enjoy yourself?'

'Yes, it was great.' Rowan grinned hugely.

'So how much do I owe you young people?' He groped around and pulled out his wallet.

'Oh no, really, we don't want any money,' Lizzie said hurriedly.

'Come. I insist. She'll want to come again, won't she? We must have it on a businesslike footing.'

He insisted on giving Lizzie £20. She thought it was a fortune, even if the lesson had been phenomenally successful. She blushed scarlet and tried to refuse it but Mr Watkins would have none of it.

'A one to one lesson – that's the going rate, I'm sure. Well done, all of you. Come along, Rowan.'

Rowan staggered to the car and got in and he whisked her away out of the yard, leaving Lizzie and Hugh staring in horror at the £20 note.

'She'll never come again! Fancy getting paid that for nearly killing her!'

They went and told Charlie and he laughed and said he would take care of it for them.

Meanwhile Rowan went home and was sick in the bathroom, but came down and talked enthusiastically about how she had enjoyed her lesson. It took an enormous effort. Her mother said she looked pale. 'It must be the excitement.'

'What are we going to do?'

On the school bus the next morning, Rowan was still a green colour and had to keep her eyes shut. 'I was so good at saying how much I enjoyed it my father says he'll bring me up again next week, and my mother's going to buy me jods and everything. She's got friendly with Mrs Prebble, and now she thinks it's all a wonderful idea.' She sighed deeply, and had to admit: 'I can't face riding Cascade again. I'll be terrified. I'm useless.'

'No. It's him that's useless. We wouldn't dream of putting you back on him.'

'What'll we do then?'

'We can just pretend you have a lesson, and take the money,' Hugh said. Was he serious? He was grinning.

'If you weren't so useless, the pony would have some manners,' Lizzie shouted at him.

Rowan's head ached abominably and the landscape swam in green arcs beyond the window. At school she kept her head down in class and hid from the teachers, and was sick once more in the lavatory at break time. She felt rather desperate. The effort at home in the evening, being bright, exhausted her. Her mother kept giving her strange looks. 'Are you sure you feel all right, dear? There's flu about, I hear. You're dreadfully pale.'

'I'm fine!' Big, bright smile. Knife stabs in the cranium.

But as the week went on she gradually recovered. Only the thought of the next lesson made her feel ill again. Was she really such a wimp? But both Lizzie and Hugh said it was quite normal to be put off by such a happening.

Unfortunately Hugh let out what had happened in front of his mother, and Joan Hawes came out to find Rowan. She gave her a lecture.

'If that ever happens again, don't take any notice of my stupid children, but tell your mother and go to the doctor. Concussion can be very serious and needs rest to cure it. I'm very angry with Hugh and Lizzie.'

'I'm quite all right now, honestly!'

'Well, you look it, I must admit. But remember what I've said. You are all old enough to act responsibly. It was really stupid to put a beginner on Cascade. I don't know what to suggest you ride – but certainly not that one again.'

It was Charlie who came up with the solution. 'You must go and see Babar,' he said to Lizzie, 'and get her to ride up here on Diamond. Then Rowan can have her lesson on Diamond and you can give Babar the money. She'll be terribly pleased.'

'Can't we keep any of it?' Hugh asked.

'No.'

'But we're the *agents*. Agents always keep at least ten per cent.'

'You didn't do anything at all, except vault on Cascade just to show off,' Lizzie said. 'So I don't see why you should even think of having any of it.'

Mr Watkins' eager gifts of £20 notes had set them all thinking what an easy way it was to make money. 'Mum's right, really. We could teach children if we had some decent ponies,' Lizzie said. 'At least, I could. Hugh was useless.'

'You could teach the beginners,' Hugh said. 'I could take them on when they were more advanced. Jumping.'

'Huh!'

Shrimp came out with 'Horse and Hound' and showed them a large coloured photograph of a pony at a show covered in rosettes and herself astride, gazing haughtily at the camera.

'Yuk,' said Hugh.

'I'm going to pin it up in the tack room,' Shrimp said. 'It's nice.'

'Don't put it near my tack. I might vomit.'

'Your tack's so filthy a bit of sick on it wouldn't make any difference.'

They were used to seeing Shrimp picked up by smart horseboxes or expensive cars at weekends to be whisked away to big shows, carrying her bag of immaculate gear. When she was younger (six) her mother had gone with her, but now she was such a professional she went on her own, the rich showing family she rode for treating her like one of their own. Lizzie and Hugh wondered why she didn't die of boredom – 'You don't even have to jump!' – but in their hearts they knew that she was worth her weight in gold to the pony owners, showing their – often difficult – ponies with a rare expertise.

'Mum says you're going to give lessons. I've come to watch.'

'Jeer, I suppose?'

Shrimp grinned. She was amazingly composed for a nine-year-old – all that show biz, Lizzie supposed. 'Do you want to do it, as you know everything?'

'No fear. Only watch.'

But Lizzie knew it would be all right with the phlegmatic Diamond. Babar was utterly reliable. She arrived at the right time and Rowan got on Diamond without any fear, so they all trailed out to the manège. Babar turned out to be an excellent teacher, much better than Lizzie, and in the end Lizzie let her take over and sat on the fence with Shrimp. (Hugh had lost interest now that Cascade wasn't involved and nobody would let him share in the money.) Babar got Rowan trotting and Diamond even lurched into a few canter steps without Rowan coming adrift. Rowan found her confidence, and thoroughly enjoyed herself. She was confident that the stolid Diamond would play no tricks, and his long flopping ears ahead of her flitched agreeably like a seaside donkey's. She felt none of the tremors of alarm that had exuded from Cascade at the feel of her insecurity. Riding was suddenly full of fun and hope, and her past week of depression and disappointment was forgotten.

'What a nag!' Shrimp whispered to Lizzie. 'I wouldn't be seen dead on it.'

'He does the job,' Lizzie said sharply. It was a long time since she had felt the enjoyment in riding that she now saw Rowan revealing. Why did she have to suffer Birdie with all her traumas, when an old steady like Diamond – well, prettier – was all her unadventurous heart desired? Perhaps Charlie could persuade their father to sell Birdie to the Prebbles. Smartypants Matty was welcome to her.

'You're a much better teacher than me,' she said to Babar, when they had finished. 'You might as well teach Rowan and let Mr Watkins know it's you.'

She looked so disappointed that Babar said kindly, 'We can still come up here and use your land. Mr Watkins needn't know anything different.'

'And share the money,' Rowan said. 'Would that be fair?'

'Babar does everything. She should have more than half,' Lizzie said.

'I don't want the money. I like doing it,' Babar said.

'We could save the money, to buy Rowan her own pony!' Lizzie said.

'Buy Swallow back!'

'What a good idea! We'll save it!'

Now Lizzie wished she could have it after all, to save to buy herself a pony. It was her idea and she had wasted it on Rowan, speaking without thinking. Then, seeing Rowan's shining face, she was ashamed.

'When you've learned to ride a bit,' she said, 'you could go over to that riding stable that bought Swallow, and have a lesson on him.'

'Oh, what a brilliant idea!'

'He's probably settled down now, with plenty of work, and he'd be much easier.'

Rowan was thrilled with these amazing ideas. Babar departed on Diamond, and Rowan and Lizzie trailed into the tack room where Rowan took her hat off and sat down in the armchair. She felt a bit feeble. Charlie came in to fetch a head collar.

'I'm going to bring Fedora in. She looks off-colour.'

'She's turned pink?' Shrimp said.

Charlie gave her a cold look. 'She's not eating. She's tucked up.'

'When is her foal due?' Rowan asked.

'Six weeks yet.'

Charlie looked worried. He went out and Shrimp said, 'Why is he so potty on that terrible old mare?'

'Because she's his own,' Lizzie said. 'Not Dad's. And he remembers her when she looked wonderful, racing at Newbury. And he thinks she can be like that again. And the foal – the foal might be marvellous.'

'I think he's mad.' Shrimp departed with a toss of her head.

'Isn't she horrible?' Lizzie said to Rowan. 'She's absolutely heartless. So cocky. We all hate her.'

Perhaps, Rowan thought, there was something to be said for being an only child.

That night, Fred Hawes had his first heart attack.

Chapter Seven

'What do you mean, a heart attack?' Mrs Watkins asked. 'How bad? Is he in hospital?'

'They took him there. Then he came home again. No, it's not bad but he's got to rest. He passed out and went peculiar.'

'Well, I expect he'll be all right. They give you tablets for things like that these days.'

'It's very hard for him to rest,' Rowan pointed out. 'He goes all over the place, buying horses.'

'That boy of his will have to do it.'

Rowan, immersed in life at High Hawes, knew it wasn't as easy as that. Charlie and Josephine worked full time looking after and tuning the horses their father brought home. When buyers came, they had to show them off. Fred Hawes hadn't sat on a horse since he was six, but he had an eye for a horse second to none, and acquired bargains which less astute dealers missed. Nobody else could do his job. Rowan had heard her friends muttering between themselves about what would happen if their father had to lay up. Gloom had noticeably descended.

But Rowan had more immediate things on her mind.

'Charlie's mare is due to foal any minute now. He says I can go and watch. But it'll most likely be in the night.'

'Well, if it's in the night, I'm afraid not.'

'It would only be half an hour or so!'

'Absolutely not. You've your school work to think of. You wouldn't sleep a wink, all the excitement.'

Rowan reported back at High Hawes. 'I've never seen anything born! Not even a kitten.'

'Oh, it's all bloody and yukky. You haven't missed anything,' said Hugh. 'Great judders and slime.'

'I bet you were slimy when you came out,' Shrimp said.

'It's wonderful,' Charlie said. 'You ought to see it.'

'I'm going to, Charlie. Promise! Promise you'll wake me!' Shrimp badgered.

'You could get out of bed and come up, Rowan,' Hugh suggested. 'They wouldn't hear you, would they?'

'How would I know?'

'We could send a signal. Light a bonfire, like the Armada.'

'I could turn on the school floodlight. You'd see that,' Charlie suggested.

'I can see that from my bed!'

'Well, then. She'll warn us, after all. I'll know roughly. If it's imminent, I'll switch on the light. Even if you miss it – it's usually very quick – at least you'll see the foal newborn.'

Rowan could tell Charlie was quite excited at the prospect. Fedora was heavy and bad-tempered and due any day. It was better thinking about the new life than thinking about Fred, and the problems with the yard. In spite of their all agreeing that their mother's idea about having a teaching sideline and a business in children's ponies was a good one, no one had said anything about it. Babar had gone on teaching Rowan on Diamond, and Rowan was pronounced to be 'quite competent'. 'You need something better than Diamond, but you're not ready yet for Cascade or Birdie,' was the general opinion.

Rowan didn't think she would ever be ready for Cascade or Birdie. She hadn't forgotten that they had planned to go over to the riding stable that had bought Swallow, but nobody had mentioned it again. She wanted to go terribly but she didn't want to go on her own.

'Will you come with me?' she asked Lizzie. 'We could use the money in the pot.' This was the money Mr Watkins insisted on paying for her lessons, which was now something of an embarrassment. They kept it in an instant-coffee jar hidden behind a box of wormers.

Lizzie looked doubtful. 'I don't really *want* to. It's such a long way, just for a ride. Why don't you ask Babar?'

Rowan asked Babar. Babar said yes, why not? She had never ridden anything but Diamond.

'We could go on Saturday morning. There's a bus. We don't want a lesson, like, just a hack.'

'Yes, I'll arrange it! I'll ring them up. I'll say a hack. And I'll ask for Swallow!'

'Tell 'um how you ride, like – not very experienced.'

'Yes, I'll say that. But you're good.'

'I'm only good on Diamond. I dunno what another's like, do I?'

Her parents agreed to Rowan's request, thinking it could do no harm to humour her this once, and Rowan duly rang to book a ride. Laura Griffiths sounded weary and hesitated when Rowan asked for Swallow. 'I suppose that'll be all right,' she said.

Rowan wasn't encouraged, but soon forgot about it in her excitement. She told Lizzie and Lizzie said, 'He'll probably buck you off, like Cascade.'

Hugh said, 'Fedora's going to go splat tonight, Charlie says.'

'You are *foul*,' Lizzie said to him.

'I'm going to stay up all night,' Shrimp said. 'Charlie's going to, aren't you, Charlie?'

'Probably. I'll see, later.'

It was a fine, soft evening smelling of summer and May blossom. The hedges up from the village were untrimmed and spilled their white flowers like confetti across the bumpy Tarmac. The fields were lush with spring grass and the buttercups that made Fred Hawes swear, and in the woods above the farm the rooks homed in on their untidy nests with a great squawking and flapping against the cloudless sky. Rowan longed to ride through the woods up onto the downs with Lizzie and Hugh, but it was impossible to borrow Diamond and leave Babar behind. She longed for her own pony. Her parents kept saying, 'Well, later, we'll think about it.'

Rowan went out across the yard to visit Fedora, who was in her loosebox round the back – 'Keep that ugly mare out of my sale yard,' Fred had ordered. But

Rowan didn't think Fedora was ugly any more, with her gaunt flanks filled out and the scars faded from her legs. Her summer coat gleamed a rich, bright chestnut, although she was never groomed, and her once-despondent eyes were now bright and – it must be said – irritable. She switched her fine red tail nervously at Rowan's approach. You had to handle her with care. Rowan only looked, out of range. Drips of milk were running down Fedora's back legs, and a sheen of sweat had broken out over her shoulders.

'Oh, come on, have it now,' Rowan urged her. 'Don't wait till midnight!'

Charlie was restless too, and came to have a look.

'She won't be long.'

'I must see it!'

'Ask your mum to let you stay. Ring her up.'

'Shall I?'

'It's worth a try.'

'Until ten o'clock,' her mother said, as a great concession. 'Then, if nothing's happening, you must come straight home.'

'She'll be later than that. They like the dark,' Charlie said. 'But you never know.'

'What do you want, a colt or a filly?'

'I don't care. Just a good one. It should be – her

107

owner knew what he was doing. He bred some good horses in his day. He's bound to have sent her to a good stallion.'

But by ten o'clock, Fedora had settled down and was munching her hay. Rowan, deeply disappointed, ran home down the hill and went to bed. She slept heavily, her window open.

Something woke her. The house was silent and it was pitch-dark, save for one bright light distant across the fields. Rowan lay looking at the light. It wasn't usually there. Then she remembered – the signal! She slipped out of bed and ran to the window. The school light – she could see clearly now where it came from. Fedora was having her foal!

Rowan dragged a jersey over her pyjamas, thrust her feet into her sandals and slipped downstairs. It didn't matter if her parents woke – she would be away before they realized. But she was neat and silent and out of the house without disturbing anybody, dragging her bike from the shed and hopping onto the pedals. Her excitement fired her up the hill. She skidded into the yard, breathless, dropped the bike and ran.

There was a light on in Fedora's box. Shrimp was hanging over the door, presumably excluded by Charlie.

'Rowan – good! I remembered the light! She's started, but Charlie won't let me in.'

Rowan looked over the door and saw that the mare was lying down. She was grunting and thrashing her legs about, and Charlie sat in the straw by her head, talking softly to her. He looked up, saw Rowan and grinned. 'Well done!'

'How long will she be?'

'No time at all, if we're lucky.'

Rowan could tell he was really excited. She felt nervous and a bit queer. Something was happening, she could see, and now she was here she didn't want to look.

'It's got white socks!' Shrimp squeaked.

'God almighty!' Charlie breathed.

Rowan didn't understand.

'It's got a white nose!' Shrimp shouted. 'Charlie, it's white!'

Rowan forced herself to look and saw a most extraordinary thing. The foal appeared before her very eyes, as if conjured, diving out into the fresh straw with its front legs pointing forward and its little head laid on its paws like a dog. It was tiny and a most remarkable colour: white with large chestnut patches. A circus horse.

'I don't believe it!'

Rowan saw that Charlie was poleaxed. He looked thunderous. Shrimp was laughing.

'What a marvellous, marvellous foal!'

'It's a travesty – a freak! It's rubbish! I don't believe it!'

Rowan could see that Charlie was close to tears with disappointment. Ignorant as she was, even she could see that this was a very strange produce from a large chestnut thoroughbred. Fedora groaned with relief and turned her elegant neck to see what lay in the straw behind her. She stretched out her neck as if to lick it, but instead she laid back her ears and bit it. A startled squeak of pain came from the little foal.

'Yeah, that's just how I feel, old girl. We don't want it, do we?'

'Charlie!' Shrimp squeaked. 'You can't say that!'

'She's going to reject it.'

The foal was already making great efforts to get to its feet. It scrabbled and swayed on its haunches, thrusting to get up. Half up, it was then knocked backwards by an angry Fedora with another thrust of her bared teeth. She started to get up, scraping up the straw. Charlie stood watching. Undaunted, the foal was struggling helplessly to get its legs back underneath it. Charlie made no effort to help it. He just stood with his hands in his pockets.

'Charlie!' Shrimp cried, 'You must do something! She'll hurt it!'

'She'll kill it. Best thing,' Charlie said.

He turned away and came to the door and unshot the bolt. Although he was framed against the light, Rowan thought there were tears in his eyes. He came out and shut the door behind him.

Shrimp screamed at him, 'Charlie! You can't!'

But Charlie was already walking back to the house. Over his shoulder he muttered, 'I'll come back in a bit, clear her up.' He disappeared round the corner of the barn.

Shrimp burst into loud blubbing tears and unbolted the stable door.

'You'll help me, won't you?' she sobbed to Rowan. 'He's *beastly*! He can't—'

Rowan was appalled. Like Shrimp, she couldn't possibly stand by and watch the little defenceless foal being bullied. Fedora's ears were flat back and she was trembling and sweating, half up, her forelegs out in front of her.

'Go and fetch a lead rope – quick!' Shrimp screamed at Rowan.

Rowan fled. Charlie had unlocked the tack-room door and the light was on. She pulled down a rope and sprinted back to the loosebox. Fedora was wearing a head collar. Rowan flung the rope at Shrimp over the door and saw Shrimp clip it onto the head collar just before Fedora, with an angry plunge, got to her feet. Shrimp was tiny at the head of the big, disturbed mare. Rowan, terrified, knew she had to go into the box to help. She unbolted the door and went in. Shrimp just managed to slip the lead rope through the ring-bolt on the wall, but Fedora flung round and it flew out of Shrimp's hand.

'Help me! Hang on!' Shrimp bellowed.

Rowan jumped forward and grabbed the rope and jerked on it with all her strength as Fedora turned and made a plunge towards the foal. Rowan stopped her, but the mare was much stronger than she was. Shrimp, like an angry wasp, leaped for the end of the rope and threaded it through the ring-bolt again, making a knot. She was so quick and deft that the mare was held before she had a chance to pull away again. Unable to use her teeth, she lashed out with her hindlegs. The foal was lying behind her, right in the line of fire. The first kick missed but the second caught the foal on the shoulder and tore off a long strip of skin. Bright blood sprung across the snow-white coat and the foal let out another pathetic squeak, dropping back into the straw.

Rowan could feel her heart pounding heavily and the tears spurting down her cheeks. They had to drag the foal away, but the mare's heels were lethal. Shrimp was as desperate as she was.

'Go and get a fork, a mucking-out fork!'

The loosebox was a very dangerous place to be. It was big, fortunately, and there was room to pull the foal away if they could brave the awful heels. Shrimp, born into horses, knew things Rowan could not fathom . . . a fork? But Rowan fled to do her bidding. Fedora was making strange noises and rolling her eyes. Rowan went in with the fork and gave it to Shrimp. Shrimp grabbed it and brandished it at Fedora. She looked like a little Boadicea, her hair standing on end, her eyes flashing with fury.

'You *beast*! You *horrid, horrid* animal!' And she jabbed the fork into Fedora's flank. 'Get over!' she roared. 'Get over!'

Fedora made one step sideways and lashed out again. But this time she missed the foal. She jerked at her head but – thank heavens, Rowan breathed – the rope and leather head collar held.

If she got free Rowan thought they would all be killed.

'Get the foal, Rowan!' Shrimp screamed at her. 'Pull it away! Quick!'

Without hesitating Rowan sprang forward. There was nothing to get hold of: the little animal was all slimy and wet and had no handles, only the enormous trembling legs flailing feebly. Its little head struggled up and Rowan looked into its bewildered eyes. She grabbed it, one arm around its neck and the other round its hind quarters. As she did so Fedora lashed out again, in spite of the fork, and the hoof whistled past Rowan's head so close that she felt the wind of its passing. Shrimp jabbed Fedora with the fork so hard that she drew blood.

'Quick! Quick!'

Rowan dragged, half rolled, the foal across the floor, at one point pulling it by the back legs. Shrimp, made strong by her fury, held the mare at bay with determined jabs at her flanks.

'Get it outside!'

Although it was small it was still a very heavy animal. Rowan reached up to push the door open and pulled the foal bodily by its back legs. There was no other way. Out in the yard she fell over, and hadn't the strength to do any more than lie there, beside the foal.

She was shaking like a sail head to wind, half with terror, half with her effort. In an instant Shrimp was beside her, kicking the door shut and ramming home the bolt. She then leaned against the door, shaking as much as Rowan.

'The beast!' she sobbed. 'The beastly mare!'

'But it's all right, Shrimp!' Rowan said. Her two years' superiority in age asserted itself as she realized what a state Shrimp was in, worse than herself. 'We've won!' she said. 'The foal's all right.'

With its instinct for survival the foal was once more struggling to get up. The sight of its antics calmed the hysterics. There was still much to be done.

'Glory!' Shrimp breathed. 'It's ours, Rowan! We've got to look after it!'

Shrimp was a girl of action, as she had already proved. She went round the barn to Cascade's box and led him out and let him loose in the field. Then she came back to Rowan and the foal. Rowan had managed, with her arms round its backside and chest, to get it to stand. The feel of its frailty and yet the urge to struggle and live moved her incredibly. The fact that they had saved its life was almost like having given birth herself and they were both now imbued with a godlike bliss. It was an extraordinary little animal, a pony foal, with an outsize will to make good. Out of the furious, nearly seventeen-hand thoroughbred . . . 'Why?' Rowan asked. 'What happened?'

'Some traveller pony got loose, I should think, and couldn't believe its luck, finding Fedora in a field somewhere. Poor old Charlie.'

Shrimp giggled. With one on each side steadying it, the foal was guided round the corner into Cascade's box. Shrimp put the light on and shut the door and the two girls stood looking at it in wonder. It was a skewbald, well marked, with bold patches of dark chestnut over white. Its head was chestnut but with a white blaze, and its front and back legs were white. It stood firmly now, just swaying slightly, and its expression was one of puzzlement and anxiety. Rowan thought: half an hour ago it was inside Fedora. The miracle of birth was hard to take in, even without the panics of this particular one. Rowan felt drained, and not quite all there.

Shrimp, looking underneath it, said, 'It's a colt.' Then, 'He's mine. My own. I shall bring him up by hand.'

'Why, won't Fedora take him eventually?'

'Once they reject a foal, that's it, usually.'

'Do you have to feed him with a bottle?'

'Yes. Every two hours at first. We've done it before,

with a thoroughbred. We took turns.' Remembering, she added, 'It was awful.' Her face dropped then, and she looked very white and little. 'I will do it, though.' She looked sternly at Rowan. 'They think I don't like work, don't they? They're always saying it. They think I'm stupid. I'll show Hugh. He wouldn't do it, I bet.'

'I'll help you,' Rowan said.

'Yes. If you hadn't come . . . it needed two of us, didn't it?' She grinned and put her arms round the foal and kissed him. He pushed his nuzzle at her, looking for its mother. Shrimp started to look worried. 'We need to feed him now. Soon.'

'What, with cow's milk?'

'No. Special stuff. We've got some, somewhere.' Shrimp considered. 'Would you go and fetch Charlie? He won't have gone to bed, because he's got to come back and see to Fedora. The foal ought to have Fedora's first milk, because it has special good things in it, to make the foal thrive. He can jolly well get that for us, milk it off. You ask him. He's more likely to do it if you ask him.'

Rowan was nervous of this job. She knew Charlie was upset, and approached the house with trepidation. He would be cross at her interfering and snap her head off. Shrimp wouldn't have been able to do it by herself, it was true. Shrimp . . . she should have been called Spitfire, Rowan thought.

The light was on in the kitchen. Rowan went in, feeling rather shaky. The clock on the wall said two-thirty. Rowan had never been out and about at two-thirty in the morning before. She certainly didn't feel sleepy.

Charlie was sitting at the kitchen table with his head lying on his arms, looking asleep. But he heard Rowan and sat up.

'Shrimp sent me,' Rowan said quickly.

'You should have gone home,' Charlie said angrily.

'She wants you to – to do something . . . when you go out to Fedora.'

Charlie didn't say anything, just sat with his head in his hands.

'We've put the foal in Cascade's box.'

He flung round furiously. 'That's a stupid thing to do! Now what? In a case like that you let nature take over. Nobody wants a runt like that – who's going to rear it? All that work, for rubbish!'

'Shrimp is. We are.'

'You've no idea!'

He was so angry, Rowan was frightened. She stood

feeling really miserable, the night that should have been so lovely shattered by his disappointment.

'I'm sorry,' she muttered. 'The way it turned out . . . for you.'

'It was going to be my own, my very own, out of a good mare . . . I was an idiot to make dreams. With horses – dreams hardly ever work out—'

As if she didn't know! Perhaps he recognized this, for he made an obvious effort to pull himself together, and gave her a hint of a smile.

'Sorry. I didn't mean to take it out on you.'

Rowan felt a great surge of passionate love for Charlie and wanted to throw her arms round his neck and comfort him, but the thought gave her a hint of the giggles, and she merely smiled instead, thankful his awful rage had dissipated. He was her hero . . . had he really shed tears? She was pretty sure he had. She was awed.

He got up and shrugged into his jacket.

'If Shrimp – and you – want to rear this foal, it will depend a bit on Father, and Mum. After all, you've got to be at school all day, and sleep at night. You don't know what you're taking on. Father will say, like me, it isn't worth it. I'm warning you. What Mum and Dad decide, that will be it. So don't count on it.'

Rowan's heart plummeted. They wouldn't let it die, surely?

'It might be best to shoot it.'

Rowan felt her throat swell as if she had swallowed an apple whole, and didn't dare say anything.

'But for now,' Charlie said, 'we'd better appease Shrimp – she's a nutter.'

Rowan went back with him to Fedora's box, and stood looking over the door while Charlie worked over her. She was still in a very disturbed state, and he was very gentle with her, talking to her softly. He cleaned the box of the mess and put a sweat rug on the mare.

'Shrimp said – she wants the milk, the first milk.' Rowan forced out her instructions.

'The colostrum? OK.'

Charlie now seemed back to his calm self. To milk the mare was a three-person job: one to hold up the front leg to stop her kicking, one to hold the bucket and one to milk. Charlie was agreeable because he thought the mare would be more comfortable and settle down better. But once the milk was in the bucket he left the girls to their own devices. He did not want to set eyes on the foal, and when Fedora was let loose and had stopped sweating and stamping, he went back to bed.

Shrimp hunted for the bottle that was somewhere in the yard's first-aid cupboard. Together, at three o'clock in the morning, Rowan and Shrimp sat in the straw and gave their funny little foal its first food. After all the excitement, they both felt overwhelmed with pure pleasure and love for the foal, each other, life, and the world. Rowan had never felt so emotional, not even over Swallow.

At four o'clock she left Shrimp curled up in the straw with the foal lying beside her, and set off down the hill for home. The sky was thin with the flush of dawn, pale and grey and soft and smelling of dew and summer. She wanted to drink it in, feeling it too rare and good to miss. Life seemed almost too much to take in; she felt as if she was bursting.

Tomorrow's – today's! – problems could wait.

Chapter Eight

It was Joan Hawes who saved the life of Fedora's foal. Fred said he should be put down, Charlie agreed, even Josephine said he wasn't worth the trouble of hand-feeding. Lizzie, Hugh and Shrimp staunchly vowed to look after him.

'Take it to school with you, on the bus?' Their father was dismissive. 'Don't be ridiculous.'

Joan, with a sympathetic glance towards the white-faced Shrimp, said calmly, 'I will feed him while they are at school. They can take it in turns at night.'

'Oh, Mum!' Shrimp flung her arms round her mother's neck. 'Rowan will share too, I know she will. Oh, thank you, thank you, thank you!'

'Good, Rowan can do my share,' Hugh said.

'Babar will help, I bet,' said Lizzie.

'But he's mine, remember,' Shrimp shouted. 'He's my foal!'

'Yes,' said her mother. 'I shall certainly remember. He is yours, and you will do all the mucking out and all the looking-after when you are at home.'

'I won't do any more shows. I shall stay at home all the time.'

'No. You can't let your owners down like that, without warning. You must go on showing until they are able to find somebody else.' Her mother was stern.

Charlie raised his eyebrows. He was going to say, 'They'll never find anyone as good as Shrimp,' but decided not to add to her already enlarged opinion of herself. Everyone was amazed that she was prepared to give up showing for the useless little scrap of a foal, which she christened Bonzo.

To give him his due, Bonzo had a strong inclination to live, in spite of his bad beginning. Although weedy, he had great determination, and scrabbled to his feet whenever anyone came near, eager for his bottle. Even Charlie admitted that he was a tough little character. Charlie even stooped to feeding him when Joan had to be away from home for more than two hours, although this happened rarely and nobody knew but Joan. Shrimp set up a camp bed in the foal's loose-box with an alarm clock nearby, and the bottled milk made up ready and keeping warm in an old hay box, and she was the one who did the midnight to dawn watch, without any complaint. Rowan was allowed by her parents to do two nights a week up to eleven o'clock, when her mother came to fetch her in the car, but she rarely went to sleep. She was quite happy to lie there watching the foal, or staring out at the dusk and the first stars, thinking how lucky she was to have this second home at High Hawes. Even without her own pony, she was happy just to be accepted into the Hawes yard.

Babar made the appointment for them to ride at the Half Moon Riding Stables two Saturdays after Bonzo was born. Rowan was crossing the days off on her calendar, and thought she would be sick with excitement when the time came.

'Reckon he'll 'ave quieted down, working in a hire stable,' Babar commented. ''E might be just the job for you now.'

Rowan still had her dream of owning Swallow and riding with Lizzie and Hugh up across the downs on her own pony. And with Charlie too – for now that Fedora had no foal to look after, Charlie had taken to riding her out, just walking for an hour or two in the evening before it got dusk. Rowan's dream grew more star-studded . . . to riding with Charlie across the downs in the cool of the evening, the horses close together on the smooth turf . . . cantering in the moonlight, following the red whisk of Fedora's tail . . .

Fedora, rid of her encumbrance, was growing back into the elegant thoroughbred racehorse she was bred to be. With work, her neck and quarters filled out with muscle, and her dull demeanour was sloughed off. Her eyes were bright again, and her coat gleamed with good health. She looked about her with her ears pricked, her gaze alert.

'She was worth an old engine, eh?' Charlie said with satisfaction. 'It didn't go, anyway.'

The Saturday morning designated for the ride at the Half Moon Stables arrived at last. Although it was flaming June, the fields were shrouded in soft rain. But Rowan's excitement was not to be quenched, and she met Babar at the bus stop dressed in her new jods and the tweed jacket she had borrowed from Lizzie. Babar looked just the same in her muddy anorak and green gumboots, swinging her grey skullcap by its strap. Rowan had read in books that it was bad to ride in gumboots and hoped she wasn't going to feel ashamed of Babar. She was then ashamed of this thought. The bus came on time, in fact two minutes early, and as it moved off she could feel her legs literally trembling with excitement. She pressed her knees hard together. It was bound to be a disappointment, she told herself. Nothing could live up to such expectations as she had woven in her dreams. As if guessing her thoughts, Babar said, 'It might not be such a wow, this riding stable. It won't be like High Hawes, you know.'

The Half Moon Riding Stables proved to be a yard of jerry-built sheds with tin roofs situated at the far end of a small industrial estate. Rowan had to adjust her expectations immediately, walking down the drive between lorries and workshops sparking out purple sprays of acetylene torches. She felt sick again, and her face was white. Babar was thinking that this visit might be a mistake, but kept her thoughts to herself. Rowan, she knew, had the usual urban view of animal life, giving animals human emotions. But a pony didn't care if its stable was falling down as long as it was fed and had its companions around it and was treated sensibly. There were more unhappy ponies overfed and underworked, overheated in thermal rugs in cosy stables, than there ever were out in the fields apparently neglected. But it was too late to start propounding such theories to the dismayed Rowan.

Sadly, the tatty stables were a sign of Laura Griffiths's trouble with money. Laura Griffiths was knowledgeable and meant well, but was a hopeless organizer and had no business head. Her stables were falling apart in more ways than one.

The usual contingent of girls were milling around outside the yard, tacking up some scurfy ponies with straw in their tails. The ponies stood dejectedly, laying back their ears as their bridles were dragged on. The saddles, although clean, were old-fashioned and worn-out. Laura Griffiths came out of the tack room and saw them. Her habitual worried frown deepened.

'Oh, you're the girls from High Hawes who booked. One of you wanted to ride Swallow?'

'Yes,' said Babar.

'Well, you're going out with Fiona and Sharon, and you can swap ponies if Swallow is—' she hesitated. 'If he doesn't suit,' she decided on.

It was only then that Rowan realized that one of the scurfy ponies was Swallow. She hadn't recognized him. He was standing with his head down and his eyes half-shut, his bright coat staring dully and all the roundness and bounce disappeared. While she stood, her jaw dropping with dismay, the girl plonking a saddle with no stuffing onto his back said to her, 'It's you that wants him? I'm going to ride Fable and if he's naughty we can swap. Your friend can have the Armchair and Sharon'll take Snowball.'

'Good,' said Laura, and went back into the tack room. If she had noticed Babar's gumboots she wasn't going to say anything.

Rowan went up to Swallow and put her arms around his neck. He made no response, beyond sighing deeply. Fiona gave his girths a great heave, which provoked a cross grunt, and Swallow took a sharp nip at Rowan's arm. She jumped back, shocked. Babar said quickly, 'Lots of 'um snap when you pull up the girth.' Then she added, despite herself, 'Poor littl'un. 'E's lost his spirit.'

Was spirit something that could be repaired? Rowan was now so disappointed that she didn't even want to ride. But Fiona was holding Swallow and expecting her to mount. She hopped up and settled herself in the excruciatingly uncomfortable saddle. Fiona shortened her stirrup leathers. Swallow stood like a pudding, head down. Rowan didn't see how he could possibly be naughty without any spirit.

The Armchair, Babar's mount, was well named, for in spite of his dirty coat and gaunt flanks, he was a naturally round and cheerful but rather ugly chestnut cob. He had a wide blaze and four white stockings and a rather humorous expression. Babar, settling herself,

said, 'Cor, I can see why 'e's called Armchair.'
Recalling Diamond's sharp spine and narrow
shoulders, Rowan imagined he felt as different from
Diamond as sitting on an apple would be to sitting on
a fence. Fable was a dull-looking light bay mare of
about fourteen two, rather like a down-market Birdie,
and Snowball was a small white pony with a mulish
look in his eyes.

When they were all mounted Fiona said, 'All right,
then,' and led the way out of a gate at the back of the
yard. To Rowan's relief she saw that they were not
going to promenade through the industrial estate, but
along quite a pleasant lane towards some woods and
fields. Swallow walked sourly with his head down, his
nose resting on Fable's tail. When Rowan tried to pull
him out to go alongside he put back his ears and
resisted stubbornly, not moving out of his track. Babar
manoeuvred herself alongside.

'This 'un isn't 'alf comfortable,' she said.

Rowan tried to tell herself that she had achieved her
heart's desire, to ride Swallow, but somehow it was
nothing like her dreams. Fiona and Sharon rode in
front, chatting, and Swallow stuck stubbornly to
Fable's tail. At one point Fiona turned round and said,
'Swallow loves Fable. He always does that.' Rowan

thought, He wouldn't if Hugh was riding him, but no one expected her to try and dissuade him from his riding-school habits. Fable, like Swallow and Snowball, walked stiffly and slowly, head down and uninterested, shuffling her ill-shod feet. Rowan sat thinking of Cascade and Birdie and Fedora, with their alert ears and bright eyes. She didn't know horses could be so different. She had never thought about it. She didn't know.

'What's wrong with them?' she whispered to Babar.

Babar shrugged. 'Tired,' she said. 'Not enough grub, too much work, I daresay. This one's not bad though.'

When the lane petered out into a leafy track through the woods the ponies all shuffled into a slow trot without being told. Swallow's head was almost on his knees and when Rowan tried to collect him, as taught by her High Hawes instructors, he pulled back at her inexperienced hands and gave a buck which shot her up onto his neck. Grabbing the copious mane, she pushed herself back into place. She did not try to collect him again but resigned herself to bumping along on the awful saddle.

At the far end of the woods a gate gave into open grass fields where a well-trodden track ran alongside the hay crop. The minute they were through the gate the ponies all started to canter. Rowan, unwarned, nearly lost her seat. She took a pull at Swallow but he stuck his head out and took no notice. He seemed to have forgotten his love for Fable for he quickly overtook her and went to the front, travelling fast. Rowan had a suspicion that she was being bolted with. She heard Babar shout, 'Sit back! Sit back!'

The track stretched away ahead of her into unbroken distance. Rowan tried to sit back although all her instincts were to lean forward and hold onto the flying mane. She was very unhappy and getting frightened, and tried to take a pull on the reins. Surely a pony stopped if you pulled hard enough? But once Hugh had said to her, 'It's not done by pulling.' Unfortunately he hadn't bothered to explain what it was done by, and Rowan had no idea. She leaned back and pulled hard. All of a sudden Swallow's neck and ears vanished and she was no longer aboard, but hitting the hard and unyielding earth with an almighty thump. All the breath was knocked out of her and she lay watching the sky reeling over her head, filled with black spots that certainly weren't birds. She made no effort to get up – it was so awful, all her eager excitement crushed by this crowning unglory. Swallow . . . her darling Swallow! Nearly killing her . . .

'You still alive?' Babar loomed overhead, looking very anxious.

'Yes, I'm all right.'

'The little beggar! He gave a huge buck! No wonder you came off.'

Babar got off and helped her get to her feet. When she looked round, she saw that Swallow hadn't vanished into the distance but had stopped to crop hungrily at the grass. Fiona had caught him and was jerking his head up crossly.

'He always does that,' she said.

'Why didn't you say so?' Babar said indignantly.

'I thought she could ride.'

'Some instructor you are!'

'You're not paying to be instructed. This is a hack. You said a hack.'

'Huh!'

'She'd better ride Fable. She won't do anything.'

''Asn't got enough strength,' Babar said. 'Just as well.'

Fiona glared at her. She held Fable and Rowan struggled into the saddle. Babar shortened the leathers for her.

'Don't worry. This 'un'll be OK.'

They all set off again at a walk. Rowan felt groggy,

but trusted the gentle mare whose long neck and ears seemed to stretch out into the distance ahead of her. She felt quite different from Swallow, and her saddle was marginally more comfortable. Babar rode beside her in her new motherly role, and Fiona took Swallow to the front, presumably able to overcome his desire to follow Fable. He went with his ears laid back, a mulish look in his eye.

'Do you want to canter again?' Fiona asked presently, over her shoulder.

Rowan didn't, but said she did, to preserve face.

Fable obviously didn't want to, and the problem this time was to make her lurch into a canter from a longer and longer trot. Rowan rolled all round the saddle in her efforts and was relieved that Fiona and Sharon were in front and not watching. Swallow didn't buck this time, but went fast with his ears laid flat back. When Fable eventually consented to canter, her stride was long and very easy. Rowan was amazed, never having found Diamond's canter very comfortable. Beside her Babar was bowling along, grinning. She too was finding out Diamond's shortcomings by comparison. But the pleasure was shortlived as Fiona turned out of the big field into a road and they dropped back into the dispirited walk. Fable had to be niggled at all the time to keep up. By the time they got back to the stable Rowan was exhausted.

They paid their money and were obviously not expected to untack and put the ponies away. Laura came out and noted that Rowan had changed ponies but made no remark beyond, 'All right then?' Meaning, 'Still all in one piece?' by the faint look of surprise on her face.

There seemed to be nowhere to turn the ponies out, as they were taken back into the low-roofed sheds. Babar asked if they had no field and Laura, looking more worried still, said no, she'd lost her bit of grass to a builder in the new year.

Before Rowan had a chance to take an emotional farewell of Swallow (and probably get bitten for her pains), Babar hurried her away, saying they had a bus to catch.

'There isn't one till one o'clock,' Rowan pointed out.

'No,' said Babar, 'but I could do with a cup of tea and a bun.' She had no desire to linger in the depressing stable. She wanted it to appear better than it was to comfort Rowan, but Rowan was not so ignorant that she could not see the truth for herself. High Hawes had set her standards.

'That's a terrible place!' she despaired, white-faced, as they went back through the industrial estate. 'Poor Swallow!'

'We should 'ave let well alone,' Babar muttered.

'How can I get him out of there?'

'Ask your dad to buy 'um.'

'He never will, when he once had him for nothing.' Rowan knew the way her father's mind worked.

'No, and Fred Hawes won't, for the same reason. Especially as 'e knows the ownership could be doubted – 'e was stolen, like.' She tried to present the best case she could. 'They're not cruel, after all. 'E's not really ill-treated.'

Rowan, who now had a splitting headache, hadn't the heart to argue. They went and got a snack in a café and sat glumly on the bus home. Babar was not a talker. The only thing she said, in surprise, was, 'That Armchair – 'e gave me a good ride, run down as 'e was. 'E could be real nice, that one.'

'He's very ugly.'

'Looks aren't everything.'

No. Swallow had the looks, but had been beastly. Fable, knock-kneed and hollow-necked, had been gentle and kind. Only tired. When Rowan went up to High Hawes in the late afternoon, Lizzie and Hugh were just coming back from the downs. Rowan saw the ponies with fresh eyes, their gleaming well-being and rounded muscle, the spring in their step.

'How was it?' Lizzie called out.

Rowan shrugged. 'All right,' she said.

Chapter Nine

Afterwards Rowan told Lizzie how awful it was. But no one could think of a way of rescuing Swallow apart from buying him, and even the notes in the coffee jar did not amount to nearly enough.

'They all need rescuing really, not just Swallow.'

When Charlie heard, he said to Rowan, 'You have to get it into proportion. Lots and lots of humans have a far worse life than Swallow. You can't save the world. He's not suffering or in pain or starving.'

'Not quite,' said Lizzie.

Hugh added, 'Charlie's suffering.'

Charlie gave him a hating look and went off to ride Fedora.

'What did Hugh mean by that?' Rowan asked Lizzie when they were alone.

'Oh, he's having a bad time with Dad. They don't get on. Charlie has to do what he's told and he doesn't like it. He ought to go and work for someone else really, but Dad can't do without him. Dad's terribly bad-tempered these days, since he was ill.'

Rowan had noticed. She kept out of Mr Hawes's way. He didn't seem to mind her being around, because she did a lot of mucking out and sweeping and tack-cleaning to pay her way, but mostly, she gathered, he gave short shrift to hangers-on. His yard was a professional dealing yard with usually some dozen or so high-class horses for sale and he and Charlie and Josephine looked after them without outside help. Charlie was the 'nagsman' who rode them for prospective buyers – or Josephine if it was a lady's horse. The front yard, which gave on to the road, was the dealing yard, with the boxes smartly painted and everything in its place. Behind the big hay barn and feed shed which made the far side of this yard, was the family yard where Birdie and Cascade and Fedora lived, and the 'problem horses' which came to be re-schooled. This was not nearly so smart, and was where the children were supposed to stay in their place. The house lay to the side, up the hill and was accessible from both yards through the garden where Joan Hawes spent all of her little spare time. The garden was rather wild but very beautiful now in the full height of summer, rampant with heavily scented roses and old-fashioned hollyhocks and delphiniums. It was protected on the far side, up the hill, by an oak copse and the huge old trees gave a lovely sense of security and history to the farm, which Rowan was very aware of. She thought High Hawes was the loveliest home she had ever come across. When she mentioned this in her own home, her father said, 'It's run-down but it could fetch half a million if it was put in order.' That was the only way his mind worked.

'Mum's a garden nut,' Lizzie said. 'She doesn't like horses.'

But Rowan was sensitive to the strains in the Hawes family and knew that times were hard and all sorts of mutinies were suppressed behind Josephine's silences and Charlie's dark gypsy eyes.

She tried to take Charlie's sensible remarks to heart and stop thinking about Swallow. It wasn't as if she had owned him ever, or ridden him before. They tried giving her a few more lessons on Cascade, but she was frightened of getting bucked again and Charlie told them to lay off. 'You don't want to put her off for life.' Instead, in the school, he let her ride Fedora, but it was only as a sort of treat. There was no future in it. As she glided round on the lovely mare at the end of a lunge line, she felt herself on the edge of paradise. It made it worse, the wonderful feeling, afterwards . . . she had nothing to ride, when she wanted to.

Her mother said, 'Next year, perhaps, we'll be able to buy you a pony. But it's such a lot of work, darling, and you'll lose interest in a year or two, you know you will.'

Rowan knew nothing of the sort. It wasn't like piano lessons, or ballet, for goodness' sake, both of which she would happily forgo.

Trying not to be miserable when she had so much anyway, she walked up to High Hawes for her session with Bonzo. Her mother would call for her soon after half-past ten. When the others had gone to bed, she settled herself on the old couch against the wall of the box and pulled the sleeping bag up round her legs. Bonzo as usual came over and pushed and shoved at her, wanting his next bottle already but she cuffed him away, as instructed – he wasn't to be spoilt – 'Some hopes!' said Charlie – and settled down to make herself comfortable. Shrimp always set the alarm clock, but Rowan hardly ever went to sleep. She was quite happy to lie watching Bonzo, or the square of soft dusk out of the top door, thinking how mostly lucky she was (except not having her own pony).

But tonight, no sooner was she settled, than Fred

Hawes came into the yard with Charlie and stopped outside Bonzo's box.

He said, 'If you let this woman try Fedora, she's ready to pay four thousand. The mare is exactly what she's looking for. She doesn't want a performer, just a good-looking thoroughbred with reasonable manners.'

Charlie said, 'I'm not selling Fedora.'

'You'll do as I tell you, my lad. That mare is in my stables, eating my grub, and using up too much of your blooming time. You're not eighteen yet. I've told you before – I'm the one who gives the orders round here.'

'Yes, I've heard the whole flaming lot before! But Fedora's mine. She's not yours to sell'

'Everything in these yards is mine to sell, lad. I think you're getting ideas above your station. This woman, Mrs Elsworth, is coming on Tuesday afternoon, and Fedora is the one . . .'

They passed on towards the house and Rowan heard no more. She lay wide-eyed, astonished by the angry words. Sell Fedora! How could he, after all Charlie had done? Cascade and Birdie too . . . he would sell those – Hugh and Lizzie had always said he would if the right money were offered. She guessed Hugh would mind terribly if he lost Cascade. But Fedora! Fedora was different. No wonder Hugh had said Charlie was suffering. Rowan's loyal soul ached for Charlie as she lay thinking what was running through his mind. Her sadness over Swallow was as nothing to how he would feel about losing Fedora.

Afterwards, she wondered if she had dozed off and imagined the conversation. When she got home she fell into bed and slept heavily, and found it difficult to get up when she was called in the morning. It was important to look bright and shiny at the breakfast table after her nights with Bonzo, in case her mother would stop her going. She was anxious to ask Lizzie if it was true that Fedora might be sold. But when she got to the school bus stop there was no sign of any of the children from High Hawes and, although the bus driver waited a few minutes extra, they didn't come. Rowan got on with Babar and they both tried to surmise what had stopped them coming.

'It's very odd, all of 'em,' Babar said. 'They can't all be ill.'

'Something must have happened.'

But what? Rowan was on pins all day, trying to connect their absence with the row between Fred Hawes and Charlie. But how could it have any consequence?

When she got home she rushed to change out of her

school clothes to go up to High Hawes. But her mother said quietly, 'You can't go up there tonight. Fred Hawes has died.'

Rowan was stunned. 'But—' He was aggressively well only a few hours ago. 'He can't—'

'He had another heart attack and died immediately. It's terribly sad. Joan Hawes is very calm – I rang her to see if there was anything we could do – but she seemed to be coping. She said she would let me know.'

Rowan burst into tears, shocked by the blow to the family. Whatever would they all do without Fred to run the stables and business? Their whole life revolved round the horses. Fred was the lynchpin. She could see her own life falling apart . . . the farm put up for sale, Charlie going away . . . the ponies . . . Bonzo . . . 'Oh no!' It was awful. For Fred Hawes she felt less compassion than for her friends, left abandoned. Her mother put her arm round her, not realizing the selfishness of her dismay.

'There, these things happen. It's very sad. Don't get upset. You can ask Lizzie and the others down here if Joan Hawes wants them out of the way – Lizzie can stay the night, perhaps, if it would help.'

Charlie needn't sell Fedora now! Rowan seized on the only ray of light and nursed it, remembering

Charlie's agonized, 'Fedora's mine! She's not yours to sell!' He was saved.

The next day, Lizzie and Hugh were on the school bus. They were subdued, but otherwise showed no great signs of grief. Rowan somehow felt in awe of them. Death was a big subject. She didn't know what to say. But Lizzie wasn't inhibited.

'Charlie wants to go on running the business, but Mum's rather doubtful. She thinks it's too much – he's too young and all that stuff. But none of us wants to move. Dad's brother's coming today – he thinks he's going to tell us all what to do but we hate him. Uncle Trevor. That's why Hugh and me decided to come to school, to keep out of his way. And Mum wants us out of the way too. Shrimp won't stop crying, she couldn't come. She thinks she might lose Bonzo. I don't think it's Dad she's crying for.'

She looked out of the window and was silent for a little while. Rowan didn't know what to say. She kept trying to think what it would be like if her father died, and couldn't. More peaceful was all she could come up with. She had a feeling that her mother might even be relieved: she spent so much time worrying about not upsetting him. Where did love come into it? Rowan loved Charlie more than her father. Or did she? It was very hard to know what exactly love was. Fred Hawes had not been very lovable, in her opinion, but if he was your father it must be different. She couldn't very well ask Lizzie if she had loved him. In the end they didn't say anything much, but talked about the end-of-term play they were going to perform in.

Joan Hawes said sharply to Charlie, 'I don't care what your opinion of Uncle Trevor is. He's coming to help and you must be civil. As it is, I haven't ten pounds in my purse at the moment and there's no way of getting anything out of the bank, the way your father has left his affairs. Everything is in his name. It doesn't seem to occur to you that I might need help just at this moment.'

'I'll help you,' Charlie said.

'Oh yes? You borrowed five pounds off me on Saturday, remember?'

Charlie glared at her and slammed out of the room. When Uncle Trevor's black Rover slid into the drive beside the house he went out the back way and made for the stableyard. Uncle Trevor was a butcher with oily hair and a smarmy manner. They all hated him. Even their father had hated him. Charlie suspected he would try and buy High Hawes; he had tried once

145

before when Fred had owed money, but had been sent packing by his derisive brother. Now he probably thought he had their mother at his mercy. She was not experienced in business affairs; her husband had kept the books and, although she knew they had little money to spare, she had been shocked at the situation outlinèd by the bank manager earlier in the day. Charlie could not bear to see his indomitable mother scared into accepting help from the reviled Uncle Trevor.

Josephine had driven off to see a dealer whom their father had been due to visit. She, without saying anything, had stepped into their father's shoes. Perhaps it was just to tell the man Fred Hawes had died. Charlie had no idea. Perhaps it was time he and Josephine should start talking. They had got on together all this time by instinct, knowing which of them did what, but always in the shadow of their father. Charlie felt as if he had been leaning against a stone wall, and the wall had fallen down. There was no ground underneath him. There was no past and no future.

A smart grey Audi drove into the front yard. He could see it through the window in the back of Fedora's box. A woman got out and looked round. She was middle-aged and well dressed in riding clothes. Someone for their father, no doubt. Charlie went round to see what she wanted.

'Mr Hawes?' she said. 'I'm Mrs Elsworth. We spoke on the phone.' She held out her hand in a business-like way.

Charlie shook it. He could think of nothing to say.

'You said you had a mare that might suit me. I haven't found anything I like so far. Could I see her?'

She looked round at the few curious heads which were looking out over the top-doors. They had turned out half the inmates, having had no time to ride them all out. 'A chestnut, you said.'

Charlie said, 'She's round here.'

He led the way to the home yard and opened Fedora's box.

'I'll lead her out for you.'

He had done it hundreds of times, trotted a horse out on the concrete, forward and back, saddled and bridled it, taken it into the manège. Mrs Elsworth watched him with keen, knowledgeable eyes. She held Fedora while he fetched his helmet. He mounted and rode Fedora into the school.

She had never gone better. Kind and willing, she circled, backed, did a half-pass in both directions, and jumped the bars in the centre. He rode as if in a dream, and Mrs Elsworth saw a perfect horse being ridden by a perfect rider. She had been looking for such an exhibition for six months and had thought, recently, it would never happen. She leaned on the gate, watching with her green hawk eyes. The boy had hands like silk, and the authority of his body communicated to the mare without any obvious signals. She was impressed by his quietness and his rather distant demeanour. His face was taut and pale and he did not smile.

When he came back to the gate he slipped off, and shortened the stirrup leathers to her length.

'You want to try her?'

'I will, but I hardly need to. She's exactly what I'm looking for.'

She rode well enough herself, but knew she would never achieve the boy's mastery. She was fifty, after all.

'I'll give you a cheque now.'

'For four thousand?'

'That's what I understood.'

'She might not pass the vet. She's got scars on her back legs, wire scars.'

'I don't want to show her. It doesn't matter.'

'Don't you want her vetted?'

'I'll give you a post-dated cheque, and get her

vetted by my own vet at home. You'd agree to that?'

'Yes.'

'Very well. I'll call and collect her in the morning.'

She gave Charlie the cheque and drove away. He took it into the house and put it on the table in front of his mother. It was made out in her name.

'That's for you.'

She stared at him. Tears were trickling down his cheeks. Uncle Trevor looked at him spitefully.

'All this playing about with horses . . . you'll have to get out and find yourself a man's job, now your father's gone.'

Charlie gave him a look of utter contempt and went out, back to the yard, slamming the door behind him.

Chapter Ten

Rowan did not go to Fred Hawes's funeral but she helped at the reception afterwards in the house, when family and close friends went back for tea. Her mother was a very good cook and offered to help Joan and, rather unexpectedly, Joan Hawes took her up on it. Joan was worn out with shock and worry, and Rowan's mother, seeing her condition, took on herself the whole business of the funeral reception, and did it very efficiently. Rowan helped her hand round cups of tea and offer cakes. There were a lot of guests, all the local farmers and horse people as well as a vast number of family. The farmhouse was packed, visitors spilling out into the garden. As at most funerals, they all seemed very jolly, considering the circumstances, many of them meeting long-forgotten friends and family after a period of years. Rowan thought it very odd, but her mother said most funerals turned out like that.

'It's a compliment to the dead person, in a way, if everyone enjoys themselves. It shows he had a lot of jolly friends. If only a few people turn up and are very mournful, it's no help to the widow and family, after all.'

Rowan hardly recognized Charlie in his dark suit and black tie with his hair combed down and his good manners on show. She had not spoken to him since before Fred died, and found it hard to believe that he had sold Fedora after all. She had told no one of the conversation she had overheard. Her heart ached for him, as she noted his strained look and the obvious effort it was taking to make polite conversation to his relations. But she had little chance to indulge her mooning over him, for her mother soon had her in the kitchen washing up. Gradually all the visitors dispersed, until, at last, only the family was left. Uncle Trevor and his fat blonde wife were the last to leave, with promises to return in a few days 'to sort things out'.

When they had gone, Charlie picked up a glass of wine someone had left and held it up.

'Here's to Uncle Trevor dropping dead like Dad!'

'Charlie, really!' Joan looked shocked, and then suddenly giggled. 'Hear, hear,' she said.

'Hear, hear!' shouted Hugh.

'Hear, hear!' shouted Lizzie.

Everyone sat down around the big kitchen table, exhausted from the strains of the day. Joan pulled a chair out for Rowan. 'You've been working like a Trojan – I can't thank you enough!'

Rowan was thrilled with a great sense of belonging, and the fact that her mother was sitting down at the table too gave her enormous pleasure. Up till now she had always had an uneasy feeling that her parents resented her passion for High Hawes, but now she believed her mother had fallen under their spell as well, as she looked flushed and happy as she poured out fresh tea. She had certainly done a splendid job.

Charlie and Josephine sat side by side at the top of the table, in Fred Hawes's old place. Josephine looked immaculate in a navy-blue silk dress, with her blonde hair pulled back from her face. She had very clear, pale skin and serene grey eyes, the same colouring as all the others, except gypsy Charlie.

Rowan saw her smile, and say something softly to Charlie. She saw suddenly a rapport between them that she had never noticed before. She saw Charlie smile as well, and a sort of glittering look came into his eyes.

'Mother,' he said.

They all looked at him.

'Josephine's got something for you.'

Josephine passed an envelope up the table to Joan.

'I sold two of the horses the day after Dad died, to Sid Palmer,' she said. 'And he gave me the money just now. Three thousand each. With the money from Fedora, that's ten thousand Charlie and I have made you this week. We think you can tell Uncle Trevor to take a running jump. We can run the business, if you'll let us.'

'Yes, yes!' shouted Hugh.

'Yes!' shouted Lizzie.

'Yes, you must!' screamed Shrimp.

Even Rowan found herself saying, 'Yes, *please*! Please do!'

Joan opened the envelope, looking dazed. 'It's in my name! I'm really rich – I've never had a penny of my own for years!'

'We've been discussing it, Josephine and I,' Charlie said. 'Will you hear our plans and let us try to make a go of it?'

'I don't want all this, you know,' Joan said. 'You must take it back, for the yard.'

'We've got six more horses to sell – of Dad's,' Charlie said, 'And the Prebbles want Birdie. With that money we thought we could set up a school, like you've always said we should. It was your idea, after all. Go more for children and children's ponies. We thought we could even take holiday weeks – kids staying here and riding out each day, and intensive week's courses. Cross-country courses, or day rides – whatever might make the money. And the Pony Club's always wanting somewhere for a course, and rallies. Dad would never have them. But we could. And we can still do Dad's dealing, with his connections, but not rely just on that, like he did. We can take duff ponies and Hugh and Shrimp can school them to sell – things like that. I'm sure we can make us all a living.'

'We don't want to go away,' Josephine said.

'No,' Charlie said. 'We belong here.'

'You *can't* go away, either of you!' Lizzie cried out. 'It would be awful here without you!'

Joan Hawes shook her head, looking rather weepy. 'I'm sure I don't want either of you to get other jobs. It's just that I don't want you to take on so much responsibility – keeping us all and the roof over our heads. You're so young for that! You want some fun in life.'

'Oh, come on, Mum, can't you see – the way Dad worked us – it won't be any different!'

'But you didn't have the worry of it. He did all that. It's probably what killed him.'

'Yes, but there's lots of us – Josephine and me now, and in no time Lizzie and Hugh and Shrimp. At least we can give it a try – surely?'

'It's very early days to take decisions. But I must say I can't stand the thought of Trevor taking us over. He's really set on interfering.'

'You know it's the farm he wants,' Josephine said. 'Helping us – so-called – is just his way of getting his nose in. Dad always steered clear of him, didn't he? Dad wouldn't want it. He would want us to carry on, I'm sure.'

'Well, your father did build this place from nothing. It was all in ruins when we came here. He was proud of what he'd done.'

'Sleep on it, Mum,' Charlie said. 'You haven't got to decide now this minute. But you've got some money now, and time to think, and you can tell Uncle Trevor to get stuffed when he turns up.'

'I must say, I would like that.'

'Well, for the time being—' Charlie glanced at Josephine again, and Rowan noticed that the strained

155

look had gone from his face and he looked like his old self. He pushed his chair back from the table. 'I'm going to change. There's work to be done.' He laughed.

Josephine got up too. 'Yes. I hate dresses.'

'So do I!' shrieked Shrimp, jumping up. 'I've got to feed Bonzo!'

Joan turned to Mrs Watkins and said, 'One thing about animals, they always need looking after, whatever happens. You can't take to your bed when there's a stableful of horses outside.'

'Yes. Quite a responsibility.'

Mrs Watkins thought it was time to go. She had only stayed so long because Joan had pressed her to. Rowan was amazed at how her mother had got on with Mrs Hawes, and how they had been accepted as part of the family.

Later, Lizzie said to her. 'It's funny, but it's much nicer at home now Dad has gone.'

Rowan was horrified by this remark.

Lizzie said, 'He only ever shouted at us. And he and Charlie didn't get on at all. There was always a nasty sort of feeling around, Dad getting at Charlie, and Josephine not saying anything, sort of stuck between them. Now it's all right. More sort of relaxed. And Josephine's started to talk more.'

Rowan was amazed. She told her mother this, and her mother wasn't amazed at all, but just said, 'Well, I understand he was a difficult man. And those older two – young people need their freedom, to work out their own lives. It's not a very good idea for a boy to work for his father, without seeing something of the world first. It makes sense to me, that Charlie's much happier now he's his own boss.'

It seemed that Uncle Trevor had been sent packing. Lizzie and Hugh giggled about it, describing how he went red with rage, and stalked out, and backed his car into the water trough and dented the wing.

'All the same,' Mrs Watkins said, 'they've got a lot on their plates. They're only children.'

Rowan didn't think of Josephine and Charlie as children, but supposed she saw it from a different point of view.

In spite of what Lizzie said, she and the others were more subdued after the funeral, and Rowan saw Hugh crying in Cascade's box when he thought no one was there. Shrimp kept bursting into tears too, and Lizzie would get into a temper about nothing at all, which she never did before. Joan Hawes looked terrible. Perhaps Fred hadn't been the easiest man in the world to live with, but it was apparent that they all missed him dreadfully. He had been the rock on which their lives had rested. Perhaps, when rocks moved, the shock took some time to sink in. Certainly the atmosphere at High Hawes had changed, and the time of grieving was something the family had to bear. Nobody talked about it, but Rowan sensed the tension, and took care to tread carefully.

It was nearly the holidays and, since the plans for a riding school had been aired, the children rather thought that High Hawes would be flooded with new ponies overnight, but nothing seemed to happen, save that Charlie bought a pony very cheap because she had a bad knee. She couldn't be ridden for the time being. She was a Welsh mountain, small and strawberry roan and very pretty, but Rowan thought she was too small for her, even when it was better. Shrimp christened it Pinkie. She was turned out in the field.

Birdie was advertised for sale. On the evening of the day the ad appeared in 'Horse and Hound' Mrs Prebble appeared in the yard with Matty.

It was hot and they were out in the field watching Bonzo learning to eat grass. Shrimp had him on a halter, finding him luscious tufts, because the novelty of staying up all night to feed him was fast wearing off. Charlie was in the manège exercising one of the yard horses which had been advertised at the same time, and Josephine was doing feeds in the feed shed.

Birdie was in, because of the ad, and Lizzie had been grooming her diligently, so that her light bay coat gleamed and her black points shone like satin, and her black mane lay neatly on one side. Charlie had promised Lizzie she could have a 'nice' pony when Birdie was sold. 'Like Babar's Diamond,' he said, laughing. 'Cheap. It will have to be cheap.' He went out looking for bargains, but they were few and far between. There was always something wrong with them. Pinkie was the only one he had come back with so far.

When Mrs Prebble came into the yard they all came to attention.

Hugh gave Lizzie a great nudge and said, 'Go on. Tell her she's five thousand pounds. She pays whacking prices for Matty's ponies.'

Lizzie got up nervously. 'Will I have to ride her? With that Matty watching?'

'Yeah. Of course.'

'Can't you?'

'She's your pony.'

While they argued, Charlie rode out of the school and dismounted to talk to Mrs Prebble. Rowan, seeing she was needed, went up and took his horse for him. Matty stared at her in her usual haughty way. She was about fourteen, slender but with a very tough look about her, her eyes hard and supercilious. She was dark, and had pink cheeks and very white teeth, and a natural scowl. Rowan hated her on sight.

'I saw your ad,' Mrs Prebble said to Charlie. 'I don't know why you didn't give me a ring first. I told your father I was interested in that pony.'

Rowan had heard Charlie say he would put the cost of the ad on to the price if Mrs Prebble bought Birdie. He hadn't wanted to make any sort of an appeal to this famously aggressive and unpleasant woman. Hugh called her Hitler. She hadn't got a black moustache, but she had black shiny hair hanging over her forehead to one side like Hitler, and wore leather boots, even on a summer evening. Rowan felt really grateful that she didn't have her for a mother, like poor Matty. Perhaps Matty scowled because she had Hitler for a mother.

Josephine came and took the horse off Rowan, but then disappeared, leaving the selling bit to Charlie. Charlie brought Birdie out of her box, and called for Lizzie to come and tack her up. Mrs Prebble examined her closely all over, as if looking for nits, and lifted up all her legs and pulled them about, and peered into the pony's mouth.

'She's five,' Charlie said.

'I'm not blind,' said Mrs Prebble.

'Only horrible,' whispered Hugh.

Lizzie was looking pale and was obviously deciding that, now the moment had come, she loved Birdie and didn't want to sell her. Charlie made her ride her in the school to show her paces, but was kind enough not to make her jump. He knew she hated riding in front of the Prebbles. But Matty wanted to jump her herself, and Charlie went off to put up the bars. Mrs Prebble leaned on the gate, frowning. Lizzie and Hugh and Rowan sat on the fence watching.

Matty was a forceful and effective rider, with none of Lizzie's misgivings, and Birdie looked surprised and rather nervous. Rowan felt sorry for her. When faced at the jump, she had no chance at all to refuse or run out, ridden with such skill and precision. Fred Hawes had always declared she had a jump like a kangaroo, and Rowan now saw how she had won this reputation, as Matty insisted that the jump was raised. Charlie looked slightly anxious, but was aware that he had a job of selling to do. To show doubt would be fatal. He put the jump up to 1.1 metres, and Birdie cleared it easily, then four foot. Again, so firmly was she presented, she flew over it.

'That's enough,' Charlie said.

'Can we have her on trial?' Mrs Prebble asked.

'No. We don't let horses go on trial.'

'Not even half a mile away? You know us.'

'No.'

'You're being ridiculous.'

Charlie flushed up. How rude the woman was! They all sat agog, intrigued. But Matty slipped off and Charlie turned to undo Birdie's girths as if the selling was finished. Lizzie went to help him.

'She felt great, Mum,' Matty said, looking eager.

Mrs Prebble glared at her.

'That's as may be. How much are you asking?' she demanded of Charlie.

'Three thousand five hundred and fifty,' Charlie said.

'I'll give you two thousand, if she passes the vet.'

'No offers. The price is three thousand five hundred and fifty.'

'That's ridiculous. She's done nothing.'

'No, but she can.'

'It's a pity I'm not dealing with your father.'

Charlie turned away, to stop himself from saying something he might regret, and indicated that he had other things to do than stay talking to Mrs Prebble. Mrs Prebble turned on her heel and strode out of the yard. Lizzie and Hugh and Rowan all went into Birdie's box to give vent to their feelings. Lizzie burst into tears and said, 'I'm not selling dear Birdie to those beastly people!'

But on the school bus the next morning she said Mrs Prebble had rung up at ten o'clock and agreed to Charlie's price, with a vet's certificate. Charlie told Lizzie he would buy some nice ponies with the money and she could have the one she liked best.

A dreamy look came into her eyes. 'A darling sweet pony who does exactly what I want, and never tanks off, or shies at things in the hedge.'

'You are *feeble*,' Hugh said in tones of great scorn. 'It's not as if you can't ride. And anyway,' he added, 'I think Charlie and Josephine ought to get horses for themselves, now we've got all this money – before you, because you're always saying you don't like it. And they do.'

'I would do on a nice pony!'

'It's not fair on them not having anything.'

'They've still got six in the yard.'

'None of them are what they want, for their own. They're all heavyweight hunters, or stupid. And

Charlie – giving his Fedora money all to Mum—'
Words failed him.

'That was noble,' Shrimp said solemnly.

'I'll say! He made a whacking profit, though. I suppose he couldn't resist it.'

Rowan said nothing. She knew Charlie could have resisted it very well. Fedora was the horse he wanted. Perhaps he didn't want another one. It was true that he was noble.

'Well, he won't have time to ride his own now, if he's got to give riding lessons to little girls. I can't see him, somehow . . .' Hugh looked doubtful. 'It's pretty yukky, after all, giving riding lessons to little girls.'

'You're a sexist pig,' Lizzie said. 'Little boys fall off and cry, and girls always get on again. That's why there's so few boys in the Pony Club, because they're always falling off and crying, and they won't come again. All the instructors say that.'

'I didn't cry! I got on again!'

'Oh, that's because you're so exceptionally marvellous and talented. Ugh!' Lizzie shuddered.

'Yes,' said Hugh.

Now Lizzie had nothing to ride she was very cross.

'No pleasing some people,' Charlie grinned.

Babar brought Diamond up again, for Rowan, but

only two could ride out together, on Diamond and Cascade.

'Where are all these ponies you were going to buy?' they clamoured at Charlie.

'I'm working on it,' he said.

It was true that he went out a lot, and read all the ads in 'Horse and Hound' with great attention, but the feeling was that he was looking for a cheap youngster for himself, and one for Josephine. They bought an unbroken three-year-old for the dealing yard, which they thought was cheap at the price (but not good enough for themselves) and they sold one of the heavyweight hunters and one of the Irish job lots that Fred had imported.

'We're not exactly doing nothing,' Charlie countered their complaints.

Two weeks before the end of term both Charlie and Josephine went out with the big lorry. It hadn't been driven since Fred died – they always used the Land Rover and trailer – and Hugh and Lizzie decided they had found two big youngsters for themselves. Or even one. Unbroken youngsters usually loaded more easily into a lorry than a trailer. They were both very mysterious about their trip and refused to take Hugh and Lizzie with them, although there was room in the cab.

'As if we want an outing in the old crate,' Hugh said sniffily.

Crossly, he went off for a ride with Babar. Lizzie, Shrimp and Rowan took Bonzo for a walk through the woods and out onto one of the downs tracks, where they lay in the grass while Bonzo practised his grazing, and Lizzie moaned about having no pony to take to Pony Club camp.

'I've never not been to Pony Club camp,' she said.

'I thought you didn't like it,' Shrimp said.

'I do now I can't go,' Lizzie said.

Rowan lay in the grass feeling its warmth underneath her and watching the little blue butterflies hovering over the flowers whose names she (being a town girl) didn't know. She couldn't imagine being back in Putney again, and yet this time last year . . . extraordinary! The sky was palest nothing-colour, the sun still high over the cockscomb of trees that crowned the nearest down. Near at hand Bonzo's new teeth and eager gums did their best on the fine turf and his bright eyes watched warily in the wide open spaces that were new to him. He hated being out in the field without a human nearby, and followed Shrimp everywhere like a dog around the yards and garden, even into the kitchen, until Joan had got cross. 'In bed next – I'm putting my foot down!' Rowan loved Bonzo and was pleased when he accorded her almost the same status as Shrimp. When he could eat grass he was going to be turned out in a small field with Pinkie, to see if she might be motherly towards him.

'Not like beastly Fedora.'

'She wasn't beastly,' Rowan said loyally. 'Motherhood didn't suit her. She was gentle otherwise. She couldn't help feeling like that.'

They got up and slowly went back down the hill, Bonzo following. From the chalk track they could hear Babar and Hugh coming back, their voices carrying on the still evening air. They went through the oak wood and down the ride that led into the fields by the manège. Bonzo cantered on ahead, bucking, but had to wait by the gate. Shrimp haltered him to lead him through the field where other horses were grazing.

'I can hear the lorry,' she said.

They were all curious as to what Charlie and Josephine were bringing back. Hugh and Babar came trotting into the yard at the same moment as Charlie pulled up. When he cut the engine, there was a lot of kicking from inside the lorry and, suddenly, a whinny that stopped Rowan in her tracks.

She looked up, as Charlie jumped down from the

cab. He was grinning. He caught her eye and winked.

'Cheer up, Rowan, it's your lucky day.'

'You've bought *hundreds*!' Shrimp shouted.

They all crowded round as Charlie and Josephine let down the ramp and opened the doors.

'A job lot,' Charlie said. 'One each and some to spare. We've got the foundation of the High Hawes Equestrian Centre here.'

He skipped up the ramp. 'Here's yours, Shrimp!'

First down the ramp was the small white pony, Snowball. Rowan recognized him immediately from the Half Moon Riding School. Also the next to follow:

'Lizzie, one for you. Name of Fable.'

The kind, thin, bay mare which Rowan had ridden stumbled down the ramp and Lizzie stepped forward dubiously to take her halter.

Next came the big white blaze of the washy chestnut cob who Babar had ridden. Babar came forward happily. 'Why, it's my old Armchair! I liked him!'

And last – 'Rowan!'

Rowan could hardly move for trembling knees nor see for helpless tears as Swallow came barging down the ramp.

'Manners! Manners!' Charlie brought him up short

with a sharp check on his head collar. He laughed at Rowan's expression.

'Your pony, madam. A High Hawes hireling.'

Swallow stood still, seeing that he had arrived safely with all his friends and an apple was being proffered on the hand in front of him. He took it delicately, and shoved affectionately at Rowan's arm.

'Oh, Swallow!' Rowan flung her arms round his neck.

'Where's mine?' shouted Hugh crossly.

'You've already got one. Cascade. And all these are yard horses. We aren't giving them to you for your own, only to look after. Muck out and feed and exercise. This is a joint exercise, remember – High Hawes Equestrian Centre.'

'Well, they are a skinny-looking lot,' Hugh said disgustedly. 'They look half-starved to me. I wouldn't want any of 'em.

'No, well, it's nothing a good field of grass won't cure. And why do you think we got them cheap? The owner couldn't afford to keep them.'

'There's another one still in the box,' Lizzie said. 'Whose is that?'

'That's mine,' Charlie said quietly.

He went up the ramp again to the horse hidden

at the back of the big lorry. Josephine was smiling.

'He's gone mad,' she said to Lizzie. 'Look at it!'

They all laughed at the scarecrow that stumbled down the ramp, a very large, very thin bay gelding with an old-fashioned Roman nose and thick, puffy legs. He looked all round, blinking, as if to see what worse fate was in store, having come so low. He had dull, patient eyes, a ragged, rubbed mane, and a thin white stripe down his face. Fedora had been poor, but compared to this one, she had been a queen.

Hugh stared. 'I don't believe it! Charlie, what would Dad say?'

Charlie looked, for him, quite sheepish.

'He's only five,' he said. 'He deserves a chance.'

'He's another for the knacker, like Fedora.'

'Exactly,' said Charlie. 'And look what I got for her!'

Hugh was squashed.

Charlie said, 'He'll be a nice horse one day. We've plenty of time. They've all had a raw deal and there's nothing that good food won't put right. For now they can all go out in the bottom field. They haven't seen grass for years, most of 'em.'

They led them out in a row, down the lane to the gate that let into an empty field. The field had been cut for hay, but already had a good new growth. Laura

Griffiths's ponies couldn't believe their luck. One by one as they were led in and let loose they put their heads down and started wrenching at the grass. They didn't even stop to explore.

'Poor things!' said Shrimp. 'They're rescue horses!'

'No,' said Josephine. 'They're our new riding-school ponies. We thought you could all go to the Pony Club camp after all.'

Was she teasing? Lizzie looked at her curiously in the dusk.

'On them?'

'There's a month to go. Why not? We'll get them wormed and well fed, and groom them, and you won't know them by August.'

'It's not very long.'

Charlie said, quite sternly, 'We haven't bought them for a lark. They've got to earn their keep, and the sooner the better. We need you all to go to the Pony Club, to show everyone we're in business now. It will get our name put around. We aren't going to make any money if we don't put ourselves out and about.'

'Us?' said Hugh. 'What about you?'

'Yes, we've already volunteered to help at camp. Josephine and I are going to do horse lines, and teach a bit. They've always wanted us – it was Dad who said we were too busy.'

'You always said it was a drag! You didn't mind not going!'

Charlie laughed. 'That's when I was always being told what to do. Now I'm going to do the telling. Nothing wrong with that.'

'You won't be teaching us!' Hugh looked alarmed. And then he added, 'At least I've got a decent pony, thank goodness.'

'Matty Prebble will take Birdie to camp, I bet,' Lizzie said, worried. 'Fable won't be the same—'

'Fable will look after you. You hated Birdie, remember?'

'I can take Snowball,' Shrimp said, 'I wouldn't mind that.'

'Thank goodness someone's pleased!'

Shrimp never went to camp ordinarily, as she had been too busy at shows. Her showing programme had dropped off since Bonzo, although she was still in demand.

And me? Rowan thought, but didn't say.

As they wandered back up the hill to home and supper, she felt isolated – scared and gloriously happy all at once. Was she really to take Swallow to Pony

Club camp? It all seemed to be taken for granted. Could she cope – that was another question? Yet it was because of her badgering on about Swallow that they had discovered Laura Griffiths and Charlie had bought his lorryload of 'bargains'. Inadvertently she had taken quite a hand in the fortunes of the new High Hawes Equestrian Establishment.

She had what she wanted. Hadn't she?

She walked back home, beside Babar riding Diamond. Babar too was quiet, and said, 'I really liked riding that Armchair. D'you think Charlie meant I could take 'um to camp, instead of Diamond?'

'I don't know.'

Rowan could see that Babar was torn, loyal to Diamond whom she had outgrown, not in size, but in satisfaction.

At the gate of the old hay field they both stopped and looked down the valley at the new horses grazing. They were spread out now, their shadows long in the golden evening. They looked magical, the dusk cloaking their scurfy hides and poor sticking-out ribs.

'I reckon they think they're in paradise.' Babar smiled.

And me, Rowan thought. It had all come true for her.

And she suddenly felt free of all her doubts and misgivings, thinking of the courage with which Matty Prebble rode, and how noble Charlie had been over Fedora, and how devotedly little Shrimp cared for Bonzo, and how Joan Hawes had not buckled over with the death of her husband ... she was amongst people who did not whinge, and to be one of them she must not be feeble and apprehensive.

She walked on down the hill beside Diamond. Her head was spinning. And Babar rode in thoughtful silence.

THE *Swallow* SUMMER

For Alison

Chapter One

'Am I going to Pony Club camp?' Rowan asked Charlie Hawes. She didn't have a pony to take, and Charlie had several.

'Of course,' he said. And smiled, as she turned noticeably first red, then white.

'It's fun,' he said gently. 'Not terrible.'

'I can't ride!'

'Lots of them can't ride. You won't be alone. And think, by the end of the week, how much you will have improved!'

'Who on?' Her voice was a whisper. She wanted, longed, above all else, that it would be Swallow.

Charlie knew her thoughts, and shook his head.

'No, not Swallow.'

Rowan tried not to let her bitter disappointment show. If she was honest, the disappointment was tinged slightly with relief. Swallow always bucked her off:

he had been labelled a rogue and only the Hawes could ride him. There were five of them and they rode like those born to it – on a horse before they could walk. Instinctive. Even Lizzie, the middle one, who was thirteen and the most nervous, and said she only rode because she had to, was an elegant and sympathetic rider. Hugh, eleven like Rowan, was (unlike Rowan) brave, brilliant and boastful. Rowan, having moved into the village only recently and discovered the magic of the horse world, knew she would never, never, never – however much she improved – be able to ride like a Hawes. But she longed to ride 'her' pony, Swallow.

Charlie disappeared into the feed shed and Rowan went round to see Swallow in his loosebox. In the stable he was the kindest pony in the world: friendly and affectionate, his bold eyes gleaming with curiosity from beneath the black wing of his forelock. He, and several others, had been bought by Charlie from a run-down riding school, in very bad condition, but a few weeks on good grass and feed had worked wonders, and Swallow was almost back to his bright self, a handsome, fourteen-hand Welshman, dark brown in colour, with a blueish sheen over his quarters that had prompted Rowan to christen him Swallow. Strange how she was drawn to this pony . . . Rowan was the first to admit the silliness of it, when he was so unsuitable. But ever since she had first set eyes on him she had adored him, and no other pony would measure up. Instead of saying she was stupid, Charlie said it worked that way sometimes. He had been drawn to the raw-boned, thin bay called Wilfred that had stood forlorn in the back of the awful riding stable. He had bought him and been laughed to scorn by the rest of the family. Rowan adored seventeen-year-old Charlie because, instead of being brisk with her dreams, he was sympathetic.

'We all have dreams,' he said, 'And sometimes they happen. Fairy tales. After all, somebody has to win gold.'

Win gold! Perhaps a mauve rosette at the Pony Club . . . that would be gold to Rowan. As she ran her hand down Swallow's warm, shining neck, she had no illusions about what lay ahead.

Charlie went into the house, which slept like a tawny lion amongst the tangle of his mother's generously planted garden on the uphill side of the stableyards. Of golden sandstone and thatch, it had looked out over the valley of Long Bottom for five hundred years and, in truth, not a great deal had changed in that time. Rowan, fresh from London with her smart parents, thought it was paradise, but sometimes Charlie wondered what he was missing. He had always assumed he would go off somewhere when the opportunity arose and find his place in the world, but since his father's death, his future had closed down. He was committed, along with his older sister Josephine, to keeping the family together at High Hawes and making a living out of the place, as his father had done. It had been a democratic vote, and he had been the first to agree to it, but sometimes . . . well, he couldn't say teaching the Blue Ride at the Pony Club camp was the most exciting thing in a chap's immediate future – slightly embarrassing, if the truth were known, mixing with the green wellie brigade, the admirable middle-aged ladies with whiskers on their chins and Labradors at their heels who steered the little girls across country with cries of, 'Legs! Legs! *Ride*, Fiona!'

His father had been a hard-bitten horse dealer and a tough master to work for. Having him off his back was in many ways a relief for Charlie, but the responsibility of having to make money out of what he had formerly thought of as mostly pleasure was daunting. It was his mother Joan who had – before her husband died –

pointed out that the area was rife with little girls who wanted riding lessons and had nowhere to go, and that High Hawes could easily fill this need. This now seemed the best course to take and the children had decided the farm would be called High Horse Stables. This was Hugh's idea. 'Very clever, don't you think?' Moderately, Charlie thought. Joan said, 'I know you think you've outgrown the Pony Club, Charlie, but it would be very valuable to the stable if you get back in there and show them that we have a private school at hand, nice ponies, and knowledgeable, friendly people to help them. Only a small proportion of them these days know one end of a pony from the other. They're all down from London like Rowan's people and they get in terrible tangles. Millie Mildmay would love you to teach at camp – you and Josephine – she told me so. And it would get the stable known and do us all a lot of good.'

Joan Hawes always talked sense. Charlie knew it. But his heart did not rise up singing at the thought of reporting to Millie Mildmay.

'The more you mix with local people, the better it will be for the business. A summer with the Pony Club will open up all sorts of contacts. Did you know, for example, that old Millie has bludgeoned Jerry

Patterson into joining the committee? I'm not sure that he knows it yet but she's after using his stableyard for Pony Club camp. He's a man after your own heart, I would have thought. Why don't you ride over and have a chat with him?'

Jerry Patterson was a racehorse trainer in the next valley. He was young, struggling and notoriously unsuccessful, but his enthusiasm kept his yard in business. His horses were hurdlers and chasers that raced in the winter, not on the flat, so his yard was largely empty in the summer. Millie Mildmay was his aunt and, such was her clout, nearly everybody did what she told them.

Charlie decided to take his mother's advice. He didn't see what good it would do him, but any excuse to visit a racing stable was all right by him, and he liked Jerry. It was a glorious day, sunny with a fresh breeze, and the more slow-riding Wilfred got to build up his muscles, the better. He went back across the garden and through the gate into the back stableyard. They kept their own horses here; the front one, with an archway onto the lane, was the smart yard, his father's old dealing yard. But it was empty now. They had sold all his horses since he had died, and the riding-school ponies which would replace them were out at grass, filling out their ribs. Teaching little girls was a start, and it was true that the market was there, but Charlie dreamed of a competition yard full of event horses (which he would ride). He liked thoroughbreds, and bloodlines that went back to Hyperion and St Simon and Eclipse. Wilfred was a thoroughbred, although he didn't look much like one at present. Charlie, because he had an instinct for such things, could see a well-made, straight-actioned young horse underneath the sad, thin-necked, dull-eyed animal he went to saddle up.

'Poor old fellow! You drew a short straw, getting into that dud stable. Trust me, Wilfred, your luck has changed.'

The horse turned his head and gave Charlie a resigned look. He had large eyes, which should have been bold and keen, long ears, and a kind, handsome head. He was a bay with black points, and no white save for a narrow stripe down his face. He stood just over sixteen hands. Charlie would have liked two inches more, for he was tall and still growing. But Charisma, a world champion, had been no more than fifteen two.

'It's heart that matters, Wilfred. And who knows how big yours is? We'll have to find out.'

He led him out and Rowan, watching, saw a very plain and boring horse, and wondered why on earth Charlie had bought Wilfred for himself. Because he was cheap, she supposed.

'Why don't you come with me? I'm hacking over to Sand House. Slowly. Find yourself a pony.'

Rowan's face lit up like the sun bursting out of cloud. She was alone because all the younger Hawes had gone, en masse, to the dentist. Josephine, the eldest, was giving a lesson in the manège. They could hear her voice: 'Use your inside leg! Feel the rein, don't yank!' A child's voice answered plaintively, 'Nothing happens!' Josephine was trying to keep her cool. Teaching, even when you knew it all yourself, was not as easy as she had supposed.

'Who on?' Rowan asked.

The 'easy' pony she generally rode, Fable, was in the lesson, as was the other easy one, a chestnut cob known as the Armchair. Hugh wouldn't want her riding his pony Cascade, and Snowball, the other possibility, was as far away down the big field as it was possible to be. Swallow put his head over his door and whinnied. Charlie hesitated.

Then he said, 'I'm only walking, all the way. How about Swallow?'

Even as he spoke, a voice inside him cried out, 'Fool! Idiot!' But Rowan, already ecstatic at the thought of riding out with him, now looked about to burst with joy.

'Swallow! Really, do you mean it?'

How could he say, *No, I've changed my mind?*

'Yes,' he said. 'Why not?'

Why not, after all? If the beast started to play up, he could put her on the leading rein. He sensibly fetched a lead rope, in case, and tied it around his waist where he hoped Rowan wouldn't notice it. She tacked up, fetched her hat, and led Swallow out. Charlie held him while she mounted, and adjusted the stirrups for her, then vaulted onto Wilfred. Already Rowan's eager face was flushed with apprehension. Her knuckles showed white as she clutched the reins.

'Relax,' Charlie said. 'Let his mouth alone. Ask him nothing. He'll follow Wilfred without your doing anything. Plenty of rein.'

To her surprise, Swallow went like a lamb behind Wilfred out into the lane. Charlie headed up the hill towards the downs above the farmhouse. There was an oak wood that circled the uphill side of the house, and the Hawes had made a ride through it that opened out onto the downs without going on the road. The path was peaty and soft and the sunlight came through the trees in golden swathes. A green woodpecker flew ahead of them like a tropical parrot, shrieking. When they came through into the open again onto a chalky path that climbed up steadily to the top of the down, Rowan felt her whole body bound with a sense of freedom and bliss, to be where she was, with Charlie alone, on her beloved Swallow . . . it had never happened before. She had ridden up here, but only on Fable or Diamond, with Hugh showing off on Cascade, and Lizzie and Shrimp quarrelling – happily, but never like this: ecstatically. White clouds soared across the horizon against a brilliant blue sky, and the warm smell of the downland turf tickled their nostrils. Rowan had never ridden over the top, where they were going now. She would follow Charlie to the world's end.

'Nice, isn't it?' he said.

Rowan could not trust herself to speak.

Swallow felt keen beneath her, but it was uphill all the way and she felt in control. She tried not to hold his mouth, and told herself to relax. Josephine had told her she was too tense, and that conveyed nervousness to the horse. 'They really do know what you are thinking, you know.' Wilfred, with his long, easy stride, walked slightly ahead, and Rowan could see how easily Charlie sat in the saddle. He was slender and wiry, his body hard as nails, and rode with an unstudied elegance. He was the dark one of the family, with thick, black hair and dark, sapphire-blue eyes – 'a gypsy like his father' they said in the village – and he had a magic, gypsy way with a horse. Unlike the other Hawes children, he had skipped a lot of school to work with his father and make money by mending and trading in old cars and agricultural machinery. The other four Hawes were studious and intelligent, but Charlie was clever in a different sort of way. And unlike the others he understood Rowan's misgivings and fear, and the strange compulsion that made her want to ride Swallow instead of sweet Fable and the harmless Armchair.

Charlie turned off the chalk track to take a short cut over the top of the down. The grass was steep and Rowan could feel Swallow's powerful quarters working beneath her. His glossy summer coat rippled over his shoulders and the wind blew back his heavy mane. Coming over the brow, the view to the next valley opened up like a map, dappled with moving clouds, the villages and roads below etched out in the sunshine like a child's toy set. Behind them, turning in the saddle, Rowan could look down and see High Hawes nestling behind its oak wood and the village of Long Bottom sprawled below it. The white dot was Snowball in the bottom field, and the piebald specks on the far side of the valley were Mr Bailey's Friesian cows with, no doubt, Barbara Bailey's knock-kneed pony, Black Diamond, amongst them. She could even see her own house in the village, and Matty Prebble's show jumps like coloured matchsticks in their field.

Swallow wheeled beneath her as Wilfred set off again, anxious to keep close. But Rowan relaxed (it was hard) and nothing untoward happened. The wind raced up towards them, flattening the grass into patterns and blowing out the horses' tails, and Charlie turned to see if she was all right, and smiled.

The village below was a haunt of racehorses, with several stableyards opening off the through-road. Gallops were marked out on the far down, sheltered by long strips of woodland, and a couple of strings could be seen working. Jerry Patterson's yard stood on its own, two miles out of the village up a long chalky drive. It was in a bowl of downland, hidden from sight, and one came upon it with surprise and – in Rowan's case – delight. Unlike most of the yards which were purpose-built and severe-looking, this place dated back to the last century and the stableyard was built round a grassy sort of green with an enormous walnut tree growing in the middle. The stables were beautiful but, undeniably, falling apart. Some of the tiled roofs had fallen in and the rows of dormers over the sagging stable doors were at odd angles as the supporting beams had given way. Outside the yard, with its back to the rising ground behind it, was a very dilapidated Victorian house.

They rode into the deserted stableyard and pulled up. Two pigeons flew out of the walnut tree and rattled away, then it was quite silent, save for the distant trilling of skylarks on the down.

'What do you think of it?' Charlie asked.

'I think it's a wonderful place. So lonely.'

'Derby winners lived in these boxes once. It was a very famous yard a hundred years ago. Look, I'll show you.'

He slipped down from Wilfred and led him across to an open loosebox. Its door creaked in the breeze, scraping on the ground. Looking in, Rowan saw a huge box lined all round with mahogany and, above that, with white tiles. The manger was of porcelain, and there were brass tie-rings above it. The floor was tiled, with grooves leading to a drain in the middle.

'They don't make stables like this any more,' Charlie said.

They led Wilfred and Swallow in and tied them side by side, one with Charlie's lead rope and the other with a bit of binder twine Charlie found, to the noseband. They loosened the girths and ran up the stirrups and shut the door on the two of them.

Jerry was in the house, making a phone call, and gestured to them to go through into the kitchen where two lurchers dozed in a patch of sunlight by the open door. The kettle was still warm and Charlie helped himself to coffee, and poured one for Rowan. The kitchen was in chaos, but comfortably so, rather than squalidly. Jerry came in shortly and greeted them. Rowan was introduced.

'I hear you're going into business – High Horse, isn't it called? And Aunt Millie tells me you're going to teach at camp – she ropes in everybody, the old bag, for her wretched Pony Club. Me too. She wants to bring the lot here! She thinks it's ideal – three miles from the nearest pub. I remember getting out at night and going to the pub was the best bit of Pony Club camp. And smuggling it back in.'

'Yeah.' Charlie grinned. His memories were more recent than Jerry's, but similar. He wasn't sure how he was going to fare, being on the side of authority.

Jerry was older than Charlie but not by all that

much, considering the responsibilities of his job. He was a large man – too heavy to ride racehorses, his life's catastrophe. Training them was the next best thing. He had a natural, bounding optimism which showed in his cheerful face and laughter.

'Thank God you'll be one of the party. I'll want some male support. She's taking the house over, you know, catering in the kitchen – I'll have to clear it all up a bit before the day. I'm going to move out, even if it means sleeping over at the stables.'

'You could come home with me. Ma'll put you up.'

'Dogs as well?'

'Sure. The house'll be empty, with the kids over here.'

'That's great! What a relief! Glad you called.'

They went back to the stableyard and the two lurchers got up and padded silently behind Jerry. Jerry inspected Wilfred and appeared to see what Rowan failed to: 'Very nice when you get him fit. Great front. Nice pony too.'

Charlie beamed. 'Yeah, we need more like him – size and type, I mean, not temperament. He's a bit of a devil.'

'There's one down the road going begging. Belongs to a girl who doesn't like riding. Her mother asked me if I could find it some work. Not much bothered about selling – they've tons of money, but no grass. It's bored rigid in a straw yard at the moment. Want to go and see it?'

'Yes! Great.'

So Jerry got in his old banger, followed by the two dogs. Charlie and Rowan got their mounts out of the loosebox and followed him at a steady trot down the drive and towards the village. He turned into the first farmyard they came to. As they rode in behind him a whinny came from one of the barns and Rowan saw an eager movement, as the pony came to see what visitors had arrived.

The pony was much like Swallow in size and shape but had a less thrusting presence. It was a dark blue roan with a pretty head, sensible-looking.

'He's called Jones,' Jerry said. 'He's quite nice, as far as I know, no vices. Shall I raise his owner? I know she's dying to get rid of him.'

'Could be one for you, Rowan,' Charlie said. He saw her expression and laughed. 'Until Swallow's settled down.'

He realized that Rowan thought one ride over the downs following Wilfred, during which she hadn't fallen off, meant that time had already arrived.

Jerry went and fetched a rather smart lady from a house a little further on, and she agreed happily that Charlie should take the pony there and then. She looked at Wilfred's thin flanks rather dubiously, but they explained that he was newly bought out of a bad home and that Jones would be more than happy where he was going. She never said anything about money.

'Wonders never cease,' Charlie remarked, after they had said farewell to Jerry and his dogs and set off back the way they had come with Jones on the lead rein. 'That visit certainly paid off.'

Rowan tucked in behind, sure that Jones, nice as he was, wasn't for her. Swallow was her pony.

Chapter Two

Jones walked calmly at Wilfred's side and Swallow jogged along beside him, rather more excited now that he was heading for home, or perhaps excited by the strange pony. Rowan tried not to hold onto his mouth, but sometimes it felt as if he would overtake if she gave him his head. She could not help feeling slightly worried, but when Charlie glanced across and said, 'OK?' she answered firmly, 'Yes, thank you.'

Charlie's mind was obviously on his luck in acquiring a free pony. He whistled as they came up over the brow of the down on the same track they had travelled on before. The wind was at their backs and the sun in their eyes, and High Hawes lay below again in the curving arm of the oak wood. Wilfred's long stride took him down easily, Charlie holding him together so that he did not sprawl, and Jones jogged at his side. Swallow tossed his head and snatched at the reins holding his mouth, and started to trot.

'Whoa, Swallow! Don't!'

Rowan heard how feeble she sounded and was ashamed, biting her tongue. It was awful trotting downhill; she was thrown all over the place, and all the time Swallow kept putting his head down by his knees, snatching at her hands. If she held on he nearly pulled her over his head.

'Sit back, Rowan!' she heard Charlie shout. He sounded as worried as she felt. If she sat back she had to let the reins run when Swallow snatched, then he tossed his head up and she had miles of flapping rein and no control at all. It all seemed to be getting worse rather than better.

At the same unfortunate moment, the younger Hawes children, released from the dentist, came cantering out of the wood below, first Hugh on Cascade, then Lizzie on Fable and Shrimp on Snowball. Rowan saw Hugh stand up in his stirrups and his shout came thinly on the wind: 'Beat you to the sarsen stone!' They were still far below and hadn't seen the riders above them. Charlie let out a bellow of warning. How does he know Swallow will take off? Rowan wondered, even as her pony's ears disappeared from view and he gave one of his characteristic bucks. By a miracle she survived the buck, but there was no way she could stop the ensuing gallop. Going downhill was terrible. She remembered that she saw Hugh look up and see her, and start to pull Cascade to a skidding halt. She lost one stirrup and then the other and her reins were all tangled up in Swallow's flying mane; the ground flew past beneath her and a terrible fear started to make a strangling feeling in her throat. Her seat was hopelessly insecure. She felt herself rolling and slipping, first to one side and then the other. One more buck would finish it. It came. Rowan went flying and hit the turf with a terrific smack, then went rolling over and over down the hill until she came up hard against a rock and hit her head.

So this was what seeing stars meant! It was true. Silver slivers of light splintered her vision, so that nothing else came into focus. She felt intense pain and couldn't see anybody, yet she was aware of action all round her and voices like needles through her skull.

'Take these horses—'

'Charlie, you idiot! You said she wasn't to ride Swallow—'

'Where's that roan beast come from?'

'Is she dead?'

'No, she's moving. Just get those ponies away.'

'Take Swallow, Hugh – what a pig! I think he needs shooting.' That was Shrimp.

'Just clear off home, all of you. One of you hurry on and tell Mum to get the Land Rover up here.'

After a lot of argument there was silence, only the thud of departing hooves in the grass under Rowan's ear. In the quiet, she thought she was probably all right, only she couldn't move or say anything. Amongst the silver glitter in her vision she saw fragments of Charlie's face, looking like a picture on television when it was a prisoner or someone who mustn't be identified.

'Jeez, Rowan. I'm sorry – it was all my fault. Can you hear me? Do say you're all right!'

'Yes,' she whispered.

She couldn't help it but she felt two large warm tears run down her cheeks, one on either side. It was Shrimp saying Swallow should be shot. Why was she so hopeless, that she couldn't ride him?

'Oh, don't be upset, Rowan. I'm sure it's OK. Can you move your legs? Say something!'

She moved her legs. They felt like lead. Then, to please him she said, 'Swallow.'

It seemed a bit easier now. 'Don't shoot him.'

'No, of course not. We'll work on him, teach him manners. I shouldn't have let you ride him out – I was really stupid. I'm sorry!'

After some minutes the stars stopped blipping in her vision and she began to feel much less close to death. 'I think I'm all right.' The relief on Charlie's face, now coming into focus like a real face, was evident. 'Thank God for that! You had me really scared. No, don't sit up. Just rest till Ma comes.'

She could think of worse things now, than lying on the warm turf with Charlie beside her. He sat picking nervously at the grass, his earlier good humour overtaken by a darker mood. 'I can't see how I'm going to get by at this new game, if I can't even take a ride out without a casualty. Ma will be furious. I should have left Jones, or whatever he's called, and gone back for him with the trailer.'

He seemed determined that it was his fault, although Rowan was convinced it was her feeble riding that had caused the trouble. When Joan Hawes came rolling across the down in the Land-Rover she obviously agreed with Charlie, for she gave him an icy dressing-down before getting him to lift Rowan into the back of the Land Rover.

'Bolting ponies are a great advertisement, I must say!

I thought we'd agreed nobody was to ride Swallow save Hugh?'

Rowan gave Charlie an anguished look. She thought of Swallow as hers, although she knew perfectly well he wasn't, and the thought of Hugh taking him over really upset her. If he was the pony she was convinced he was, Hugh would never give him up, not when he started winning. Charlie knew what she was thinking.

He said crossly, 'For now – but Rowan will learn. She's not a wimp.'

When they got back to the yard Hugh and Lizzie and Shrimp had put away Wilfred and Swallow, tied up Jones awaiting further instructions, and were ready to start off on their ride again. Hugh looked in and said, 'It's OK. She's still alive.' Then he ran up behind his pony Cascade and jumped on over his hindquarters in his showing-off way. Cascade put back his ears but did not budge: a stocky grey pony built like a small tank. He had as much spirit and talent as his rider; they were a well-matched pair. They were Pony Club stars, although Hugh affected to despise Pony Club – 'all those girls.' Rowan guessed that if he couldn't beat the girls, he would stop going. Boys were like that. In spite of Charlie's kind words, she felt she was definitely in the category of wimpy girls. Lizzie, two years older than Hugh and much nicer, said kindly to Rowan, 'Anyone would've fallen off, Rowan – that buck! I would. He's really beastly, that pony.'

She meant it as comfort, but it wasn't much, although Rowan raised a sickly smile. Lizzie got back on Fable, who was a dear: a well-bred, light bay mare with black points, the one anybody could ride. Lizzie, although a very good rider, had been glad to see the back of her old pony, Birdie, an idiosyncratic thoroughbred who had been sold to the show-jumping girl, Matty Prebble. She had appropriated the gentle Fable with relief. Not everybody wanted to show off like Hugh.

They all wanted to know who Jones was and why, so Charlie explained that to them, and they put him out in the field and rode away, and Charlie and his mother took Rowan into the kitchen and sat her down tenderly in Fred Hawes' old armchair.

'I shall have to ring your mother and tell her what's happened,' Joan said. 'You must be checked out after a fall like that. You might be concussed.'

Rowan nearly said, 'Like last time,' then remembered she hadn't told anyone how ill she had felt for a week after banging her head the first time (another of Swallow's bucks).

'Must you tell her?' Charlie asked, echoing Rowan's own feelings. 'You know how anti-horse her dad is.'

'Yes, I must. I'm sorry. You should have thought this through before you put her on Swallow. You've got to learn, Charlie. The hard way, by the look of it.'

Josephine came in while Joan Hawes was telephoning and, seeing Rowan's wan face, and the egg-like lump that was fast emerging over one eye, wanted to know what had happened. Her reaction was not unlike her mother's.

'Oh really, Charlie, you're an absolute idiot.'

'Don't you start! The pony was as good as gold until the last mile when that brainless goon Hugh burst out of the wood at flat gallop. And Rowan sat it very well – the first buck, fine. It was just bad luck she came off.'

'His bucks are dynamite. I think he needs a bullet.'

'Oh, shut up!'

Rowan was mortified by putting Charlie in such a predicament – all her fault that the whole family was castigating poor Charlie, because she was so hopeless! Joan Hawes came back from the phone and told Rowan her mother was coming up to fetch her in the car.

'Just as I thought – she said your father would be annoyed. I don't think he thinks we're a very good influence, after your nice London friends.' But she smiled encouragingly. 'Never mind, Rowan. We'll see that you never have to ride that pony again.'

The last words she wanted to hear! She bit her lip, and saw Charlie's eyes on her, contrite, but he didn't say anything. She sensed that Joan was crosser with Charlie than she wanted to reveal in front of Rowan. She had a very firm set to her lips and her eyes could be flinty at times. She looked haggard since her husband's death, and almost ten years older. Her mother remarked on this fact as she drove Rowan home.

'She does look ill! What a situation to be in – that place to run and all those children – I don't know how they'll keep their heads above water. Especially if they do stupid things like this. I thought you could ride now, Rowan?'

Her father said exactly the same thing, but with rather more heat. 'I've paid over three hundred pounds so far to that place to teach you to ride! What's wrong with them? Or is it you?'

'They didn't *want* the money!' Rowan cried out angrily. 'You made them take it. Of course I can't ride properly yet – it takes years!'

He had been so effusive, pressing the notes on Hugh

and Lizzie, which were still pushed, unappreciated, into an instant coffee jar behind the wormers in the tack room. He never understood that they were teaching her as a friend, for fun. Everything was money to him, Rowan supposed, because he was an accountant. He had very odd ideas, as he now started to prove.

'Surely to learn the basics of riding, so that you don't fall off, can be covered in the amount of lessons you've had? I'm not expecting you to jump an Olympic course, just stay on safely. What is so difficult about it? I can't see that family making much of a living if they can't din that much into you.'

Rowan felt it best not to say anything. But after she had seen the doctor and been told to rest at home for a couple of days to counter a hit of concussion, her father had another outbreak of high-mindedness and said she was not to ride again.

'It's too dangerous, and I don't think consorting with a load of gypsies is doing you any good.'

At this Rowan burst into tears and screamed at him, her mother became highly indignant and started to shout, and a family drama erupted. Rowan had noticed that her parents had been having a lot of rows lately but this one, instigated by herself, was a real corker.

She retired to her bedroom and neither of them noticed her go. She lay on her bed and sobbed, and her head throbbed, and the row below continued unabated until she fell asleep. She could not believe she wouldn't be allowed to go up to High Hawes again. If her father insisted on the ban, she thought she might as well die. She hiccupped herself to sleep and slept heavily.

When she awoke in the morning it was very quiet and there was no sound of her father getting up and going to work, although it was time. He drove up to the motorway and commuted to London every day, although to Rowan it felt as if London was on a different planet. It certainly was quite a long way. Sometimes, in fact, quite a lot lately, he didn't come home at all. He was always saying how much it cost them, living so far out in the country. Rowan had always shut her ears to this. She thought her father was a pain.

She had rather thought her mother would bring her up a cup of tea and be all sympathetic, but nothing happened, so she got up and got dressed. She felt all right save the egg on her forehead which looked weird and was going purple. Quite a few bits of her were going purple. She felt terribly stiff. She went downstairs and found her mother sitting alone in the kitchen in her dressing gown, doing nothing. This was unheard of. She didn't even have a cup of tea by her. She was just staring into space. Her face was white and peculiar-looking.

'What's the matter?' Rowan asked.

'Your father's gone.'

'To work?'

'No. Gone. He says he's not coming back.'

Rowan wasn't quite sure how to take this. Her first thought was, Hooray, now I can still go up to High Hawes. But when she looked at her mother again she saw that this was a very wicked thought and it was quite serious. The phrase 'one-parent family' came into her head. (At least it was the right one parent . . . she had always got on well with her mother.) Then she felt a bit peculiar too, like her mother looked, and sat down opposite her.

There was a long silence between them.

Then Rowan said, 'He'll come back, I should think. When he's cooled down.'

And her mother said, 'No. I don't think he will.'

And he didn't.

Chapter Three

'Both our families have had bad shocks, losing their fathers,' Joan Hawes said to Rowan's mother. 'The best thing the children can do is go off to Pony Club camp and enjoy themselves.'

'I don't know if I can afford it now.'

'You can use the money out of the coffee jar. We've never spent it,' Lizzie said.

'What money?'

'He – Mr Watkins – kept paying us for giving Rowan lessons. We said we didn't want it but he insisted. There's a hundred pounds.'

'That's splendid,' said Joan Hawes. 'Well done.'

'It won't cover the hire of one of your ponies, surely?'

'Rowan does enough work up here to cover all that. We'll make her work harder!'

'I like it!' Rowan declared. She still wasn't at all sure

about camp. She looked doubtfully towards Charlie. 'Who shall I ride?'

'Josephine thinks you ought to try Jones. Lizzie's ridden him in the field and he shows no signs of tanking off or not wanting to leave the others. Lizzie wants to take Fable, Hugh's having Swallow and Shrimp wants to try Pinkie. We can always swap around if it doesn't work out.'

'I've never ridden Jones!'

'I'll give you a lesson on him,' Josephine offered unexpectedly.

'When?' Rowan quaked. She was very nervous of the severe Josephine.

'In a minute. As soon as we've finished lunch.'

They were all sitting round the kitchen table eating ham and salad and hard-boiled eggs. Rowan's mother had come up and been prevailed upon to stay. Since she had been left alone, three days ago, she had been wandering round in a state of shock, and was only just coming to. Rowan felt much the same, deeply disturbed, as if she had been sitting on a chair that had been snatched from underneath her. It was hard to take in, and each time she came home from High Hawes she expected to see her father's car in the drive, but it never was. In a way she felt a sense of relief, seeing the empty drive, but underneath, deep down, she felt outraged that he didn't care enough for her to come home. It was terribly hurtful. Each time this hurt came, she turned her brain back to High Hawes and made it concentrate on her luck, not on the family disaster. At least her mother was never going to stop her going up to High Hawes. Hugh said fathers leaving was very common. Rowan said she supposed it wasn't as bad as him dying, like Hugh's father, but it did seem rather weird to think that her father was still around, but not connected with them any more. Her mother hadn't worked since she had married – when she had been her father's secretary. She was now saying she would have to get a job, and looking rather hopeless.

Rowan had always wished her mother was slightly less feeble and more rock-like, like Joan Hawes. Her mother, whose name was Pauline, was much prettier and smarter than Joan Hawes, but Joan Hawes gave off an aura of strength and total reliability that Rowan found very reassuring. She was a big, untidy woman with a majestic posture, rather slow-moving, but a wizard at producing meals from nowhere and saying the right thing at the right time.

'You needn't worry about looking for a job while camp is on. You'll be asked to help with the catering –

that'll keep your mind off your troubles for a week. We can go over together. You'll meet a lot of nice people.'

'I haven't really met anybody since I came to live here.'

'No, you don't unless you join things. We don't go out of our way to be friendly, on the whole. But if you're in trouble, you'll find people will come out of the woodwork.'

Rowan felt very good about her mother being friends with Joan Hawes, less good about her lesson with Josephine.

'Go and tack him up. We'll sort you out.'

Rowan did as she was told. She wished desperately it was Charlie. Everything was fun with Charlie, but Josephine was a serious girl, and did not smile a lot. She was tall and rather beautiful in her cool blonde way and, although they were so different, was very close to Charlie since the two of them had taken on the brunt of running High Hawes to make a livelihood. Rowan had noticed how it was weighing on them.

Josephine said, 'You've got to get to know this pony, and I've got to practise my teaching.' She even smiled. Rowan felt better.

She found Jones very nice to ride, obedient and

comfortable, and able to understand her inexperienced demands. He didn't give her the feeling that disaster was imminent, as Swallow did, that she was tiptoeing round the edge of a sleeping volcano. He was laid-back but not unwilling, and Josephine taught her how to try and collect him so that he held himself together when he trotted, but admitted that it wasn't easy for a beginner. 'You do it with your back and leg muscles, and these have to develop. The "seat" is everything, and it takes a long time to develop it.'

Rowan was not encouraged, feeling she had started too late. But Josephine laughed at her fears and said, 'You have the right attitude, that's what matters. Hugh, for example, thinks he knows it all. He can ride Swallow's bucks, no trouble, but he has no finesse. One day he will find out.'

'Has Charlie got finesse?' Rowan dared to ask.

Josephine said crossly, 'Oh, Charlie's got everything. I hate him!' But then she smiled. 'It's no good trying to copy Charlie. He does it by instinct. He can't teach to save his life because he can't understand why other people can't get the same results as he does.'

'But I thought High Hawes was going to be a riding school and Charlie was going to be a teacher?'

'It's not going to work out that way.'

'Charlie said—'

'Charlie doesn't know!' Rowan got the impression that Josephine was crying out to her what she hadn't voiced to anybody else – the worries that kept her tight and silent and depressed. Her cool look was suddenly quite passionate. 'Charlie knows he doesn't like teaching but he doesn't understand why. It'll never work – Charlie teaching children. And me – I'm not a lot better. I haven't got the right temperament to be a teacher. I get cross if people are stupid, instead of laughing and making it fun. It isn't fun to me. It's deadly serious.'

'But how can you start up a riding school with no one who can teach?'

'Exactly,' said Josephine. 'That's what keeps me awake at nights.'

Rowan was amazed at Josephine's confidences. She suspected that they had not been voiced to anyone else in the family, and Josephine confirmed this by adding, as they went to put Jones away, 'Don't tell the others any of this. I always worry about things. I can't help it. I might have it all wrong.'

Rowan said, 'I think you're a good teacher. I think that was the best lesson I've ever had. Better than with any of the others.'

And Josephine said, 'Yes. That's because you think the same as me. You're deadly serious too.'

Rowan was astonished.

There were forty applicants for Pony Club camp. The only others Rowan knew besides the Hawes were Barbara Bailey, the farmer's daughter who lived just along the road from her, and Matty Prebble, the show-jumping girl – although she only knew her a bit, by sight. Barbara was known as Babar the Elephant by the Hawes (she was a large girl and did not mind, Babar being such a nice character). In spite of her laid-back manner, broad speech and bun face she was brilliant at school and knocked spots off all of them. She had a weedy old pony called Black Diamond who couldn't do anything, and lately, since Charlie had bought the job-lot of riding-school ponies, she had taken to riding the chestnut cob, Armchair. She had found the difference, after Diamond, amazing and was now torn with guilt at preferring Armchair over poor old Diamond.

'I would love to take Armchair to camp,' she confided to Rowan, 'but I can't abandon poor Diamond.'

'Ask Charlie what he thinks.'

Charlie said, 'Yes, take the Armchair. It will do him

good – and you. You'll have far more fun on him than on Diamond. If you like, Diamond can come up here, and we can use him for nervous pupils – if we get any, that is. He can earn his keep.'

Babar's large round face lit up at this. 'That would be great! I don't want 'im to think I don't love 'im any more.'

'Horses don't get huffy, like human beings,' Charlie said.

'He likes it up 'ere, because of the company. 'E's only got cows at home.'

'That's it, then. Everyone's happy.'

Rowan knew Charlie would solve it. The pressure on Babar's loyalty was dissolved and she started to take a more proprietary interest in the Armchair, grooming him diligently and schooling him over small jumps. She had never been able to get Diamond to jump even a cavalletti. The Armchair was a very amiable animal, no oil painting, but a rather flash bright chestnut, fourteen-and-a-half hands high, with stout legs and hairy heels, a hogged flaxen mane and a bushy, unmanageable cream tail. Rowan had once seen Josephine riding him and had been surprised how very smartly he went and how good he looked, almost like a show cob. She did not know that a sign of a good rider was not necessarily how they handled the difficult horses, but how they made the slugs perform. Not that the Armchair was a slug, but he didn't look quite the same for Babar as he did for a talented Hawes. Babar's enthusiasm for camp, now she had a new horse, inspired Rowan to rather more excitement herself. There was only a week to go, and she got out her list of instructions to make sure she would be well prepared.

She was to be in Orange Ride and share accommodation with a girl called Roma Glade. 'Roma Glade' conjured up a rather dreary vision in Rowan's mind; it sounded like an air freshener.

'Never heard of her,' said Hugh. He then went on to explain that the Orange Ride was for older but fairly useless riders. 'Green Ride is for younger but better riders. Blue Ride is top, Red Ride second top. I'm in Red. I should be in Blue really, but I'm too young. Shrimp's in Green. Lizzie's in Red with me.'

Lizzie said, 'Don't take any notice of him. Orange is not for "fairly useless riders" – it's for people without a lot of experience. And it's only rough anyway – nearly everyone complains they're in the wrong ride. Hugh can't believe he's not in the top ride – he has to say it's because he's too young, but Charlie was in the top ride when he was eleven.'

214

'He didn't have a difficult pony like Cascade,' Hugh said hotly.

'His pony didn't have a duff rider like you!'

'I don't stand a chance of winning anything on Swallow anyway.'

'Poor diddums!'

At this point Shrimp came in and stopped the conversation by saying, rather tearfully, she didn't see how she could take Pinkie away to camp for a week without taking Bonzo too, as Bonzo was now so attached to his surrogate 'mother' Pinkie that he would pine if she went away. 'He'll have to come too. I still have to feed him anyway, and Ma won't want to do it for a week.'

Bonzo was Shrimp's orphan foal which she had hand-fed since birth. He was now a very pushy colt of two months, turned out with the little strawberry roan mare Pinkie to whom he had struck up a fierce attachment. Pinkie was another of Charlie's bargain buys, having been discarded for a knee injury, but the injury had cleared up completely with rest. Shrimp, who had always ridden show ponies for professional show people and never had her own pony, now lavished attention on her two darlings, Bonzo and Pinkie, as if to make up all the time she had lost out in the family, being away at shows.

Apparently 'Auntie Millie' gave permission for Bonzo to come too, for when the morning arrived when they all set off to ride over the down to camp, he was let out to run free behind the group of ponies. Children and ponies were unrecognizably smart. The children sported snow-white shirts and gleaming badges, well-brushed jackets and spotless jods, and the ponies shone, their manes and tails freshly washed and hooves polished. Rowan could not keep her eyes off Swallow, whose blue-black coat showed faint dapples across the belly, chinking his bit against Hugh's restraining hand. He looked like a little fairy-tale charger, all spirit and strength, tossing the heavy forelock with impatience.

Charlie's instructions were to walk all the way, fiercely reiterated to Hugh. Babar was in charge, riding the Armchair. For once her gumboots had been replaced by proper riding boots, and her mothy anorak by an equally ancient but correct tweed jacket. Following her through the wood, watching Swallow, Rowan was relieved to be on sensible Jones and for the first time felt a slight optimism about the week ahead. Her mother, still in a state of shock and frequently in tears, had cheered up notably at the prospect of the hard work in the catering department that awaited her over at Sand House, the abode of Jeremy Patterson. Jerry was now thankfully defecting to High Hawes for the week. Joan Hawes and Pauline were driving over with all their children's gear to see them settled in, and Josephine and Charlie would follow in the Land Rover after lunch, when their services would be required.

The ride to Sand House was uneventful, due to the firm restraining influence of Lizzie and Babar on Hugh who, in spite of instructions, kept suggesting 'a nice canter'. Although kept under restraint, he didn't sulk, just laughed, which was the nice thing about him and why, although he was so horrid, one couldn't help liking him. Rowan rode along thinking how incredibly lucky she was to have fallen in with this amazing family and nice Babar, when she could have been marooned at home all the holidays with her neurotic mother. And her mother too, taken in hand by Joan Hawes, turned cheerful when she came up to High Hawes, and was really keen to start cooking Pony Club dinners. Rowan had a bit of a guilty feeling then, for thinking herself lucky when her father had left them to run off with his secretary, but she couldn't help how she felt. Certainly she missed him, but mostly it was a relief to be free of his bad temper. Perhaps now he was with his secretary he was all smiles.

'Put Bonzo on a lead rope,' Babar commanded, as they came down the track to join the road. Horseboxes and trailers were approaching the drive to Sand House, and cars full of gear, stirring up the somnolent valley. It was a hazy, close day, and their ties felt hot – Hugh had pulled his apart and rode with his jacket flapping open. Swallow had behaved like a lamb all the way, Rowan noticed crossly. She felt very nervous as they crossed the road and followed an enormous cream horsebox up the drive, choking in its dust.

'That's Priscilla Hicks,' Hugh said, and made his being-sick face. 'She's never come to camp before because her horse is too valuable to come slumming. But now Auntie Millie has collared Jerry's yard, she thinks she'll honour us with her presence.'

Behind them the Prebbles' equally large box, driven by a groom, throttled down, deciding not to overtake. They pulled off the drive onto the grass verge to let it by, and Rowan saw Matty's pale face looking down at them, unsmiling.

'She's another who's only come because we've got posh stables this year. She never comes ordinarily – not when we were at the farm and the ponies had to be tied up in the cow byre.'

Rowan wondered how big Roma Glade's horsebox

would be, as she was going to sleep in it for a week. Priscilla and Matty were going to be in luxury in the living accommodation of their vast horseboxes; Lizzie and Shrimp were going to share space in one of the few safe dormer rooms over the stables and Hugh was sharing a trailer with a boy called Alan Finch who he said was all right. Just before they reached the stable yard another trailer passed them, this time a very rickety affair pulled by a wheezing Land Rover. On the trailer's tailboard a notice announced: 'Glade's Pigs. Organic Bacon from Free Range Farms.'

'That's your home!' Hugh shouted with great glee. 'A pig trailer! Jeez, Rowan, I hope they've hosed it out!'

Even the girls thought it was funny, so Rowan tried to smile gamely, but her expectations were plummeting by the minute. They turned into the old stableyard, which was now humming with activity. The horse-boxes had driven through it to the far field, where the ponies were being unloaded, and Auntie Millie was inspecting the arrivals under the walnut tree, and allocating stables, helped by Matty's mother, the sharp Mrs Prebble (who was not the most popular mother in Long Bottom) and Jerry Patterson. Rowan was much encouraged by Jerry's smile of recognition.

'So Jones is at work already? Do him the world of good. How do you get on with him?'

'He's lovely.'

Had Jerry heard about her accident with Swallow? she wondered.

'Get off and trot him out for me, will you?'

Rowan got off. She had no idea what she had to do to trot him out, but luckily dear Lizzie saw her hesitation and said quickly, 'I'll go first!' It appeared that one led the pony away up the yard and trotted him back in a straight line, aiming straight at Jerry. This was to make sure no lame ponies were passed in. The stalwart Millie Mildmay watched grimly. She was a four-square, sixtyish-year-old woman in a green quilted jacket and fawn trousers, who moved with a strange rolling gait born of many injuries from falls in point-to-points. She had gimlet eyes, a mousetrap mouth, and hairs on her chin. But her dark eyes were full of a zest for living; they raked over Rowan and her pony and came to rest challengingly on Rowan's terrified face.

'Who are you then? You're not a Hawes, are you? Or is my mind going?'

'I'm Rowan Watkins. I ride with them – the Hawes.'

'Ha! Good for you. Run your stirrups up. Never leave

them dangling after you've dismounted. How shall we arrange your ponies then? All good friends, are they? Which one is that ridiculous foal attached to?'

Shrimp scowled. Bonzo was a skewbald and did look slightly ridiculous, standing there with his long rabbit ears pricked with surprise at the goings-on, all legs and cheek.

'He'll have to stay shut up while you're riding, for goodness' sake. He won't kick the box down, I hope?'

She let out a great guffaw at the idea and clapped the foal on the hindquarters. Shrimp scowled at her and received a beaming smile. 'And you, young lady, we've got to teach you to ride properly, haven't we? No more sitting up there in your red hair ribbons smiling and just looking pretty. Take that foal and your pony to the box in the corner and put the other mare in with them.' She pointed at Fable. 'If you think that's best. You know them better than I do. And you, Rowan, does your pony get on with Hugh's new beast? Will they share?'

'I want to share with Alan Finch,' said Hugh.

Lizzie said, 'Yes, Swallow and Jones are friends.'

'Good. Put them together.' She ignored Hugh. 'And you, Barbara—'

They led their ponies to their boxes. Hugh was

furious and Shrimp was almost in tears at the insult to her riding. 'I bet she couldn't show a horse to save her life. She only knows about crashing cross country and falling off.'

Lizzie said, 'You'll just have to show her then, won't you?'

Shrimp glared at her, even while digesting the truth of her sister's remark. She had something of the same nature as Auntie Millie herself, Rowan thought, remembering the night Bonzo had been born, and her courage in saving him from the berserk dam. Shrimp's week was already set up – to *show* Millie Mildmay. Her eyes were blazing. She was nine, and small for her age, but her character enlarged her presence remarkably. Poor Pinkie was going to have a tough week. The pretty little mare, a pure Welsh mountain, twelve hands high, was already searching the large porcelain manger for signs of sustenance and Bonzo was quickly copying her.

Rowan reckoned she had got off lightly from the formidable Mrs Mildmay and untacked Jones in his allotted box while Hugh muttered crossly over Swallow. How nice, Rowan was thinking, that she would be sharing the box with dear Swallow. As she slipped off the bridle, Hugh looked out over the door and said, 'There's Princess Priscilla. Look at her! Mummy Prebble's buttering her up, you can see.'

Priscilla Hicks was extraordinarily handsome, along with her young thoroughbred. She had long, red, very curly hair which was immediately eye-catching, and large amber-coloured eyes like a cat's. Rowan was stunned by the elegant, imperious way she stood at her horse's head while Mrs Prebble gushed away. She was said to be sixteen, but had the authority of an adult; her confidence no doubt built upon her arresting beauty. Rowan could not help but admire such a picture, in spite of Hugh's yukking noises. She was what most insignificant mouse-coloured girls like Rowan dreamed they might turn into one day, and knew quite assuredly they would not.

'Daddy Hicks bought that horse from the Whitakers. He cost a packet. They've only brought him to camp to get him used to going in company and roughing it a bit. Auntie Millie said he's too uptight. She thinks mixing with the likes of us will do him good. Princess Priscilla is having trouble with him, you see.'

Rowan tried to digest that people with 'millions' to spend and with looks like a top model had the same sort of troubles as she did. Difficult. She couldn't see it.

Lizzie said, 'Look at Mrs Prebble! Her darling Matty is always top dog at camp and now Princess Priscilla's decided to come she's going to get her nose put out of joint.' She grinned at Rowan. 'Aren't we catty? The trouble is,' she explained, 'when it comes to being in the teams, we all want to be in the Pony Club team, but people like them take the places. And they aren't real members, doing all the nitty-gritty – they only come to the minimum number of rallies to qualify – they never do any of the fun things, like treasure hunts and tet and things.'

Rowan supposed she would learn what 'tet' was in due course – there was too much to take in all at once. It struck her that a lot of members might think the Hawes were privileged – were they always chosen for the teams? She was sure Charlie and Josephine must have been. On the other hand they did it by sheer hard work – no one ever bought them expensive ponies. Even Cascade, the star, had been obtained almost for nothing, as he was considered dangerous.

Jones and Swallow seemed perfectly happy in their shared box, both looking out over the half-door to watch the goings-on in the yard. Nearly everyone else arrived by lorry or trailer, most of which parked in the field beyond the yard to become living accommodation for the week. There was a gate from this field into the garden of the house, where a large mess tent had been set up for eating in, convenient to the kitchen. The two big fields on either side of the drive, next to the road, were where the riding would take place, and Hugh said there was a cross-country course up the lane a little way in the grounds of a National Trust house. Apparently, such was Auntie Millie's clout, she could arrange these things. The tenant of the house was one of her many relations. Apparently she had twenty-six cousins, mostly horsey.

Princess Priscilla's beautiful horse had been given a loosebox all to himself, where he was tossing himself around in circles and scraping his bedding into heaps. Rowan heard Auntie Millie say to Jerry, 'I think we've all bitten off a bit more than we can chew in that department,' with a nod in the gelding's direction, to which Jerry replied with a grin, 'Pass her over to Charlie. He'll sort her out.'

Rowan felt rather disturbed on Charlie's behalf, and a nasty jealous feeling turned in her stomach, which she squashed by making herself concentrate on Roma Glade, who had just led her pony in from the horsebox field and given her name to Mrs Mildmay. To Rowan's relief she was not in the Princess Priscilla league, but a rather earnest-looking, twelvish girl with untidy hair sticking out from under her hat and an equally earnest-looking pony, a rather stout dun who she said was called Honeypot.

'Right about the pot,' remarked Mrs Mildmay. 'Not very fit, by the look of him. You're sharing with that new girl who came with the Hawes, so you'd better put your pony by theirs, up there. Rowan and Roma – you sound like a circus act, on the trapeze, eh!' She let out one of her bellowing laughs.

'Go and talk to her.' Lizzie gave Rowan a shove.

Hugh marched up beside Rowan and said, 'Hi, Roma. This is Rowan who's going to share your pig lorry.'

'I scrubbed it out last night, honestly. It doesn't smell of pigs at all, only a bit of him.' She nodded at her pony, and looked dubiously at Rowan. Hugh marched off to find Alan, Lizzie went to see if Fable was all right, and Roma said to Rowan, 'I was really worried when they told me I was sharing with a Hawes.'

'I'm not a Hawes!'

'You've got a Hawes pony though. It's bound to be brilliant.'

'No. They've only had it a week. All their ponies are new. They're rescued ponies.'

'Hasn't Hugh got Cascade and Lizzie got Birdie?'

'No.'

Roma looked much happier all of a sudden. 'I thought you'd be brilliant like them. Honeypot won't jump, you know. Not even a cavalletti. He just won't. I didn't want to come but my mum made me.'

'I can't jump. I can't even ride, really,' Rowan confessed.

'Oh, good,' said Roma.

They warmed to each other at once after these confessions, and went back to the field to the pig trailer. Joan Hawes and Pauline Watkins had arrived with all their gear and backed up the estate car to unload Rowan's stuff. There was barely room for the two camp beds side by side, with a little slice at the top for their bag of clothes. They had to sit on the beds as there was no gap between. Pauline looked appalled but Rowan thought it looked very cosy.

'At least we'll have no housework to do,' Roma said. 'We get marked each morning for how tidy it is. Priscilla will have to get the Hoover out to do her floor, and wipe round the fridge every morning! Have you seen her horse? It's called Out of the West, and cost ten thousand pounds.'

Rowan thought Out of the West was a most beautiful name, if not very handy, and couldn't help feeling that the lovely Priscilla was possibly dreading the week ahead even more than she had been. She must know how everyone was gossiping about her. Now it had started, and Roma seemed quite normal, Rowan was beginning to enjoy herself. It was nearly lunch time and when they had tidied up they had to go back to the yard, and hay and water their ponies under the eagle eye of a fierce girl called Octavia or, more usually, Otty. She was a sort of budding Mrs Mildmay, not yet weathered and lame. She had short, dark hair and a brown face and was very quick and strong.

Roma said, 'I think she might be teaching Orange Ride. I hope so. She's nice.'

Rowan had prayed Orange Ride would get Charlie, but he had been given the top ride with Priscilla and Matty Prebble. It was all up on a noticeboard outside the mess tent. Hugh and Lizzie were in Red Ride with Mrs Prebble in charge and Otty was, as Roma surmised, down for Orange. Josephine had Green, which Shrimp was in. Roma said she would have had Red save for Lizzie and Hugh being in it, as apparently it wasn't good to be taught by a relation, if it could be

helped. There was only one ride below Orange, called
Yellow, which was for very small children. Rowan was
relieved to see that there were older (possibly worse?)
riders in Orange. She felt much better now she had
discovered there were other members as diffident as
herself.

They went into the mess tent and sat down for
lunch. It was an easy one of ham, salad, tinned fruit
and ice cream because the kitchen was not yet
organized. When they had eaten Mrs Mildmay gave
them a harangue about being helpful, manners,
behaviour, going to sleep at Lights Out ('Some
hope!' Rowan heard Otty remark) and remembering
that their ponies deserved the first and best of their
time.

After a final glare her face immediately switched to
sweetness and light and she let out her great laugh and
said, 'Remember, it's fun! Enjoy yourselves!'

They all filed out (except the duty group for the day
who had to wash up and clear away) and got their
riding clothes and tacked up their ponies. The first
afternoon was a sorting out with their instructors.
Hugh, tacking up Swallow, was moaning about having
Mrs Prebble.

'You're all right – Otty's nice. Mrs Prebble's

downright cruel . . . hours of sitting trot and on the bit and stuff. Swallow'll hate it.'

'You will, you mean,' Lizzie said.

Otty had changed from shirt and jeans into pristine jods and boots, white shirt and tie and a jacket. When Rowan led Jones out she saw Charlie talking to Mrs Mildmay. He was dressed similarly, and looked amazing. For a moment she didn't recognize him, not until he turned away and saw her, and grinned. In spite of being told how lucky she was to have Otty for an instructor, Rowan wished desperately she had Charlie. Charlie's ride consisted of six girls of about fifteen; Matty Prebble was the youngest. She rode Birdie, the thoroughbred pony that had once been Lizzie's.

'She's welcome,' Lizzie said, as they watched her mount. Birdie was uptight as usual, spinning round nervously. Charlie went across and held her. Matty scowled furiously and rode away across the yard, out into the field. As soon as she had gone Priscilla came out of her loosebox with Out of the West. Out of the West was sixteen-and-a-half hands high, with an arrogant and commanding outlook that made him seem bigger. He was beautifully made, up to weight, and very eye-catching with his gleaming black coat.

Rowan saw the look on Charlie's face, of pure admiration. She hoped it was for the horse, and not its rider, who had an instinctive way of looking at the opposite sex, with a bold come-hither smile and then a lowering of the eyes and a flutter of the long dark lashes. Rowan, staring, was terribly impressed.

'Get a move on, Rowan,' Otty said.

The five rides were marked out in the two flat fields on either side of the drive with coloured cones, and the riders went to their colour and lined up to have their tack examined by their instructor. If it was all new to Rowan, it was obvious that most children knew the drill. There was plenty of laughing and teasing, save – noticeably – in Mrs Prebble's ride. Otty was kindly and not over-critical, and Rowan was confident that her pony and tack were in good order and had no worries. It was the actual riding she was nervous of, of not being good enough.

But she need not have worried. To her astonishment she found there was nothing that she couldn't cope with, and at the end of the afternoon Otty said to her, 'Well done, Rowan. You've made a good start.'

Rather different from Hugh, to whom Mrs Prebble was saying in her acid voice, 'I don't know why you bother to come when you make it so apparent you know everything.'

Lizzie said to Rowan, 'Her own darling daughter was having trouble with Birdie, did you notice? She could see, out of the corner of her eye. It's made her terribly cross. I'm so glad it's Matty on Birdie, and not me any more. Fable's a darling.'

Rowan was surprised how hungry she was when they went in for tea.

Chapter Four

Rowan adored this new, strange life: sleeping in the pig trailer; getting up at midnight to trail across the moonlit field to giggle and trade crisps with two others of their ride living in comparative splendour in a caravan; dodging the night patrol by rolling into a ditch (dry fortunately); and overhearing a gem of gossip from the lips of Auntie Millie herself as she walked past with Otty: 'I'm afraid Lucy Prebble is very unsuited to Pony Club life. She's a pain, and I'm sorry for the children who have to bear with her. But it's difficult to give volunteers the sack. We just have to make the best of it.'

To this Otty replied, 'According to Charlie, Matty Prebble's not getting on very well with that new pony of hers. If she's having trouble, Mrs Prebble will be upset and that makes her temper worse.'

They walked on, and Rowan and Roma stayed lying

in the ditch for a bit, to be on the safe side. The friends in the caravan had given them a glass of cider each, and Rowan was impressed by how the stars were circling round the sky and how the ditch seemed to swing gently like a hammock, so that it was more comfortable to stay than to go. It was very warm, and the dark downs seemed to wrap round them in a friendly fashion. Rowan felt fantastically, incredibly happy.

Roma said, 'It's a bit embarrassing for the Hawes if they sold Birdie to the Prebbles and she's no good.'

Rowan said, 'Mrs Prebble insisted on having her. She answered the ad. She tried to beat the price down, but Charlie wouldn't. He didn't hide anything about Birdie. She is a difficult pony. That's why Lizzie didn't like her. But Mrs Prebble knew all that. I suppose she thought Matty was good enough to cope with her.'

'It's funny,' Roma said, 'how some ponies are just right for a person, and all wrong for another. I don't think Honeypot is right for me somehow. Or perhaps it's just me.'

'Yes, I think that.' Rowan knew Jones was right for her, but she wanted Swallow. Lizzie wanted to keep Fable although her family scorned her lack of ambition. Hugh and Cascade were made for each other. Rowan thought of dear Swallow in his mahogany-lined stable, picking at his hay-net. 'I *will* ride him!' she whispered to herself. She looked up at the sharp half-circle of a sickle moon lying above the downs and made a fierce vow. Roma had got up and walked on and Rowan supposed she had to go too, but for a moment it was the most important thing in the world, to lie in the ditch committing herself to dear Swallow. Roma came back, rather worried.

'Are you all right?'

'Oh, yes!'

It was all to do with being so lucky and so happy, not living in Putney any more but having landed up with the Hawes, and having Jones to ride and Swallow to aspire to. She got up and started back for the pig trailer behind Roma.

'Swallow was stolen, you know, and nobody really knows who owns him properly.'

'What are you talking about?'

Rowan couldn't remember.

The next day Mrs Prebble picked a row with Charlie, accusing him of upsetting Matty with his 'inadequate teaching'. She said to Mrs Mildmay, 'He's too young and totally unqualified to teach a Pony Club top ride.'

Auntie Millie stuck out her famous jaw. 'Yes, you're right. But I have faith in him. I don't think the trouble lies with Charlie. I think it lies with Matty.'

'Then I'll have her in my ride and sort her out myself.'

'Yes. Try it.'

Mrs Mildmay asked Lizzie to go and tell Charlie she wanted him. The rides were just preparing to go out, and he was giving Priscilla a leg up on Out of the West. They were laughing together and Rowan, hearing them, felt a stab of the old familiar jealousy. Charlie was hers!

He came over, looking slightly nervous.

'Mrs Prebble is going to take Matty into her own ride. She's not satisfied with your teaching.'

Charlie did not look too worried.

'Am I supposed to be upset?'

'No. I just want your side of the story.'

'Matty doesn't get on with Birdie. She hypes her up and Birdie's losing her confidence. The more Matty has a go at her, the more Birdie decides she doesn't like it. They give her too much hard feed and they haven't let her out in a field since they bought her. What do they expect?'

'Have you told Mrs Prebble this?'

'I'm not daft! I've told Matty. I've tried to get her to relax, let the mare down, stop over-feeding her, not ask too much of her. They've only had her three weeks and the mare needs sympathy, not force.'

'You sold the pony to them. Did it occur to you she might not suit?'

'I advertised the mare for sale and Mrs Prebble answered the ad. Dad always knew she wanted her, because of the jump she's got, but I purposely didn't offer Birdie to Mrs Prebble because she's such a pain, and when it comes to show-jumping she asks such a lot of youngsters. You know Dad didn't worry about things like that if the money was offered. But Mrs Prebble turned up and haggled, and when I refused she coughed up the price. What could I do?'

Mrs Mildmay frowned.

Charlie said, rather tentatively, 'It's difficult for me, having sold them the mare. But I think they're going to have trouble if they carry on the way they are. It could be dangerous.'

'But Lizzie rode Birdie. You didn't think she was dangerous then, surely?'

'No. Lizzie was nervous of Birdie, that's why she didn't want to keep her. But she was never dangerous. We didn't keep her hyped up like the Prebbles do and

237

Lizzie tried to keep her calm. Perhaps you could tell them to cool it a bit, take their time? It's no good my saying anything.'

'I think I agree with you, my lad. I'll see what I can do.' She looked far from confident. 'Pity. How are you getting on with Miss Hicks? Or should I say her horse?'

Charlie flushed up slightly. 'Her horse is magnificent. Much too strong for her. Heaven only knows what will happen when she takes him cross country.'

'Well, I must say, you fill me with confidence! I think I'll go and check up on our insurance policies.'

Charlie laughed.

Rowan overheard a lot of this while she was tightening her girths and waiting for Roma on the plodding Honeypot. They rode together out to their orange markers in the field and Otty told them they were going to ride along the road to the cross-country course and hack through the woods, up and down banks, across ditches and over a few logs. This caused a fair amount of panic amongst the motley members of the Orange Ride, although Rowan felt quite happy about it. Otty led the way on a cob called Ben which she had 'borrowed'. Its rider had been sick in the night and deflected into 'Welfare', a sagging tent with two moth-eaten camp beds in it.

The road led up a narrowing valley where the downs rose up steeply on either side. It was hot and sleepy out of the wind and the ponies clattered along behind Ben. Roma was complaining to Rowan, 'Honeypot won't jump a thing, nor a ditch either. I shall be useless doing this. I should have gone sick like Tracy.'

After half a mile, the land on the left side of the road flattened out and became the old parkland of the National Trust house. The parkland merged into woodland and Rowan could see the jumps the Pony Club fathers had built: some island jumps in the grass and then others leading into the woods.

'We'll never jump those!' Roma muttered.

The Red Ride was already circling on the parkland. They were using the Hunter Trial course for that session and Mrs Prebble shouted imperiously to Otty to make sure she didn't get her children in the way. She turned away and Otty stuck her tongue out. Rowan could see Swallow lined up with Hugh on board, and Lizzie on Fable and, at the top of the row, Matty on the sweating Birdie. Even Rowan, with no experience, could see that Birdie was far more of a handful for Matty than she had ever been back home when Lizzie rode her. She would not stand still, but pranced and swung round and tossed her head. Matty was red-faced and cross. Hugh sat on the immobile Swallow watching her with his usual expression of smug conceit.

Mrs Prebble wanted them all to jump a log that had blown over from the edge of the woodland. It was huge at one end and quite low at the other. They all went over one by one, mostly in the middle, but when it was Hugh's turn he put Swallow into a fast canter and turned him for the largest part of the jump. Rowan's heart missed a beat as she watched. But she might have known . . . Hugh was a true Hawes, and Swallow jumped perfectly, ridden with such confidence and skill. Rowan was thrilled – not so Mrs Prebble, who scolded Hugh angrily for showing off. Hugh just smiled. When it was Birdie's turn, she got so steamed up that she refused twice, and then tried to run away after cat-hopping awkwardly over the lowest part.

Otty smiled and said, 'Poor Mrs Prebble!' Her eyes gleamed.

They rode into the parkland and Otty took them down to the far end away from Mrs Prebble's voice and lined them up to jump a very modest log, all of nine inches high. Some of the ponies took it in a trotting stride; Jones gave a beautiful little jump and Rowan managed to stay in place, then Honeypot waddled up to it and stopped dead.

While Otty went to sort him out, Rowan went into a dream of flying over jumps on Swallow, looking for the highest part. She would lie up with her hands on his neck whispering encouragement into his lovely little ears and he would jump for his team . . . for his country . . . for silver cups as high as your chest . . .

'Get off, Rowan, and let Roma have a try on Jones.'

Roma was nearly in tears. She gathered up Jones's reins, muttering, 'I could *kill* Honeypot.'

'You get up on Honeypot, Rowan, and see if you can make him jump,' Otty said.

Honeypot only wanted to graze. Rowan felt it was like sitting on a barrel, and the feeling of approaching the log at a sluggish trot and slowing to an irrevocable walk and a halt just as he got there was very depressing.

Otty got impatient and said, 'We can't spend all day with him, Roma, I'm afraid. You'll just have to have turns on the others.'

They changed back and Rowan realized once more how lucky she was. Jones was an obliging pony and never gave her frights. She thoroughly enjoyed scrambling through the woods, over banks and ditches and the odd small logs. He was the best pony by far and made it easy for her. Some of the others wouldn't go over ditches nor through a small stream, and Honeypot wouldn't do anything. Roma cried. Otty succeeded in getting the others round, but not Roma. Rowan lent her Jones again to cheer her up and rode Honeypot back to the park with the others along a peaty ride. She wondered if Charlie could make him jump the log, or even Hugh.

They came to a well-built jump which gave onto the ride and, hearing crashing noises and screams approaching through the wood, they pulled rather nervously into a clearing to wait. In a moment a bay pony appeared, very fast and looking largely out of control. Rowan recognized Birdie at once, her long ears flitching wildly and her eyes frightened. Matty was riding hard, looking very tense. The jump was solid, made of telegraph poles, but it wasn't very high. Birdie straightened up for it, saw it, and at the last moment refused, digging in her feet and tearing long streamers out of the peat. Matty screamed at her and gave her a huge belt with her whip behind the saddle, at which Birdie jumped wildly from a standstill. She caught her front feet against the log, being in too close, and turned a mighty somersault, flying through the air and landing with a flump in the middle of the ride. Matty was thrown clear, but Birdie, trying to scramble to her feet, slipped on the wet leaf mould and fell again, heavily on her side, on top of Matty. Matty screamed. Birdie flailed wildly, lurched up and galloped away through the trees.

Matty lay still.

The members of the Orange Ride were, for a moment, too terrified to move. The wood was suddenly immensely silent, all the action stilled. The sun filtered down through the trees, making patterns across the ride, and a thrush was singing serenely as if nothing had happened. Rowan stared at Matty's sprawled figure, expecting every second to see it move, but nothing happened. She got off Honeypot, as no one else seemed to be doing anything, and started to walk towards Matty. She felt very sick.

Matty lay on her front with her arms flung out, her face buried in the earth. There was no blood or anything but somehow, to Rowan, there was an intangible indication of seriousness about her position that was terrifying. One of the others shouted at Rowan, 'You aren't supposed to move them!' She knew that.

While she was standing there she heard suddenly a steady thrumming of hooves from behind. It was too late to stop anybody, so she just had to turn round and stand in front of Matty to protect her. She looked up and saw Swallow approaching, head up, ears pricked.

'Hugh! Stop!' she screamed.

She saw Hugh's face above Swallow's streaming mane, very cool. He steered into the corner of the jump and took it very neatly, well clear of Matty, and pulled up at once.

'Jeez, what's happened?'

'Birdie fell on her!'

'Serves her right,' Hugh said. 'I'll go and fetch her ma.'

He wheeled round and galloped full pelt away down the ride towards the park. The others pulled themselves together and posted someone to stop further riders, and someone cantered back to fetch Otty, and soon Rowan was no longer alone with the casualty. Otty arrived, and Mrs Prebble herself came storming along on a borrowed pony. Hugh came back and said to Rowan, 'I'm going to look for poor Birdie. Coming?'

'Yes.'

Rowan was thankful to have a job to do, and pleased that Hugh had asked her. They followed the Hunter Trial course and Hugh jumped the jumps. Rowan went round. She felt a bit queasy and cold, and couldn't take pleasure now in watching Swallow, unnerved by Matty's so-sudden demise.

They found Birdie in the far corner of the wood, grazing, her reins tangled up under her legs. Hugh got off and sorted her out, talking to her kindly. She was sweating and very nervous.

'They've ruined her,' he said. 'Mrs Prebble is really stupid. She goes on and on at Matty.'

Rowan sat on the solid Honeypot, holding Swallow's reins. Swallow rubbed his nose against her knee. Hugh loosened Birdie's girths, and stroked her sweaty neck.

'The trouble is, they'll blame us. I bet you. They'll say Birdie is dangerous. Probably want their money back.'

He got back on Swallow, and Birdie walked between them, quiet now, as if she recognized she was back with friends. Rowan felt better, relaxed by Hugh's calming of Birdie. He wasn't the big-headed Hugh now, but the nicer boy that was sometimes seen lurking underneath. How strange it was, Rowan thought, how different it was for everybody with their ponies – Roma crying because she couldn't jump a twig, Matty being pushed by her dreadful mother, Priscilla having the best that money could buy . . . the Hawes seemed to get it right.

Once again she recognized her luck, being under their wing.

'Charlie said there'd be an accident with Birdie,' she remembered.

They started back through the woods. They were at the far end now, beyond the National Trust house, and had to take a walkers' footpath to get back to the road. Hugh led Birdie from Swallow, and she walked calmly between them.

'Whatever are you riding?' he asked.

Rowan explained. 'He won't jump even a pole on the ground.'

'Too fat,' Hugh said.

'Could you get him over a little jump?'

'Of course.'

'I bet you couldn't!' Rowan remembered the dispiriting feeling of Honeypot slowing down beneath her, in spite of her flailing legs.

'Bet you.'

'Go on, I bet you can't!' He was so conceited!

'I'll show you. What will you bet me? Your pudding at supper? It's treacle tart. I saw it this morning.'

'All right, pig. I bet you my treacle tart.'

'Let me get on him. You ride Swallow.'

Rowan blinked, not foreseeing this move, but her

heart leaped with excitement. Hugh gave her a leg-up on Swallow and handed her Birdie's reins. He moved off ahead of her down a grass ride that led back to the road and Rowan followed. She felt as if she had turned into a member of the top group, ready to ride in the team, not nervous at all. The sight of Swallow's thick blue-black mane and little ears pricked ahead of her made her shiver with joy. There was a handy log lying on the side of the path just ahead of them, about a foot high.

Hugh turned Honeypot towards it and managed to get him into a trot. Rowan thought he would jump, but at the last minute he stopped dead. Hugh sat like a rock and would not let him turn aside, pressing him on with his legs and, after a little dithering, Honeypot actually jumped – a proper jump, not a step-over.

'There.' Hugh tried not to look pleased but the thought of the treacle tart evoked a self-satisfied grin.

How was it done? Rowan wondered crossly. Roma had tried it and she had tried it, all to no avail. Hugh took Birdie's reins from her, but didn't ask to change ponies again, and when they came to another log she turned Swallow to face it and pressed him into a trot. What possessed her to do this she had no idea, only the memory of seeing him flying over the timber in the wood with Hugh leaning on his neck and remembering her feeling of longing that it might be herself . . . and Swallow lengthened his stride and flew the log, so effortlessly that she did not budge in the saddle. True, it was only small, but Rowan felt as if she were riding for England at Badminton. Her confidence swelled and took off like a hot-air balloon, so that it was all she could do to stop belting off down the inviting path for the sheer hell of it.

'What on earth do you two think you're doing?'

An angry voice interrupted her moment of glory and she looked up to see Charlie coming down the track ahead of her, riding Out of the West. Swallow skidded to a halt and Hugh ambled up on Honeypot. To Rowan's dismay Charlie was obviously furious, and his dark blue gaze was directed straight at her.

She had no excuse at all.

'Don't lose your rag. We went to look for Birdie,' Hugh said. 'No one else bothered.'

'Not surprising, considering what's been happening. Birdie was the least of their worries. Get off that pony, Rowan, before we have another broken neck. At once!'

His voice was icy. Rowan felt a terrible flush of shame engulfing her. She slithered off immediately, all her Badminton feeling squashed flat, and Hugh said, 'It's not her fault. I told her to swap ponies.'

'You are completely irresponsible,' Charlie snapped at him.

'Just because you're instructing the top ride you needn't get so uppity. You sound like Mrs Prebble,' Hugh said, giving Honeypot back to Rowan and taking Swallow. 'What are you in such a stew about?'

'Oh, come off it, Hugh – can't you see how bad things look, without taking any more risks? Matty's really damaged herself – it's not just peanuts, and Mrs Prebble's going to blame us, I can see it coming. Everyone else has gone home and I'm sent to look for Birdie and find you two idiots playing about on your own. You know that's forbidden.'

'Why's everyone gone home? I thought your ride was going to do cross country after us?'

'Well, the accident's cast a gloom. It all looks rather serious. Auntie M couldn't face the prospect of Prissy Hicks going cross country on this beast on the same afternoon. She thought two in hospital on the same day might give her a bad name.'

'I thought that was what they bought her for, so that Princess Priscilla can win everything?'

'Yes, that was the idea. But this horse is far too

high-powered for Prissy. She's not had much experience. Her parents are potty, getting her this.'

Hugh cast a reflective eye over the gorgeous horse. Rowan could see the way his mind was working . . . five years from now . . . 'Pity we couldn't get a horse like that in the yard.'

'We've never had that sort of money. Dad bought some good ones, but they're the ones that sold the fastest.'

For all Charlie's skill, he had never had a good horse of his own, Rowan realized. Even Bonzo's mother, Fedora, had been sold, and broken Charlie's heart for a little while. He looked splendid on Out of the West as he walked out beside them, the gleaming coat shadowed against the afternoon sun above the down. Rowan, falling behind on old Honeypot, was grateful his wrath was short-lived. She could not bear to be seen wanting by Charlie.

A gloom lay over the camp that evening. Word came from Mrs Prebble that Matty was being airlifted to Stoke Mandeville, the hospital for spinal injuries. Mrs Prebble would not be returning. This was far worse than the usual mild concussion, broken leg or collar bone, and outside the Pony Club's experience so far, although Auntie Millie knew plenty about such injuries. Her face was very stern and unhappy that night. Rowan was on washing-up duty after supper and found the atmosphere in the kitchen amongst the mothers on duty equally gloomy, all of them thinking it might have been their child.

'It's a risk every time a child mounts a pony, we all know that,' said one.

'Well, if she wants to buy her child such a difficult pony, what does she expect?' said Roma's mother, who did not know that Birdie had been sold to the Prebbles by Charlie Hawes, the mother of whom was drying dishes at her side.

Two other mothers, who knew the facts, exchanged worried looks at the turn the conversation had taken. Joan Hawes said nothing but her old look, which had started to dissipate over the last few days, had come back, Rowan noticed. Rowan thought of poor Roma, whom she had left weeping in the pig trailer, being stranded in her ambition on the hopeless Honeypot who was undoubtedly safe, but so safe as to make Roma's pony life a complete waste of time.

When she went back to the pig trailer she tried to cheer Roma up, but Roma said her parents would never buy her another pony until she grew out of Honeypot. Rowan had another idea.

'Perhaps if you bring him up to High Hawes – High Horse,' she corrected herself quickly, 'they might get him to go.' She told her about Hugh making him jump the log.

Roma looked slightly more optimistic at this idea, and said she would ask her parents. Rowan thought perhaps she had got the stable a customer. When she went to the stable to see Jones was happy for the night she mentioned it to Lizzie, but Lizzie was too upset about Birdie to be much interested. She too had been crying.

'Poor Birdie, it wasn't her fault. Now everyone's saying Mrs Prebble will have her shot.'

'She wouldn't! I saw it happen – it was a complete accident!'

'You saw it?'

'Yes. I was right there. Birdie slipped up. She didn't fall on Matty on purpose.'

'Oh, Rowan, you must stick up for her! If you actually saw it, you're the only person who can say this.'

'And Roma. And a few of us. We all saw it.'

'Oh, good. I thought nobody saw. And Mrs Prebble is so beastly! She's been blaming Charlie for selling her the pony, and we all know at home how she insisted on

252

having her. It will be terribly bad for setting up High Horse, if she goes round telling everyone this. And Matty in Stoke Mandeville!'

'Auntie Millie knows it's not your fault – I heard her talking to Charlie and she backed him up.'

'We'll just have to show everyone on Saturday. Shrimp and Hugh and you on Jones. How perfectly *safe* all our ponies are. You especially, Rowan, because you're a pupil, not family.'

Rowan was a bit appalled at this, but did not say so. On Saturday all the parents came for the last day and they had a big competition – show-jumping and cross country, even for the smallest ride. She had been fairly confident about it, so obliging was dear Jones, but now the thought of such responsibility put her off a bit. Suppose she let them all down by falling off and breaking something? Apparently, in spite of the Hicks's clout, Prissy was not going to be allowed to go cross country on Saturday. Auntie Millie had put her foot down. Prissy was saying her dad would be furious.

'We can't risk it, Priscilla.' Auntie Millie had her rat-trap expression on. 'We can't wave a magic wand in one week flat. You need long, steady training with a good instructor to get together with that young horse.

I shall speak to your father. It will be me he will be angry with, so don't get upset.'

Prissy looked rather marvellous when she was angry, her chestnut mane bouncing with indignation, her amber eyes flashing like traffic lights. She turned away and went back across the yard to her loosebox. At the same moment Charlie came to fetch the old Land Rover to drive home in, and Priscilla stopped to talk to him. Rowan came out of Jones's box in time to see Charlie put his arm round Priscilla and give her a comforting hug. Priscilla's expression changed. Instead of sending out sparks, she now looked like the cat who had found the cream. Her lovely amber eyes shone full beam on Charlie.

Rowan watched, goggle-eyed, as Charlie gave Priscilla a really soppy smile. His hand came up and caressed her hair, then he realized they were not alone and stood off, and grinned in his usual way, and Rowan heard him say, 'Don't worry. We'll sort it out with your dad. It's not your fault. You're great.'

Yuk, thought Rowan. She was furious with jealousy. How could he! *Her* Charlie! With that really revolting girl! Her day was ruined. She stomped back to the pig-trailer and Roma gave her a Mars bar.

'We've been invited to a midnight feast over at the

stables tonight. With your lot – Hugh and them. Hugh's pinched one of the trifles for tomorrow's dinner. It's in Swallow's stable with a bucket over it. You're not to tell anyone else though.'

Rowan forgot about Charlie for the time being.

Chapter Five

The midnight feast turned into a rather sombre discussion, not surprisingly, since the events of the day. After they had eaten the trifle they sat in a circle in the moonlight that shone through the dormer window and gossiped. (Rowan kept her revelations about Charlie and Prissy to herself.) Hugh and Lizzie and Shrimp were there, and two boys from the Red Ride: Alan Finch and a weedy blond boy called Bas, and Babar had been invited too. She had been having a thoroughly satisfactory week on the Armchair and was quite a changed character, Rowan thought, far more outgoing and cheerful.

''E's wonderful,' she said simply. ''E does just anything.'

'Huh,' said Roma crossly.

'It's not looks, is it?' Lizzie said. 'He doesn't look anything, and neither does Fable, but they're both lovely.'

'So's Jones,' said Rowan loyally, noticing that no one was saying how wonderful Swallow was.

'Blue roans are horrid,' Hugh said.

'They're not!' said Shrimp. 'Roans are lovely. Pinkie's wonderful. And Jones is a dear. It's just your ponies that are horrid. Cascade and Swallow.'

'Cascade—'

'Oh, shut up,' said Lizzie. 'It's Birdie we want to talk about. What's going to happen to Birdie? We've got an idea.'

'Who's got an idea?' Shrimp asked.

'Me and Hugh, and Charlie a bit. We mentioned it to him but he's rather doubtful. It depends—'

'Charlie said don't tell him, he'd rather not know,' Hugh said.

'Tell him what?'

'We want to ride Birdie cross country on Saturday, just to show everybody how good she is, and safe. She could easily win the Intermediate, with a proper rider.'

'Who's we?' Babar demanded. 'You, I suppose?'

'Well, I could, but it would be better if it was Lizzie. Birdie knows Lizzie, and everyone thinks Lizzie's – well – they think she's—'

'Not much good,' said Shrimp amiably.

Lizzie said firmly, 'If Hugh gets her round they'll just

say, 'Oh, Hugh can get anything round,' but if I get her round they'll be impressed.'

'That's what I meant,' Hugh said.

Babar gave him a disgusted look and said, 'You are *pathetic*, Hugh! 'Ow about me riding 'er? – that would show 'em!'

'Or Rowan,' suggested Shrimp.

'We're serious,' said Lizzie earnestly, not put off by Hugh's insults and the others' sarcasm. 'I am sure she'll go for me and it would just show everybody that she's not a rogue. Mrs Prebble will go round telling everyone – you know she will.'

In the moonlight Lizzie's face was flushed with earnestness. Rowan knew perfectly well that when she used to ride Birdie she was nervous of her and longed for an easier pony. It was only her loyalty that was spurring her to attempt this proving of Birdie's good name. Rowan thought it was very risky, remembering Birdie's wild behaviour under Matty.

'It was only that she didn't like the way Matty rode her,' Lizzie said.

Babar looked very doubtful. 'Surely 'er bad experiences this week can't be cured overnight? You can't be sure she'll go round for you. And 'ow will you start? When they see you they'll shout and scream at you to get off.'

258

'Auntie Millie and Otty and them all station themselves in the wood to watch people go round. By the time I pass them they won't be able to stop me. The starter's going to be Jerry Patterson and he won't know Birdie from Fable, and the stewards at the start are all parents who don't know either. It's just a question of riding her up the lane when no one who matters is looking. To most people she looks much like Fable anyway. It's only afterwards, when we've shown them how good she is, we'll make sure everyone knows it's Birdie.'

Rowan was terribly impressed. She thought Lizzie very brave indeed. The others, she could see, were impressed too.

Hugh said solemnly, 'It matters to the stable, to High Horse. It would be marvellous for Mum and Charlie and Josephine, if we proved to everybody that we don't sell duds. That Birdie is as good as gold. Especially for Mum.'

'As long as she is,' Babar said.

There was a long silence. Rowan found she was getting the shivers, a sort of excitement mixed with fear, and the glory of being involved with these daring plans. It was dark in the loft save for a wide sheet of moonlight that slid in through the dormer window, and their anxious faces had a blueish cast, in keeping with the seriousness of the discussion. Below them they could hear ponies shifting, sighing, munching hay, the occasional snort.

'Suppose she isn't as good as gold?' Babar asked.

'She will be. I know she will be.' Lizzie leaned forward earnestly. 'I know her better than anyone else.' Her great mass of springy pale hair flared round her head like a ghostly halo. She was very intense and caring, not like her brash brother. 'I can't bear the thought of beastly Mrs Prebble blaming it all on her.'

'And us,' said Hugh.

'No.' Babar was thoughtful. After a long silence she said, 'I don't think you ought to let Charlie and Josephine know what you intend to do.'

'They'd agree with us!' Hugh said. 'They would want—'

'They might want, but they can't. Not now that they're instructors. Don't be stupid. They have to take the other side, being good and correct. Josephine is terribly instructorish, isn't she, Shrimp?'

'Yes. Almost as bad as Mrs Prebble. She's not a bit nicer to Babar and me in the ride.'

'Charlie's nicer to Princess Priscilla,' Alan said, and laughed.

'They were holding hands in the feed shed,' said Bas.

'What? Charlie?' Lizzie squeaked.

'He says she needs a lot of help.'

'That's true,' Rowan said staunchly. 'He says Out of the West is too strong for her.'

'Lucky for him,' Alan said with a smile.

'But she's awful!'

'Very pretty,' said Bas.

The boys started wrangling about something else and the plot for Birdie was forgotten for the time being. But every time Rowan thought about it she got shivers again.

'I don't know how she dares,' Roma whispered when they were back in bed.

'No.'

Both Rowan and Roma knew the Hawes were made of sterner stuff than they were. Yet Rowan knew that it was much harder for Lizzie to do such a daring deed than it would have been for Hugh. When she groomed Jones beside Fable in the morning, Rowan could see that Lizzie was pale and fraught. She had asked to look after Birdie too, and had been in to feed and groom her, but Auntie Millie said no one was to ride her.

'I said she needs exercising, but Auntie Millie said no. Absolutely not.'

'She'll be a real handful by Saturday, if she's not ridden out.'

'Hugh says we'll ride her tonight, when the night patrol's gone off. He's going to smuggle her tack out of the tack room before it's locked up and hide it in the loft, and come with me on Jerry's bicycle. You mustn't tell anyone!'

'No fear!'

'Lucky she's in the end box, on her own. We think we can get her out without anyone hearing, if we keep on the grass. Just hope none of the ponies whinny. Then I'll be able to see if she's her old self with me.'

'You are brave!'

'It matters,' Lizzie muttered fiercely. 'For our stable. Now Dad's gone.' Rowan was appalled to see tears running down Lizzie's cheeks. She did see that life was very uncertain for them since Mr Hawes had died, and tried to be as sympathetic as possible.

'If I can do anything to help—'

Lizzie said, 'Thanks. You might. I can't bank on Hugh helping tonight. You know what he's like – if the boys decide to get up to some fun he'll want to stay. So if he lets me down, you can help instead.'

Rowan nearly died of fright. When she had offered

to help, she hadn't meant that! Her fingers trembled as she pulled up Jones's girths.

'I'll come for you,' Lizzie said. 'When the night patrol's finished.'

Rowan rode out feeling very anxious. Unlike Hugh, Lizzie was a worrier, and Rowan rather thought she was the same. Seeing Lizzie cry gave her a guilty qualm, for the plain fact was that she had scarcely given her deserted mother a thought during the week, so taken up was she with this amazing new life. She had no father either any more. She hadn't really taken it in yet. Her mother came to camp every day to help in the kitchen, and they had scarcely had any conversation beyond, 'Do you need a clean shirt?' and, 'Can you bring me another bucket? Jones trod in it and squashed it flat.' But her mother hadn't looked particularly deserted; she had always appeared to Rowan quite cheerful.

At lunch time that day she took the trouble to observe her mother. Unlike Joan Hawes, she looked about five years younger than she remembered, and was laughing with Roma's rather dour mother over a strange trifle that someone had brought in as a supper contribution.

Rowan said to her, 'Are you all right?' Her mother gave her a startled look and said, 'Yes, of course.'

'About Dad – you're all alone now I'm away too.'

'Oh no, I'm staying with Joan at High Hawes. And Charlie and Josephine come back in the evenings, and Jerry's there, and we have a high old time with the youngsters – all the gossip and the stories they have to tell about you children. I'm really enjoying myself.'

'But what about Dad?'

'What about him?' her mother said sharply. 'If he prefers other company, the same goes for me too.' Then, more kindly, 'Don't worry, Rowan. We'll be all right.' And she put her arm round her and gave her a hug. 'Are you missing him?'

'No. I thought you were.'

And her mother laughed.

Rowan wondered why people got married in the first place. Did it all change afterwards, from being all gooey like Charlie and Prissy, to shouting at each other like her mother and father?

'Are your parents happily married?' she asked Roma.

Roma said gloomily, 'Yes, I think so. You could fool me sometimes.'

Joan Hawes was obviously grieving over Fred: it showed. Yet he had shouted quite a lot and had not been what Rowan thought of as lovable. Auntie Millie had a dear old farmer husband, always smiling. Mrs

Prebble seemed to have discarded Mr Prebble, as he was never mentioned. Mr and Mrs Hicks seemed to be on speaking terms. Perhaps Rowan was unlucky. But, curiously, like her mother, she couldn't say she was sorry her father had departed. He had been so bad-tempered, and not enthusiastic about her new-found obsession with ponies.

At the end of the afternoon Otty said to Rowan, 'On the last day, when we all go cross country for the competition, I think it would be nice if Roma could go round on Jones. It would give her so much confidence, and he's such a genuine pony, he's bound to get her round. It means he'll have to go twice, but he's quite up to it, if you don't mind.'

'No, of course not.'

'She's so unhappy with Honeypot.'

Rowan didn't mind, but was slightly put out by the implication that Jones would go for anyone, even a duffer. She supposed it was true. No one would have offered Roma Swallow to get round on.

When she put Jones away, Lizzie came back with Fable and said, 'I've told Hugh I'd rather go with you tonight. I don't want him letting me down at the last moment. He's like that.'

Lizzie must have noticed Rowan's face turn pale.

She said, 'There's nothing to worry about. Otty's going to lunge Birdie after tea, and she's going out for a bit in the schooling meadow, until it gets dark. So she won't be too fresh.'

Rowan thought Lizzie was trying to convince herself, as much as reassure her. She felt sick when she went to bed. She told Roma what was going to happen, and set her alarm clock for three in the morning. Lizzie had said it would be going light, but Rowan was sure it wouldn't. Roma wanted to come too, but Rowan said she couldn't. 'Instead of' would have been all right, but not 'as well'.

The news had come through from Stoke Mandeville that Matty had a spinal injury and her legs were paralysed. The only good thing about it was that they didn't think it was a permanent injury. They thought she would recover, but it would take time. Mrs Prebble had rung the news through to Auntie Millie, but was staying at the hospital. Lizzie had cried again when she heard. Rowan knew it was for Birdie more than Matty. But the seriousness of the accident was certainly very depressing. Nobody thought that sort of thing happened to anybody like them, only to a few adults out racing. Collar bones cracked by the dozen, but that was nothing. Welfare had only had one black eye and a trodden-on big toe the whole week, and that was the usual sort of haul, not dreadful things like Matty's injuries.

Rowan lay in the darkness wondering what would happen if Lizzie was wrong about Birdie, and Birdie tossed her off tonight, and she was left to pick up the pieces. It didn't bear thinking about! She could not sleep and was wide awake when her alarm clock went off. She squashed it immediately so that Roma wouldn't wake, and crawled out of her sleeping bag. She was already dressed and only had to pull on her anorak. She felt stiff and awful, and shivered uncontrollably as she peered out across the field. She couldn't tell if it was cold or fright. Both, probably. Her teeth chattered. The field was silent and bathed in bright moonlight, and when she set off for the yard she made a bright trail in the dew for all the world to see. All the horseboxes and caravans slumbered, the midnight antics long finished. Rowan longed to be back snug in her sleeping bag.

She made a detour round the back of the stables and crept in from the drive to Birdie's box, which was nearest to the gate. She was afraid going through the yard might provoke a greedy whinny from an alert pony. They did not necessarily sleep all night, any more than their riders did. Her shivering stilled by the time she got to the loosebox and she felt slightly more optimistic, especially when she found Birdie ready saddled and bridled, and Lizzie waiting for her.

'I couldn't sleep,' Lizzie whispered. 'I came out early.'

'I couldn't either.'

'This is the worst bit, getting out.'

Birdie was nervous, excited by this strange routine, and churning about. They had to cross the tiled bit outside the stable before they could get onto the grass, then cross to the gateway where the scrunchy gravel took over. Lizzie had 'borrowed' the bike from Jerry in the afternoon, and it was leaning against the end of the stables.

'Keep your fingers crossed,' Lizzie whispered.

Rowan could see that she was now absorbed in the task at hand and her white fear had changed to excitement. They opened the door, lifting it so it didn't scrape, and Lizzie led Birdie out quickly towards the gate. The next-door pony put its head out and whinnied. Rowan, her bloodstream pulsing with fright, grabbed the bike and scurried out after Lizzie.

'Go back and shut the door,' Lizzie hissed. 'If anyone comes to look—'

Rowan did as she was told. The pony watched her

expectantly, but did not whinny again. Rowan dragged the door to. Lizzie had already hopped on and was disappearing down the drive, riding on the grass verge at a rapid trot. Rowan grabbed the bike and pedalled madly after her. She was out of breath, but the worst of the frights had receded. When they got to the road, Lizzie pulled up and waited for her. She was laughing.

'Piece of cake!'

Rowan felt slightly indignant, knowing that her part in the adventure was to sort things out in case Birdie was difficult and Lizzie got carted or thrown. It wasn't over yet. Birdie was excited, not unnaturally, at this unusual outing, and pranced about as Lizzie held her. Her hooves made a ringing clatter on the road which seemed to echo across the silent fields. It was cold and the grass was heavy with dew. The sky was clear and the enormous yellow disc of the full moon seemed to stare at them as if outraged. They were the only signs of life in the whole world. Rowan was still half a town girl, used to street lights and traffic all night, and hadn't yet become accustomed to the austere silence of the country night. She cycled along beside Birdie feeling that all her senses were on full alert, half afraid, half in wonder at the beauty of the sleeping valley whose shadows seemed to reach out to enclose them.

She dared not say anything. On Lizzie's face was what she recognized as a typical Hawes expression: a glowing satisfaction at taking on something rather more than she knew she could chew. Birdie's shadow stretched across the road and up the hillside.

'What are you going to do?' Rowan asked.

'Just school around the park, go over a few jumps, that's all.'

They came to the park and Rowan opened the gate for Birdie, taking care to close it behind her – good Pony Club practice as she had been taught. Lizzie rode away and Rowan watched her. Birdie was a beautiful-looking pony, nearly all thoroughbred, a bright bay with black points and a lovely fluent mover. But her thoroughbred spirit was not suited to a child rider and she quickly became excited and eager to go. Lizzie, knowing her well, kept her working calmly, trotting in large circles, stopping, turning, standing still. Only after half an hour did she put her at the fallen log, riding into it at a steady trot. Birdie jumped without hesitation, then tossed her head, wanting to go on. Lizzie brought her back to a walk and trotted some more steady circles. Again she jumped, and this time Birdie was calmer.

Lizzie brought her back to Rowan who sat shivering on one of the tree stumps.

'There. She remembers me, how we do it. According to Charlie, she never settled down with Matty at all. She'll go cross country all right.'

They rode home slowly.

Lizzie said, hesitantly, 'I'd forgotten how lovely she is. After Fable.'

'But I thought you hated her! You said—'

'I know what I said. Yes, I love Fable because she's so easy. She never gives me frights. I'm always frightened on Birdie. She always feels as if she's going to take off. She's sort of super – super-charged. When we used to ride out on the downs I was always a bit frightened. Now, with Fable, it's fun.'

'What about Saturday then? Doing cross country – will you be frightened?'

'Yes,' said Lizzie. 'I shall be terrified.'

'You haven't got to do it!'

'Yes. Yes, I have.'

Rowan tried to digest all these difficult pronouncements but was beginning to feel rather tired, not to say frozen. Birdie jigged about, but Rowan kept out of her way and cycled ahead of her up the drive to the stableyard. She propped the bike up against the wall and went to open the stable door. Birdie came in through the gate and as her hooves clattered momentarily on the tiles her neighbour stuck his head out over his door and let out a loud welcoming whinny. Birdie threw up her head and neighed back. Fable, hearing her from the other side of the yard, threw her head over the door and called a greeting, followed by Jones and Swallow. The night was suddenly rent by jolly equine conversation.

'Oh, lor', someone'll come looking! Hark at them!' Lizzie hissed.

She dragged Birdie through the door. 'Shut it!' she said to Rowan. 'Quick, take off her bridle!'

She undid the girths while Rowan fumbled with the bridle. They pulled off the tack and Lizzie threw it in the corner and covered it with straw. Then she grabbed a handful of straw and furiously rubbed the saddle marks off Birdie's back. Birdie put her head out of the door and whinnied some more and then, always a greedy pony, turned to attack her hay-net.

Lizzie looked out over the door to see if anything was happening and shot back immediately.

'Someone's coming. I saw a torch! Jeez, what shall we do?' Then, taking a hold of her panic: 'They might not come right down here. We must sit tight.'

'Where?' Rowan squeaked.

'Here!'

Lizzie grabbed her and sat down on the floor hard against the wall beside the door. They pulled some straw over their legs but there wasn't enough spare to cover them. Even some of the tack showed, they noticed, but it was too late to do anything about that.

'What'll happen if they see us?'

'We'll be sent home in disgrace.'

Sent home! Rowan wanted to weep. She could not imagine a worse fate – and her mother so happy making dinners, and she with all the competitions to ride in on Saturday . . . perhaps, if she was terribly lucky, a rosette to be won . . . all her dreams would be shattered. Just because she was nobly helping out instead of beastly Hugh. She *hated* Hugh!

A voice called out imperiously from the top of the yard, 'Anyone there?'

The flash of the torch made wavering beams outside the door as it travelled round the yard.

'It's Otty,' Lizzie whispered.

Rowan felt a flicker of relief – not Auntie Millie herself. Otty slept in a caravan near the gate. It was her job to see to disturbances in the night, pony scuffles and the odd kick and one mild attack of colic so far. Nobody had thought of people disturbances. Otty's voice sounded slightly uncertain. Perhaps she was as frightened as they were?

But Otty was made of stern stuff and came boldly down the yard shining her torch into every box. They could hear her murmuring to the disturbed ponies, her voice coming nearer and nearer.

Rowan could feel her heart pounding; almost wanted to shush it to be quiet. The palms of her hands were sweaty and she felt sick. Birdie snatched at her hay as if she had been away for a week.

'It was you making that row, wasn't it?' Otty stopped at the next-door box. 'What set you off, you old idiot?'

There was a long silence while the 'old idiot' regarded Otty in the torchlight with innocent eyes. Lizzie and Rowan crouched lower, holding their breath.

The torch beam sprang in through the door. Birdie jerked her head up and stood looking, a mouthful of half-snatched hay dropping from her jaws. The torch took in her head and travelled down her back and dropped to her legs. Rowan saw the glint of a stirrup under the manger.

'You look warm,' Otty remarked curiously.

But Birdie, as if in league with Lizzie and Rowan, turned back to her hay to show her unconcern. She did not come nuzzling up to the two girls who crouched in agony below the half door.

Otty turned away, and fell over the bike.

'What on earth—?'

They heard her swear and the bike crash down. The torch light jumped about.

'God almighty, that hurt!' Otty kicked the bike.

Would it occur to her that the bike was not usually there? There was a long, long silence outside. The two girls crouched together, holding their breath. What was she doing?

Rowan thought she would burst. Then they heard a bit more swearing, and Otty's head went past the door, making back for her caravan. They waited ages longer, but the terrible frights were over and now they were exploding with giggles, which had to be muffled. They sorted out the tack and Lizzie said she would take it back to the loft with her. Rowan had to walk out across the field. Otty would be lying awake, or perhaps had her eye open still for a possible intruder.

'I'll go down the drive and come in round the back, behind the hedge,' Rowan decided.

What a night of frights! When Rowan at last got snuggled down again into her sleeping bag it was going light and nearly time to get up.

Chapter Six

Rowan woke up feeling a hundred years old. She knew it was no ordinary day and only rather slowly remembered why. She was going to ride Jones in competition, and had to display her talent as a product of the High Horse Equestrian Centre. Everyone would be watching. And Lizzie was going to ride Birdie cross country . . . Rowan felt sick again, as well as a hundred years old. As she had only had about two hours of sleep she supposed she had good reason.

Seeing the carefree Hugh at breakfast incensed her. He had nothing to worry about at all since Swallow had proved during the week that he was a winner (which, of course, Rowan had known all along) and Hugh expected to win his usual number of cups and rosettes, just as if he had been riding Cascade. He knew the practice with Birdie had been successful, and saw no reason why Lizzie should be in a stew about her afternoon's prospect and certainly did not expect her to beat him. Rowan could see that Lizzie was, in fact, very frightened, more of the trouble she would get into afterwards than of the ride itself. But when Rowan tried to suggest it might be wiser not to do it, she said defiantly, 'I've got to. It's to prove to everyone we don't sell duds.'

It was true, Rowan noticed, as the parents started to arrive to help arrange the course, that there was a lot of gossip going around about the accident and the reasons for it. Quite naturally it was the great talking point. Rowan heard someone say, 'They bought the pony off the Hawes – makes you wonder a bit, doesn't it? They must have known.'

She tried not to think about it, knowing that if she was in a dreadful nervous stew Jones might get worried too. It was a beautiful day and there was a terrific lot to do, and she wasn't the only one in a panic about not making a fool of herself in the afternoon.

Another crisis was looming in the Princess Priscilla department, as apparently Auntie Millie had forbidden her to take Out of the West cross country.

'My parents will be furious!' Prissy wailed.

'Send them to me. I will explain,' Auntie Millie barked. 'A week is not long enough to work miracles.'

This remark upset Priscilla. She sobbed to Charlie, 'Why is it a miracle for me to ride Out of the West cross country?'

Hugh reported that Charlie went all sloppy and told her she was marvellous but the horse just needed more schooling, instead of saying (according to Hugh), 'Your parents were mad to buy you such a high-powered horse when you're a right dozy rider who couldn't get round on Jones, let alone Out of the West.'

Rowan was riled that her pony was used by everyone as the one *anyone* could ride. But Prissy and her parents bought mounts for looks, for vanity. Dear Babar, Rowan was heartened to see, was all smiles to be riding the Armchair, who was just as ugly in his way as her own Black Diamond, whom everyone had laughed at for years. With his too-large blaze and carthorse legs, Armchair had a heart of gold.

Mr and Mrs Hicks arrived at lunch time in their Mercedes and parked conspicuously alongside the vast horsebox that Prissy had lived in all the week. They joined her inside for their gin and tonics, and Mr Hicks emerged ten minutes later with a face like thunder, demanding to talk to Mrs Mildmay. Everyone pretended to go about their business but managed to get close enough to overhear the exchange.

'What's this ridiculous instruction about my girl not riding in the competition this afternoon?'

'I don't want another accident, Mr Hicks. Priscilla is not yet experienced enough to take such a difficult horse cross country.'

Mr Hicks turned from red to purple.

'Priscilla is perfectly capable! That horse is a trained and schooled jumper. We had it from the best hands. We were only interested in the best, and that's what we bought. I dispute your opinion.'

'Yes, well, you may. But I run this camp and my word here goes.'

'You told me a week at camp would work wonders with the horse. You led me to believe—'

'It has worked wonders, but more work has to be done, Mr Hicks.' Auntie Millie's jaw was sticking out like Land's End. 'Priscilla's instructor speaks very highly of her progress. But more time is needed.'

'I would like to speak to her instructor!'

'By all means. Go and find Charlie,' Auntie Millie snapped at Hugh, who was goggling nearby. 'Tell him Mr Hicks wants a word.' She turned back to Mr Hicks and said scathingly, 'This is the Pony Club, Mr Hicks. Not Gleneagles. Perhaps Priscilla has grown out of it.'

Rowan felt herself getting steamed up at the thought of poor Charlie facing this irascible man. She heard Otty say, 'I thought it was supposed to be a fun day,' sadly, and Auntie Millie reply, 'We've got Lucy Prebble gracing us with her presence this afternoon as well. This is just the start.'

Mrs Prebble! Of all the people likely to torpedo Lizzie's attempt to ride Birdie Mrs Prebble herself was the most likely. With luck she would be given a job far away from the start of the cross country. She must!

Charlie ambled up, fortunately dressed in his instructor's best, with a tie and his boots shining, and said, 'You want me?'

Mr Hicks looked him up and down as if he were a yearling at the sales and said cuttingly, 'How old are you?'

'Twenty-five,' Charlie said.

Mr Hicks didn't know how to answer this, obviously not believing him, but not actually brave enough to accuse him of lying.

'I understand you've been teaching my daughter all the week?'

'Yes, sir.'

'And what's this nonsense about her not being allowed to go cross country?'

Charlie shot a hopeful glance at Auntie Millie for help but Auntie Millie was glaring unhelpfully into the middle distance.

'It would be wiser to give it a miss. She hasn't had enough time yet, to get used to the horse.'

'She's no good, you're saying?'

'No. She's very good. But the horse gets rather steamed up. He's likely to take off with her. And that wouldn't be very useful.'

'I want to see my horse perform, that's what I'm here for. If you're such a fine instructor I suggest you take him round.' He spoke in a sarcastic tone of voice that clearly implied he thought the challenge would be refused. But Charlie immediately said, 'Certainly. I'd like to.'

Auntie Millie opened her mouth, then shut it again. Mr Hicks stormed off to make trouble somewhere else and Auntie Millie said to Charlie, 'Was that wise?'

'No. It's a bit stupid really.'

They looked at each other and grinned. Auntie Millie shrugged and laughed. 'That's my boy.'

Otty, taking all this in, shook her head.

'They're all batty in this Pony Club,' she said. 'All of them.'

Rowan thought she didn't know the half of it yet.

She groomed Jones until he gleamed dark bluey-grey like a suit of armour and then went to lunch with a white-faced Lizzie and a gloomy Roma. Hugh and Babar looked happy enough, Hugh because he knew he was going to win everything and Babar because, for once, she knew her pony would jump when asked, not spectacularly, but with an amiable heave that generally left the obstacle in one piece. Lizzie had to go away and be sick in the loo.

Rowan and Roma were to do their cross country first, being in the Junior group. Shrimp, Babar, Lizzie and Hugh were all in the Intermediate, but only Hugh was expected to do any good. Lizzie's Fable, whom everyone thought she was going to ride, was too slow to win and sometimes stopped; the same applied to the Armchair, and Shrimp had found Pinkie had a mind of her own and hated leaving Bonzo behind, having become attached to him like a real mother. Hugh said she should go cross country with Bonzo running behind, and Shrimp actually asked Auntie Millie if she could but received a not unexpected refusal. She was determined to prove to Auntie Millie that she was not just a pretty show rider with red hair ribbons. Her hair was now severely secured with brown rubber bands. She was preoccupied with her problems, which loomed to her as large as Lizzie's. Pauline Watkins came up to them as they finished their lunch and said, 'Why do you all look so miserable?'

Nobody replied.

She said, 'I suppose because it's all going to finish this afternoon.'

The others went back to the stables but Rowan ran after her mother and asked her what she was going to do during the afternoon.

'They tell me I've got to fence-judge. I've no idea what it entails. I'm hoping someone will tell me before the off.'

'What's Mrs Prebble doing? Is she fence-judging?'

'Yes, I think she is.'

As long as she was well stuck in the wood all would be well, but if she was anywhere near the start, Lizzie's ride was doomed. As it was, whatever happened, Mrs Prebble would recognize Birdie and make a great fuss. Rowan's gloom deepened, and she wished that Lizzie had not set her heart on this noble action for the stable. She was going to get little thanks.

Being in the lowest cross-country ride she was one of the earliest to go. As Jones was going twice, Rowan was going to go first and Roma last in their group, to give him plenty of time for a breather. Rowan had had strict instructions to go straight back after she had ridden and help them with the Birdie plan, and the Birdie plan was so much more difficult than riding Jones over the course that she found she was through the start almost without noticing it.

Her mother was fence-judging at the first obstacle, an easy row of straw bales, and Rowan saw her excited face as Jones whizzed over. Lizzie had told her to find out where Mrs Prebble was fence-judging, but Rowan suddenly found that Jones was far more of a handful on his own than when they had practised the course all together and rather forgot about everything else. Her seat was still very insecure and she wasn't too proud to take a large handful of mane at each approach. 'Much better than hanging on by the reins,' sensible Otty had told her. She was going quite a lot faster than she had meant to, but it was rather exciting. Her course was only very low, with scrambles over banks and through ditches, and it was more a matter of steering accurately than anything else. It sometimes crossed the Intermediate course which was much more respectable, and the last bit came back into the park alongside some horrific jumps for the Seniors which were left over from a proper One Day Event. Otty had told them that one day they would sail over these and enjoy every minute of it. Who on? was the question. Hugh said Swallow would fly them and thought he ought to ride in the Senior group, but he had been squashed. For a moment, coming home, Rowan felt a surge of confidence that made her feel that Jones too would fly them if she faced him in the right direction. He was such an honest pony, and she hadn't disgraced herself as she had feared, but was jumping into the park with her feet still in the stirrups and her reins nicely arranged, not out like the washing, and was even able to pull up, unlike some who were apt to disappear from sight into the hinterland of the National Trust gardens.

'Well done!' shouted Jerry Patterson, who was time-keeping (no doubt pleased that the pony he had recommended hadn't blotted his copybook).

Her mother was making excited, arm-waving gestures from her place by the hay bales and in her excitement missed out the next competitor (which was later to cause confusion in the scoring caravan).

Rowan realized she had never looked for Mrs Prebble. But she was so excited by her successful round that it was hard to feel bad about it. If she never saw her, with luck she wasn't there at all. She couldn't help bubbling over with pride – a clear round! – even if it was potty stuff . . . she hadn't fallen off. She was a credit to the High Horse Equestrian Centre! Even Hugh would be pleased with her. But her duty was back at Lizzie's side. She handed Jones over to Roma, who said she would ride him round quietly, and got onto fat Honeypot who was only too pleased to be headed back to the stables and waddled along keenly. Several riders were going up to the course and asked her how she had got on, and it was sweet to smile and shout, 'Clear!' They shouted back, 'Well done!' and the whole Pony Club thing seemed suddenly a very good idea. If it wasn't for the Birdie issue, this last day would be absolute bliss.

People were charging about all over the place, some going out to show-jump in the field, the little ones gymkhanaing, cross-country competitors coming and going down the lane. In the confusion it was easy to tack up Birdie in her box. There were no instructors around; they were all out organizing things, and the yard was relatively peaceful. Roma had had strict instructions to hurry back after her round so that they would know when the Intermediate was due to start. The Green Ride was to jump first – that included Shrimp and Babar, then the Red Ride which was Hugh and Lizzie. Shrimp and Babar said they would stay down there in case they could be useful. Lizzie was down to jump second in her section after a girl called Anna Bambridge on a bay cob, and Hugh followed her on Swallow. In spite of all the tension, Rowan's good feeling after her successful round stayed with her, and she found she could be quite helpful calming Lizzie, because she felt so good herself. Roma came back on Jones grinning all over her face saying how wonderful he was, and Rowan exchanged him for Honeypot before they all rode off down the drive in a group, with Birdie in the middle.

'I'll ride Birdie in the National Trust woods until it's my turn,' Lizzie said. 'No one will see us there.'

It all seemed more optimistic now they were under way. They got down to the park without anyone noticing Birdie, and Lizzie rode on to the woods. Birdie was very much on her toes, sensing all the excitement, but Lizzie was now calm and stern, not shivery any more.

There were two riders to go before Shrimp. Pinkie, having left Bonzo behind, was being cantankerous and Hugh said he betted she wouldn't start.

'She will,' Shrimp said.

She was white and her jaw was stuck out like Auntie Millie's. She took Pinkie down to the start and made her trot in circles, and Pinkie kept pulling towards the gate.

'She'll never make her,' Hugh said. 'She should've brought Cascade.'

'I could give her a lead,' Babar said. 'She'd follow Armchair.'

'She'd be disqualified.'

At this moment Auntie Millie's Land Rover came bouncing into the field and she pulled up near Jerry.

'That's torn it,' said Hugh.

Auntie Millie got out, and plonked down on her shooting stick, chatting to Jerry. Shrimp was given the nod to start. Jerry clicked his stopwatch and Mrs Mildmay's gimlet eyes followed Pinkie's bucketing canter down to the first jump, where she stopped dead.

'Told you so,' said Hugh.

Shrimp did not turn away from the jump, but sat in the saddle and kicked Pinkie into it. Pinkie tried to swing away but Shrimp wouldn't let her, legs and heels drumming to stop her. For such a small figure her determination against the stubborn pony was formidable. It was only when Pinkie took a step backwards that Shrimp swung her round to present her for a second time, because she knew that a step backwards counted as a refusal. (Whether Rowan's mother, the fence-judge, knew this was doubtful.) She did not take her far back, and rode at the innocuous jump again with legs flailing. Three strides away she landed Pinkie a terrific clout with her whip behind the saddle, and Pinkie shot over as if the jump were Becher's Brook itself, and Shrimp did not get left behind or even dislodged, but landed beautifully poised to drive Pinkie on into the wood.

Hugh and Babar cheered madly, and Auntie Millie was heard to shout, 'Well done!'

'She'll get round now,' Hugh said. 'But one refusal – she won't win.'

'It was good enough,' Babar said. 'I couldn't 'ave done that.'

When it was her turn she strode off at her rocking-horse canter on the trusty Armchair and proceeded to do a steady clear round.

'Too slow,' said Hugh.

'I thought we wanted good advertisements,' Rowan said. 'That was a very good advertisement.'

Babar came back beaming. Rowan knew the feeling. There was nothing like it. After Babar there were only three more in her class to go, then it was the next section and Lizzie was second to go. Shrimp had spotted Mrs Prebble in the wood at the well-named coffin jump, and Auntie Millie seemed to have settled herself permanently at the start, which was not at all convenient. Hugh decided to go down and distract her when it was Lizzie's turn to go. Lizzie was keeping a watch-out and when Anna Bambridge started she emerged from her hiding place.

Jerry Patterson, looking at his clipboard, said to Hugh, 'Your sister's next to go. Where is she?'

Hugh nodded towards the bay in the distance and said, 'She's coming.'

Jerry bawled in Lizzie's direction, 'Number thirty-three next!' Then he turned to Hugh and said, 'What's she riding? Looks like the Prebble beast.'

His voice was loud and clear but Auntie Millie was at that moment, by a stroke of magical luck, trying to make her walkie-talkie work, which was always a great effort for her. She was clicking away and talking very loudly into the microphone. Hugh rode up to Jerry and hissed, 'Don't say anything, *please*! It's for Mum, and Charlie – you haven't *noticed*!'

Jerry looked astonished, as well he might. The insouciant Hugh was the last character to look so fraught: that in itself was a shock. Perhaps Jerry thought Charlie was in on the venture, for he didn't say any more but merely looked very worried. He kept his head down, examining his stopwatch. Hugh rode boldly across to Auntie Millie and sat where she had to turn her back to the course to speak to him, and started on a long ramble about when they cleared up could they leave their stuff in the hay loft until tomorrow because they had to ride home because Charlie was transporting somebody else in their horsebox, for money, which they needed ... etc. etc. Swallow was very excited, sensing that he was about to go cross-country, and Auntie Millie had to jump off her shooting stick at one point to save her skin, after which she said rather tersely, 'Of course, Hugh. Do stop fussing. It's not like you. And take that dangerous pony out of my way before you do me a damage. Are you next to go?'

'Yes,' said Hugh, because Lizzie had taken her opportunity and sped through the start the minute Jerry had clicked his stopwatch for Anna's finish.

Jerry said blandly, 'Lizzie Hawes on Fable. Hugh next.'

It all happened so smoothly and so fast that Rowan and Babar and Shrimp could not believe Lizzie's luck. Birdie sped down to the straw bales and flew over them in her stride before Pauline Watkins could catch her number. (Fence-judging was much harder than making sandwiches, she was thinking; she would make sure she didn't get this job again.) 'Who was that?' she shouted to the fence-judge who guarded the jump into the wood and he shouted back, 'Thirty-three! Lizzie Hawes on Fable.'

Birdie was excited but Rowan could see that Lizzie was so hyped up to do well that – like Shrimp earlier – she was riding out of her skin. When it *mattered* . . . Getting started was the hardest – whatever happened next would be an anti-climax. The deed was done. Unless Lizzie hit a tree or had an accident . . . Rowan realized she was trembling all over. She looked at Shrimp and noticed she was white as a sheet, staring towards the wood, and Babar was silent, sitting motionless on the Armchair. Only Hugh was not concerned with Lizzie, his hands entirely full with a super-charged Swallow, who was tearing long strips of grass up with his eager plunges, frantic to go. Rowan gulped, thinking of herself in Hugh's place, where she always thought she most wanted to be. Did she? Swallow was daunting. Even Hugh, the brilliant, conceited, best rider in the world, was looking worried.

In fact, so disturbed was Auntie Millie about Swallow's behaviour that she got off her shooting stick and closed it with a snap and got back into her

Land Rover. Out of the window she shouted at Hugh, 'I hope you know what you're doing, young man! I shall have a word with Josephine about that animal.' And while Hugh was taking her attention, Lizzie cantered back through the finish on Birdie, and Mrs Mildmay was back to stabbing buttons on her walkie-talkie set and shouting, 'Over to you! Roger!' and did not even see her.

Lizzie trotted back to the others and almost fell off in her relief and delight.

'She was brilliant. Clear! She didn't put a foot wrong! She was wonderful.'

She was so excited she burst into tears. They none of them watched Hugh depart, but gathered round Lizzie all with the same flooding feeling of incredible relief that the plan had been carried out so successfully. In fact, now it was over, and had been so easy, they started to wonder about why they had all been so worried.

'She went so well! No hesitation at all! She loved it!'

'Auntie Millie never even noticed!'

'But what if you've won,' said Shrimp, 'and when they give out the results they say Fable, instead of Birdie? They've got to know, else there was no point doing it.'

'That's true. You've got to tell 'um,' Babar said.

'Go and tell Jerry,' Shrimp suggested. 'Then he can tell Auntie Millie.'

'Ride over there and just see what happens,' Rowan suggested.

Lizzie was on such a high that she was no longer worried about the prospective row. She gathered herself together and started to ride back to the start. As she did so, there was a startled shout from the fence-judge at the last fence out of the wood.

'Loose horse! Loose horse!'

'It's Swallow!' shrieked Shrimp.

Riderless, the bay pony came belting back up the field towards his friends, reins and stirrups flying. He pulled up wildly, his nostrils wide and red like a Derby winner's, sweat streaking his dark flanks. Babar nudged her pony across to cut him off and called out, 'Steady, boy! Steady on, Swallow, there's a good fellow!' He twirled around once or twice, but Babar managed to grab his reins and hang on. A fence-judge was yelling from the edge of the wood, 'Ambulance! Ambulance! Stop the next rider!' and Auntie Millie, just as Lizzie approached her on Birdie, started her engine and drove away towards the gate that led into the wood.

Rowan found it all rather hard to believe. Nothing

was working out as planned. Hugh had fallen off! She didn't realize it was possible. Lizzie had done an exemplary clear round on Birdie and hadn't even been noticed. The ambulance people, parked on the edge of the wood eating their sandwiches, couldn't get their engine to start. Rowan watched it all going on like a spectator at the cinema. Lizzie, unable to catch Auntie Millie, was talking earnestly to Jerry, so at least someone would know how clever Birdie had been. The ambulance got started just as Hugh appeared, climbing over the last fence looking noticeably furious but unbloodied. Behind him, panting, came Mrs Prebble, also noticeably furious.

Babar gave Swallow's reins to Shrimp and said to Rowan, 'I'm going back to the stables. Coming?'

'Yes,' said Rowan. And they rode off together.

Chapter Seven

It was quite late in the evening when they all rode back together over the downs to High Hawes. Bonzo ran behind bucking and kicking, relieved to be free after his week of confinement. All the ponies, even Swallow, went rather wearily, but the mood was one of satisfaction, and the late, golden light still flooding over the open grass sent their shadows in long, bobbing patterns behind them as they breasted the steep hill. The eternal breeze up there lifted the ponies' manes off their sweaty necks and cooled the riders' hot and dirty faces, and the skylarks sang as if the day would last for ever.

I shall remember this, always, Rowan thought, again deeply aware of the pleasure that had come into her life with the High Hawes ponies. There were all sorts of problems ahead for them, but just now none of it mattered, the small successes of the day – the week –

more important and more rewarding than anything they might encounter. It was far, far from Olympic gold, but the rosette that fluttered on Jones's browband meant more to Rowan, and always would, than any more illustrious ones that might come later. It was only a second, as one beastly girl had gone faster than Jones, but Rowan could not keep her eyes off the bright ribbon nestling in his thick mane. He should have worn another one, as he had gone third for Roma, but Roma had kept it. It was her first ever too. Her delirious joy had rather impressed her gloomy parents and her father had half promised to bring Honeypot over to High Hawes for 'a bit of schooling'. ('Starving is what he'll get,' Charlie had remarked, 'before anything else.')

Birdie's silver cup and rosette, for the overall Intermediate winner, had been appropriated by the incensed Mrs Prebble. She had rattled Birdie away in her trailer at angry speed, promising that they would all hear more from her 'very shortly'.

'More what?' said Charlie afterwards. 'Lizzie showed everybody Birdie is a really good pony.'

Lizzie was the heroine. Mrs Mildmay, presenting her with the cup, made the most tactful speech of her career, managing to infer what a brilliant pony Birdie was and declaiming how everyone at camp wished Matty Prebble a speedy return to health and action. She phrased it so cleverly that it made it seem that the applause and cheering that followed was all for Matty, so Mrs Prebble was overwhelmed with people's general niceness and unable to utter a word. It was only later that her habitual resentment returned.

Roma remarked, 'Matty might be quite nice underneath it if she didn't have her for a mother.'

'Perhaps we ought to visit her in hospital,' Lizzie said. 'It must be terribly boring lying there. The summer holidays too.'

They vaguely decided that they would.

Mrs Mildmay had given Lizzie a real piece of her mind after she had realized what she had done, but Lizzie said, even thought she was foul, you somehow knew that it was more for the sake of form, and underneath she thought it was great. 'Her eyes weren't cross,' Lizzie said. And afterwards, after the scorching words, she had put her arm round Lizzie's shoulder and given her a sharp hug, before walking away very quickly.

'People say she was really wild in her youth. Dad used to tell stories about her,' Hugh said.

He hadn't lost his conceit for very long, although he

couldn't bear to recall the humiliation of watching everyone else taking his glory, of not being called up to receive a single rosette. Not even a white for effort, like the dunces. It had never happened before.

'So how come the brilliant Hugh Hawes *fell off?*' his friend Alan Finch had asked derisively. 'Only lesser mortals *fall off.*'

By the time Hugh had sorted out his tale, it was one of high endeavour over impossible odds. 'Swallow bolted down the ride and some idiot of a fence-judge came out waving her arms like a lollipop lady and Swallow shied like an idiot into the trees and I got wiped off by an overhanging branch. Somebody caught him and brought him back, and I knew I'd lost my chance so I decided to come back and do some of the senior jumps. I did two – he really flew over them – but over the third my stirrup leather broke and he did a colossal buck on landing and I flew off.'

Rowan had surreptitiously looked at his stirrup leather and it didn't look very broken to her, but she didn't say anything. Hugh had convinced himself quite quickly that he should have won. It was only other people's stupidity that had prevented it. Charlie, hearing this story, had just smiled.

Even Shrimp had come away happy because Pinkie

had got a fourth with only one refusal and Mrs Mildmay, when she presented this rosette, whispered to her, 'I take it all back. You're not just a pretty show-girl. You're a damned good rider.'

Shrimp, even at her tender age, sensed that there was no way to explain to such as Mrs Mildmay that it wasn't just peanuts riding a show-pony to win a cup, so she sensibly smirked and said nothing. But the rosette meant a lot to her, more than the many championship ribbons she had been in the habit of tossing nonchalantly to her owners in the past.

By the time they had got home and dried off the ponies' tack marks and turned them out in the field it was almost dark. Rowan hung over the gate after the others had gone in and watched Swallow rolling down in the wet patch by the stream. Jones went down to join him, and when he had got up and shaken himself with a blubbery noise like a wet dog he stood head to tail with Jones and they started scratching each other's necks with their teeth. After Hugh's failure, Rowan knew she would never ride Swallow, yet her ambition did not waver. Her dogged devotion to 'her' pony had never faltered. In the dusk he gleamed with wellbeing, and his fatal exuberance, even in repose, was evident in the proud way he stood and the impatient way he switched his tail at the midges. The sweet sour smell of the evening grass, already wet with dew, freshly trampled by the ponies, hung in the air. Rowan stayed there until the ponies had all separated and started to graze hungrily, and the sky had turned a deep, brilliant blue, with just a few lights showing below in the village. She shivered. She wanted to cry, for no reason. Yet she was so happy. And afraid. And, she realized, suddenly, incredibly tired. She couldn't take any more in.

Her mother took her home in the car and she slept until noon the next day. When she awoke she could not believe the time. When she got downstairs her mother was just putting out lunch.

'Joan Hawes warned me,' she laughed. 'She says it takes a week to recover. I must say, I didn't wake up till almost ten myself. It's rather blissful to think there's nothing to do today.'

Life without camp did suddenly seem strange. As if she had been there for ever.

'It certainly took my mind off things,' Mrs Watkins said thoughtfully. 'It made me think what a lot of time I've been wasting all these years, just dusting and cooking and ironing your father's shirts. Going to the hairdresser.'

She certainly didn't look as if she had been to the hairdresser recently. Her blonde hair was rather scraped back and unkept and her face was brown and her nose was peeling. But she looked fit and well and didn't have the worry lines that had habitually marked her forehead. Rowan didn't like to remark on it.

'Joan was talking about going into cooking – professionally. To make some money. Cooking for dinner parties, or do wedding cakes, or sandwiches for businessmen or something. She asked if I was interested, to set something up.'

She seemed to be asking for Rowan's opinion, although not directly. But Rowan noticed her new lively expression, and recognized the importance of this almost casual remark.

'You're a real wow at icing cakes – all that wedding stuff, roses and things. I bet Mrs Hawes can't do that.'

'I love doing that sort of thing.' Her mother's voice was wistful.

'Why don't you, then? I think it's a great idea, if you get on with Mrs Hawes so well. Do you?'

'Yes. We're not a bit alike, but we seem to get on. I think she thinks I'm rather frivolous. I've really enjoyed this last week, meeting all those people. I shall miss it now.'

They neither of them mentioned the missing Mr Watkins. Rowan found she really did not want to think about him. If he preferred somebody else to them, and cared so little that he just left them, without compunction, it hurt in a way that was very disturbing. Her *father*! Don't think about it.

'Yes. I think it would be great if you worked with Mrs Hawes.'

'I do admire her courage. It's quite dreadful, her loss. Not like mine at all. And the worry of the business and all those children. I've really had my eyes opened this week, seeing such a different sort of life – all those horsey people and farmers' wives – they're all so – so – tough. So busy all the time.'

Rowan looked round the tidy, sterile room that was their dining annexe, with her father's row of model cars on the top of a bookcase filled with *Reader's Digest* volumes and a picture of a vase of flowers over the mantelpiece whose fireplace was filled with an electric fire pretending to be a real one, and realized how unlike it was to any room in the Hawes's house, or Babar's or Jerry Patterson's. It didn't speak of any interest in life, beyond conformity. She wondered what Mrs Mildmay's house was like. It was said to be full of cobwebs, vast silver cups, ancient sofas and pictures of her grandfather's hunters and steeplechase winners. Hugh said it had mice. You could hear them scuttering about. Hugh had a mouse in his bedroom but wouldn't let his mother put a trap down. He said he liked it. Mr Watkins would have died if he thought there was a mouse in his bedroom.

Mrs Watkins had gone into a sort of trance, eating her salad and thinking about the horsey women she had discovered, and Rowan, after offering her a few more words of encouragement, got on her bike and cycled up to High Hawes. She had to work very hard up there, to earn riding lessons. At the back of her mind she had decided to ask Josephine to teach her rather than Charlie. It was so important to her that she learned quickly, and being with Charlie was a distraction because she wanted him to think well of her all the time. It meant not making a fool of herself in front of him and sometimes, when you were learning, you had to risk making a fool of yourself. She thought she would concentrate more with Josephine.

When she arrived at High Hawes there was a large Audi in the front yard. For a moment Rowan thought it was Mr Hicks and her heart sank. Charlie had ridden Out of the West clear in the Senior cross country and done the fastest clear round by miles, but as an instructor had ridden *hors de combat*, which meant, Rowan had discovered, not eligible for a prize. The fence-judges had been heard disputing as to whether he was in control or not – the general opinion was presumably, as he hadn't hit a tree, that he was, but he had gone past so fast most of them never got his number. Otty had also gone well on her youngster Hadrian. But Priscilla had won no rosettes and Mr Hicks had not been a happy man. Lizzie and Hugh were slumped out in the hay barn, doing nothing.

'Don't say you've come up to ride!' Hugh exclaimed in disbelief.

'I've come to work. Whose car is that?'

'It's Uncle Trevor. He says he's been trying to get Mum all week. He's got a buyer for High Hawes.'

'What!' Rowan was shocked. 'But you're not—'

'No, *we're* not,' Lizzie said. 'But the others—' She shrugged and made a face. 'It's all doom and disaster in there this morning. That's why we've got out.'

Rowan was appalled. She could not believe anything so bad could happen to her, that her paradise could disappear! Uncle Trevor was the deceased Fred Hawes's brother, and after the funeral he had come up with this idea that High Hawes should be sold. He said the family could never make a living out of the place without Fred. Joan Hawes had disagreed and said they would run the place as a riding school, and Josephine and Charlie would teach, and buy and sell ponies. They all hated Uncle Trevor, a large bullying man, a successful butcher with a string of shops. He had offered to buy High Hawes himself to use as a fattening farm.

'I thought – I thought you had all told him – you were going to run the place between you—'

'We did,' Lizzie said. 'But you know what he's like. He's a bully. The trouble is–' Her face was white and miserable. Even the ebullient Hugh was, for once, squashed and quiet.

Hugh said, 'He rang up last night, quite late, and said he was coming over. The timing was bad because Josephine and Charlie had spent the whole evening saying they weren't cut out to be teachers. They hated the week at camp – the teaching part, at any rate.'

'But—'

'They enjoyed being there and that – they just don't actually like teaching,' Lizzie said. 'Charlie says he doesn't know how to put it into words, and Josephine says it just makes her cross. Of course, they've never learned how to teach. It's something you have to learn. Just because you can do it yourself—'

'They don't want to learn anyway,' Hugh said gloomily. 'And if you want a proper riding school you have to have letters after your name. Qualifications.'

Both Mrs Prebble and Mr Hicks, Rowan remembered, had remarked on Charlie not being qualified.

'Charlie'll never get qualified,' Lizzie said. 'He can't spell.'

'He can't write,' Hugh said.

Rowan thought they must be exaggerating. 'Josephine could.'

'Not if she doesn't want to,' Lizzie said.

'But you can't sell up and go away!' Rowan wailed.

'That's what we said, and Ma told us to go away and get lost. They'll all in there yakking away, all very bad-tempered.'

'But Mum said your mother was thinking about setting up a food business – for dinner parties and weddings and things – and my mum was talking about going in with her—'

'Yeah, well, they can still do that. You don't need fifty acres and two stableyards to make sandwiches. That's what Uncle Trevor is after, the land and the stabling.'

'And the house, he said. He said we can get a house in the village.'

'But where will the horses go?'

'We sell them, daftie. What do you think?' Hugh snapped out.

Rowan could see that Hugh was as upset as she was herself. She could not believe, after such a wonderful day yesterday and all their successes, that this bombshell could have exploded.

'Josephine and Charlie go out to work and we all go to boring school and Mum makes sandwiches, I suppose, and we watch telly in the evenings,' Lizzie said. 'Shrimp rushed out and started crying over Bonzo. She called Uncle Trevor a big fat pig and Mum sent her out.'

All Rowan's plans lay in ruins. Swallow! What would happen to Swallow? No one in the Pony Club would buy him, he was too naughty. He would go to market again and go from bad to worse. Those sort always did, she remembered Charlie saying once. And Cascade . . . she glanced at Hugh, and thought he looked as if he had been crying. They sat in a glum row on the feed bins.

'I can't believe it,' Rowan said.

'We're too far away from anywhere to be a riding school, he said,' Lizzie remembered. 'No one will come.'

'Roma's coming, and Prissy might. That's all we got

from camp. I suppose it's true. Even if Josephine and Charlie were to love teaching . . .'

Rowan couldn't bear it. She went out and down to the field gate where she had stood the night before, and remembered her feelings. Now, although the sun shone and the same ponies grazed in the same place, it was as if an enormous black cloud had blotted out the sky. The change was so sudden and unexpected, she felt numb with it. Surely, to stop it happening, Josephine and Charlie could learn to like teaching! Otty did. She had said so. She loved it.

Not long afterwards, Uncle Trevor came out and Joan Hawes came down to the yard with him and stood talking by the car. They seemed quite amicable. Then he got in and drove away. Lizzie and Hugh rushed out of the feed shed and Shrimp came tearing around from Bonzo's box and they all shouted at her, 'What's going to happen? What did you tell him?'

'Nothing immediately. Don't be silly,' Joan said in her calm way. 'You know perfectly well there's nothing to worry about for the time being.'

'The time being, but what about the time after the time being?' Shrimp sobbed out.

Joan put her arm round her. 'It will be all right, pet, don't worry. You won't lose Bonzo, I'm sure.'

'What about Cascade?' Hugh said gruffly.

Joan Hawes did not answer him, but said instead, 'Come in and I'll make some lunch. None of you have eaten. And you, Rowan – are you fit this morning, or worn out?'

Rowan muttered something, unable to explain how she felt. They all went in to the kitchen and sat round the big table where Joan put out all sorts of leftovers from camp: stale rolls which she heated up in the oven, tired salads, a couple of quiches, half an apple pie and an unpopular trifle. Charlie and Josephine were sitting together looking fed up and tired.

'What did he say? What is going to happen?' Lizzie and Hugh wanted to know.

Charlie looked glum. 'We don't move, but I work for him, here, raising his bullocks. We turn the yards into cattle yards.'

'What, Dad's lovely stables? He built them!' Hugh said. And then, almost growling, 'He wouldn't like that. Dad wouldn't like it.'

'Dad, unfortunately, isn't here any more.'

'And what does Josephine do?' Lizzie asked.

'Josephine can work as his secretary in town. A generous offer, he said. Well-paid and three weeks' holiday a year.'

Surely she'd rather teach riding than do that, Rowan thought! Josephine was looking rather stunned.

'All the horses and ponies would have to go. He'd want all the grass.'

'No!' shrieked Shrimp. Rowan felt herself shrieking with her, but stayed in her seat, silent and white-faced.

Lizzie said wildly, 'Have you agreed to all this? Is that what is going to happen?'

'We discussed it. No decisions have been made. He only said it was his idea, his offer to us. We didn't accept. We said we'd think about it.' Joan cut the quiches into equal portions. 'It's largely up to Josephine and Charlie, what they want to do.'

'We don't either of us want to do it. But it does mean we can all stay here and not move,' Charlie said.

'But we were going to have a riding school – High Horse! It was all arranged,' Hugh shouted out. 'Why can't we do that?'

'It won't make enough money, not that alone,' Joan said. 'I thought it might, but it means both Josephine and Charlie getting their teaching diplomas – I learned quite a lot at camp, things I hadn't realized. Everyone has to have qualifications these days, or you get into trouble if anything goes wrong. We're in trouble anyway – a letter came from Mrs Prebble's lawyer. She's going to sue us over Birdie.'

'You never said.' Charlie sat up abruptly. 'When did it come?'

'Yesterday. I only read it late last night.'

'They wrote it before Birdie won the cup,' Charlie pointed out. 'They can hardly say we sold them a dud!'

Mrs Hawes studied the date and her face lightened. 'Yes, you're right. The date is Friday's. Well done, Lizzie! You've saved our bacon!'

'And we were planning to visit Matty in hospital! How can she be so piggy? It wasn't Birdie's fault!' Shrimp cried out.

'I still think you should visit Matty, all the same,' Joan said. 'It isn't her fault her mother is – as she is.'

'How lucky I rode Birdie!' Lizzie was hugging herself with delight. 'And I was so terrified – the trouble I would get into!'

'You were great, Lizzie. Full marks,' Charlie said.

Everyone agreed. Lizzie went pink with pride. But it made no difference to the overall sense of doom that hung over the lunch table. It seemed that Josephine and Charlie had the chief say in what was to happen, but Joan Hawes said they should carry on as they were for the time being, and give themselves time to decide.

'We're not going to be bullied by that fat butcher. He's only after what's good for him. Not what's good for us.'

Rowan went home sadly and told her mother what had happened. She cried, and her mother said, rather desperately, 'Don't, Rowan! I'll do my very best to buy you a pony, whatever happens, if it means so much to you.'

'I only want Swallow!' Rowan bawled, like a baby.

'Oh, but they say Swallow is—'

'Swallow's what? What do they say?'

'They all think he's dangerous. Even Mrs Mildmay. Why don't you want Jones? He's a lovely pony.'

'I want Swallow!'

'Oh dear,' said her mother in her old helpless way.

The day had fallen to pieces.

The next day Mrs Prebble delivered Birdie back in her horsebox and said she would sue for her money back. Mrs Hawes said they were happy to have Birdie back but would not refund the money. 'If it goes to court we can produce several witnesses – Mrs Mildmay and Mr Patterson, for example, who will testify that the pony was ridden cross country successfully by a far less capable rider than your daughter.'

Mrs Prebble – so the story went (the scene had been eavesdropped upon by Hugh, behind the kitchen door) – immediately burst into tears, and Joan Hawes put her arm round her and made her sit down at the table and made her a cup of tea. 'We would like to visit Matty and cheer her up. We don't want to be enemies. I am sure we can sort this Birdie thing out without going to court. We've all got enough troubles at the moment.' Perhaps then Mrs Prebble remembered that Mrs Hawes had recently lost her husband for, according to Hugh, after she had finished blubbing she turned quite nice and very nearly apologized. She said, 'Sometimes I expect too much of Matty. I can't help it. I am too competitive.'

Hearing this story, Charlie and Josephine were stunned.

'Mother works miracles! Talk about turning the other cheek!'

'Even foul Uncle Trevor – she was quite nice to him. I don't know how she can do it.'

Then, more practically, 'What on earth are we going to do with Birdie? She's neither ours nor theirs now.'

Josephine said, 'I suppose Mrs Prebble just wants her off her hands. No one to exercise her, and she'll be away a lot visiting Matty.'

Josephine was rather like her mother, Rowan thought, calm and sensible.

Charlie said, offhandedly, 'It'll sort itself out. The kids can ride her.' He had been gloomy since Uncle Trevor's visit and spent most of his time working on broken-down combiners for which he was much in demand or, in the evenings, going for long rides on Wilfred across the downs, alone. Jerry Patterson offered him a job in his racing yard. He didn't know what to do. Nor did Josephine. Uncle Trevor called again – 'Just a social call. I was passing,' he said, but his eyes kept roving round the barns and stables, and out over the fields. 'You can see he's really itchy for them,' Hugh said.

It somehow made them all the more determined to thwart him.

'I couldn't work for him,' Charlie said. 'Even if he takes the yards and land. I won't be his stockman.'

'Well, that's one decision taken,' Josephine said. 'Nor could I. But what do we do? Jerry's job won't pay. Jerry's got no money himself.'

'No.'

Joan Hawes was serious about visiting Matty, whilst not pressing her two eldest in any way to come to any decisions. 'There's plenty of time.' She was going ahead with her cooking idea, and Rowan's mother went up for consultations. They reckoned they could go ahead with that, whatever happened to the farm.

Lizzie and Rowan succumbed to the hospital visit. Two was enough, Joan decided, and Hugh would be bound to say all the wrong things. They drove to the hospital on a fine August afternoon past fields of harvested corn and water meadows where the cows stood dozing in the shade of willows and alder, swishing their tails rhythmically at the flies. Lizzie and Rowan went into a decline, thinking of losing the long days pottering around with the ponies. Roma's Honeypot had arrived for 'schooling' and Roma came to ride, and Otty came over sometimes on her young horse Hadrian to school in the manège, and various small children turned up for lessons but, as was painfully obvious, not enough. 'And this is the summer,' Josephine said. 'It's dark after school in the winter and no one will come.' But it was blissful just riding whatever pony was convenient, through the woods on to the downs; the knowledge that it was coming to an end was agonizing. Where would the ponies go? No new homes would ever be as good as their lives at High Hawes. The depression hung like a black cloud.

Perhaps Joan Hawes thought seeing Matty would

make them realize that things could be far worse. It really did. Rowan had never been in hospital and hadn't even visited, and Lizzie's knowledge was almost as sketchy. The atmosphere was welcoming and cheerful but the sight of people in bed strung up by the legs to various contraptions was awesome, and Rowan kept her eyes glued to the floor, following Joan Hawes's feet, feeling her heart thudding with apprehension. She was aware of the health of her own legs and back; she had never thought about it before. A sideways glance at Lizzie showed her that Lizzie was feeling much the same. She looked like she did when she had decided to ride Birdie in the cross country.

'Have you two gone dumb?' Joan said suddenly.

They looked up numbly and saw that they had arrived at a bed with Matty in it. She wasn't strung up at all, although she was lying down. She was reading a magazine. On the cover it said, 'Is your Sex Life Satisfactory?' She looked dumbstruck when she saw who her visitors were. Her white face blushed.

'Oh,' she said. Then, 'Mum didn't say—'

Neither Rowan nor Lizzie could think of a word to utter. Matty had always been Enemy Number One, but this fresh view of her rather turned the conception upside down. Joan Hawes managed to yak away without embarrassment until the two girls recovered their tongues and Matty's initial horror subsided. Then she said she was going to look for a cup of tea and departed. The three girls stared into space. Suddenly Matty said, 'Why have you come?'

'It was Mum's idea,' Lizzie said. Then, realizing how that sounded, she added politely, 'But we had thought of it too. We thought—' Words failed.

'When are you coming out?' Rowan asked.

'Quite soon. I'm not really bad, not going to be in a wheelchair or anything dreadful. Just it'll take a long time and my right leg doesn't work properly. It won't for ages, apparently.'

'Won't you be able to ride?'

'Well, not jump. Sit on, yes.'

'Your mum's sent Birdie back,' Lizzie said. 'You could swap her for something – quiet, perhaps.'

'Swallow?' Matty actually smiled.

'No. But Charlie could find you one.'

'I heard he went round on Out of the West?'

After the camp news was broached, conversation rattled ahead. Matty had a very jaundiced idea of what had gone on, no doubt relayed with much prejudice by her mother, and she was obviously pleased to get an unvarnished account, including one of Lizzie's ride on

Birdie with Mrs Mildmay not even noticing. By the time Joan Hawes came back the three of them were shouting and laughing, and the nurse who accompanied her said, 'My word, you sound a lot more cheerful all of a sudden, young lady,' to Matty.

They made their farewells and Matty said, 'Do come again,' almost imploringly.

They departed and the nurse came with them down the corridor and said, 'That's really what the poor child needs – someone for a laugh, not that awful mother of hers forever asking how long it will be before she can compete again.'

'Does she really? Poor Matty.'

Going home in the car Lizzie and Rowan were subdued, thinking of Matty and her lot, and of how they had always hated her, and now, away from her mother, she had seemed positively nice. She hadn't bragged or sulked or said anything uppity like she usually did. Nor made any snide remarks, nor anything bad about Birdie. Lizzie said, 'I think she's enjoying having a rest, away from show jumping.'

Joan Hawes laughed. 'Funny, I'm always trying to get you lot to do something useful instead of riding those ponies and you can't be prised away from them. And Matty, being forced all the time, doesn't really want to do it. What perverse little beasts you are!'

But afterwards, Rowan couldn't get Matty's white face and bright eyes out of her mind. She might think she had troubles herself, but they were not much compared with Matty's lot, her injury and her mother. There was no magic cure for Matty. Somehow, she thought, there must be one for the High Hawes dilemma, but nobody seemed to be able to think what it was.

Chapter Eight

It was raining; soft, summer rain making the fields smell of earth and, depressingly, of winter ahead. The leaves were already beginning to turn brown and the swallows' babies were hatched out and as large as their parents. Rowan had been to two Pony Club rallies with Lizzie, Hugh and Shrimp, and ridden Fable, because Roma had bagged Jones (her father *paid*). Lizzie had ridden Birdie and Hugh rode Cascade, and Swallow had been left at home. Hugh said he was unreliable, and it was clear he did not want to be left out of the ribbons again. Even on Fable, Rowan had loved the rallies. Auntie Millie kept saying things like, 'Next year, at the rate you're progressing, we might get you in the Prince Phillip team.' Rowan supposed gloomily she might borrow Honeypot off Roma, after she had taken over Jones. Honeypot was thinner now and rapidly becoming more active. 'He's not a bad little pony,' Charlie said, and got on him and jumped two cavallettis, lifting his feet so as not to kick them over. Rowan's inside voice wailed, 'I don't want Honeypot! I want Swallow!'

They were now back at school. Although Joan Hawes never badgered Josephine or Charlie, it was clear that decision time was due. Uncle Trevor had taken to dropping in once or twice a week – 'Just passing – dying for a cup of tea' – and every time he came he stood in the yard looking at the building with narrowed eyes, and leaned on the gate looking down over the pastures towards the village. Now school had started, hardly any children came for lessons. Anyone who came had to be driven by a parent who had to wait during the lesson – 'Nobody's got that sort of time any more,' Joan pointed out. All their high hopes lay in ruins.

'Everything's horrible now,' Shrimp said. 'Charlie's so bad-tempered all the time.'

'And we hardly went to any shows at all,' Hugh said. 'Charlie wouldn't take us. Dad used to take us all the time in summer.'

'Only because he took the big lorry, and Josephine and Charlie showed the horses that were for sale. He didn't do it for us – we just went along because there was room in the lorry,' Lizzie pointed out.

'He liked it when we won.'

'He liked it better when Charlie or Josephine won.'

'He used to sing all the way home. And buy us ice creams.'

They were very quiet after that. Rowan could feel the gloom palpably descending. They were riding home, the four of them, from an after-school canter across the top of the downs. The evenings were drawing in and soon, all too soon, there would be no riding after school. The valley basked in the evening sun below. They could see the other horses grazing in the cool by the stream at the bottom of their fields, Swallow and Wilfred and the Armchair, and, nearer the gate, ever hopeful for a feed, Honeypot and Bonzo. Looking down on the scene, Rowan pictured it as Uncle Trevor's, the horses departed and a herd of Aberdeen Angus taking their place. She knew the others were thinking that too. She was relieved when they passed into the wood, and the great oaks shut out the view. The ponies' hooves made no sound on the soft peaty ride and none of them spoke any more.

As they came out onto the lane beside the entrance to the yard, a large car came over the hill behind them and swept past very close. Hugh yelled, 'Hogface!' and waved his fist in the air. The car slammed on its brakes and started backing up towards them. Hugh rode rapidly into the yard and the others followed, half alarmed, half giggling.

'He can't come in here,' Hugh shouted. 'I'll tell him he's trespassing.'

The car reversed past and came into the yard, and a large burly man got out. Hugh went rather pale but rode boldly towards him.

'You—'

'Charlie Hawes live here?' the man demanded. 'I want a word.'

Hugh gawped. The man looked familiar. Hugh noticed the numberplate on the car, HIX 1, and realized who it was.

'Mr Hicks?'

Priscilla was getting out of the passenger seat. She gave him a cool look. 'Is Charlie around?'

Hugh got off Cascade and tried to pull his wits together. This surely wasn't a social call? Was Charlie in trouble with Mr Hicks? The man never smiled; it was hard to tell. He was a hard and astute businessman, said to be mega-rich.

'He's probably in the house. I'll fetch him, if you like.'

'You do that.'

The way he talked, you ran. Hugh chucked Cascade's reins at Lizzie and scuttled towards the gate. Left with the ponies, the three girls weren't sure what to do next. It seemed rather rude to walk through to the back yard and leave Mr Hicks and Prissy standing there.

'Would you like to come through?' Lizzie said. A sort of invitation.

The Hickses followed them and looked around the back yard and at the manège and down the fields. Just like Uncle Trevor. He surely didn't want to buy the place? Lizzie and Rowan both got the same thought at once.

'Oh, lor', what's he after?' Lizzie snuffled, tugging at her girth. 'Of all people—!'

'Perhaps it's Prissy – wants lessons – because she loves Charlie,' Rowan murmered.

As they turned the ponies out into the field Hugh came back with a startled-looking Charlie.

'Can I help you?'

'Yes, you can,' boomed Mr Hicks. 'Don't know how you're fixed workwise, but I've a job I'd like you to take on. That horse of ours, Out of the West – we've had top trainers in to help Priscilla but they all say the same thing – great horse but not for a girl. A lot of work to be done. You want it?'

Charlie looked stunned. The others all stood round gawping, too fascinated to politely move.

'Want it? How? What are the conditions?'

'I own it, keep it here at livery. You ride it in events, train it up to advanced level, make it worth a bomb. I'm told it's a potential star. As well as that, you find a suitable horse for Priscilla, and train it here. She can come over for lessons and compete when she's ready. Just about a full-time job, if you're free to take it on. You have the facilities. And, I'm told, the skill.'

There was a long, long silence. Rowan looked at Charlie and saw him standing like a startled deer, staring. His navy-blue gypsy eyes looked huge, wild. He didn't say anything.

Priscilla was looking at him, grinning. She wore a cream sort of tunic and tight brown trousers and her chestnut hair floated in a great cloud around her head. Was it her idea? Was it a magical offer or a minefield?

Charlie then recovered his composure and said, 'We would need to discuss it.'

'We can discuss it now.'

'Perhaps you'd better come up to the house,' Charlie said.

'Certainly.'

They departed.

Lizzie, Hugh, Shrimp and Rowan stood staring after them, their mouths hanging open.

Then Lizzie said, quite simply, 'We're saved.'

'What, by him?' Hugh said, uncertain.

'Two eventers at livery, to be trained, and lessons for Priscilla – that is very expensive. Charlie will make his name on Out of the West, and Mr Hicks will pay all the bills. That is how it works.'

'Then he'll sell Out of the West for a hundred thousand pounds to a foreigner.'

'Yes. But by then High Horse will be on the map.'

'Do you think—?' Rowan wondered if Charlie would seize this offer with the alacrity Lizzie seemed to assume. He did not like Mr Hicks. Charlie was very independent, and hated to be told what to do. But he adored Out of the West, and was soft on Prissy. Life was a compromise, after all. She felt a flicker of hope, and saw that the others had sort of come alight, but were afraid to put anything into words. Their cheeks were flushed, and Hugh's lower lip trembled in an odd way. He turned away, almost crossly.

'We haven't got to stay out here, just because of him. I'm starving. Mum will have tea ready.'

'I must go home,' Rowan said, routinely. But she

couldn't bear to go. She didn't stay to tea after riding, not on school days.

Lizzie, understanding, said, 'I'll ring you up when Mr Hicks has gone, and tell you what happens.'

'Yes. You must!'

It was as if life was on hold, suddenly. A whole new picture had opened out before them, but it was hard to believe in it. Rowan realized suddenly how depressed they had all become lately. Every time they went riding they could only think of how it was going to stop soon, and the more they enjoyed themselves the worse the misery. It had become an accepted ache.

She cycled home in a dream.

Her mother had made tomato soup and a salad using up some prawns that they had decided were a bit dicey for the sandwich trade. Rowan was used to heating up leftovers, or trying out new mixes. Mr Hicks or no Mr Hicks, the Hawes and Watkins cooking partnership was making slow but steady headway. The only trouble was that the sandwich-eaters, like the children who wanted to learn to ride, lived too far away. Pauline Watkins did the delivering but the cost of the petrol ate into the profits.

'We want a big factory or something, where we can sell a lot in one place.' Pauline Watkins was always alert for opportunities, and went out looking. Rowan had noticed that her mother got steadily more cheerful, just as she had got steadily more uncheerful.

She told her what had happened.

'My word! Mr Hicks is a big cheese, I gathered. Although nobody likes him much. Poor Charlie!'

'Well, not if he gets such a good horse to ride.'

Rowan was on pins, waiting for Lizzie to ring up. She pictured Joan Hawes being calm and polite to Mr Hicks, just as she was to Uncle Trevor. They were not unlike, Mr Hicks and Uncle Trevor, wanting to take people over and tell them what to do. But Rowan didn't think anyone could tell Charlie what to do.

She helped wash up and then tried to settle down to her homework, but couldn't. When at last the phone rang, she leaped up to grab the receiver.

'Yes, Charlie's going to do it,' Lizzie said breathlessly. 'It's all right! They're going to bring the horse over, and there's going to be a sort of probationary period to see how it goes. Charlie's going to be terribly tactful. He's over the moon about getting that horse – beyond his wildest dreams, he says. He was trying to make Mr Hicks see that it takes quite a long time, especially as Charlie thinks everyone has tried to make Out of the West do too much too soon. He's only five, after all, and Mr Hicks thinks he ought to go round Badminton next year! Charlie explained all this and Mr Hicks took it quite well. He actually listened! Charlie called him 'sir' and Mum gave him a brandy and ginger and he was quite nice in the end. He laughed! Apparently he'd had a long talk with Auntie Millie and this was all her idea. All the people he spoke to told him Auntie Millie knew everything, and he got to believe it, he said. He almost admitted he didn't know much, which we think is a very good sign. And Charlie's got to buy another horse, for Prissy – that's two at livery! Now he's gone we're dancing about and celebrating. Can you hear us?'

Rowan could.

'Mum's going to ring Uncle Trevor and tell him what's happened. She keeps telling us we mustn't count our chickens before they're hatched, and Charlie could easily fall out with Mr Hicks and then where will we be? But we say we won't let him. He's got to keep saying 'sir' and bowing and scraping.'

'What happens if he has a row with Prissy?' Lovers always did, after all.

'Well, apparently the Out of the West deal is nothing to do with Prissy. And we've all thought that out – if they have a tiff, Josephine can take over Prissy.

She might anyway. She'd be better than Charlie.'

'Perhaps Wilfred would suit Prissy?'

'Yes, he might. But Charlie's got instructions to go out and buy something suitable. Money no object. What a lovely job!'

'And the ponies will stay!'

'Oh yes. Everything will be the same, only better!'

Rowan hadn't realized just how bad she had felt about the whole thing, until suddenly the awful threat was lifted. She felt like a new person, floating on air. When she met the others at the school bus stop in the morning, they were all bouncing again, like old times.

'Out of the West is coming tonight. You must come and see him. Charlie and Josephine are making the yard look beautiful and scrubbing out his box and turning out the tack room and mending the gate and all those things. And Ma has started singing again. You know, when she's cooking. She's a new person.'

Rowan came home, changed, and flew up to High Hawes without waiting for her tea. It was a fine evening, the air sharp with autumn and the promise of frost, and a faint mist like gauze gathering across the stream in the valley. Rowan looked at her favourite view with a feeling that it was never going to rain any more; the clouds had rolled away and God was smiling on High Hawes. Their luck had turned.

The front yard had never looked so smart. Charlie had knocked out a partition and made two boxes into one really big one, and it was filled with deep straw and a huge net of best hay hung ready. Charlie wore clean jodhpurs and a white shirt and had had a haircut, and kept saying, 'Yes, sir. That's right, sir,' so that they all got the giggles. In the event, just as it was going dusk, the enormous horsebox arrived driven by the Hicks's groom, without Mr Hicks at all, so that Charlie's efforts to look smart and clean were wasted.

The groom, an older man, climbed down from the cab and came round to open up the cab.

'Can't say as I'll be sorry to lose this one,' he said. 'Too much energy for 'is own good. Nothing but trouble.'

'Too strong for Miss Hicks,' Charlie said politely.

The man grunted contemptuously. 'Should go back to racing, what 'e was bred for. The Grand National should suit 'im nicely.'

Charlie looked in no way abashed by this information. Rowan knew that he thought most horses were underworked and overfed. Out of the West hadn't been turned out since he had been bought by the Hicks.

They dropped the ramp and the groom led out the gorgeous horse. He stood looking all round him with his large, intelligent eyes, then let out a challenging whinny. Wilfred, already installed as his neighbour, answered with his sweet, high-pitched nicker and danced about behind his door. They led Out of the West into his new box and let him loose and he walked all round sniffing and pawing at the straw and generally making a great mess of the carefully arranged bedding, then came to the door and let out some more bellows. From way down the field behind the yard the ponies answered him. Charlie laughed. Then he took the groom into the tack room and they discussed feeding and the horse's foibles. Joan Hawes offered the man a drink in the house, but he said he had better be getting back, so the impressive horsebox departed and left the younger Hawes and Rowan capering round the yard with excitement, until Charlie told them to clear off and leave his horse to settle.

Rowan stayed for tea and afterwards went to see Swallow in the field. His winter coat was starting to grow, with its blue-black lustre deepening across the flanks, faint dapples stippling his belly, and his muzzle softening to gingery brown. Out of the West was much the same colour – perhaps even the same character? –

Rowan was struck by the comparison. Swallow was sweet and affectionate in the field and stable, and wouldn't hurt a fly. Why did he have to be such a difficult ride? Perhaps, as Charlie maintained, if he was ridden and worked hard every day, he would settle and become more amendable. But even in the holidays he did not get that much work. And in school time – there just wasn't that much time in the day. Rowan stroked his velvety muzzle.

'I *will* ride you,' she vowed. 'I *will* get good enough.'

It was amazing to think that she had even got this far in only seven months. A year ago she hadn't even set eyes on Swallow. She found it hard to think back to her life in Putney before they moved to the country, and to the days before she had discovered ponies, and the Hawes.

Out of the West was not an easy horse. Charlie decided to let him out and work him over the downs on long hacks, and not jump him nor do dressage training until he had settled into his new home and got over some of his hang-ups. He had told Mr Hicks not to expect quick results. It was one of his conditions. Mr Hicks, advised by Auntie Millie, had agreed.

After a week, Out of the West was turned out into

the home field. He careered round madly, while Charlie stood anxiously watching, but eventually he settled and started to graze. The ponies had all come up to the fence from the bottom field and stood in a row staring at him. The big horse moved about restlessly, switching his tail. Charlie leaned over the fence, chewing a piece of grass.

'As long as he doesn't jump out, we're OK.'

Rowan didn't know this was something horses did.

'Big horse like him – the fence across the end, against the down, isn't really high enough. All right for the ponies, but we've had a colt jump out once, when some people went by on horses that way.'

Charlie had never had to handle horses that didn't belong to him, and found the valuable horse a worry he hadn't foreseen. Standards at High Hawes were somewhat slapdash, and the whole regime would have to be tightened now he was virtually a professional.

'The ponies need clipping. They look like wild things. You can fetch them in and get the mud off them for a start, and get their boxes cleaned out and ready.'

The days were shortening and the leaves were blowing about the fields. Charlie and Josephine spent a lot of time out looking for the right young horse for

Priscilla. 'The sooner we get it in the yard, the sooner our income increases.' Meanwhile she came once a week for lessons with Josephine on Wilfred, but she didn't like Wilfred. He didn't go for her, because she was a weak rider and exerted no authority, so he dropped back into his lazy riding-school habits. Both Charlie and Josephine realized quickly that to get a suitable horse for Prissy to compete on – and hopefully win – to keep her father sweet – was going to be difficult. A push-button jumper, which did not hot up . . . which could win in big company with a passenger rider.

'They're rare.' Charlie discussed it at length with his sister. 'Like gold dust. I think we shall have to persevere with Wilfred. We know he's safe, and willing enough if she gets her act together.'

'I reckon she might well get on with Birdie,' Josephine said.

'More than our life's worth. Officially Birdie still belongs to Mrs Prebble.'

'We'd better start sending her bills for keep then.'

'I think Rowan could ride Birdie, given time, if she'd drop her fixation for Swallow.'

'She wants her mother to buy Swallow.'

'That would be unwise. He has a very dubious past –

336

on the loose and lost for several weeks, then stolen, sold on the market – who knows that his real owners might not turn up one day, especially if we take him to shows or events? Somewhere along the line he was very well-schooled and taught to jump. It's really weird nobody ever enquired after him.'

'All I can say, he must have had a pretty good rider.'

'Yes. He's for Hugh, if he's for anybody. He's a boy's pony.'

Rowan did not hear this conversation, busy carrying out orders, carting new straw into the ponies' boxes. The ponies were to be trace clipped, and their rugs sorted out from the tack room.

The next Saturday Rowan went to High Hawes to find that Joan Hawes had decided to take Lizzie, Hugh and Shrimp – much against their will – shopping for winter school things. 'Everyone else does it in August,' she snapped at them, as they grizzled. She didn't like shopping either. Charlie and Josephine had gone to look at a horse in Devon. Charlie had ridden Out of the West earlier, and he was now turned out, with instructions to be brought in when the shoppers came home. All the ponies had been clipped except Swallow, who was shut in his box to keep clean until Charlie returned, when he said he would do him.

The others were out down the bottom of the field in their freshly scrubbed New Zealand rugs.

'So you're in charge, Rowan,' Joan Hawes said as she backed her ancient car out of its shed. 'We won't be away for long – you can all ride after lunch.'

'I'll groom Swallow, and sweep the yard.'

'Otty might come over to school Hadrian.'

'OK.'

They departed. Rowan went and leaned on the fence and watched Out of the West for a bit, who looked fantastic, unclipped and with a coat gleaming with wellbeing. It was very easy to waste time just looking at horses. Out of the West, with his beautiful but not handy name, had been rechristened Jack, and was grazing peacefully with Wilfred. All the ponies except Swallow were in their favourite spot at the bottom of the field, too far away to talk to, so Rowan fetched a box of grooming tools and set to work on Swallow. Charlie had taught her how to groom, throwing her weight behind the brush – 'Not just a tickle. It should be really hard work!' – so Rowan conscientiously did the job properly and had the satisfaction of seeing the dark coat coming up from under the layer of dried mud with its accustomed shine. Funny how she didn't mind this sort of hard work . . .

Strangely, in the distance she could hear voices. She looked out of the stable and saw a couple of riders coming up the hill from the village on the far side of the top field. Quite a strong wind was blowing, and one of the riders was having trouble with his horse which was bucking and trying to take off. They were shouting and laughing, and Rowan heard one of them yell, 'Oh, come on! Let them go – they want to!' They were far away but Rowan could sense the fun and excitement and found herself smiling. But Out of the West sensed it too, and started to trot along the fence beside them. The riders went on, taking no notice. Out of the West reared up, the wind in his tail – he looked magnificent – spun round and galloped back the other way, down towards the ponies, then he reared up again, flung himself round and, in one almighty jump, cleared the fence out of the field.

Rowan, watching and laughing, felt her jaw drop in horror. What had been a bit of fun was now major disaster. The horse was galloping away up the hill, bucking as he went with pure spirits, excited by the horses far in front of him. Whether their riders would see him and try to catch him Rowan had no way of knowing, for very shortly the edge of the wood above the house cut them off from her view, and Out of the West as well.

She dropped her grooming tools and stood fastened to the ground like a zombie. She was completely alone, and the whole future of High Hawes was on the loose out on the downs. Out of the West could go for miles, come to a road and get hit by a car, he could fall down the chalk quarry, break a leg, or get completely lost and distressed, not to be found for days . . . her imagination pictured the worst.

Before he got too far away, she ought to make an effort to keep up with him, see where he went. What would Charlie do? He would get out the Land Rover and drive after him over the downs. She couldn't do that. Her bike would be hopeless up there. The answer was to ride after him, take a head collar and try to catch him. With a pony, he might even follow her back.

She looked out of the door. All the ponies were miles away, and had their winter rugs on. By the time she had got one out of the field, which was always a tangle for her, opening the gate and shoving the others out of the way, and stripped and saddled and bridled it, Out of the West would be miles away. The answer, of course, was standing right beside her, breathing down her neck – Swallow. His saddle and bridle were in the tack room next door and he was groomed and polished and ready to go.

Rowan ought to have hesitated, but strangely her heart leaped up at the challenge – she had no alternative! Nobody could blame her for taking Swallow.

'You *will* behave, won't you? You *will*, Swallow!'

Was it an appeal or a command? She didn't know, sliding the saddle hastily onto his back and grabbing for the girth. She remembered to run for a big head collar, and stuff her pocket with horse nuts which always helped with catching. In two minutes she was leading Swallow out and scrambling into the saddle. The stirrup leathers were right, thank goodness – she kicked him heartily in the ribs and he was out in the lane making for the path through the woods at a surprised trot. Normally, like good children, they always walked for the first ten minutes. Now, once on the path under the trees, Rowan asked him to canter.

Swallow liked this. He set off with a preliminary buck to show what a good mood he was in, but Rowan sat this without any trouble. Her blood was up and she almost wanted him to buck again, and again, because she knew she wouldn't come off. She had never felt this confident before. It mattered so terribly – dear Charlie's whole life depended on it! She could hardly believe what was happening, the suddenness of it!

Out of the woods and onto the downs she asked Swallow to gallop up the long grassy hill. There was no sign of Out of the West below, nor of the two riders, but she thought once she breasted the top of the hill and could see in all directions, she was bound to see them. With luck the two riders would help her – they might already have had the sense to catch the loose horse. Swallow loved going fast and when he slowed for a breather she kicked him on again, and he responded like a little racehorse, although beginning to blow. Rowan was beginning to blow too. She had never ridden so fast so far before. The hill got steep near the top but they scrambled up, and the wind met them, whistling up from the other side. Swallow put in another buck, this one more unexpected, and Rowan lost a stirrup.

'Bother!' The first fine rapture of the chase was now starting to wear off a bit, and anxiety was taking its place. What if she couldn't even find out where the horse had gone? The downs were huge once you were on the top, rolling north, east and west like the backs of great basking pigs, hazed in the distance with the soft mist of autumn which almost hid the maze of lanes and villages beyond. Out of the West could eat up miles with his long stride.

Rowan looked back down the home valley and there was no sign of anything moving. She continued up onto the ridge and looked down the other side towards the site of the Pony Club camp. Nothing. The world was totally deserted. She almost wondered if she had been dreaming, that Out of the West was still happily grazing in his field. But, looking down, she could see that he wasn't, unless he was in the corner hidden by the wood, which was unlikely. She had to ride on and see over the ridge to the east, then she would have covered all directions. He must be there.

She put Swallow into a trot. He seemed to have sensed her seriousness for he did not play up again. Perhaps the gallop had taken the tickle out of him. As she rode she wondered how on earth she was going to catch the big horse – she had never even led him before, feeling scared of his size and her puny strength should he disagree with her. Now she was planning to lead him tamely home on a leading rein like a pet dog. But find him first.

The ground flattened out ahead of her and then started to run downhill, and at last she could see the whole of the landscape to the east. She pulled Swallow up and frowned into the distance. A chalky lane wound up from the valley between high banks of trees, and she could see the two riders disappearing down it, but Out of the West was not with them and it was apparent that they were not aware of him, for they seemed relaxed. Something moving caught her eye to the right, half hidden by a rise in the ground. Swallow swung his head round suddenly and stood staring towards the same spot, his ears pricked tight. Then he gave a whinny.

Rowan waited, very tense. Then a familiar head appeared over the rise in the ground and Out of the West trotted into view about a quarter of a mile below her, coming in her direction. Swallow saw him and gave another whinny, piercing this time and plunged forward so suddenly that this time Rowan nearly fell off. She just managed to grab a handful of mane and haul herself to safety, then had to gather up the snatched reins to pull him up. Out of the West was coming towards them now at a canter, kicking up his heels every now and then with excitement, just like Swallow.

Rowan had no idea what to do. She wasn't sure she had control over Swallow, and now the idea of catching Out of the West and leading him tamely home seemed preposterous.

So she stood there and felt Swallow dancing beneath her as the big horse approached. In her nervousness she tightened the reins and as Swallow snatched at his bit she knew she was doing exactly what Josephine always warned against, tensing up and making Swallow cantankerous. But how could she relax? She was frightened.

Out of the West came up, snorting and tossing his head. Rowan could see that he was very excited, his nostrils flared wide and red. He came so close she felt the heat of his breath, then he spun round and let out the most enormous bucking kick. His shod hooves whistled past her leg and landed on Swallow's flank with a jolt that Rowan felt beneath her. Swallow gave an angry squeal, snatched himself round and let fly in return, which Rowan felt as a large buck. She shot up Swallow's neck, landing round his ears, and all but came off, but pure fear and a healthy sense of self-preservation compelled her into doing the right thing, shoving herself back in the saddle, turning Swallow quickly round to face Out of the West and driving him on to ride past, heading for home. She had to exert command.

Swallow nervously went on and Out of the West, to Rowan's surprised relief, followed. But there was no indication that he was going to stay for long, for he was looking all around him, stopping and starting, and seemed likely to lose interest in Swallow quite shortly. The thought of him plunging off over the top of the downs after she had actually found him was chastening. Charlie would never forgive her if she let him get away now.

But catching him was a two-handed job. Could she manage it without letting go of Swallow? Handling one pony was all she had been asked to do up to now: the job before her was horrific. Unless the horse lowered his head she could not even reach high enough to get the head collar on.

But she had no choice.

She got off Swallow. Her hands trembled as she shook out the head collar and got it the right way up. Out of the West wandered off while she was doing this and started grazing. At least his head was in the right place now. If only there was something to tie Swallow up to! But there was nothing for miles. She knew she couldn't let him go, because if he decided to kick up his heels and gallop off and Out of the West went with him she would be in worse trouble than ever. So she pulled his reins over his head and looped them over her arm, and approached the big horse warily. From the front, as Charlie had taught her. Swallow tried to graze too, but she pulled him up with a yank.

She had a pocketful of nuts, she remembered. As she got close, and Out of the West made no move to go, she threw some of the nuts down in front of his nose. Forgetting Swallow – that was a mistake – for he greedily dived forward . . . Out of the West tossed up his head, turned and trotted off for several paces. He stood, looking round. Rowan was almost weeping with tension.

'Come on, Jack – look what I've got!' she wheedled, holding out her hand with the nuts.

Swallow barged in and gobbled them up before she had a chance to shove him off.

'You beast!'

But Out of the West saw that she had something of interest and took a step forward.

Risking everything, Rowan scattered the rest of the nuts on the ground and let go of Swallow. As Out of the West's head went down she managed to hold out the noseband of the head collar in just the right place, getting it under his chin before his lips touched the grass. To her everlasting relief, he let her halter him without a fuss, and she got the buckle done up safely. He went forward with his ears back, warning Swallow off the titbits. Rowan made a sideways dive to grab Swallow's reins, but couldn't reach them. Swallow turned round and walked away, the reins trailing on the ground.

Now she had Out of the West, but Swallow was loose, saddled and bridled.

Rowan didn't know whether to laugh or cry.

She had no more nuts left to tempt Swallow with. Out of the West seemed disposed to go on grazing. If only someone would come! But in her experience, they hardly ever met anyone up here. She knew perfectly well that Jones would have been easy to catch, so would Cascade and even Birdie, but Swallow was often difficult, unless you carried titbits.

At least she had the valuable one. She was very nervous of his size, and getting her feet trodden on, but when she walked forward he came with her quite happily. She decided to take him home first, and hope Swallow would tag along. She hadn't even run his stirrups up, and the trailing reins invited disaster, but there was nothing she could do about it now.

She walked firmly on. In spite of Swallow being loose, she felt shakily triumphant at having caught

Out of the West. She felt rather tearful, and it seemed an awful long way back to High Hawes, the way she had come so fast on Swallow.

Swallow seemed disposed to come with them, but every time she went towards him to try and catch him he trotted away, treading on his reins and pulling himself up short, then trotting on. Rowan decided to leave him. She didn't want him to excite Out of the West, for if he decided to pull away from her she knew she would never hold him.

How wonderful if the family were to come back early and come sweeping up the hill towards her on their ponies! But nothing happened and it was a long, anxious walk. Out of the West came tamely for the most part, but sometimes he would stop and pull back, and gaze out over the valley as if in two minds to gallop off, but each time she spoke to him softly and urged him on and, all in his own good time, he came. Swallow, stopping mostly to graze, dropped away behind, and eventually became lost to view.

When she got back she put Out of the West in his box, and burst into tears. She couldn't stop trembling and crying, and kept thinking how stupid she was. She knew she had to go back and find Swallow, and she guessed he would be harder to catch than Out of the West. This time she took several handfuls of nuts in a bucket and trudged back through the wood onto the down. But there was no sign of Swallow anywhere, and it was a long way to the top without a pony. She decided the best thing would be to saddle up Jones and go searching, so she turned and started trudging back. But as she did so she saw Charlie's Land Rover coming back up the hill and swing into the yard, and all her troubles fell away. She ran.

From the wood she could hear the telephone bell ringing in the yard (it was wired to be heard in the manège, although the telephone was in the tack room). She thought nothing of it until, turning in through the gateway, she saw Charlie come running out of the tack room and jump into the Land Rover again.

He turned it round furiously and shouted at her out of the window, 'Who told you to go out on Swallow? There's been an accident on the road and they say it's one of our ponies!'

His eyes blazed. Without waiting for her, he shot out of the yard and roared away up the hill.

Chapter Nine

This time Rowan really cried. She howled. Poor Swallow was killed and it was all her fault, and no one would ever believe what had happened.

She had forgotten all about Josephine who suddenly came out of the tack room to see what the noise was.

'What—?'

'It's not fair!' Rowan heard herself crying out, like a baby. 'I – I didn't—'

'Rowan! Shut up!'

'I couldn't help it! I did – did – what I thought – was best – and Charlie – Charlie shouted at me!'

'Oh, Rowan, calm down and tell me what happened.'

The voice was calm and sympathetic, not cross like Charlie's, and Rowan managed to control her sobs, although she felt shaken to the core.

'I only rode out on Swallow because Out of the West

jumped out of his field and galloped away. I caught him, but then Swallow ran off—'

'Rowan!'

Josephine looked thunderstruck. Through her tears Rowan saw the shock on her face. The older girl came up close and put her arms around Rowan and hugged her.

'Stop crying! You're a heroine! We wondered why Jack was back in his box and the others not home – and he'd been sweating. We were just talking about it, and then the phone rang—'

'What did they say about Swallow? He's not hurt, is he?

Another great outpouring of tears at the thought of darling Swallow lying mangled in the road . . . the first time she had set eyes on Swallow was when her father hit him with his car on the road – it seemed years ago now. And it was all her fault, because she had been too stupid to catch him.

'I don't know. They didn't say the pony was hurt, only that a car was in a ditch. He'll probably be OK, if the car swerved. Don't worry! Ponies have a great sense of self-preservation, not like thoroughbreds. Tell me what happened—'

Rowan, calming down, told Josephine the story of

chasing Out of the West. Josephine was full of praise and admiration.

'You did wonderfully well to catch him! That matters more than anything – whatever would we have done if we'd come home and found him missing! Letting go of Swallow was the best thing to do. You're brilliant!'

Josephine gave Rowan a real hug, and Rowan's despair gave way to an unusual flicker of self-esteem.

'Poor Rowan – all that and then Charlie bawls at you – come along, let's go and make a cup of tea.'

Rowan followed her across the garden to the house. Rowan had never had much contact with Josephine before, apart from during her riding lessons, and her warmth now surprised her. She was always rather quiet, cool and beautiful, and – Rowan had always felt – unapproachable. But she had never been alone with her before, nor in such a state. Sitting down at the familiar kitchen table, she now felt ashamed of her hysterics. She felt tired, as if it were bedtime instead of not even lunch time. Josephine produced a strong cup of tea and a large tinful of chocolate biscuits.

'Don't worry about Swallow. On the phone it was all about the car, and the driver who was in a rage. They never said anything about injuries.'

'Oh, good. But will you have to pay for the car?' A terrible thought now assailed her, that a large bill for damages would be forthcoming.

'We're insured for that. We're not that stupid. But losing Out of the West like that – I can't think of a worse disaster! I shouldn't think any of the others could have done better, getting him back like that.'

Hot tea and praise warmed Rowan through. She felt as if she were going to melt, exhausted by her traumas. After unburdening of all her troubles, she remembered what Josephine and Charlie had gone out for.

'Did you buy a horse?'

'No. But we liked it.' Her eyes went dreamy. '*I* liked it. Oh, I would like it!'

'You mean for you, not for Priscilla?'

'Yes.'

It had never occurred to Rowan before that, of them all, Josephine didn't have her own horse. She was always riding, but always other people's, schooling or training – like Charlie, who had lost Fedora and bought only cheap, thin Wilfred for himself.

'Charlie thinks it will be too much for Priscilla.'

'Like Out of the West.'

'Yes. But not as unsuitable as him. I just thought—'

Her voice trailed off. Rowan waited, interested. 'I suppose it's dishonest.'

'What?'

'Buy this one for Priscilla, and it will be unsuitable for her. But Charlie and I could make it – I know we could – and perhaps – perhaps—' She hesitated, then shrugged.

'Mr Hicks will say, you ride it? Like Out of the West?'

Josephine grinned. 'Yes. It's dishonest, isn't it?

Rowan considered. 'A bit, I think. If you really think it isn't suitable. But then Mr Hicks could always say sell it again, and you would have improved it, and you can make him a profit.'

Josephine looked hopeful. 'Yes. That's very sensible. You're really bright, Rowan.' A long pause. 'Not very fair on Priscilla, though.'

They both laughed.

At that moment the telephone rang again. Josephine answered it.

'Oh, Jerry, hello!'

Rowan, thinking it might be Charlie about Swallow, sank back in her chair and took another chocolate biscuit. Jerry seemed to do all the talking and Josephine kept saying yes. After some time she said,

'Yes, I'm sure we're interested. When Charlie gets in I'll tell him.'

She put the phone down and came back to the table.

'You won't believe this, but that was Jerry Patterson saying he might have a horse that would suit Priscilla.'

'Oh dear,' Rowan said.

Josephine grinned. 'Bad timing.'

'Perhaps she could have two horses. If Mr Hicks is so rich.'

'This one is a racehorse, but so laid back Jerry says it will never win a race. But very good-looking, a very easy ride and a good jumper. And cheap.'

'Probably too cheap for Mr Hicks. He likes expensive things.'

'Yes.'

'He might like the idea of Priscilla having two horses. She could start on Jerry's and improve enough to ride yours.'

Josephine laughed. 'Well, we're not short of ideas, dishonest or otherwise. We'll see.'

Rowan was on pins waiting for Charlie to come back. She couldn't be sure Swallow wasn't hurt, in spite of Josephine's encouraging words. If Swallow was all right she would feel fantastic, Josephine having told her she was a heroine, brilliant, sensible and bright. Not bad for one morning.

But it wasn't long before the rattle of the Land Rover echoed across the garden. Rowan leaped up.

Josephine said quickly, 'I'll tell him what happened,' and went out ahead of her. Rowan trailed behind, her heart thumping with apprehension. She hung back as she watched the two of them talking, Charlie still sitting in the Land Rover. Then, after a bit, he got out and slammed the door. He looked stunned, as Josephine had at the news of the near disaster, and went instinctively over to the horse's box and looked him over.

Rowan, judging the smoke had cleared, advanced.

'Is Swallow all right?'

Charlie swung round.

'Yes.' He looked lost for words, obviously still thinking what he might have had to be saying to Mr Hicks if Out of the West had been lost. 'I – jeez, Rowan—' Words failed him. He came forward and put an arm round her shoulder. 'I'm sorry I shouted. You're a marvel.'

'What happened to Swallow? Is he all right?'

'Yes. What a near squeak, eh? What an idiot I was, not to think—' He gave himself a mental shake. 'Yes, your Swallow's OK. He just ran out into the lane at the top of the hill as a car was coming down. The car swerved into the ditch and more or less crumpled up, but the driver's all right. Only a bit mad – you can say that again. Guess who it is?' A wide grin stretched across his face suddenly.

'Who?'

'Mrs Prebble.'

'No!'

They couldn't help roaring with laughter, until Josephine recovered herself and said, 'Oh, no, we mustn't laugh – poor Mrs Prebble! She can't do without a car, with Matty in hospital.'

'Matty's coming home tomorrow,' Charlie said. 'That was part of the diatribe – what she's going to do without a car to fetch Matty in? I said she could borrow ours.'

'She wouldn't be seen dead in ours!'

'Yes, she more or less told me that. Well, I did my best.' Charlie shrugged. 'At least the pony's all right. She always drives too fast. Visibility's perfect on the hill. She should have had plenty of time to stop. We'd better go and collect him. I left him tied up in Mr Herbert's barn, till Hugh gets back.'

'I'll go,' Rowan said. '*Please!*'

Charlie looked at her and gestured to the Land Rover. 'Hop in.'

She hopped. Charlie turned round and drove out of the yard.

'What you did today . . . you know how important it was, don't you? My life, just about.'

'Yes.'

'I shall never be able to thank you enough. None of the kids could have done better.'

'They might have caught Swallow. Hugh would have.'

'Blow Hugh.'

Charlie changed gear as the Land Rover met the brow of the hill. Then he said, 'Look, for better or for worse, think of Swallow as yours. Between us, we'll make him behave. I shall never let you ride an unsafe pony, but I don't think we'll let him beat us. He's got so many qualities. He just needs to learn a bit of sense. We can teach him sense between us, you and me and Josephine. We'll take time with him.'

Rowan wasn't sure if she'd got it right. 'Mine?'

'Yours, with provisos.' Charlie laughed. 'You know perfectly well we can't sell him – no one'll have him. You must do as you're told. Never, never ride without supervision. Not until he's safe. Unless Out of the West jumps out of his field, of course.'

'Oh, Charlie!' She couldn't speak.

They came to Mrs Prebble's Audi lying crumpled in the ditch, with the breakdown van labouring towards it up the hill from the other side, then Charlie drove away down a farm track and pulled up in a barnyard. He stopped the engine and turned and looked at her.

'You're a great girl, Rowan,' he said.

Then he opened the door and got out.

Rowan followed him into the old barn, high and cool like a rough-hewn cathedral. Swallow stood resting a hind leg, his nose in a corner. When he saw them, he lifted his head and fluttered his nostrils. Rowan went up to him and buried her face into his forelock. She was crying again and wanted to hide it. She felt so stupid, crying all day long like a ninny, in spite of being a heroine and a great girl. It was all too much for her. But when she looked up, Charlie was taking the saddle off.

'Lead him back,' he said.

'But—'

'This time, Rowan. He's had a very disturbing morning. Running away, nearly hit by a car – it would be very stupid to have your first authorized ride on him after all that. You lead him home quietly for now.'

'Yes.'

It was true. If Swallow felt anything like she did, he would keel over before they went far. They untied him and led him out into the sunlight. Charlie put the saddle in the car. He went to get into the driving seat, and turned back.

'Another thing,' he said. 'It might not work. Remember that.'

'What do you mean?'

'For all we school him, he might always be too strong and dangerous for you. And there'll be no answer to that. You'll have to accept it. Accepting disappointment is the biggest thing of all to learn when it comes to horses. Ask anyone – Auntie Millie, Jerry, Mrs Prebble – from racing right down to ponies. Don't forget, Rowan, that I told you that.'

His gypsy dark eyes were very serious.

'No. I won't forget.'

He drove on and she started to lead Swallow down the farm track. Her head was swimming. So many things ahead of her – all sorts of things starting to happen: Josephine scheming to get the horse she had fallen in love with, Out of the West to be proved a star eventer, Priscilla to be made happy, High Hawes to thrive, and Swallow . . . Swallow to learn to bend his will to hers. Charlie's warning rang in her ears.

But for now ... the sun was shining. She was a marvel and a heroine, and Swallow was walking beside her, quiet and gentle. The downs stretched before her, disturbed only by the lane snaking down to High Hawes. Where I belong, thought Rowan. Me and Swallow. There was certainly nothing to cry about any more.

Swallow,
THE STAR

For Meg

Chapter One

Rowan got depressed sometimes, thinking she couldn't ride and never would. She was small for her twelve years, mousy in colour and quick and bright, but with an inferiority complex – especially when faced with her horsey friends, the Hawes, who had all ridden from age one. She kept her pony Swallow at the Hawes' farm, just up the road from where she lived in the village of Long Bottom. Swallow was a high-spirited and difficult pony, a great jumper but wild with it, and the Hawes could ride him better than she could and she knew, in her heart, that they all thought she should give him up for something easier. Hugh, the fourth down of the five Hawes, coveted Swallow, although he had a very good jumping pony of his own, called Cascade. Hugh was brash and boastful, the same age as Rowan.

'I've had a very interesting letter – it concerns Hugh.'

Rowan was in the Hawes's big kitchen when Auntie Millie Mildmay, the boss of the local Pony Club, came in waving a typewritten screed. Auntie Millie was an elderly, extremely tough, ex-point-to-point rider whom everybody loved and was scared stiff of at the same time. She was crippled with old injuries, had hairs on her chin, and eyes that went straight through you and out the other side.

Mrs Hawes waved her to a seat at the large table where her children and Rowan were in the various stages of eating fried potatoes and scrambled eggs which she was lobbing out at the stove.

'Make Mrs Mildmay a cup of coffee, Lizzie,' she said.

Lizzie was Rowan's best friend, although two years older. She was a thin, quick girl with pale frizzy hair that made a halo round her head. She, too, had an inferiority complex because Hugh, who was younger, was a better rider than she was – or so she thought. He was much bolder and braver, but their older brother Charlie said having sense counted for a lot and she had more sense than Hugh. Charlie was eighteen and the best of the lot. Rowan adored him.

'What concerns me?' Hugh asked. 'Something nice?'

'Very,' said Auntie Millie. 'But it's for your mother to say. Wait till she sits down.'

'I want something nice to happen to me,' said Shrimp, who was the youngest.

'Don't we all?' said her mother, coming to the table. 'Why is Hugh so lucky?'

She sat down next to Millie Mildmay and took the letter Millie handed her. She read it through, then read it again, while everyone politely waited to find out what it was all about. Impatiently.

Hugh said, 'Well?'

Mrs Hawes looked at Auntie Millie and grimaced.

'I thought Hugh,' Auntie Millie said. 'Unless, of course, you disagree with a child of yours being involved in this sort of thing.'

'What sort of thing?' Hugh shouted.

His mother looked at him thoughtfully. 'It's a film producer, looking for a boy to play a part in a film, involving some very difficult riding.'

'Hugh can't act,' Shrimp said. 'He was a terrible Mr Toad.'

'I can ride!'

'That's what they want,' Auntie Millie said. 'I think they say it's just the riding – there's already a boy playing the part, but he has to have a stand-in for the riding. That's the job that's going. They've written to several Pony Clubs to try and find someone.'

'Of course I can do it!' Hugh shouted.

'Well, I'm not against it,' his mother said. 'They should pay you for it, after all.'

'Of course. And hire of the pony. I think you supply your own pony. If you agree to it, I'll ring the producer and say I've got the man for the job.'

'If Hugh wants to, I'm quite agreeable,' his mother said.

'Of course I want to!'

'It'll make him unbearable,' Lizzie said. 'A film star! He's big-headed enough already.'

'We can all go to the first night, in Leicester Square!' Shrimp said.

'If we can fight our way in through Hugh's fans,' Charlie said solemnly.

'I'll get famous!' Hugh shouted.

'Famous for being a swollen-headed show-off!'

'He's bad enough already!'

'Do you mind?' their mother said sharply. 'Finish your disagreements outside, please, not at the table.'

Charlie said curiously, 'What do they mean by difficult riding? Underwater? Cantering backwards?'

'I'm sure I don't know,' said Auntie Millie. 'The young man will come down and see you, I dare say.

The producer is a stepbrother of one of my godsons. Whatever it is, I'm sure Hugh will cope.'

Hugh grinned. His blue eyes jeered across the table at the girls. He had short blond hair and was wiry and tough and was obviously going to be rather handsome, which depressed them utterly. Lizzie and Rowan slipped out to the stables as soon as they had finished.

'Trust him to get a job like that! Why didn't they want a girl?' Lizzie moaned. Then she added crossly, 'But if they'd wanted a girl, I suppose Shrimp would've got it.'

Not only did poor Lizzie think that her younger brother rode better than she did, she also suspected that ten-year-old Shrimp did. Unlike the rest of the Hawes, Lizzie was not totally committed to The Horse.

'I suppose you want to go for a ride?' she said to Rowan. 'Not just mess about?' she added hopefully.

'Yes, I want to go for a ride.'

Rowan wasn't allowed to ride out on Swallow alone. If there was no one to ride with, she had to ride in the school or in the small fenced field, which was boring.

'I'll ride Jones,' Lizzie decided.

Jones was the pony everyone thought Rowan ought to buy because he was good and honest and did everything right without frightening the living daylights out of his rider. He was a dark blue roan of nondescript breeding, but well made. Not as handsome as Swallow, of course – was any pony? (No.) Swallow put his head over the door of his loosebox and gave a low knucker of welcome when he saw the girls coming. He had been got in from the field and groomed before tea and he knew a bit of fun was now in the offing. It was April and his blanket clip was growing out, his nearly black coat gleaming with wellbeing, showing the slightly blueish cast which had prompted Rowan to christen him Swallow. He was just over fourteen hands, a Welsh with a dash of thoroughbred, Charlie said (although nobody knew for sure), aged about six. He had a mysterious past, having been found roaming, and although Rowan technically now owned him, he had been stolen in the past and no one had ever found out who his original owners had been. Rowan had nightmares sometimes about them turning up and claiming him.

Rowan hugged him and kissed his soft, golden brown nose as she pulled his bridle on. In the next box Cascade kicked the door and put his eager white head out to see where Hugh had got to. He wanted to go out too, but Hugh wasn't allowed to ride with Rowan and Swallow, as he would never go steadily. Charlie insisted that Swallow was only ridden steadily out on the downs, with no galloping; and only a short canter *uphill* in one or two special places. And no cantering coming home. He was very strict.

'I want you to succeed on Swallow, Rowan,' he said. 'Not get carted and frightened to death.'

Rowan was slowly getting more confident, but the pony's nature wasn't going to change.

'This sort,' Charlie said, 'they're tearaways still, even when they've gone thirty.'

The two girls saddled up and rode out into the lane. High Hawes lay near the top of the long down that enclosed the village, and they could ride out through an old oak wood above the house straight onto the fine old turf of the down. Rowan loved the spring evenings, riding through the uncurling green of the woods and smelling the fresh growth pushing out of the earth, and the damp peat turned up by the ponies' hooves. Swallow went eagerly as always. She never had to touch him with her heels and often had to remind herself not to hold onto his mouth too strongly.

'Don't fight him,' Charlie said. 'Give and take.'

Except she did the giving and he did the taking.

But dependable Jones kept a steady pace coming out through the gate onto the lovely turf. This is where Cascade always bolted off with Hugh encouraging him. Swallow curvetted and pranced to show what he wanted, but Rowan tucked him close to dear Jones and tried to make herself relax and flump in the saddle. A relaxed bottom told him no go, Charlie said. Pretend you're a big fat lady. (Auntie Millie said Charlie wasn't a brilliant teacher, more a doer.)

'I wish I could be a film star,' Lizzie said. 'Why does it have to be Hugh?'

Rowan desisted from pointing out that as they wanted a boy it was unlikely they would choose Lizzie.

'A stand-in's not a film star,' she said. 'More like a stuntman. They spend all their time hanging about waiting, I think. It might be miles away. I don't suppose we shall see anything of it.'

'It'll be fun to watch. They might have a famous film star in it, and we could talk to him, get his autograph.'

'Hugh might get discovered.'

'Like Shrimp said, he can't act. I don't suppose it'll be anything much. Shall we trot here?'

Lizzie was kind enough to ask. Hugh would have been away like the clappers by now. Rowan eased Swallow cautiously after Jones, feeling him bouncing beneath her. If he didn't get what he wanted he would buck. Rowan had learned to sit his bucks, but didn't like them. Charlie had told her that she must be firm with him. 'But try not to make it a fight. He's bound to win if it becomes a fight.' Lizzie was understanding, and kept her eye on Swallow as she increased the pace. If he behaved, there was a lovely long canter up a grassy track that made for the brow of the hill, and a steep bank at the top acted like buffers for a grateful Rowan. At last she had learned to keep Swallow in hand as she cantered, answering to the bit, no longer in danger of bolting . . . at least she thought she had . . . but she usually felt anxious. She recalled Hugh's total confidence and courage in riding, how he laughed as he turned in the saddle to see who was keeping up with him. She knew she had a long way to go. She was determined to be good enough to master Swallow completely, and laugh too, instead of biting her lip nervously. It was all right for Lizzie – she didn't care; she just wanted to enjoy herself, no more. With her lifetime's practice, she couldn't help being good. But Lizzie had no competitive spirit. Rowan knew *she* had a competitive spirit, although she had done no more so far than win a Pony Club rosette in the Junior cross country on Jones, who did it all for you. (In the same event Hugh had ridden Swallow and been bucked off.)

Coming to the bank, Swallow dropped his nose and came back to a walk, and they scrambled up calmly. Rowan felt a great joy swell in her as they breasted the top of the down and saw the green humpbacks of the hills beyond basking in the evening sun – it seemed far more than eighteen months since she had been a city child with only roofs for a skyline and the smell of buses in her nostrils. She could scarcely remember her before-Swallow time – whatever did she *do* in those days? Piano lessons and extra dancing . . . what a waste of time! As the wind spun in her face she looked down the way they had come and saw the golden stone and thatch of the High Hawes farmhouse nestling beneath the oak wood as if it had grown there, surrounded by its old barns and horse yards. Below, the Hawes' fields ran down into the valley where the village lay, to meet the lazy river that wound through the bottom. The ponies stood there when it was hot, under the scraggy willows, and it was miles to catch them unless they decided to gallop up at the rattle of pony nuts in a bucket. It was a magic place to Rowan and she never stopped thinking how lucky she was.

When they got home they found Hugh in the yard working on Cascade with Charlie's clippers.

'Whatever have you done!' Lizzie shrieked in horror.

Cascade's mane lay in large chunks all over the yard and his crest was now bare and shaved. Hugh was standing back regarding it critically.

'It suits him, don't you think?'

'No, it looks terrible! Poor Cascade!'

The pony turned his head, ears pricked, as Swallow and Jones came past. Rowan thought the hogging quite suited him, as he was a chunky pony, a flea-bitten grey, with a strong crest. It made him look chunkier still, like a little battle horse.

'I like it,' she said, to be fair.

Lizzie said, 'It's only because you can't be bothered to keep his mane pulled and you hate plaiting.'

Hugh grinned. True. Cascade was in the Pony Club teams and Auntie Millie expected the ponies to be properly turned out for competitions.

They brushed the ponies off and turned them out together. Rowan had to go home to get her homework done, so she fetched her bike and whizzed down the hill into the village. She lived in rather a smart house converted from a barn, but since her father had departed to live with his secretary, her mother was looking for a smaller house. It was too big for two.

'It's absolutely got – *got* – to be near High Hawes,' Rowan had stipulated.

'You could always rent one of their looseboxes to live in,' her mother said with a grin.

Luckily they got on well and, after the shock and strangeness of being left, they were happy enough, although short of money. Mr Watkins had been a very ambitious and impatient man, difficult to live with. He had regretted leaving London to live in the country, but Rowan and her mother loved it.

'Hugh's going to be a film star!' Rowan told her mother the exciting news. 'Pity it's him, mind you.' She thought Charlie would be a brilliant film star, with his gorgeous dark eyes, gaunt cheeks and tousled black curls. All the Hawes were fair, except Charlie. (Rowan wanted to marry Charlie later.)

'He'll like that, I should imagine. He's not a shrinking violet, is he?'

Visiting the estate agents, Rowan's mother found out that there was a cottage in the village for sale, but it had once been a shop and was more or less derelict. Long Bottom consisted of only one street, meandering along the valley beside the river, and as there were only about a hundred houses in it finding one for sale was not easy.

'Your father will say it's rubbish, but it could be done up. It's got a really long garden at the back, goes down to the river, and a stable. The shop used to deliver with a horse and cart, years ago. I thought perhaps it was meant – you know – you being so pony-mad.'

'Oh, yes, I know it. It's next door to that funny old woman Mrs Brundle, who takes in injured animals. She rescued Birdie – Lizzie's pony – that's where they got her from. It's nice. I'd love to live there.'

Rowan spoke with enthusiasm, as the cottage was even nearer High Hawes than their present house. The old shop was on the corner where the lane that ran up the hill to the farm left the village street.

'Do buy it! It would be lovely. I could bring Swallow down to stay the night sometimes.'

Her own stable! She knew perfectly well Swallow would hate it, being separated from his friends, but the thought was lovely.

She got out her homework and set to.

Chapter Two

'They're coming! They're coming!' Shrimp rushed into the kitchen. 'A great big car! A woman in shades and a man with a cigar – they've parked in the front yard. Charlie's talking to them.'

Joan Hawes said firmly, 'If you children are going to stay in the kitchen and gawp during this interview you're to behave yourselves. No interrupting!'

Hugh was unusually quiet, looking as if he had rather gone off the idea of being a film star.

Rowan and Lizzie and Shrimp huddled up at the end of the table and tried not to feel giggly.

Charlie came in and said, 'The film people are here.'

He stood back and ushered in two people. There was no sign of the cigar, but the woman was wearing dark glasses, and looked very sharp and towny, and had jangling bracelets and a large file clamped to her flat bosom, and the man was rather shaggy-looking in a purple anorak and suede boots. He was quite young and had a friendly face, and eyes that roved everywhere. He came forward to shake hands with Joan Hawes.

'I'm Ron Phillips, in charge of locations, and this is Debbie Manners, our casting director. I think you've been told what our brief is?'

'Joan Hawes,' said Joan Hawes, shaking hands. 'This is my son Charlie, who is in charge of the horses here, and this is Hugh, who Mrs Mildmay thinks might fit the bill for the riding part.'

'Oh dear, he's fair,' said Debbie Manners.

'Nobody said what he needed to look like.'

'No, of course. The boy we have starring in the part is dark, but if Hugh is suitable it's easily overcome with a wig.'

Lizzie gave Rowan a great nudge of glee and Shrimp nearly fell off her chair trying not to laugh.

'He won't be seen in close-up, of course.'

'What is he required to do? Will you have a coffee, or a drink?'

Charlie pulled out seats for the visitors and Joan made coffee and Ron Phillips said what a lovely place it was and Hugh sat in silence digesting the bit about the wig.

When they were all settled Debbie told them what the film was about.

'It's a film about the life of a famous jockey, Fred Archer, who rode in the eighteen seventies and eighties. At the beginning, we have scenes from his childhood. He has to be shown being schooled by his father on a rather wild pony – then there are some hunting scenes in which he is required to give the lead over a difficult jump, and then one scene where he has to jump a racehorse over a hedge. That's all. The boy we have in the role can't ride well enough. He made out he could in the audition, but I'm afraid he was exaggerating.'

'Hugh could do that,' Joan said. 'I was thinking it was going to be something stunty, but that's just plain riding, isn't it?'

'Oh, yes. But of course he has to show that he is an outstanding rider. That's the point we're making – an outstanding rider at an early age.'

Hugh began to look more enchanted. 'Do you supply the pony, or us? And the racehorse?'

'Mrs Mildmay said you had your own pony who would do whatever was wanted.'

'Yes, I have!'

Charlie said, 'And there's a string of racehorses just

over the hill, belong to a friend, if you want a race-horse that jumps a hedge.'

Ron Phillips said to Debbie, 'That's a point. We could shoot the whole thing in one site.'

'You mean here?' she said.

'From what I've seen of it, it would be ideal. The field down the bottom there, by the stream, with those willow trees and the old village behind – it's perfect for the schooling scene. And Auntie Millie said she could lay on the hunt and find a good jump for that – and if the racehorses are to hand as well – brilliant! Everything from one base. The guv'nor will love that.'

'Yes, you could be right.'

Ron turned to Joan Hawes and said, 'We hadn't been anticipating this – that we should shoot the scenes here. But, having seen it, I think it would be great if we could. How would you feel about having the film unit here for a few days?'

'What does it entail? Total disruption?'

'Not total. Some disruption, yes. There will be a lot of vehicles and people – everyone is amazed at how many people it takes to shoot a bit of film. And we would need vehicle access into the fields. We wouldn't need to come into the house.'

Joan Hawes looked at Charlie. 'It's up to you, really. You're in charge of outside.'

Since her husband Fred, a horse dealer, had died several months ago, the two eldest Hawes, Josephine and Charlie, had taken over the running of the yard, providing for the family. Times were hard.

'I don't see it as a problem. We can move the ponies, and the fields are dry enough to take the lorries. The pony fields, that is – you can't use the hay fields until after the hay is cut.'

'No. We'd only want one field. Perhaps we could have a good look round? And the pony – perhaps see Hugh in action?'

'Yes, fine.'

They all retreated outside, the girls following, agog not to miss anything. Charlie whispered to his mother, 'They should pay us well for this. We're in luck.'

Hugh ran ahead with a head collar and fetched Cascade out of his loosebox.

'Oh, my God, he's got no mane!' cried Debbie. 'We can't have that!'

Charlie said, 'Ponies were often hogged in the last century!'

'They might have been, but I can't see Tom wanting that. A wild pony, lots of mane and tail flying, that's what we want.' She looked round and saw Swallow's head over the door, taking in the excitement. 'Like that,' she said.

There was complete silence among the Hawes. Rowan felt her stomach tell her she wanted to be sick.

'Is that your pony too?' Debbie asked Hugh.

'No.' Then Hugh added, 'But I ride him. He's very wild, like you want.'

Charlie said sternly, 'He's not yours.' He turned to Debbie and said, 'He belongs to Rowan here,' and indicated the shrinking Rowan.

Debbie smiled at her brightly. 'Would you lend your pony, dear?'

Rowan couldn't answer. For Hugh to show off on! To gallop wildly and jump great hedges – everything they were keeping away from to calm Swallow down. But if she said no, there wasn't another pony, not to do those things. Fable wouldn't, Jones wasn't showy enough, Birdie didn't belong to them, Snowball was too small, the Armchair too ugly. Diamond likewise. Hugh was looking at her with an expression that almost frightened her: such an intense, defiant stare from his sky-blue eyes . . . why, she found herself thinking, he could well be a film star with his strong personality and instinct for showing-off . . . how could she stand in his way at the start of a great career? She looked helplessly at Charlie.

Charlie said sweetly, 'Can we think about this one? It's not as simple as it seems.'

'Of course. But could we see the pony? Could he ride it for us?'

Charlie looked at Rowan.

'Yes,' she said chokily.

Film people tended to stampede over ordinary people, she had heard her father say once. They thought if you paid enough, people would agree to anything. All the Hawes had dropped rather quiet at the turn in the proceedings, for they all knew exactly how tricky it was.

Charlie helped Hugh saddle up and Hugh stood Swallow out in the yard in front of Debbie and Ron. It was quite obvious, in the April sunlight, that he knew he was being admired. Hugh knew how to get him to stand, as if in a show, with his legs square and his head up, rein loose. He looked boldly at the film people and the wind blew his heavy mane up over his crest and he sold himself: Swallow, the star. Rowan knew she didn't stand a chance.

'Charming!' cried Debbie. 'Delightful! Tom will just love it!'

'Can you just move around the field, show us some action?' said Ron.

Charlie opened the gate and said something fiercely to Hugh as he went through, which Rowan didn't catch. They all stood in a line along the fence, watching, and Hugh made Swallow trot down the hill, then turned him and came back at a very strong canter, nearly a gallop. Swallow bucked three times, and Rowan was pretty sure that Hugh had made him do it, although she had no idea how. She spent all her time trying to make him not do it. He pulled up very abruptly and Swallow churned around, excited, head up. He did look splendid, there was no doubt.

'Wonderful!' Debbie cried. 'And he's good at jumping?'

'I'll show you!' Hugh shouted.

'You will not!' Charlie shouted back. And to Debbie, 'Take my word for it, he can jump anything.'

Whose side was Charlie on? Rowan had no idea. Dear Charlie saying Swallow could jump anything . . . and she too nervous to ask him even to canter . . . it was pathetic. She felt a great despair come over her, and couldn't bear to look.

'That's enough,' Charlie said to Hugh. 'Put him away.'

The film people made to depart, going through into the front yard. They all followed. As they went to get into their car, Charlie's eventer, Out of the West, stuck his head out over his door, all ears and eyes. Debbie the casting director was immediately smitten by his gorgeous head.

'Oh my word, what a beautiful beast! Can we get him in our film as well? Could he be the racehorse that jumps the hedge?'

'Hugh doesn't ride this horse,' Charlie said.

'I could,' said Hugh.

'What a looker!' said Debbie, peering in over the door. Certainly they all knew Out of the West was a looker, also that he was young, wayward and a very strong ride. He was being trained by Charlie for a rich man who thought they would all make a fortune out of him some day. Charlie thought they might, but not as soon as Mr Hicks thought. Mr Hicks had bought him for his sixteen-year-old daughter Priscilla, but had come, with great difficulty, to accept that the horse was much too much for a young girl. Charlie lived in hope that his own horse Wilfred might prove a more suitable horse for Priscilla, and was training them both together towards that end. The finances of High Hawes now depended largely on Mr Hicks.

'Well,' said Debbie, smiling, 'you seem to have everything we need here. We didn't realize it would be so good. Perhaps if we ring you tomorrow, we can talk terms and make some plans? When I've got back to our director . . . we are ready to start quite soon and it would be great if we could have a quick decision.'

She spoke in such a way that suggested she did not expect to be told no. Nobody ever told her no, Rowan thought, looking at her hard, bold face and piercing eyes. Rowan wished she was like that, bossy and tough. She knew she had lost before she started. How could she stand in Swallow's way, any more than Hugh's? He was a natural star. A little bit of her felt excited at the thought of seeing him in the cinema. She could have a DVD and watch him over and over again, being a star. If only it wasn't Hugh on his back . . . if she'd been good enough she could have got the job, even if she was a girl . . . had a haircut, and been filmed from the back . . . She went into a dream, seeing herself as the infant Fred Archer. She knew about Fred Archer, because she had a book at home which described his sad and dramatic life.

After the film people had departed they all went back to the house to discuss what had happened. Rowan immediately said she didn't mind Hugh riding

Swallow, because she knew she couldn't stand in the way of this great bonanza for the Hawes.

Lizzie whispered, 'Liar! You *do* mind.'

'Shut up,' Rowan hissed back sharply.

Hugh said complacently, 'Charlie did give him to you, after all. You didn't buy him.'

This was so patently a twisting of the complicated route by which Rowan had come to own Swallow that the rest of the family turned on Hugh and told him to shut up. But Hugh was on a high of excitement, thinking he was going to be a film star, and only laughed.

Rowan said hurriedly, 'I wouldn't want to stop the whole thing happening. She did seem to want Swallow.'

'He's the only one suitable,' Charlie said, 'apart from Cascade.'

Josephine, the eldest Hawes, who gave Rowan most of her lessons, said quietly, 'You haven't got to, Rowan. We don't mind either way.'

'I do,' said Hugh.

'We don't care about you. It's Rowan that matters.'

'No. Honestly. It's all right.'

In spite of their consideration, she knew perfectly well that they all wanted the excitement – and the money – of the film being made.

'Well, I dare say it will only take a day or two,' Joan Hawes said, 'It's not a whole epic – only a little scene. You needn't get big ideas, Hugh.'

But everyone could see it was a good part. What had she said: the point of the scenes was to show that the boy was an outstanding rider? No wonder Hugh had such a cheesy grin on his face.

Of course, they were all very excited and gabbled about it all the evening and Rowan came round to seeing that it wasn't really a great disaster, but a great honour for Swallow, and she went home eventually with her jealous feelings dissipated. It just made her all the more determined to be good enough to ride Swallow.

But when she got home she found her mother had gone off to look at the cottage-cum-shop down the road. She went out of the house to go and find her and met Babar coming up to post a letter. Barbara Bailey was the farmer's daughter from Low Bottom Farm, who rode up at High Hawes where she had fallen for the chestnut cob known as the Armchair. All her life she had ridden her own knock-kneed, ewe-necked black weed called Diamond, and now she was suffering a guilt complex for having transferred her affections. The Hawes family called her Babar the

Elephant because of her shape, but she didn't mind. She talked like a yokel but was terribly clever at school, better than all of them.

She came along to the cottage with Rowan, and Rowan told her about the excitement up at the farm, and about Swallow being the chosen pony for Hugh.

'Cor, that's rotten on yer.' Babar understood immediately.

'Well, I don't mind,' Rowan said valiantly.

'Aye, but Hugh! Anyone but Hugh, I'd say. 'E's got designs on your pony, you can see it a mile off.'

'He hasn't!'

'Yeah, 'e wants 'im to ride in the team. Cascade's good, but 'e's not as good as Swallow, anyone can see that. And Mrs Mildmay, like, she said Swallow would be a JA if 'e got trained right, 'e's got such a lep in 'im.'

'What's a JA?'

'It's the top class for show-jumpers, ponies, that is. J stands for Junior.'

'I couldn't do that!'

'No, but Hugh could.'

Whose side was Babar on? Rowan wondered wildly. Her confidence was draining away by the minute. They had reached the cottage and Rowan could see her mother inside with the estate agent.

'You goin' to buy this old place?' Babar asked.

'I don't know. It's got a stable.'

'Aye. Old Mr Markham used it for his 'oss to deliver with. Ages ago, that is. It were a grocer's store.'

They went in a side gate and walked through into the back garden which was a tangle of elder and nettles. There were some old sheds, and the last one was quite a decent loosebox with a half-door, a brick floor and an old wooden manger along the back, its edge polished smooth with the rubbing of generations of horses. Rowan rubbed her fingers over the silky wood. She thought suddenly she would be happy with just any old pony, living here, and no competition. Just to hack out on, and enjoy, no traumas. No trying to keep up with the Hawes. Ride with them, but not compete. They were all natural competitors, even Lizzie, who pretended she wasn't. They couldn't help it. She would always be the one trying to keep up, and she didn't see how she ever would, not against them. Was it worth trying?

'Perhaps Swallow suits Hugh better than me,' she said sadly.

'They're two of a kind – bossy, pig-headed. Doesn't mean as they're suited though.'

'Hugh could ride anything.'

'Aye, but to get one that clicks with you, just right –
that's another thing. He clicks with Cascade, you see.
But Hugh – 'e's never satisfied, always looking for the
next thing, that's 'is trouble.'

'Lizzie didn't click with Birdie,' Rowan said,
considering Babar's philosophy. 'She likes Fable much
better.'

'That's what I mean. And yet Birdie's a much better
pony.'

'Matty didn't click with Birdie either!'

Birdie was a very pretty bay mare who had been
Lizzie's but, because she didn't like her, had been sold
to Matty Prebble, the village's show-jumping high-
flyer. But at Pony Club Camp there had been an
accident. Matty had been badly injured and the
aggressive Mrs Prebble had sent Birdie back to High
Hawes demanding her money back. As she had no
evidence that the accident was Birdie's fault – in fact,
the evidence was to the contrary – Charlie refused to
pay her, and Birdie was now residing at High Hawes in
a sort of limbo, belonging to no one.

'Poor Birdie,' Rowan said.

'Birdie came from next door here,' Babar said. 'Mrs
Brundle rescued her. Did you know that? Like she
rescues everything.'

By looking through a window above the manger they could see into Mrs Brundle's back garden and, to prove the point, they could make out a large aviary housing two barn owls and several pens containing a seagull, some hedgehogs, a small badger and lots of ex-battery hens with no feathers. Grazing on the lawn was a thin donkey and an even thinner pony. Lots of cats and dogs lay out on the back terrace of the once very beautiful house, the Old Rectory, which now looked as if it, in its turn, needed rescuing.

'You'll 'ave 'er for a neighbour, come you live 'ere,' Babar said. 'She's bonkers, like. All right, but bonkers.'

Rowan tried to picture her mother being neighbourly with old Mrs Brundle, who wore a terrible old gabardine mac tied round the middle with a piece of baler twine. Mrs Bundle, she was called by the Hawes. Rowan had thought her mother was making very good progress at turning into a countrywoman, mostly helped by her friendship with Joan Hawes and getting involved with the Pony Club. Coming from Putney, she had been frightfully smart and gone to the hairdresser's every week, and the house had been like an advertisement for polish and floor cleaners, but now dishevelment was setting in on all fronts and Rowan didn't have to keep changing her shoes outside the kitchen door, and they ate off their laps watching the television instead of at a polished table with a bottle of wine.

Rowan and Babar left the stable and went in by the back door to the kitchen, as it was open. The kitchen was ancient, still with a stone sink and a pantry and no sign of any machinery except a terrible old gas cooker. The room beyond, with the shop window, was large and light and had stairs going up out of it to the bedrooms, which all seemed on different levels.

'It's awfully small,' Rowan said to her mother.

Her mother had obviously changed her mind about earlier dreams of a sweet little country cottage, and was looking rather depressed.

'No bathroom,' she said glumly.

And the loo was outside, Rowan discovered.

'But only just,' the estate agent beamed. 'It could easily be joined on, a downstairs cloakroom added.'

'It needs such a lot doing to it!'

'Oh, come, a property of character!'

'Too much character.'

The estate agent drove off and they all walked home together. Mrs Watkins said they ought to go up and visit Matty sometime.

'She's out of hospital now and very bored, I understand, poor child.'

'She could come and watch the filming,' Rowan said.

Her mother said, 'I'm glad it's Hugh they wanted and not you!'

'However could it be me?' Rowan asked in tones of deep scorn.

'I thought you were a good little rider now,' her mother said brightly.

'Well, you thought wrong.'

Her parents were hopeless. After six lessons her father had thought she could ride. He thought anyone could do it. Her mother was nearly as bad.

'I'm just a beginner. I shan't be any good for years!'

'Oh dear. Well, you haven't got to do it, you know. It's supposed to be fun, not a disaster.'

Fun! Just at that moment Rowan couldn't see it.

Chapter Three

Great excitement stirred in Long Bottom at the news of a film company coming to perpetuate their sleepy valley. High Horse Equestrian Centre was suddenly on the map. Dates were fixed. Rowan groomed Swallow every day until he shone as never before. 'You'd think Hugh would do it – he's getting all the glory,' Lizzie said, but the girls knew Hugo never groomed or cleaned his tack unless violently coerced. Mrs Prebble called to see what was gong on, and Joan Hawes invited her to bring Matty up to watch. They all loathed Mrs Prebble, but they were desperately sorry for Matty. Matty was fourteen and, away from her mother, all right. Mrs Prebble had been very ambitious for her and taken her show jumping all over the country but, since her accident on Birdie last summer, she was stuck in a wheelchair most of the time, or lurching about on a pair of crutches.

She came out into the stableyard in her wheelchair and sat watching Rowan brushing out Swallow's thick tail.

'Where's Birdie?' she asked.

'She's in the field.'

'Doesn't anybody ride her?'

'She doesn't belong to us, does she? She's still yours. Charlie won't let us ride her.'

'Well, she's no good to me any more. Why don't you have her back?'

'I think it's money,' Rowan said. 'Your mother wants her money back and I think Charlie's spent it.'

'Oh, what good's money?' said Matty sweepingly. 'Ma's got tons. It's a shame if nobody rides her and she doesn't do anything. I'd forget about the money.'

All very well Matty saying that, Rowan thought, but Mrs Prebble had threatened to sue the Hawes family over Birdie.

'I thought you didn't like Birdie,' Rowan said.

'She didn't like me,' Matty said.

Charlie had said that the Prebbles expected too much of Birdie and got her all uptight; she was only young. Remembering her conversation with Babar, Rowan thought that poor Birdie hadn't found anybody yet to click with. Like me, she thought. Clicking with

397

Swallow wasn't really happening, however much she tried to pretend it was.

'When's the filming starting?' Matty asked.

'Tomorrow. That's why he's got to look good.'

It was the week of half term so they were all going to watch. Joan Hawes had asked for it, not wanting Hugh to miss school, and the film company had agreed, mainly because it suited them as well. Apparently the rest of the film was already shot, and only the childhood scenes remained to be made. Tom, the director, said that, if all went according to plan, the film would be in the cinemas before the end of the year.

Rowan kissed Swallow's soft muzzle. Swallow gave her a gentle, friendly rub. If only he was as sweet when you were on his back!

'I'd like to be a film star,' Matty said. 'Wish it was me.'

Rowan felt embarrassed. Poor Matty! She was rather beautiful, with pale skin, large violet-blue eyes and shining black hair. But she'd never be a film star now, with her damaged leg. It wasn't for ever, apparently, but walking again was going to take a long time.

Rowan said, on an impulse, 'Couldn't you ride a quiet pony – instead of the wheelchair, I mean? Just for transport. You could come up here then without your mother having to bring you.'

'I don't know. Perhaps I could. My mother keeps talking about when I will ride again.'

'I don't mean show jumping. I mean, like a bicycle,' Rowan said.

Mrs Prebble was such a forceful mother. Thank goodness I don't have one of those! Rowan thought. They were quite a common breed in the Pony Club. Matty was an only child, and poor Mrs Prebble was now frustrated by no longer having a competitor. If Matty became able to ride again, she wouldn't get a bicycle sort of pony, but no doubt another show-jumper.

Now that the filming was imminent Hugh had gone much quieter and they all guessed he was quite nervous. He had had interviews with the director, Tom, a terse, short-tempered man whom everyone jumped to attention for, and the cameraman, who was called Ernie and seemed very laid back. Hugh had to appear in three scenes: one in the bottom field in which he was being schooled over jumps by his father (who was quite a well-known actor), one in which he had to give a lead over a jump to his elders and betters while out hunting, and the last scene, which was set in a racing yard where he had to ride in a string of thoroughbreds at exercise and jump a hedge at the whim of his trainer. All these scenes had been discussed with Charlie and Mrs Mildmay, and Mrs Mildmay had arranged for some suitable people to come along for the hunting shot, and Charlie had arranged for his racing friend Jerry Patterson to bring six of his horses over for the day, with riders, to shoot the hedge-jumping scene. In the film story the racehorses had been young flat racers who had never jumped in their lives, and the young Fred Archer had jumped the hedge at the bidding of his master on a horse that had never been asked to jump before, which he did with consummate ease. In the film, of course, they would use a horse who knew how to jump a hedge. Nobody had quite decided which horse this was going to be, as Jerry said his horses only jumped hedges when presented at them flat out from fifty metres off, and in the film the horse was required to jump almost from a standstill, turning out of the string to do so.

'There's only one horse around here that will do that,' Charlie said. 'And that's one we can't use.'

'Out of the West.' They all knew who he meant.

They all assumed Auntie Millie would turn up with

a suitable animal on the day. That scene was to be shot last.

They hadn't counted on how the attractions of getting in on the act affected people. When Priscilla Hicks heard how Out of the West had been admired by Debbie, the casting director, she had cried out with enthusiasm, 'Oh, do let him be in the film! It would be marvellous!'

Charlie said, 'It would be crazy!'

'But you know he can do it!'

'He could if I was riding him, but I haven't got the part,' Charlie pointed out. 'Hugh's got to do it.'

'But Hugh's a brilliant rider! Everyone says so.'

'He rides ponies well. He's never ridden a horse like Out of the West.'

'But – surely? – Dad would love to have the horse in a film.'

'It's very spooky conditions for a horse, filming. The cameras and the sound boom overhead – all that sort of thing. Anything could happen.'

'Oh, do, *do* get them to use Jack!' (Out of the West was called Jack for every day.)

They all knew that Debbie, the casting director, still hankered after using the horse. It was true that Out of the West was spectacularly good-looking, with a natural presence. He was black, with a coat you could use as a mirror covering rippling muscle. He was shortly to take part in his first One Day Event, ridden by Charlie. Priscilla still thought she would be good enough to ride him eventually when Charlie had schooled him sufficiently, but Charlie said he would never be a girl's horse. Not Priscilla's, at least. He hadn't exactly said this to Priscilla yet. One had to be so tactful with the Hicks family, for Mr Hicks was another of the Mrs Prebble variety, an ambitious parent. Fortunately Priscilla was getting on quite well with Charlie's horse, Wilfred. She came for lessons three times a week, having recently left school. She was a rather spoilt rich girl, almost as good looking as Out of the West, with spectacular long, curling red hair and large brown come-hither eyes which she used to good effect on the susceptible Charlie. He was much attracted to Priscilla, but disappointed to find her rather stupid.

Rowan suspected that Priscilla would be in her element on filming day, posing in front of the director. In that she was not mistaken, for the Hicks' car rolled into the yard shortly after the director's on the first filming morning. There was no shortage of spectators, for Mrs Prebble had brought Matty over and Rowan and Lizzie and Shrimp were all lined up to see Hugh go through his paces. Charlie had taken on the job of horse adviser, the director having little idea of how one schooled a pony over jumps.

'The script says that Fred was more frightened of his father than the pony, which was very wild. His father ran after the pony with a whip and threw clods of earth at it to make it jump.'

Tom Ballantyne, the director, talked to Charlie in the yard while the crew drove the gear down to the field where the filming was to take place. The ponies had all been gathered up and put in the stables for the day. There seemed to be an amazing number of vehicles, with vans for dressing rooms, make-up, costume and an office as well as trucks containing the filming gear and cars full of electricians, and people with titles like grips, best boy, gaffer and runner. Catering was to arrive later in another cavalcade of kitchen, serving and dining-room vehicles.

The Hawes family and their friends looked on in astonishment as all this paraphernalia came up the lane to park around the farm. Half the village trailed up behind it to see what was going on. Hugh by now had gone as white as a sheet but had been rousted out of hiding by the film people and taken to the costume and make-up vans, presumably to be turned into a lookalike of the young actor, Sam Marshall, who played the part of Fred.

Sam Marshall, the Hawes could see, bore no resemblance to Hugh at all, save that he was the same shape.

Charlie did not look too happy to hear what was required by the script.

'I hope it won't need too many takes – throwing clods of earth and all that. He's a pretty excitable pony without someone running behind him with a whip and chucking things.'

'Good,' said Tom Ballantyne. 'Exactly what we want.'

Luckily Rowan was too far away to hear this exchange. She was busy getting Swallow ready, for Charlie had said, as it was her pony, she could bring him down the field and be his handler. Everyone else had to stay out of the way. Swallow was already pop-eyed in his loosebox, excited by all the unusual traffic, and twirled round in the yard when she brought him out. Such was her lack of confidence that Rowan was now frightened he could tear out of her hands before she got him to the required place. But Charlie came over and Swallow calmed down.

They went down the field together. The technicians had set up their gear and there was a sort of railway line with a trolley on it that ran along carrying the camera and the cameraman. One of the large willow trees had keeled over some time ago and the director seemed to think it was just the thing for Swallow to jump.

He came up to them and said, 'What we want – first, Archer senior and young Fred on the pony – we see them back-view going down the field. That will be your boy. Then we have a close-up scene of the father telling young Fred to ride the pony round, put it through its paces, etc. – that will require Sam on the pony. Then – cut – the pony cantering away and jumping etc., with young Hugh on it. He'll have to do it a few times as we shall want both long shots and close-ups.'

Rowan felt quite nervous, so what on earth must Hugh be feeling? He came out of the costume van with the young actor, Sam, and Rowan hardly recognized him. They both wore identical clothes, old-fashioned boys' gear, knickerbockers and stockings and Norfolk jackets, and ugly caps pulled well down, and they did look amazingly alike. Sam was said to be fourteen, but his voice hadn't broken and, close up, he was naturally dark with large soulful eyes accentuated by make-up.

Hugh came up to get Swallow, and had the grace to blush when he came face to face with Rowan. He mumbled something and pulled the stirrups down. He rode away to meet the actor playing his father, who looked familiar to Rowan, but she didn't know who he was.

Sam came over to Rowan and stood watching.

'That your pony?'

'Yes.'

'Why didn't they give you the job, riding? It's all long shot. You're the same shape.'

'I can't ride as well as Hugh.'

'I'd have thought, if it was your pony, you'd be better.'

Rowan didn't like to say he thought wrong. She didn't know what to say after that, not knowing anything about the acting trade. It seemed to her that it involved a lot of hanging around doing nothing. But Sam, although so glamorous, seemed a patient sort of boy and stood glumly watching.

'Do you get off school for this?' Rowan asked.

'I'm at acting school. We get time off for jobs.'

'Do you like it?'

'It's all right,' he said, unenthusiastic.

It occurred to Rowan that he too might have an ambitious parent in the background, enrolling him in an acting school. It wasn't the sort of thing a child did for himself.

When he was called for his scene, talking to his father while mounted on Swallow, it was quickly apparent that he couldn't ride and that Swallow was not going to stand still for even a few minutes. Charlie had to dive in quickly to catch Swallow by the bridle and stop him tearing off.

'He's got to stand still,' Tom said tetchily.

Charlie said shortly, 'We were asked to supply a wild pony. This is a wild pony.'

'Well, for this shot he's got to stand still. You must hold him out of view.'

Rowan had to come up and stand at his quarters to stop him swinging away from the camera. If she bent down she wouldn't be seen in the film. At the front end Charlie had to block Swallow from swinging forward and duck down when the camera rolled. Sam had to sit undismayed, listening to a harangue from his father.

This took six takes. Rowan couldn't believe the frustration of it. When they got Swallow right, a helicopter came over, drowning out the sound. A second time a tractor went up the lane. Once when Swallow stood really still, Sam fluffed his lines. Twice Swallow swung out of shot, in spite of his sweating handlers, and Rowan got trodden on painfully. When at last the take was successful, it seemed to have taken all morning.

Then they had to film the father saying his lines against the correct background which – without Swallow's involvement – took only two takes. At Tom's bidding Hugh came and mounted Swallow again and Sam disappeared back to one of the numerous vans. A props girl came down the field with a driving whip which she gave to the actor, and then proceeded to empty a bucket of clods of earth around a marked area.

Charlie and Rowan had to retreat, and left Hugh riding an already agitated Swallow round behind the cameras to 'get him hyped up'.

Charlie looked as worried as Rowan felt.

'He's hyped up enough already.'

Hugh shouted, 'If I jump the log, that'll get him tizzed up.'

'Idiot,' Charlie muttered.

It was apparent that Hugh wanted exactly what the director wanted, but for a different reason, to show off.

He was rising to the part, seeing himself on the wide screen. He turned Swallow and went bombing off towards the log. Swallow plunged and bucked and tore towards the jump with his ears pricked, soaring over with nearly a metre to spare. Hugh came belting back and Swallow put in three huge bucks which made Rowan wince. And no one had thrown any clods of earth yet or waved the whip.

'Great!' shouted Tom.

Hugh had to come and stand by his actor father while the clapper boy banged his boards together, and then set off at a great wave from the whip. The actor picked up one of the convenient clods of earth and flung it and shouted, 'You're racing, Fred, not out for a hack! *Racing!*' and Swallow, never having been subjected to such treatment in his life, went off down the field with a series of plunges and bucks that Hugh had considerable difficulty in sitting. The actor chased him furiously, waving the whip, and Hugh turned for the log.

Charlie groaned. Rowan felt herself come out in a cold sweat, thinking of herself in Hugh's place.

Swallow flew over the log, but on landing gave the biggest buck Rowan had ever seen and Hugh soared over his head with a terrific crump in the grass.

Swallow turned and came up the field, bucking and kicking, stirrups and reins flying. Rowan ran towards him, horrified at the turn of events, and shouted out to him, 'Whoa, Swallow! Steady, boy, steady!'

So used to these words from his owner, Swallow did in fact slow down and when Rowan ran towards him he dropped his head and allowed himself to be caught.

Charlie, meanwhile, had to run down to see what had happened to Hugh. Tom was shouting 'Cut!' and then, 'Great stuff! First rate! Get that pony back here!'

Hugh, however, seemed to be a long time getting up.

'God almighty, don't say he's hurt himself!' Tom said angrily.

He waited, tight-lipped, as Hugh came limping back with Charlie. Hugh was pale, but not noticeably damaged.

'OK?' barked Tom.

Hugh nodded.

'We'll do that again, but don't fall off this time.'

Rowan could see quite plainly that all the stuffing, along with the arrogance, had been knocked out of Hugh, and that Tom had no idea, absolutely no idea, of what the situation was. He saw only his film. He said to his PA girl, 'You got the boy insured, I take it?' and she nodded and said, 'Yes, of course.'

Charlie said, 'Give him ten minutes. He took a hard fall.' He spoke with such authority that Tom gave him a stern look, but did not demur.

'We'll shoot close-up on Stan.'

Stan was Fred's father, who then went through his shouting and swearing with the camera close to his face. Hugh sat on the grass, silently, and Charlie stayed with him, while Rowan led Swallow around, letting him snatch at the grass. He was sweating and nervous, but her presence reassured him. Rowan was thinking that even if Hugh was now regretting his role, he had no option but to go on with it. Perhaps he was wishing he had broken his leg?

But Hugh was made of stern Hawes stuff and when the close-up filming was finished he remounted Swallow without a word and turned him away sharply for a repeat performance.

This time he had to canter some circles, with the earth clods flying, which went without a hitch.

'It's jumping that gets that little beggar going,' Charlie said to Rowan. 'He adores it, you can see. He's got enormous talent.'

He regretted his words, for he saw Rowan's thoughts plainly registered in her abject eyes: if only I could ride him well enough to do him justice! Rowan didn't say

411

anything, actually thinking she would never be able to ride him at all after this.

'Now jump the log again!'

This time the jump was filmed in close-up.

'It doesn't matter if you fall off this time!' Tom shouted, as if to comfort. 'We just want you going over.'

Once again, Swallow went over with about a metre to spare, and the camera looked up, from behind, so that Hugh's face wouldn't show. Rowan could see that it was a spectacular shot, all swirling tail and flying hooves. Swallow bucked again on landing but Hugh stayed on.

'Cut!'

Tom was transparently pleased. Rowan could see that directing was a very fraught business, getting it right when there were so many things to go wrong, from passing car noises to death of actor, and began to appreciate why the man got so uptight.

He even came up to Hugh and said, 'Well done! How are you feeling?'

'OK.'

But Rowan thought he looked terrible as she took Swallow's bridle to lead him back to the stable.

'We shoot the jump with the hunting men at three

o'clock. You report to the costume van at two and come up with the actors. Meanwhile you can go and get your lunch in the canteen. You too,' he added to Charlie and Rowan.

Charlie said to Hugh, 'You might do better to come back home for an hour.'

Hugh shook his head. 'I'm OK.'

Rowan sensed that he was humiliated by having fallen off, and didn't want to meet Lizzie and Shrimp and all the hangers-on in the yard. She felt a small pang of sympathy for him, surprisingly.

Auntie Millie had some strong words when she met them at the gate.

'If I'd known how that madman was going to treat that boy and the pony, I'd never had put them forward for it! Ridiculous! He's no sense at all!'

'No horse-sense,' Charlie agreed.

Rowan put Swallow in his box and untacked him and gave him a haynet. Charlie didn't want to eat in the canteen and nor did she – they went into the kitchen where her mother had helped Joan Hawes lay out a tableful of ham and Scotch eggs and salad.

'Where's Hugh?' his mother asked.

Charlie explained.

'I hope he's not knocked himself silly.'

'He's silly enough already,' Shrimp said. 'He *fell off*, Mum, right in front of the camera!'

Charlie said, 'You wouldn't have sat that buck either.'

'So what happens next?' Joan asked.

'He's only got to jump a fairly easy jump,' Auntie Millie said placatingly. 'It's that bit of fence in the corner of Sandpile field. He can ride up there when he's ready. Mr Sedgefield and his son are going to bring their horses up. They always refuse, so when they've tried and refused, the idea is that Hugh nips in and jumps it in front of them and gallops away. That seems to be what that madman wants. Really, if I'd known how stupid he is about horses I wouldn't have offered to help.'

'I think he might have got some good film, all the same,' Charlie said.

Rowan supposed Swallow would look pretty magnificent on the screen, but how would he behave when she came to ride him again?

In the lunch hour they discovered that Priscilla had been beguiling the film director and Debbie, the casting girl, with eulogies of how well Out of the West would jump the hedge in the scene that was to be shot the next day. They also discovered that the local press

414

had arrived and were taking photos of all and sundry. Priscilla led Out of the West out of his box and told them he was going to be the star the following day, and they took a photo of him with Priscilla smirking at his head. Charlie shook his head in despair. Rowan, furious, fetched Swallow out and got his photograph taken as well, and then Hugh came up from the canteen – 'Jolly good – roast turkey and roast potatoes, sprouts, Yorkshire pudding, gravy, apple pie and custard' – 'You're a fat pig already!' Shrimp shouted. 'Swallow will collapse!' Hugh now wore a smarter outfit with a white stock and breeches and boots, as befitted a boy going hunting in 1868. He was already mounting, to get his photo taken as well.

'Everyone's gone mad round here,' Charlie decided.

They all had to decamp up the lane to the field Auntie Millie had chosen for the hunt jump, and the same hanging about then ensued as the camera was set up and shots discussed. The horses that always refused arrived in their lorry and their riders were kitted out in ancient hunting gear, and mounted and sent down the field with Hugh and Swallow.

Everyone lined the fence to see the fun, Rowan once more with a sinking heart and Charlie distinctly worried. Hugh was cantering Swallow in circles to get him warmed up, but it was hardly necessary.

'When they started the first take, one of the refusing horses actually ruined everything by jumping the fence. His rider was so amazed he fell off and the horse galloped away and was quite a long time getting caught. Swallow, having got the idea, started bucking again before he was even asked to move. Tom was shouting angrily.

'Take two-hundred and sixty-one!' The clapper man leaped back and the three horses came hurtling up the field again. This time the first one refused and the second one crashed into its backside. Hugh was supposed to pull round to jump but there was no room and Swallow skidded into the ditch at the side of the fence and Hugh landed up his neck, and all but in the thorny hedge. Pushing himself back into the saddle he shouted angrily, 'The jump isn't wide enough!'

'You're supposed to be a brilliant rider, for heaven's sake!' Tom shouted back. 'That's the whole point of it. Find room!'

'That man is seriously brainless,' Auntie Millie snapped.

She started to climb the fence to stride into battle but before she could do so the horses went into action again. This time, as the two hunters jolted to a stand-still, Hugh pulled out wide and charged the hedge instead of the rails that were set in them.

Rowan heard Charlie's gasp of alarm.

Auntie Millie shouted out, 'You stupid boy!'

Swallow took off miles back and made a stupendous leap at the huge obstacle. He crashed through the top, sending twigs and leaves flying, and landed well out into the next field. Although he pecked and nearly went down Hugh sat him like a limpit, gathered him together and galloped away, no doubt feeling hugely smug and pleased with himself.

Tom was conferring with the cameraman, frowning – was he ever pleased? The sound man was complaining about someone shouting 'You stupid boy!' in the middle of the action. It would have to be done again.

'I don't believe this!' Auntie Millie snorted. 'Is this really how films are made?'

Apparently the seriously brainless Tom managed to convince her that it was, and when Hugh came back grinning all over his face he discovered that his mean feat of riding was all in vain. It had to be done again. But he didn't seem to mind.

'How he is enjoying showing off!' Shrimp groaned.

Swallow was dancing on his toes, unable to stand

still, and Hugh had to ride him around to calm him down. This time the two refusers were told to try and keep to one side so that Hugh would have room to pass them. They set off one after another, but after the first horse refused the second one swung out to avoid him right across Swallow's take-off, and there was an almighty pile-up in the ditch. The horse and Swallow both went down in a great flailing of hooves.

'This is ridiculous!' Charlie decided.

After a long argument with the director it was decided, mostly by Auntie Millie, that Charlie should ride the second refusing horse as he was a strong enough rider to stop it veering off in the undesired direction. Its owner was only too pleased to agree, and swapped his clothes with Charlie out in the field to save time. 'Else we'll be here all night. The light's beginning to go already,' Tom complained.

Swallow had a great gouge of skin out of his near hindleg which was bleeding, but not badly, and the horse Charlie was to ride now had a marked aversion to going anywhere near the fence, not surprisingly. Charlie rode him around for a bit to calm him down and Auntie Millie came stalking back from the fray saying, 'Damned thing will probably jump with

Charlie on his back. It always refused because that idiot can't ride.'

It did seem to Rowan that a certain discipline seemed to descend on the operation now that Charlie had taken over and in two subsequent takes Swallow was given just the right gap to nip through. Each time he cleared the fence perfectly. Tom was satisfied. Charlie said to Auntie Millie it was a nice horse and would jump perfectly well if given a chance, but exchanged commiserations with its owner when he went to get his own clothes back. Hugh gave Swallow back to Rowan, smirking at the congratulations, and the party started to dribble back down the hill to the farm.

'What a circus!' Auntie Millie boomed, but Tom was now all sweetness and light, having got his day's work in the can.

He was now ready to discuss the next day's jumping of the hedge. Everyone else departed but he stayed, wandering down the field with Charlie to find a suitable spot, discussing the various options. The girls turned the ponies out in their field and Swallow galloped away, bucking and kicking with delight after his exciting day.

Rowan stood watching him go.

Shrimp said, 'He's a fantastic jumper. I wish he was mine.'

'Don't be stupid. You'd get carted,' Lizzie said derisively.

They went in for their supper and Rowan got her bicycle out to whizz home. She felt very low.

It was almost dark and the ponies were shapes in the dusk, grazing on their favourite patch at the bottom by the river. Rowan stopped at the gate to watch them, too stirred up to go home immediately. Over the bridge she could see the back garden of the old shop she had examined the night before and the horseless stable with the elder tree growing against it. The vision of her own perfect pony, who never gave her a moment's fright, looking out over the top door, came back to her with a painful twist of longing. She leaned over the gate, close to tears of frustration.

Swallow, Fable, Jones, Birdie, Snowball, the Armchair, Pinkie and her shadow Bonzo, the skewbald yearling of Shrimp's, cropped contentedly. The evening smell of the river was familiar and soothing. Rowan could see the yellow flowers of the marsh marigolds like stars scattered in the water and the green weed streaming on the current. It was a trout river – perhaps she should have taken up fishing, so restful . . .

As she lingered, one of the ponies lifted its head and looked across at her. It was a bright bay, built like a small thoroughbred, very elegant, with black points and a fine black mane and tail, two white stockings and a narrow white blaze.

'Birdie!'

Rowan called to her, but the pony tossed her mane and walked slowly away after the others. A mist was creeping up the valley, and in a moment they had all disappeared.

Chapter Four

When Rowan went up to High Hawes the next morning, Lizzie said to her, 'You'll never guess – Priscilla has got herself into the film! She's going to ride Wilfred in the string of racehorses. She fluttered her eyelashes at Tom and he agreed.'

'But she's a girl. They never had girls then.'

'No, but she's going to be dressed like a lad and Tom says it'll be all right if she stays at the back. She's so pushy! They're going to use Out of the West too, in spite of Charlie's not wanting to. Hugh wants to, of course.'

Rowan thought it might be quite a good idea to keep out of the way. It sounded as if it would be far more fraught than the day before. While she was thinking this, Josephine came into the kitchen, saw Rowan in her jodhpurs and said, 'Oh, good, you've come for your lesson. I thought you were off gawping with the others.'

'Well, I was going to, but I'd rather have my lesson.'

'If it's anything like yesterday, you can do both. It takes them hours to get going. We'll have finished by then.'

Rowan got on well with Josephine who, at twenty, seemed rather remote from the rest of the family. She was quiet, and did not join in the bickering. She had qualified to teach, but didn't care for it much save one to one, which she enjoyed. She helped Charlie school Out of the West and Wilfred and went out teaching quite a bit, to people who had their own horses at home. She still didn't have a horse of her own, and Charlie was losing Wilfred to Priscilla. They both said it was a waste of money when you could ride other people's. But Rowan knew the Hawes were short of money since Mr Hawes died.

'Who shall I ride?'

Josephine looked surprised. 'Swallow?' Then she laughed. 'Or have you gone off him after his rodeo displays yesterday?'

Rowan dared not admit it. Hugh hadn't done him any good.

Josephine put a friendly hand on Rowan's shoulder.

'We'll be very quiet, bring him back to square one.'

Rowan was relieved. Josephine was sympathetic, and

knew about her lack of confidence. Rowan didn't mind her knowing but she minded the others knowing.

The others had got the ponies in and Rowan had only got to brush Swallow over and tack up. She had her lesson in the manège where, whatever else, Swallow couldn't bolt. The film people hadn't yet arrived.

Rowan led Swallow out to the school and Josephine shut the gate behind her. She mounted and immediately Swallow stiffened beneath her, and snatched at his bit, tearing the reins out of her hands. Then he pranced backwards into the fence, cracking the top bar, and immediately made to leap off but Josephine caught his bridle and restrained him. Rowan felt as if she were sitting on a keg of dynamite. All her worst fears were immediately realized.

Josephine kept hold of the bridle and said to Rowan, 'Get him to walk on. Use your legs. Gently.'

Rowan couldn't believe that she had to be led, like a four-year-old. She bit her lip to stop the tears of despair blurring her eyeballs. She inched out her reins. Swallow walked, switching his tail, his neck bent like a German show-jumper. He seemed to Rowan to be quivering with pure mischief like a naughty child.

'Relax, Rowan. Give him some rein.'

Josephine let go, but stayed walking close to Swallow's head. Rowan sensed that Swallow respected Josephine's authority, for he too relaxed and after a couple of circuits of the school Josephine dropped to her place in the middle. Swallow walked on, switching his tail.

'Get him really settled. Walk him in figure of eights. He's got to forget he's a film star.'

It was boring, but better than being bucked off.

Josephine said, 'I don't know what his past history is, but I think he probably belonged to a nut-case like Hugh, who just galloped and jumped.'

'Charlie said Swallow adores jumping. He was great yesterday.'

'He's very bold, no doubt about it.'

But there was lots of doubt about his being a suitable pony for Rowan Watkins.

After half an hour, having done serpentines and circles and changes of rein, Josephine decided they could risk a slow, steady trot. Rowan did two circuits of the school and was just starting her third when Swallow snatched at the reins, put his head down and broke into a sort of bucking canter. His head seemed to disappear altogether. Rowan sat back and tried to haul in her reins, having had a fair amount of practice, but

– remembering yesterday's bucks (even *Hugh* had come off) – felt very frightened. But Josephine, springing up like a gazelle, was at his head before he had gone halfway down the school.

'You *bad* boy!' Then, severely, 'Walk on. Wa-a-a-lk on.' Rowan was being led again.

They walked for the rest of the hour, Josephine tactfully retreating as before. But she did not ask for another trot. When they finished and Rowan thankfully slid off, Josephine grimaced and said, 'Not good. I'm sorry. That filming has gone to his head.'

Rowan burst out, 'I shall never be good enough for him! Babar said that Mrs Mildmay said—' She hiccuped with tears again – 'He's a JA or something, and Charlie – Charlie said – he—' What had Charlie said? She couldn't remember now, only that Swallow adored jumping. She was keeping Swallow from his true role in life, walking him in endless circles because she was too feeble to do anything else.

'Come on,' Josephine said. 'It's not just you, Rowan. Calm down. It's something we've got to work through. It'll take time and nobody's in a hurry. Let's put him away and you can have half an hour with one of the others. Do a bit of jumping. Which one do you want? You choose.'

426

'Birdie,' Rowan said.

She never knew why she said it. The name just slipped out.

Josephine gave her a somewhat shocked look and said, 'She hasn't been ridden lately. I'm not sure if it's wise.'

'She couldn't be worse than Swallow!'

'True.' And then, 'Well, why not?'

They had the place to themselves. Birdie was snoozing in her box. Rowan ran to fetch her saddle and bridle out of the tack room, leaving Josephine frowning over the turn of events. She thought Rowan needed humouring, needed to prove herself. Riding Jones or Fable or the Armchair wasn't going to prove anything, because they were all darlings, but if she rode Birdie successfully it would cheer her up no end. Josephine, like all the Hawes, was not averse to taking a chance. Nothing ventured, nothing won.

Birdie felt completely different from Swallow, sort of slippery, Rowan thought. She felt much higher off the ground, and the pony's shoulders were much narrower and she was more delicate. The reins felt light and soft from her mouth. Rowan couldn't believe that she'd had the nerve to ask for Birdie – what had come over her? But somehow she didn't feel frightened of her like she did of Swallow. Although Birdie did not go very smoothly, but curvetted and danced about, Rowan was quite happy. She felt that Birdie was pleased to be ridden again, and her prancings were of delight.

Josephine was very careful, watching Birdie like a hawk and assessing just how much she could ask of her without getting her tizzed up. They did trotting poles, and Josephine taught Rowan how to extend Birdie on the long sides of the school and shorten her up at the ends, which she did beautifully. Rowan had never been able to do this with Swallow. Birdie's long stride was very comfortable, and it was easy to feel the difference, shortening and lengthening. Then Josephine put a cavalletti at the end of the poles and Birdie popped over it. Twice more and she tried to break into a canter, but at Josephine's command Rowan was able to steady her back into a trot. When she had trotted over them a couple more times, slowly, Josephine told Rowan to pull up.

'That was very good. We'll finish there. She's been so good!'

If Josephine was relieved, Rowan was even more so. As she slid to the ground, she was filled with the true exhilaration of success. It was only a potty success but, after Swallow, Rowan was thrilled.

'You *can* do it,' Josephine told her. 'You can ride her in a lesson again, if you want. She went very well for you.'

Rowan remembered what Babar had said about 'clicking' with a pony and wondered if, perhaps, Birdie had liked her. Perhaps Birdie lacked confidence, like she did, and felt a kindred spirit. Lizzie had never liked Birdie, and nor had Matty. But she didn't dare say this to Josephine. Josephine, like Charlie, could ride anything and looked marvellous on Out of the West and on Wilfred, with her long legs and deep, elegant seat. She schooled the two thoroughbreds in their dressage.

After the lesson Josephine went to tack up Wilfred. Rowan watched her. She longed to be able to ride like Josephine – more than being able to ride like Hugh. Even she, a beginner, could see the finesse of Josephine's riding. Charlie said anyone could bash across country on the right horse, but riding a horse in the school, doing perfect circles at a slow canter, changing legs so smoothly onto the other rein, was real riding. Rowan sensibly thought you wanted a bit of both – but, oh, how she wanted to succeed!

Josephine, as if she guessed what she was thinking, laughed and said, 'Why are you so ambitious, Rowan? It should be fun, you know. You mustn't get upset.'

'I want to ride like you. And Charlie.'

Josephine pulled up Wilfred's girth. Then she said, 'You won't learn on Swallow, you know. You're making it very hard for yourself.'

'Not ever?'

'Perhaps. But on such a strong pony you will learn bad habits.'

'Even if we go very slowly.'

'You can't change a pony's nature, Rowan. It's like people. Hugh is quite different from you. Training doesn't make you alike, does it? You will always be just how you were in the first place. Training can only improve what is already there. It can't turn a timid horse into a great cross-country winner, or a really stupid clumsy horse into a dressage champion. Swallow is a natural-born jumper, and very head-strong. He's not able to teach a girl like you how to ride.'

Rowan digested this information sadly. It was what she knew, in her heart, but couldn't bring herself to admit.

Josephine said, 'I'm being honest with you, because I want you to succeed. Because you want it so much yourself. If you just want to be tough and career about like Hugh, fine. You will learn to handle Swallow, if you're brave enough, but you won't be successful, because there will be no groundwork underneath. Hugh, for all he's so crazy now, learned the basics of riding on a dear little pony called Pommie who was as good as gold. Pommie looked after him like an angel. We all learned on Pommie, even Charlie.'

Rowan was silent. There was nothing to be said, although Josephine's words hurt like a physical pain. Josephine knew they did, but she thought Rowan had to know. Charlie had been an idiot to give her Swallow in the first place, in her opinion.

'Come on, Rowan, it's not the end of the world! These things have a way of working themselves out. We'll think of something, between us.'

Rowan watched her ride away into the school on Wilfred. Wilfred had been bought out of the same bad riding school as Swallow and had looked like a scarecrow when Charlie had brought him home. They had all laughed. But now he had filled out and looked like the well-made thoroughbred he was. Charlie had seen what lay underneath the skin and bones. He had a very amenable nature and learned quickly and had turned out to be just the horse for the not-brilliant (but thought she was) Priscilla.

Priscilla finding Wilfred was a success. They clicked.

Rowan and Swallow was not a success story, and Rowan knew it.

Before she could get too deep into the waters of despair, Rowan was distracted by the arrival of the Hawes' Land Rover. Joan Hawes was back from a shopping expedition with Shrimp. Before the car had come to a proper halt Shrimp was leaping out, shouting at Rowan, 'Look, Rowan! Have you seen the newspapers! Look! Look!'

She came running over with a sheaf of newspapers in her hand.

'We bought lots, one for everybody! Look!'

Rowan looked and saw a magnificent shot of Swallow staring at the camera with his ears pricked up and his mane blowing in the wind. Hugh sat on his back, glowering in his flat cap and old-fashioned clothes.

The picture was captioned, 'Local Boy Helps Out Film Makers'.

Underneath there was a smaller picture of Swallow jumping the log with about a metre to spare.

'Local rider, Hugh Hawes, of High Hawes Farm, Long Bottom, stood in for young star Sam Marshall when filming took place in the village recently. Chosen for his riding skill, twelve-year-old Hugh successfully jumped his pony Swallow in several scenes showing the early life of the famous jockey Fred Archer. The film is being made by . . .'

Rowan didn't bother to read any more, gazing with glowing eyes at Swallow's undeniable beauty.

'*His* pony, it says!'

'What a cheek!' Shrimp shouted. 'We'll tell him what a liar he is! Where are they all? We must show them!'

'They're all over at Jerry Patterson's racing yard,' Joan Hawes said. 'There's been a change of plan. They're going to film over there. They're sending the horsebox for Jack and Wilfred. You two can go over in the horsebox when it comes, save me ferrying you.'

Such was the excitement, Rowan's misery was forgotten. Shrimp had bought Rowan her own copy of the newspaper – perhaps they could write and get a glossy copy of the original picture? It was such a beautiful photograph.

Charlie arrived shortly, driving Jerry's horsebox, and was made to enthuse over the newspapers.

'Luckily they didn't get him falling off. It was far more dramatic,' he said unsympathetically. 'Good photo though.'

Josephine brought Wilfred in from the school and

boxed him up, and Charlie fetched Out of the West. Soon they were on their way round to the next valley where the racehorses lived, several miles by road but quite quick by pony over the top of the down.

'We'll see what drama we have in store today,' Charlie said gloomily. 'I fear the worst.'

'Have you chosen the right bit of hedge?' Shrimp enquired.

'Yes. The lowest bit I could find.'

All the chaos of the day before was now being re-enacted around Jerry Patterson's yard. He was watching, bemused, as Tom ordered his string of race-horses about. A man with bushy whiskers in a black suit and a high silk topper, and another man dressed in the same fashion with a flower in his buttonhole, were chatting together in the middle of the yard while Jerry's 'lads' were being ordered to let down their stirrups and sit with their legs pushed forward and their toes down and turned out.

'This is supposed to be the eighteen sixties. That's how they rode then, none of your crouching stuff.'

They rode round, practising and larking about, while Charlie tacked up Out of the West. Priscilla came forward to take Wilfred, dressed in breeches and boots and a tweed jacket, with all her gorgeous hair pushed up into one of the ugly flat caps. She looked terrible. Rowan hoped Tom might tell her so and get Charlie to swap her, but nothing happened and she mounted and joined the back of the string, trying to sit in the way Tom wanted.

Knowing what to expect, and not having Swallow to dote on this time, Rowan found the filming rather boring.

'It's all the waiting!' Lizzie complained.

Jerry's racehorses, who had mostly been out at grass on their summer holidays, stood dozing but Out of the West, fit and hard, got progressively more fidgety while Tom messed about with his cameraman. In the end, when he was asked to jump the hedge by Hugh, he refused.

Charlie came forward crossly and said what did they expect? He got on and schooled Out of the West for ten minutes in the field, then jumped backwards and forwards over the hedge four times. Then he slid off and said, 'Film it now, while he's expecting it.'

He legged Hugh back on and Hugh joined the string on the now fizzing Out of the West. They walked down the hedgeside and Hugh pulled him away from the others, circled him and jumped the hedge. He pulled up on the far side, and then jumped back as instructed.

Then he had to do it again. All went well.

Then Tom had to take some close-ups of Sam Marshall sitting on Out of the West, listening to his instructions from the trainer, which Charlie said they should have done first, for now the big horse was excited by his jumping and wouldn't stand still. It took Charlie and Jerry between them to manhandle him into position, bending down out of shot when the cameras rolled.

Hugh had no more to do, and got changed into his own clothes, and then all the excitement was over.

It seemed a terrible anti-climax.

Charlie and Priscilla rode away over the down for home and the rest of them were given a lift back by one of the technicians. Only the fantastic photos of Swallow remained to remind them what had happened.

As Hugh and the others enthused over them, Rowan felt the cold web of despair wrap her again – *her* pony, yet not really hers at all, and never would be, if Josephine was right. Lizzie was taunting Hugh; 'It says "on his pony" – I bet you told them that – I bet you told them Swallow was yours!'

'I never!' Then he added, 'I wish he was!'

'Poor Swallow, if he belonged to you!' Shrimp shouted.

'Why don't you all go for a ride and get out of my kitchen?' Joan Hawes appealed.

They scattered out into the yard to fetch saddles and bridles. Rowan knew she couldn't ride Swallow if Hugh was coming. She had an overwhelming urge to tack up Birdie, but knew the others would think she had gone potty. While she stood dithering in the tack room, Lizzie said, 'I'm riding Fable, so you can take Jones,' so that decided it.

Jones was a really good pony, but Rowan had never felt any proprietary interest in him, mainly because a girl in the Pony Club called Roma Glade came for lessons on him and was going to buy him. The snag was she had been going to buy him for almost a year but somehow the money had never been forthcoming. If Josephine meant what she said, Rowan supposed she would now be having lessons on him instead of on Swallow. She could not bring herself to dwell on what Josephine had said. It was like a bad dream. She wasn't even going to tell Lizzie. It hurt too much.

When they got back she went home for lunch on her bicycle. Her mother was rather quiet but Rowan supposed she was thinking about moving house and getting a divorce, which preoccupied her quite a lot these days, so she tried to be helpful and said nothing about her own woes, which – although it didn't feel like it – were probably not much compared to her mother's. She told her mother about the beautiful photos of Swallow in the local paper.

Her mother said, 'Oh yes, Joan rang up and told me about them.'

She then gave Rowan a rather odd look and said, 'Joan wanted me to tell you—' She hesitated.

'Tell me what?'

'While you were out riding a man rang up. He'd seen the photos and said—' Her voice failed her again.

'Said what?'

'He said the pony belongs to him. He recognized it. It was stolen out of his yard a year ago, when he was abroad. He's only been back a couple of months and saw the photo in the paper today. He's coming over tomorrow morning.'

Chapter Five

Rowan knew what it felt like, because it had happened before. She had rescued Swallow after he had been found wandering and abandoned, and a man had claimed him dishonestly and taken him away and sold him in a market. The same dismay she remembered so clearly overwhelmed her again. Her mother commiserated sincerely, knowing that her love for Swallow and her new pony life had helped enormously in deflecting Rowan's grief from the family break-up. Now everything seemed to have fallen to pieces again.

Charlie said, 'It's not cut and dried. Swallow has been sold twice since this man lost him. He can't expect just to come in and take him away.'

'What did he sound like? Nice?' Rowan asked timidly.

Joan Hawes had taken the call. They were having a family conference the following morning.

'Cheerful. Confident. Pleasant enough. He said he'd gone abroad and left the pony with friends. The friends had then been in a car accident and had to stay in hospital and it was disaster all round, and Swallow going missing was the least of their worries apparently. It's his son's pony. Competition pony, he said.'

Rowan's worst fears were realized. A cocky boy like Hugh, no doubt, with heavy hands and big feet, all out to win. Not a sweet girl with a loving heart.

'What's his name?'

'Bill Trugg, he said.'

The Hawes family, even Hugh, were all sombre at the news. Nobody wanted to lose Swallow, for all his faults. Rowan was sure that Hugh had been hoping he would get him, after she had failed to cope with him, and have him to compete on.

Shrimp said sadly, 'He'd never have known if Swallow's photo hadn't been in the newspaper.'

And they had been so proud!

Everyone was on edge, waiting for Mr Trugg to arrive. It was a cool day, threatening rain, which fitted in with the general mood, and the ponies, let out, had all rolled in the mud. But Swallow had stayed in and been groomed, to show how beautifully he was kept. His coat already shone like an advertisement for polished furniture; he was well-rounded but fit, the picture of a perfect pony.

At half past eleven a smart BMW pulled into the yard.

'He's not short of a bob or two, at least,' Charlie commented.

Rowan was shivering and felt sick. She quickly saw that her worst fears were realized, for Mr Trugg – 'The name's Billy' – was a big brash man, the sort that exhorted his child from the ringside, and his son Tom was a well-built boy of her own age, with a neck as wide as his face, a bristly head and hard, pale blue eyes behind thick glasses. Rowan took an instant dislike to them both.

'Tom Trugg,' Lizzie whispered. 'More like Tom Thug.'

'Billy Brag,' Shrimp whispered and they got the giggles. 'Billy Brag and Tom Thug.'

Rowan didn't feel like giggling.

They all went over to Swallow's box and Charlie led him out and the Truggs exclaimed with satisfaction.

'That's our boy! That's our little beaut!'

Tom Thug did show a slight enthusiasm, and patted Swallow on the neck.

'Hi, Hottie,' he said.

441

'Hottie?'

'His name is Hotspur.'

Even Rowan had to admit that it was a good name for him. Even that it was probably better than Swallow. She could see how it was all going to happen, and was convinced already that the pony was lost.

Charlie was telling Billy Brag that he had paid good money for Swallow, and that his present owner was Rowan. He put a hand on Rowan's shoulder and propelled her in front of their cheerful visitor. Rowan glowered.

'It's a long story. Perhaps we'd better go indoors and I'll explain what's happened.'

Nobody knew what the legal position was. Swallow had passed through several hands since the Truggs had lost him.

'We don't want to get a load of lawyers involved, surely?' Billy Brag said. 'Their bill would be ten times what the pony's worth.'

'Two families went to court about the same situation recently,' Joan Hawes remarked. 'It was reported in the paper. But at the last minute they settled and the original owners let the current owners keep the pony.'

'Well, we want this pony back, don't we, Tom?'

'Yes,' said Tom bluntly.

'He's a winner, you see. And Tom's not out of his class yet.'

'He's fairly big for him, I would have thought,' Charlie said equably.

'Getting on that way. But we've a whole summer of competing ahead of us.'

'We can't just give him to you,' Charlie said. 'You must see that. We can't afford to lose the price of him.'

'I'll pay you what you paid for him, or whatever it was he fetched on the market. That's fair enough. You won't be out of pocket, and I'll be happy to pay a reasonable sum to have him back.'

Charlie was silent. Even Rowan could see that it was an amicable, even generous, offer.

Joan Hawes, seeing the dismayed faces around the table, said, 'Perhaps, when Tom has grown out of him, there might be a chance for us to have him back?'

'Possibly, but he won't be cheap, I can promise you. Not after Tom here has got him back on the circuit. I take it you haven't been competing on him?'

'Only in the Pony Club.'

'And Hugh fell off,' Shrimp said.

Hugh kicked her under the table and she screamed.

Mr Trugg laughed and said, 'He's not an easy beggar, is he?'

Charlie, seeing Rowan's face, made a despairing try: 'We really would like to keep him if we could.'

'No way,' said the man. His expression changed and it was plain that he was no man to have for an enemy. 'I've made you a very fair offer.'

It was indisputable. He had.

'You can go to the law if you want, but I'll fight you all the way.'

'Well, no, none of us want that sort of hassle.' Charlie shrugged. 'I agree you're being fair. It's just — you know — kids get to love a pony—'

He looked embarrassed and Rowan felt she had to jump in and help.

'It's all right, honestly. You know I can't ride him properly.'

'It isn't all right!' Hugh hissed at her.

'Hugh!' his mother snapped.

Through all this exchange Tom Thug sat stolidly, without emotion. There was no way, Rowan thought, he had ever loved Swallow, save perhaps as a money-maker. But perhaps Swallow didn't want love. He had certainly made no bones about removing her painfully from the saddle if it suited him. Perhaps she was just a stupid sentimental twit. But Charlie had cried when he had had to sell Fedora. Love? No, frustration probably. She would be well off without Swallow, considering she only ever had trouble with him. She boldly smiled.

Charlie, surprised, said, 'All for the best.'

'You're happy, kid?'

Rowan forced a sickly smile.

'Good on yer!' Billy clapped her on the shoulder so that she nearly fell over, and pulled out his cheque book.

'What's your price?'

So the deed was done. The Hawes all watched in silence as Charlie took the cheque, and then went out with father and son to make the travelling arrangements. The Truggs only lived ten miles away.

'Oh, poor Rowan!' Lizzie wailed.

Hugh was sulking and Shrimp casting round for alternative rides for Rowan. 'You can have Jones! He's lovely. Or Diamond – Babar doesn't ride him any more. Or Bonzo when he's old enough!'

'I'm sure Charlie will find you something suitable,' Joan Hawes said. 'The money is yours, after all, because he did give Swallow to you.'

They were all extra nice to her and Rowan had to

show that her heart wasn't broken, although she was quite sure it was. She turned her mind resolutely away from Swallow, and tried to make it concentrate on a lovely pony that stopped when she asked, cantered like a dream over the downs without pulling her arms out and came to the gate with a welcoming whinny whenever she came into view. She would win all the Pony Club competitions and be chosen for the team. Somehow she kept thinking of all this happening with Birdie, yet she knew Birdie was impossible. Birdie had cost a lot of money and belonged to an irascible Mrs Prebble and no one was supposed to ride her.

Everyone was terribly nice to her for the rest of the day, even Hugh, who said she could ride Cascade (only she didn't want to; Cascade was pig-headed, just like Hugh). With extraordinary timing, Roma Glade's mother rang up in the evening with the news that they had sold a prize pig and decided to use the money to buy Jones for Roma. 'At last! We've messed you about so long – I'm sure you'll be so relieved we've made our minds up after all this shilly-shallying!'

Joan Hawes made all the right noises, but when she put the phone down she said, exasperated, 'What timing! Just when he would have done for Rowan!'

But Rowan, strangely, felt a great sense of relief. She

did not want Jones; he was too easy. He was everyone's pony. A 'press-button' pony, they called him. She wanted a pony that would go better for her than it would for anyone else – like only Charlie could get Out of the West round a cross-country course without being carted, and only Hugh could get Cascade to jump clear rounds. She wanted a challenge. Josephine knew this.

'What now?' she said to Rowan in the evening when the ponies were all turned out, save Swallow, who was to be collected in the morning. Rowan was sitting in his manger, talking to him, not having to be brave any more. Tears streamed down her cheeks. Josephine found her when she came back from a ride on Wilfred.

'It's a good home, after all. He'll be well looked after. They're quite well known on the jumping circuit, the Truggs.'

'I know.'

'It's not like he belonged to some idiots, who don't know anything. They've got two grooms and several horses.'

'I know.'

Rowan remembered that Josephine, who was brilliant, didn't have her own horse either. And she never moaned. She leaned over the door, pulling her long blonde hair loose and shaking it out. She wore an old brown jersey and her cream jodhpurs with holes in the knees, yet she looked as elegant as always.

'You've got the money. You can buy another pony. Your mother might give you a bit more, to get a decent one, if you ask her.'

Rowan did not answer.

'Come on, Rowan, it's not the end of the world. You'll still see Swallow around. Ponies are always getting outgrown and passed on, it's a fact of life. You just have to get used to it.'

'I know.'

She had got used to the idea by now, but she couldn't get used to her new idea. Birdie.

'I—' She couldn't get it out.

'What is it?'

'I would like—' Her voice failed her. But she knew Josephine, of them all, would understand.

'I want Birdie.'

'Birdie! Heavens, Rowan, you go looking for trouble!'

'I like her.'

'She went well for you. But – oh, Rowan! She's nearly as difficult as Swallow – in a different way, I grant you. And her price! Mrs Prebble paid three and a half thousand for her. That cheque for Swallow – it's only half of that! Your mother'll never pay that much, will she?'

'I shouldn't think so.'

'If you ask Mrs Prebble, I suppose she might let you ride her until she's sold. Or until she decides what she's going to do with her.'

'Am I being really stupid?'

'Yes.'

'But I liked riding her. Better than any of the others. She felt—' Rowan couldn't think of the word. 'Slippery' was the word she remembered but that wasn't right.

'Sensitive?' Josephine suggested.

'Yes!'

'You're a very sensitive rider. Perhaps you felt she responded to you? Matty wasn't right for her; she was too forceful, she asked too much. And Lizzie couldn't get together with her at all. Perhaps she is right for you, Rowan, who knows?'

Josephine smiled, and Rowan for the first time that day felt that all was not completely lost. Josephine didn't completely throw out the idea. Josephine understood what she scarcely understood herself.

'Do you want me to see what I can do?'

Rowan looked up in astonishment. 'You think—? I'm not just being really idiotic?'

'Well, fairly idiotic. But it just might – might – work.' Josephine smiled, and then her smile turned off and she said severely, 'If it doesn't you'll be in a worse way than ever, won't you? Is it worth the risk?'

Rowan didn't answer.

'You make it so hard for yourself!' But then the cool face softened again. Josephine leaned against the door, gazing into space. Then she said, 'Perhaps— if we ask Mrs Prebble – she might lease you Birdie, for long enough to see if you can get on with her. And then, if you do, you could buy her. And if you don't – well, you will have learned sense, and be ready to opt for something suitable.'

'Oh, please – could you ask? And not let the others think I am – am—' She supposed the word was conceited. The others were so brilliant and she was such a duffer; they could think her conceited that she thought she could ride Birdie successfully.

'All right, nut-case. I'll stick up for you.'

The enormous price tag on Birdie was something Rowan thought she could forget about for the moment, for it was very likely she would never get to the point of actually being able to ride Birdie well enough. Josephine laughed and went in for her supper, and Rowan stayed with Swallow until it was nearly dark.

'I'd rather have you, all the same,' she said. She felt slightly guilty that she was thinking of the next before Swallow had actually gone. She sometimes felt she got things wrong all the time. Perhaps she should try and be more like Hugh, sure he was always right even when it was patently obvious that he wasn't. He always bounced up like a rubber ball.

But Swallow's going hurt badly enough to make her forget all her plans for the future. When the horsebox came for him the next morning she stayed well away and lay on her bed, howling, until her mother told her to come and visit the estate agent with her about buying what they called 'the shop'. Her mother had thought it might be rather fun doing it up. 'Take my mind off things,' she said, meaning the divorce and the hurt and the sense of failure. She had been very low for a few months, but now seemed to be getting a lot more cheerful. Rowan was chastened by thinking how pre-occupied she had been with her potty pony problems, and forced herself to turn her mind onto what was now interesting her mother: kitchens and lavatories and central heating. The shop was the only house for sale in Long Bottom, and the thought of moving out to another village beyond cycling range of High Hawes was horrific, so it made a lot of sense to be enthusiastic. Actually the shop seemed more and more possible the more they examined it. The room that would be Rowan's, at the back, had a view straight up the pony fields and into the back yard of High Hawes – fantastic! – and when the house agent pointed out to Pauline Watkins that she could turn the house round and make the back the living room, opening into the garden, and the front – the shop – into a kitchen-dining room, instead of vice versa as it was at the moment, everything started to take shape. Excitement quickened.

'Why, I think it could be really sweet! And we could spend money on the improvements when it's so cheap.'

And the stable, Rowan thought with a glow – I can scrub it all out and paint it inside and make it for Birdie to come to sometimes! She got as excited as her mother. They went out for supper in a smart place that night and celebrated the future.

'It doesn't do well to dwell on what's past, what can't be helped. On with the next thing, I say,' her mother said.

She wasn't really thinking of Swallow, but it worked for him too.

Mrs Prebble was invited to call, to discuss 'a plan for Birdie'. Joan Hawes shooed everyone out of the kitchen. Only Josephine was to stay and do the deal. Charlie had taken Out of the West to an event, which Josephine said was a good thing as he wasn't very keen on their idea. He didn't want to be beholden to Mrs Prebble, he said. Leasing was a messy idea. 'Oh, rubbish, not with a good insurance cover,' Josephine countered. 'She'll say you're ruining her, and insurance only covers injury.' And Josephine said quietly, 'Rowan wouldn't ruin any pony, you know that.' Rowan felt proud to have Josephine's trust, but couldn't help being frightened by her own ambition. If Mrs Prebble had been a kindly old soul, like Auntie Millie – 'Of course, darling, see how you get on with her! What a splendid idea! How lovely!'

But Mrs Prebble wasn't like that. She had flaring nostrils and dark, suspicious eyes. She had a haughty, upper-class manner and could be extraordinarily rude. She had been a brilliant rider herself in her heyday but now seemed embittered and without laughs (even before Matty's accident). Mr Prebble supplied the money, but was only interested in golf himself and was rarely seen at a horse event.

When she arrived she disappeared into the house, leaving Matty out in the yard on her crutches, which she handled with considerable aplomb. Her right leg trailed dispiritingly and wouldn't be much good, Rowan could see, for a bicycle, but a nice quiet pony . . . the thought of having to be taken everywhere by Mrs Prebble was really depressing.

'Can I have a go?' Hugh asked.

Matty handed the crutches over and leaned against the stable wall.

'What's this about Birdie?' she asked as Hugh went lurching away.

'Rowan wants her,' Lizzie said.

'To try her,' Rowan corrected, blushing scarlet. She could tell by the way they all looked at her that they thought she was out of her mind.

But Matty just said, 'She's no good to us. I don't want her.'

'Don't you want to ride again?' Shrimp asked.

Lizzie and Rowan felt embarrassed at Shrimp's indiscretion, but Matty only laughed and said, 'Not Birdie anyway.'

Then she said, 'I would like a horse of my own. But it doesn't exist, what I want.'

'Why?'

'I don't want a dumb squit, but that's all I can ride now. I've always ridden class horses. I'd rather not bother if I can't, you see.'

Her words were swanky but true, and the way her voice dropped on the last sentence sounded apologetic. Rowan saw that her idea of a bicycle-pony was not going to appeal.

'But it's awfully boring, stuck like this,' Matty said.

They didn't know what to say, feeling awkward. But Hugh came swinging back and shouted, 'I say, this is great! How fast can you go, Matty?'

'Give them to me!'

She showed him, and they all had a go, and Hugh got one of the Pony Club stopwatches out of the tack room and they all went round the yard being timed. Matty was miles the best; even Hugh couldn't touch her time. Lizzie put out some cavalletti and they tried it with jumps, but Shrimp fell flat on her face and cut her chin and when Mr Prebble came out with Josephine they were all in the tack room putting wound powder on her. Matty went out to deflect trouble.

'Have you sold her?'

'No, but if she suits, Mrs Watkins will buy her.'

'Mrs Watkins!'

Rowan couldn't help overhearing the astonishment in Matty's voice. Nobody thought it was going to work, she could see that. Only Josephine held out a faint hope. And even Mrs Prebble's announcement was scary. Where was her mother going to find the money, even if it did work out? Rowan wondered how on earth she had managed to get herself in such a mess.

Mrs Prebble drove off with Matty, and Josephine said to her, 'Cheer up, Rowan! It went well. She agreed to lend Birdie, as long as we insure her – and with an option to buy at the end of the summer holidays.'

Rowan tried to look pleased, but the old, cold fear of failure seemed to grip harder than ever. Whatever had she done?

'Dad'll never pay that money,' she mumbled.

'Rowan!'

Josephine's voice was stern. Rowan raised her eyes nervously.

'Your father is a businessman. Birdie is worth that money if you can ride her. It's up to you. She's only young. Your father will buy her and make a profit when you've grown out of her, because you'll make a good pony into an even better one! You told me once that money is all your father thinks about. So where's your resolve?'

'It's – it's—'

'Look at me, Rowan!'

Rowan looked. Josephine's eyes were flinty.

'You will do it. You've got to do it, haven't you? There's no alternative.'

Chapter Six

'I don't know why I get myself into such muddles,' Rowan said to Babar. Babar was the only person she could confide in now, all the Hawes except Josephine thinking she was potty. Even dear Charlie did not approve, because he hated being involved with Mrs Prebble.

And she hadn't dared tell her mother yet that at the end of the summer she was going to have to fork out £3500 to keep Birdie.

'Aye, you're a right 'un,' Babar said, and laughed. But kindly. 'That's some fair price, eh?'

Rowan said, 'You know they want to buy another horse for Matty?'

'She can't ride no horse now!'

'No, well, the right horse. Matty herself said she would ride the right horse. Mrs Prebble said if Charlie found her the right horse for Matty, she would let us have Birdie.'

'For nothing?'

'Well, for much less, she said.'

'I reckon she said it because she knew there ain't no right 'orse for Matty. That's wishful thinking, that is. Unless she wants my ole Diamond. 'E's quiet enough.'

'Well, I don't think so.' Rowan thought it would be imprudent to repeat that Matty didn't want 'a dumb squit', which was an exact description of Diamond.

'If I were you,' Babar said, 'I'd get on and enjoy myself. No use worryin' over what might never 'appen. You ride Birdie and show 'em, and your ma'll marry a rich farmer and come he'll stump up to make you 'appy.'

'You think?' Rowan couldn't help smiling.

'Well, look at it this way. You're better off than Matty?'

'Oh yes!'

'You got what you wanted?'

'Yes.'

'Well then.'

Put that way, there was no argument. Babar's stolid philosophy pulled Rowan together. For the time being, Birdie was hers.

'Well,' said her mother, 'that's very lucky for you!

Such a pretty pony! And Mrs Prebble says you can have her for your own?'

'To see if I get on with her. With an option to buy, if I do.'

'That's very generous. I'm sure we'll be able to buy her if she's suitable.'

Even then, Rowan could not bring herself to mention the price. As Babar said, why worry about what might never happen? For the moment, Birdie was hers.

'Shall we go for a ride?' Lizzie asked her when she went up on her bicycle. Rowan had missed the day of Swallow's departure, and the sight of his empty box – although she was prepared for it – gave her a fresh pang of grief.

'Yes!' It was what she most needed, to think ahead, put Birdie in Swallow's place.

They went down the field to catch the ponies. Birdie, not used to coming to work, was surprised to be wanted, but made no demur as Rowan flipped the head collar round behind her ears. She had a long walking stride and Rowan had to almost run to keep up with her.

She tied her up in her box and groomed her. Her summer coat was just about through, and Rowan's vigorous brushing revealed it, smooth and shining, beneath the mud and old hair. The light, bright bay turned to black round about her knee and hock joints so that she had black legs, and the gleaming white stockings behind gave her a showy appearance. As she was beautifully put together this accentuated her presence. She was kind in the stable, but quite different from Swallow, gentler and much less pushy. She had a way of looking into the distance, as if she were listening to something, ears pricked up, her eyes were soft and purple-dark and unfathomable. Rowan laid her hand on the hard muscle of her neck. What did ponies think about? When you stared into their eyeballs you could not tell. Did they care who owned them? Did they know how badly you wanted them to make it all come right?

Rowan didn't think they did.

Birdie's real name was Bird in the Wilderness, she remembered. Perhaps that was what she was, until now. Perhaps she was waiting to find her way out.

She tacked up and led Birdie out into the yard. Josephine and Charlie had gone out in the horsebox and there was no sign of Hugh or Shrimp. It was a still, grey day, not cold, and the hedges were full in leaf and the hawthorn just beginning to flower, with its thick, summery smell. A little shiver of excitement – pleasure or fear? – made Rowan's hands tremble on the reins as she sat up on Birdie, waiting for Lizzie. She could hear her own heart beating. Yet she was only going for a hack, for heaven's sake! What was wrong with her?

They set off cautiously up the lane. 'Better not go on the downs, until you are used to her more,' Lizzie said wisely. It occurred to both of them, although neither voiced it, that they hadn't asked if they could go out. Deep down, Rowan had a strong idea that she would only be allowed to ride in the school at first, if she asked, and not asking was instinctive.

Birdie walked on calmly with her long, easy stride, so Lizzie had to keep trotting to keep up. Fable, Lizzie's pony, was common compared to Birdie, but kind and generous. She had no vices at all and Lizzie loved not being scared. With good feeding and plenty of work, Fable had filled out and got her spirit back, hardly recognizable as the sad little plodder they had bought from the riding school. (Nearly all the Hawes' animals had come cheaply from poor homes – 'Only ones we can afford,' Charlie said cheerfully.)

Birdie was so different from Swallow that Rowan couldn't stop being amazed. She felt much more like a horse, although she was only half a hand higher, and she was much narrower and much smoother and her mouth was so light she hardly needed a touch on the reins to turn or stop. Swallow had needed quite a lot of yanking, which had never had much effect. When Birdie trotted, she was so smooth Rowan scarcely had to rise in the saddle.

'She's rather spooky, remember,' Lizzie warned, and no sooner had she said it than Birdie gave a violent jink sideways across the road, and Rowan was pitched over her shoulder. She almost didn't fall off, her foot desperately hooked over the saddle, but in the end it was a very slow-motion fall, depositing her quite gently on the tarmac. She held onto the reins, and Birdie started cropping the grass verge.

'Whatever was that for?' Rowan asked indignantly.

'That gateway – the notice,' Lizzie said. There was a white notice which said HALL FARM, not at all terrifying as far as Rowan could see.

'You have to watch out for things in advance. She always does it. You get to see things before she does – even cigarette packets.'

While Rowan was hopping about getting back on, Lizzie lay down with the back of her head on Fable's rump and laughed, 'You can't do this with Birdie. You can't relax.'

So, now she was learning!

'What else does she do that I ought to know about?'

'The spooks is her worst. You never know. Sometimes she spins round and tries to go home when you're not expecting it. Sometimes when you're cantering she puts her head up in a horrid way, or sometimes down, so that she sort of disappears from in front of you. She doesn't bolt like Swallow, but she gets quite excited when you go fast.'

'Does she buck?'

'No.'

Something to be thankful for!

They continued on their way, following a track down into the next valley, where Jerry Patterson and the racehorses lived. Then they had come so far that to go back by the road was miles.

'We'll have to go back over the down,' Lizzie said dubiously. 'It'll be all right if we walk.'

'We could canter up,' Rowan said. 'Some of the way.'

'I suppose so.'

Rowan was rather cross with Lizzie for being so careful, as if she were convinced that Birdie's rider was completely incapable. But everything that had happened so far (apart from the spook – and she was ready for spooks now) filled Rowan with a confidence and joy that she really had never felt on Swallow. Yes, she might be tricky, but Birdie liked her – Rowan knew she did. She could sense it. Rowan felt at one with Birdie, even if she wasn't much of a rider. (Yet.) So when the chalk track up the hill out of the valley petered out onto the lovely down turf Rowan turned in her saddle and shouted, 'I'm going to canter.'

She scarcely had to tell Birdie. The mare knew, springing straight into a canter from a walk. Rowan managed to go with her, feeling a great surge of adrenalin rushing through her body, half fear, half excitement, at the amazing feel of Birdie in full flight, so strong and smooth and willing. She didn't bolt like Swallow, nor did she put her head up, but rather bent her power to Rowan's message on the reins, very kind, even when so fast. And fast she was! Her long thoroughbred legs swept her up the hill, leaving Fable toiling far behind, for all she was much fitter than Birdie. Like a racehorse, thought Rowan, almost delirious with joy at the feel of it. She had never, ever, felt this heaven on Swallow. She wished for a heady moment that there were great jumps ahead of them that the mare would take in her stride, for she knew – she just *knew* – that they would fly over them without hesitation.

As it was, Birdie wasn't fit and came back to Rowan immediately she decided to slow down, her breathing coming flared through her nostrils so the membrane showed red. As she dropped to a walk she flitched her black tail and dropped her nose as if to say, that was good. Rowan leaned forward and stroked her hot neck.

Fable came toiling up and Lizzie shouted, 'I thought she'd taken off with you!'

'No, she never – she's just so fast. I never felt she was out of control.'

After that they walked all the way home, anxious to show that they had been very quiet and good. Rowan rather thought she would get a telling-off, but nothing would take away her feeling of triumph, that Birdie was going to be right for her. She now knew what everyone had tried to tell her about Swallow. She had never listened to them. She had always been frightened of riding Swallow. But Birdie—!

She did get a telling-off, from both Josephine and Charlie, but even they noticed the look of bliss on her face and had a laugh when they left her.

'At least she's still in one piece. What a case!' Charlie said. 'Talk about single-minded!'

'People like that succeed,' Josephine said.

'If they don't kill themselves first.'

'Hark who's talking!'

'I just wish Birdie didn't belong to that Prebble woman. She's perfectly capable of throwing a spanner in the works, however well it goes for Rowan. I wouldn't trust her further than I could throw her.'

'The answer to that is to get poor Matty riding again. Then Mrs Prebble won't give a toss for what happens to Birdie. But I can't see how, exactly – I thought side-saddle, perhaps with her right leg being useless. But the right horse . . .'

'One in a million. They still want pure class, and yet utter reliability – docility. Rare as ice in the desert.'

'It's got to be very special for Matty.'

'Yes. And I'm not wasting time looking for it.'

It seemed amazing to Rowan that something in her horse life was going right at last. Her colossal gamble had come off – Birdie did go for her; they suited each other. Twice a week she had a lesson in the school with Josephine, and other days, as the evenings grew longer, she rode out with Lizzie and Shrimp, and even Hugh, whose antics on Cascade did not disturb Birdie as they had Swallow. It was true she had to watch out for the mare's spooks, and sometimes she did fall off, taken unawares. She also found that Birdie could sometimes

467

get impatient and silly if schooled for too long. Josephine said she was a bit of a baby and had been spoilt in her youth, and it was best to humour her, and make the lessons short. But the schooling was more to teach Rowan to ride better rather than to teach Birdie anything, so sometimes Josephine would give her a lesson on Wilfred, or the Armchair, to show her how different horses felt and how differently they needed to be ridden. Rowan, now she had her confidence, felt she was improving at an amazing rate. Josephine must have thought so too, for she said one evening, 'If you don't watch out, Auntie Millie will have you in the Pony Club team.'

'But—' Confident as she felt, Rowan knew she was far from being a Hawes.

'Birdie's a very good jumper.'

Rowan wasn't sure if her new confidence stretched to competing against the likes of Hugh – or Tom Thug. She wasn't a natural show-off like Hugh. But the season for shows was upon them, and Charlie was taking Hugh and Lizzie and Shrimp in the horsebox . . .

'You can enter for novice jumping,' Lizzie said. 'Birdie's still a novice; I never won anything on her and nor did Matty – she never had time before she got hurt.'

The others took it for granted that she would come. Josephine said gently, 'Not if you don't want to. But I think you're ready. It's not affiliated, only a potty little show for charity. Otty runs it.'

Otty was one of the Pony Club instructors. She had a young horse called Hadrian, and was funny and nice. Rowan was persuaded.

'It's not Wembley,' Lizzie said in scathing tones, when she saw Rowan's nervousness.

It was all right for them – they had been to shows since they were born. Shrimp had almost lived in shows until recently, having ridden show-ponies for rich owners. Charlie was taking Out of the West to jump, for practice, and Priscilla was going to jump Wilfred in the Novice. With six animals entered, Josephine agreed to take the trailer for two of them, as the horsebox didn't take more than four comfortably, only if illegally squashed up. Everyone took it quite for granted, but Rowan was awake all the night before, and felt sick with nerves when she got up. Lizzie couldn't believe it, seeing her so pale and quiet.

'It's just the pottiest show – however can you be nervous? Birdie jumps far better than Fable and I'm not nervous.'

Rowan tried to be cool. The two of them bagged to go with Josephine. Rowan did not want to be unnerved by swanky Hugh, who had the Challenge Cup for Junior Jumping newly cleaned and gleaming on his lap, to take back from last year. He nearly didn't clean it, so convinced was he that he was going to win it back again, but his mother made him. At least he wasn't in the same class as Rowan. He was in the Open under 14.2. Cascade was no novice.

It was a sunny day, not too hot. The show was in a big flat farm field beyond the next village, only a few miles away. Rowan's mother was coming in her car with Joan Hawes and a picnic. If Rowan was quiet, nobody else noticed. They parked the lorry and trailer and went off to the secretary's tent to get their numbers and find out who the opposition was. Otty was there and pleased to see them.

'Who are you riding, Rowan?' She was curious, giving out the numbers. 'Swallow? Jones?'

'No. Birdie.' Rowan explained what had happened.

'Very interesting. I think she might go very well for you. She needs understanding, that one.'

It was a compliment, but Rowan didn't take it in. The Novice jumps were quite small but arranged in a complicated sort of course with some sharp changes of direction.

'It's a rider course,' Josephine said. 'Not to go too fast, Rowan, and keep your eye on the next jump all the time, that's the best way. The first round isn't against the clock, remember. I'll walk the course with you.'

Josephine showed her where to take it steady, how to make a straight approach, where she could cut corners if she went into the timed jump-off.

'Watch the others. You can learn from their mistakes. And think of it as a lesson, not an ordeal! You've never done it before, but you've got a pony who loves jumping. She's not going to refuse unless you get her into a complete muddle, and I'm sure you won't do that.'

At least the Novice class was first, thank goodness. Lizzie was jumping Fable in it, and Jones arrived in the collecting ring with his new owner, Roma Glade. She came up to Rowan and said, 'Cor, that's Birdie, isn't it?'

'Yes.'

'Cor, rather you than me.' Roma, the pig farmer's daughter, was not noted for her way with words, and reminded Rowan that poor Birdie, although it had in no way been her fault, was still regarded as the pony that nearly killed Matty Prebble. A small crowd was collecting as the class was announced, and Rowan saw her mother at the ropes, looking more frightened than she felt herself. Neither Roma nor Lizzie seemed to be bothered at all, and pushed in to go early.

They both went clear. Rowan knew that Birdie could jump far better than both their ponies and if she made a mess of it, it would be her fault. She would have no excuse. Her number was called and she turned towards the ring entrance.

'Don't start until you hear the hooter,' Josephine warned her.

Birdie was excited, knowing what it was all about, and needed no urging as Rowan trotted her in a circle while the judge took her number and gave them the hooter. Now she was started, Rowan found that every-thing seemed much less alarming and the first jump looked only knee high and positively beckoned across the soft green turf. Birdie wanted to go faster than she did, but Rowan wasn't sure about whether she ought to rein her in as she approached the jump – decided not to, and Birdie flew over it so big that Rowan was nearly thrown out of the saddle. Half out – and then she wasn't ready to gather the mare together on the other side as she had intended . . . Rowan bit her tongue and almost panicked as Birdie bore down on the next set of rails at a very fast canter. She took a pull out of a sense of self-preservation, nothing to do with horsemanship, and Birdie came back fractionally, bounced up and down on the spot – or so it seemed – and then plunged wildly over the rails. Rowan heard nothing fall, but thought she had probably gone deaf as well as stupid – her senses seemed to have left her. Where was the next jump? She had no idea.

Birdie was now heading for the ropes and looked set to jump them too, but suddenly Josephine was there, hissing, 'The red wall on your left! Slow down!'

Rowan, anguished at the thought of being found wanting, desperately pulled her wits together. Charlie must be watching too! The thought was like ice on her fevered brain. She saw the next jump clearly and the one beyond it, and pulled Birdie gently, firmly, out of her sprawling canter and back to a trot, collected her exactly as Josephine had taught her in the school and, three strides away, kicked her on to jump the wall. Perfectly!

Now Rowan saw the course ahead of her, the order of jumps neatly in her brain, knew exactly how she must calm Birdie and present her straight and collected. Suddenly she was in charge and – wonder of wonders! – enjoying herself. Birdie, although hyped up, was still controllable, quite unlike Swallow whom she could never have jumped in public. Well, fairly controllable . . . Rowan knew they were going too fast, but safely fast, or so she thought. She just had to steer. Nothing fell, and they flew through the finish and did two circles to pull up.

Josephine was severe. 'If those jumps had been anything at all, you'd have knocked half of them down.'

Rowan listened to her but, now it was over, she was so fantastically thrilled with the feeling that she hardly took it in. She had gone clear!

'But for the grace of God—' Josephine said darkly. 'Much too fast!'

'I couldn't help it.'

'You've got to help it, muttonhead! The jump-off will be against the clock, but if you go even faster you'll end up through the ropes. This is your first show, Rowan – it's a practice for the future. Much better in the jump-off to be under control and riding well all the way and coming fourth or fifth, than to win in a crazy, lucky gallop. Of course Birdie can do it – we all know that – but you were no help to her at all.'

'You've got to be a credit to us,' Hugh said smugly. 'Nobody's going to ask Josephine for lessons if you're any advert.'

It was Hugh saying this that put steel into Rowan's soul. The pig!

They drew lots for order of going for the jump-off. There were about a dozen clears and Rowan drew near the end, after both Lizzie and Roma.

Josephine said, 'Don't think about winning this time. Think about doing a copybook round. Show them you can.' Show me, she meant.

Rowan could see how Lizzie, even though Fable was no great jumper, got her round very fast by pure riding. No jerks or skids, but economical turns, perfectly controlled. Fable was not a natural goer, and had to be kicked on all the way, but she did a fast clear. Roma, on Jones, tried to emulate her but, without Lizzie's experience, got a refusal when her attempted fast turn got her into the jump all wrong. But Jones was a real trier and did well in spite of his rider's over-keen riding. Rowan saw that that was what she mustn't do.

As it was her turn to go, she got a glimpse of Charlie turning round from chatting to someone to watch her. It stiffened her resolve – she would do exactly as Josephine said! Don't think of winning. Then she saw Hugh grinning, and her resolve changed to deep indignation. No advert indeed! So she rode out in a great wash of excitement and whizzing adrenalin, not knowing what on earth she was going to do.

At least she now knew the course – the same, luckily. The thing was to go fast between jumps, but come back to jump them all in hand, and be ready on landing to turn quickly. But she wasn't yet secure enough on landing to gather the pony together quickly enough. She still felt on landing that she was jolly lucky to have made it, and she needed several strides to congratulate herself and sort herself out again. Of course, while she was doing this, Birdie was flying off in the wrong direction. Even so, although in no way as expert as Lizzie, she got a clear round and was only a few seconds slower.

When she came out Josephine was smiling and said, 'Jolly good effort, Rowan. For your first show that was brilliant.'

Hugh gave her a sort of pitying sneer, and Charlie said, 'You rode that very well. Well done.'

For this accolade, her day was made. She came fourth. Lizzie was third and two people they didn't know were first and second. Her rosette was green and glittered proudly on Birdie's browband. Rowan leaned forward and put her cheek against the hard, sweaty neck. 'You're wonderful, Birdie. It's only me that's no good. I promise you I'll get better, and then you'll win.'

Her mother was thrilled, and Rowan, after all her cowardly fears, found that the day was suddenly all sunshine and she went to the secretary's tent and collected a sheaf of schedules for future shows.

Shrimp won the under 12.2 Open and Hugh won the 14.2 Open and got his cup back. Grudgingly, Rowan had to admit that he was brilliant. He had his photo taken by the newspapers, one hand on the cup that he had so unwillingly cleaned the night before. He wasn't nearly as thrilled with his win as she was with her fourth.

'Oh, he's such a big head,' Lizzie sympathized.

They were going to watch Charlie jump Out of the West, but Rowan went back to the horsebox first to make sure Birdie was all right. She had her haynet and a summer sheet on and was tied outside the trailer with Fable.

There was a man looking at her with a young girl at his side. When Rowan hitched the haynet up better, he said to her, 'Is this the pony that came fourth in the Novice?'

'Yes.'

'Is she yours?'

'Yes.'

'You're not thinking of selling her, I suppose?'

'No!'

'I like her very much,' the man said. 'Just the sort we're looking for. If she does come on the market . . .' He handed Rowan a card and smiled. 'No offence, I hope?'

Perhaps he was nervous of the glare Rowan gave him. He retreated, leaving Rowan with a wildly beating pulse. It was almost as bad as all the uncertainties with Swallow, owning Birdie and yet not owning her. She did not even look at the card, but shoved it deep into her jodhpur pocket. Thank goodness Mrs Prebble wasn't around! Just as well none of the others had overheard either . . . the offer was something she was going to keep to herself.

But when she went to watch Charlie, and stood beside Josephine at the ringside, she remembered that her two heroes did not really own the horses they rode either. Prissy had jumped Wilfred in the Novice and knocked down a triple bar, which made Josephine mad – 'The stupid girl – *legs*, for heaven's sake! She rides like a mashed potato!' But, Rowan thought, if Josephine was riding him he could get round the Open without much trouble. She jumped him at home and Wilfred went splendidly for her.

But Out of the West – he was another matter. He

was so super-powered that it took all Charlie's expertise to keep him calm enough to jump. As a three-day event horse, he had to be equally good at dressage, cross country and show-jumping. He settled fairly well for dressage and his superb paces and Charlie's incredibly tactful riding got him quite good marks in spite of lack of experience. His power and enthusiasm in cross country made him one of the best, but the same enthusiasm in a constricted show-jumping ring tended to lead to his downfall. He got so excited at seeing the jumps that he couldn't wait to fly over them and, so long and powerful was his stride, he was onto the next out of control – just like me, Rowan thought – and apt to send the poles flying. Charlie was trying to teach him to listen to instructions but Out of the West was a bighead like Hugh and hated to be told.

'He's so brilliant cross country,' Josephine sighed, 'and throws everything away show-jumping. He's just got to learn. Poor Charlie!'

Mr Hicks had come to watch and stood by the ropes beside them. He was gloriously rich, Rowan remembered, sneaking him a look to see if he had a sweet, kind face and might buy Birdie for her out of kindness of heart. But he had a face like flint, hard with doing deals in the city. Rowan remembered her father saying that kind people didn't get rich very often. 'You have to be ruthless to make megabucks,' he had said. (He was fairly rich and fairly ruthless, in Rowan's opinion, but now that he had two families to support – the secretary had three children, it transpired – he kept saying suddenly that he was poor.)

The difference between her and Charlie was that, whatever Out of the West did, Charlie stayed with him, and in the jump, however wild, Charlie was like a part of him, never jabbing his mouth or budging one inch out of his perfect position. Now she had tried it herself, Rowan was in even more awe of Charlie's expertise. Calming, calming – he never got cross or too strict, letting the horse run on enough to make him happy, yet sensitively, so tactfully, collecting him enough to make a good presentation at the jump.

Josephine said, 'If you collect him too much he sulks and knocks them down. He's so bold! But he's learning, slowly. This sort of outing is just what he needs.'

He didn't win because he knocked the last triple bar flying, but Charlie was very pleased with him. He came out of the ring patting his neck and saying nice things to him, and grinned happily at old flint-faced Hicks.

'Great, eh? He'd have flattened the lot a couple of months ago.'

'Well, if you say so,' Mr Hicks said tetchily.

'It takes time.'

'You're always saying that.'

No congratulations or encouragement . . . 'He's cross because Prissy didn't win,' Josephine whispered. 'And that was no fault of the horse's. Only her feebleness.'

But, as if she didn't think any of this, she went cheerily up to Mr Hicks and said, 'A great round, don't you think, Mr Hicks, considering he's only a baby? He must have a real future. You know how to pick them, eh?'

Such blatant flattery – even Rowan could see it a mile off – worked wonders on Mr Hicks. A thin smile cracked his lips and he was obviously pleased to be admired by the girl turning her beautiful clear blue eyes on him. It was completely out of character for Josephine to act in that way, but it had the right effect. Their livelihood depended on Mr Hicks for the time being and they were defending it valiantly with their deference.

When they were in the lorry going home, Rowan sat next to Charlie and he said, 'Stupid old twit – I don't know how I keep my cool! Josephine's brilliant.'

Rowan realized he had worse troubles than she had with Birdie, with far more at stake if he lost his horse.

She told herself this, but it was no real comfort. When she brushed Birdie down in her box, she kept thinking of her having a second home in the stable behind the shop, where she would be truly, utterly hers ... and they would go to shows and she would learn to control her and ride like Charlie, and when someone offered to buy her she could turn and say coolly, 'A million wouldn't be enough to buy this mare.'

'Oh, Birdie, you are so lovely!' And she flung her arms round the mare's neck. Birdie nudged her for a polo mint, and for a moment Rowan thought of Swallow and felt terrible. Then she saw the green rosette lying in the manger and felt wonderful. And she laughed, and nearly cried, and went home for her tea.

Chapter Seven

Pauline Watkins bought the shop and a builder made the required improvements. The builder had a black bathroom suite cheap from a demolition job so they had that installed with gold taps and red shower curtains.

'Great, isn't it?' Pauline Watkins was thrilled and Rowan thought she'd never have dared have a wacky bathroom like that when her husband had been around. It would have been pink or avocado. Like her bedroom, there was a view up the pony field and no frosted glass – 'Whoever's going to watch us having a bath, for heaven's sake?'

As she had suspected, Rowan soon learned that there was no money over from doing up the cottage. Her father disputed all the bills, in spite of having sold their smart house in the village for plenty of money.

Her mother said, 'Half each, it isn't a fortune,' as if to defend him.

Rowan plucked up courage to tell her mother Birdie's price.

'Do you think he'll buy her for me in the autumn?' The lease agreed with Mrs Prebble was up at the end of October.

Pauline Watkins was stunned. 'At that figure! I should think it's highly unlikely! However can she be worth as much as that?'

'It's what Mrs Prebble paid for her. She just wants her money back.'

'But what a lot! The Hawes sold her for that?'

'Yes. They are horse dealers, after all, and Charlie put the price up because he didn't want Mrs Prebble to buy her. But she did, all the same. Birdie's got what they call potential.'

'Haven't we all, given the chance?' Pauline said rather bitterly. 'Oh, darling, I can't see him paying that much! Half, perhaps. He does love you, after all.'

Rowan thought there was no price on love. Wrong again. She could see her mother was very cast down.

'There's no extra cash. I'm earning a bit with the cooking but only enough to barely keep us, there's nothing to save. We might hit the big time, but not before October, I shouldn't think.'

She did sandwiches and local dinner parties with Joan Hawes and they seemed to enjoy themselves working together. They were both very good cooks.

Rowan had come across the card in her jods pocket from the man who had offered to buy Birdie at her first show and, without saying why, asked Lizzie if she knew who he was.

'Oh, yes,' said Lizzie. 'Big show-jumper. Hickstead and all that. Charlie knows him.'

Had he said anything to Charlie? But Rowan knew she was safe until October, even if they were queuing up to buy Birdie after that. And it didn't help that she was steadily improving and that the green rosette tacked to her bedroom wall (something else her father wouldn't have allowed) was quite soon joined by several others: red, blue, and yellow. In spite of her inadequate rider, Birdie was doing clear rounds, and their confidence was growing show by show. Rowan thought of nothing else. She was deeply committed to Birdie and her new life and everyone said exactly what they hadn't said about Swallow – 'You two seem made for each other.'

By the summer holidays Birdie was out of the

Novice classes and was jumping against Hugh – and Tom Thug. She couldn't beat them, although she came third once.

In spite of Tom Thug being so beastly, worse than Hugh, Rowan saw that he and Swallow were extremely well-suited. Tom Thug was a laconic, undemonstrative boy with, as far as Rowan could see, no redeeming features at all. He sat hunched on Swallow in the collecting ring, watching his fellow competitors going over the practice bar with his pale, spiky-lashed eyes saying nothing behind his sportsman's glasses. If Swallow fidgeted he growled at him and Swallow stood still. Rowan had never got Swallow to stand still. Swallow wore a twisted snaffle and some severe gadgetry with which Tom Thug was able to control him – although Tom was no more severe on him than was necessary and was undeniably a very strong and able rider, as good as Hugh. He usually beat Hugh, which made Hugh furious. Hugh was not a good loser, especially as Rowan knew that he'd had his eye on Swallow for his own after Rowan failed to ride him.

'It's all your fault – showing off on him to the newspaper,' Shrimp said candidly. 'If he'd never had his photo in the paper, the Thugs would never have seen and we'd still have Swallow. And you'd probably be riding him by now because Rowan—' She shrugged and laughed.

'Rowan never would,' Rowan finished for her. She could say it now, without being upset. Swallow, she now saw, was a bit of a thug himself. Birdie was a lady. Swallow's film was to open in London in the autumn, and they were all going to the opening night, amongst the film stars (they hoped).

Just as the summer holidays were starting, Auntie Millie, the Pony Club boss, came to High Hawes to have a chat with Joan Hawes.

'I've got to make up a team for a competition in the holidays. The Barnfield Hill Pony Club is running a One Day Event, and we've got to send a team. Their DC is such a dreadful woman – she's only running it because she thinks she can beat us all. She's got the Truggs, for a start, and that very good gel Melinda Bottomly. She thinks it's all buttoned up. But we've got Hugh and we've also got Rowan now. I just want to know if you think Rowan's ready to be thrown in at the deep end?'

'I would have thought so,' Joan Hawes said. 'She'll shiver and look terrified, of course. She still can't believe it's happening to her, poor mite. But I'm sure Josephine would agree to it. Ask her.'

'Well, I'm banking on it. We stand a chance then. I'm afraid Fable isn't up to it, although of course Lizzie is. I suppose—?'

Joan Hawes laughed. 'No, we're not looking for a better pony for Lizzie. Hugh, perhaps, but not Lizzie. She doesn't want to be in your teams, does she? She's happy with Fable.'

'She's no ambition, that girl!'

'We don't all want to be winners, Millie, thank God! There's enough in this family without Lizzie too.'

'No, I can't complain. Pity we haven't got Matty Prebble these days, although at least we've got her pony. What's the situation there, by the way?'

Joan Hawes explained it. 'We can't see poor Rowan keeping Birdie, somehow. Not at that price. Lucy Prebble says she'll do any exchange, or part exchange, if we find a suitable pony for Matty to start riding again, but of course Charlie won't take the risk. If it doesn't turn out perfect we'll get the blame. That woman is such a pain!'

'Oh dear, poor kids! What a muddle.'

Rowan couldn't believe she was being asked to be part of the Pony Club team. Josephine said to her patiently, as if to an idiot, 'It's what happens, Rowan, if you are successful. You – are – a – success.'

Rowan felt shivery even thinking about it.

'Of course' – more severely, being an instructor, Josephine continued – 'I think it's a little premature, but a brilliant chance. You must take it. Your dressage is easily as good as Hugh's and Tom Thug will have to be brilliant to get decent marks with Swallow, so you should start with an advantage. Then it's up to you.'

'But I haven't done any cross country!'

'You have round the fields here. But, true, that's where you need the practice. We'll ask Charlie.'

Charlie said amiably, 'We'll take her to Sparrow Farm and have a morning round there. Birdie will love it. The three of us can go, not the others. We can take Jack and Wilfred.

Sparrow Farm was a cross-country course ten miles away where you paid to practise. It had jumps of varying sizes, to suit novice and experienced horses. When Hugh heard they were going he wanted to come too but Charlie said crushingly, 'You don't want any more practice, idiot. Your pony'll be clapped out by the time of the competition, the way you career about.'

'There's room in the lorry!'

'Not in the cab,' Charlie said. He knew that the last thing Rowan wanted was Hugh's company. He would turn it into a competition from the first fence.

Josephine thought it would be good practice for Priscilla, but they then decided they didn't want their day spoilt by Priscilla's company any more than Hugh's.

'Just us three,' Charlie decided.

Rowan was thrilled to be so privileged. She knew Charlie had pressure on him from Mr Hicks to start Out of the West in serious competition in the autumn and cross-country practice was useful for him too. Charlie thought it was too soon, but Mr Hicks paid the bills. It was up to Charlie to make it a success, in spite of his misgivings. He too might lose his horse, just like Rowan, if things didn't go right. Moaning about Mr Hicks, Charlie sighed and said, 'It's a hard life!' then laughed, because they were driving over the downs in their horsebox to go jumping, not standing in a dole queue or working in a car factory or sweltering in the Stock Exchange.

'Money's not everything,' he said.

And Josephine said, 'It is if it means buying Birdie and keeping Jack to make us a living and things like that.'

Charlie changed gear as the lorry started to labour up a hill and his expression changed and he said, 'It's horrible if you start thinking seriously — that our family's bread depends largely on this beast in the back of the lorry jumping cross country well enough to please old Hicks.'

'Not really,' said Josephine. 'Everyone has to please their employers to keep their jobs.'

'I wish Jack understood that!'

Rowan saw that her Birdie thing was really quite minor beside Charlie's problems. All the same, there was nothing she could to help him and he refused point blank to help her.

'No way am I going to get involved in finding Matty a pony! Even for you, dear Rowan.'

'What do you think Matty wants?' Rowan thought she might find one herself if she knew what she was looking for.

Josephine said, 'Matty's growing quite fast. It's got to be fifteen two-ish with a fabulous temperament, impeccable manners and obedience, very good-looking – our Mrs P is a terrible snob about looks – possibly an older horse, with spirit enough not to be boring yet utterly trustworthy. Altogether, a rare beast.'

'What she *ought* to buy is something like our Armchair,' Charlie said, 'but of course she wouldn't have such a common-looking horse in her stables.'

'Quite. After all, looks don't matter a jot if the horse is right for the job,' Josephine said.

Rowan tried to remember the requirements. She would have to look herself. Where on earth to start? Perhaps Lizzie would help her. It was her only chance of keeping Birdie, she could see. But stupid to spoil the day with worrying, when she was out with her two idols to jump dear Birdie cross country. Who could ask for more bliss than that?

The cross-country course was set in rolling farmland, with a wood in the middle and a water complex, which was what Charlie wanted for Out of the West. The horse was already jumping freely over big fences and ditches, but needed practice with trickier and more unusual obstacles, such as steps and jumps into water. There were large fences for Open horses and, beside them, medium and smaller ones for Novice horses and the likes of Birdie, built in similar style. Hugh had already told Rowan that Cascade had jumped the course several times, and done the Novice course twice. It was only Lizzie's presence, Rowan thought, that stopped him from saying he'd been round the Open course as well.

'You'll have to take Rowan,' Charlie said to

Josephine. Once mounted on Out of the West, his whole attention was occupied.

They saddled up and mounted and rode the horses in, then Charlie went to 'play in the water' and Josephine on Wilfred said she would go round with Rowan.

'Just a jump at a time, very steadily, Rowan. Birdie's done this before – she'll be fine.'

'What about the water?' Hugh had told Rowan about the water complex. The thought of jumping over a fence into water terrified her.

'Birdie's OK. Think positive. She'll do it.'

When someone like Josephine said she'd do it, Rowan believed her. As it was, Birdie set off through the start first. Josephine followed her and they had no trouble. When they came to the lake they pulled up as Out of the West was standing in it.

'Cooling off.' Charlie laughed and rode out. 'He's done them beautifully – the two bottom ones. I'm going to jump the top one and call it a day.'

The top one was, Rowan thought, horrible, with an earth bank built up in front of the water. On top of the bank there was a heavy telegraph pole, not very high but, with the bank, making quite a steep drop into the water. The middle one had a smaller drop and the bottom jump – hers – no drop at all, just a telegraph pole about two feet high immediately in front of the lake.

Birdie flew over it and Rowan was so surprised and pleased she did it again. Nothing to it! Josephine jumped Wilfred over the middle one and then they pulled up to watch Charlie.

'When he's done, you can go round again on your own,' Josephine said. 'Just keep her steady, that's all, no rushing.'

Birdie with her soft mouth was much easier to steady than Swallow. Rowan felt confident and keen to go again. Birdie swung beneath her as she pulled her up out of Charlie's way. She sat beside Josephine and watched Charlie canter Out of the West slowly round the back of the bank, keeping his stride short. The horse, as always, was pulling hard and bounding up the bank with kangaroo-like leaps. But at the top, instead of taking the last leap out wide over the top, he seemed to suddenly lose his confidence. He stopped dead with a snort, then made a half-hearted half-rear to clear the bar, caught his toe on the top and cart-wheeled spectacularly over into the lake, landing with a huge splash on his back.

For a moment there was nothing to be seen but

churning spray and flashing iron hooves. Rowan sat paralysed with horror.

'Oh, my God!' Josephine cried out.

She wheeled Wilfred around and trotted sharply over to the end of the lake to where Out of the West was set to emerge, streaming water. Charlie was secondary to the valuable horse. With fraught alacrity she caught the trailing reins just in time to stop him galloping off. She leaped off and shouted to Rowan. 'Come and help me!'

Charlie was staggering out of the lake, wet to the skin. Rowan clumped her heels to Birdie's side and cantered over to Josephine who, with one look at Charlie, said, 'Collar bone?'

'Yeah,' said Charlie.

Josephine said to Rowan sharply, 'Get off and hold Wilfred for me.'

Charlie was clutching his shoulder and looking rather white. He said, 'We can't let Jack finish on that.'

'No, I'll take him over it,' Josephine said.

'Get Rowan to give you a lead. I'll hold Wilfred.'

'What, over the top?' Rowan nearly fainted with fright.

Charlie, in spite of everything, laughed. 'No, you twit, the little one!'

He took Wilfred's reins from her, half laughing, half groaning. His left arm wasn't working, and as soon as he had the reins looped over his right arm he went back to holding the injured arm in place. He said to Rowan comfortingly, seeing her fear, 'I've done it twice before, I know the drill.'

'Is it broken?'

'Yes, but it's only a collar bone. They mend quite quickly.'

Rowan thought he was incredibly brave. It put her on her mettle, not to let him down in the cause of Out of the West's schooling.

'Just go like you did before,' Josephine said. 'And we'll follow. It will reassure him, after that fall.'

Rowan gathered Birdie up and cantered her back round the bank. She felt hyped up and had no doubt at all as she faced the lake for the second time. Birdie flew it and the big horse followed her without hesitation. Rowan turned in her saddle and shouted, 'I'll do the middle one, if you like!'

She did not see the look that passed between Josephine and Charlie. They knew they should stop her, but neither of them did. They both took chances, knew they shouldn't, and still did.

Rowan, in her wonderful new role of confidence-

496

giver, cantered boldly round the back of the bank again, and faced Birdie for the middle jump. As she approached and saw the drop ahead of her she wondered suddenly what on earth she was doing, gulped, and drove Birdie on. The water seemed awfully far down this time – whatever did the top jump feel like? It was like the high board in the swimming pool; she had stood there but never jumped. This time there was a loud splash as she hit the water and for a moment she thought she was going to go in, pitching over Birdie's shoulder. But her seat was improving all the time and miraculously she stayed in the saddle and was able to canter out in great style before being overtaken by the exuberant Out of the West. Josephine did two circles before she could pull up.

'I feel sure he'd do the top one now!' she shouted at Charlie.

But Charlie shook his head.

'Don't risk it. He's done well. Just cool him off and we'll get home.

The day hadn't gone as planned, but Rowan felt that Birdie would do anything she asked. Her confidence was increasing all the time. Half of her was thrilled with her success, the other half cast down by Charlie's accident. Josephine had to drive the lorry.

She tied Charlie's arm up with Jack's tail-bandage.

'It's not too mucky. I'll drop you off at Casualty and come back in the car later.'

'Losing time now – I can't afford it—'

Charlie, Rowan could see, was now feeling his pain and disappointment, huddled beside her in the cab and looking, strangely, rather like Hugh in one of his bad moods.

'No – well – I'll keep him going for you till it's mended,' Josephine said. 'The rate Rowan's improving I reckon she'll soon be up to it!'

Rowan flushed with pride. At that moment she felt the remark wasn't far-fetched at all. Jumping the middle water had been magical, feeling Birdie's commitment – joy, even. The little mare loved it. Yet with Lizzie she had been difficult, and even Matty hadn't liked her. She is *mine*, Rowan thought fiercely, she is *meant* for me. But in her triumph she had to commiserate with Charlie. It was he who had warned that doing anything ambitious with ponies was all ups and downs – huge disappointments followed great triumphs.

'How long will it be, getting better?'

'I can ride again quite soon after if I take bute,' he said.

'What's bute?'

'It's a painkiller.'

Josephine laughed and said, 'Painkiller for horses.
But lots of riders take it.'

'Don't tell Ma,' Charlie said quickly to Rowan.

'Collar bones are ten a penny,' Josephine said. 'But
they mend easily because they don't move about like
arms and legs. They hurt though. I've only done it
once.'

'Ribs hurt most,' Charlie said.

Josephine duly made a detour to the local hospital
and pulled up outside the Casualty entrance to let
Charlie out. Rowan offered to stop with him, seeing
his miserable face, but he told her not to be daft.

'You can do all my work next week if you want to be
helpful – mucking out and grooming.'

'Yes, I will!' Rowan breathed.

Charlie laughed, groaned – 'You are a nut, Rowan' –
and disappeared through the Casualty door. Out of the
West was kicking in the lorry, thinking they had
arrived somewhere, but stopped as they drove away.

'Mr Hicks'll be cross,' Josephine sighed. 'Poor
Charlie. Jack pulls so hard – only Charlie can get him
round a course; I can't. One or two jumps, then after
that I can't hold him.'

Rowan knew the feeling well. 'Like me and Swallow.'

'Exactly. They're two of a kind.'

Rowan felt muddled when she got home, on a high with her Birdie feelings but then even more anxious about the future. She wished she wasn't such a worrier. None of the Hawes seemed to worry like she did. Perhaps she got it from her mother. But her mother, in the new cottage, seemed much happier.

'Why don't you clean out that stable?' she suggested. 'Make it nice for Birdie? It would be great for you, having her in the back garden.'

'Only sometimes,' Rowan said. She didn't think Birdie would want to be away from her friends much. And she didn't want to be away from the Hawes. But the thought of her own snug stable at home somehow made her think that she would actually own Birdie one day. But Lizzie told her gloomily that the better she did with Birdie the more easily Mrs Prebble would be able to sell her.

'You win at Barnfield Hill and lots of people will want her.'

'Win! There's no chance of that, not with Tom Thug and Hugh going round. And that Melinda girl.'

'Gel,' said Lizzie.

'I'm dreading it.'

'You're daft,' Lizzie said. 'Mum says she's taking us to the circus tomorrow, d'you want to come? It's a modern circus – you know, no tigers or things. Only the flying trapeze. People getting zapped instead of animals.'

'Are there any horses?'

Might be. I don't think horses count.'

Rowan didn't see the point of a circus without horses.

'Ma says we're all too serious. Not me. Just the others. Charlie's in a great gloom because of losing time with his collar bone and Mr Hicks was on the phone and Mum took the phone off Charlie and told him – Mr Hicks – to shut up – not exactly *shut up* but in a polite sort of way, you know. But quite fierce. "We're not bowing and scraping to him just because he owns that horse!" she said – quite put out, for her. Then Charlie said we'd all starve without Mr Hicks and they had a row, so then Ma said we'd all go to the circus, just like that. She told us to ask Matty too. We said only if her mother didn't come, and that's arranged. But we don't mind your mother if she wants to come.'

Rowan supposed it would be quite fun, all of them. She and her mother never went anywhere new but, with High Hawes up the road, she never wanted anywhere else. They went in two cars, the two mothers driving, and Lizzie and Shrimp and Matty came with Rowan and her mother. As they sat squashed in the back, following the Hawes' Land Rover up over the long hill out of the village, Matty said to Rowan, 'I hear you went round Sparrow Farm on Birdie and jumped the water?'

'Not the top one. Only the middle.'

'Were you surprised?' Shrimp asked Matty. 'We were, when we heard.'

'You are rude, Shrimp!' Lizzie snapped. 'You're not supposed to say things like that.'

'Well, it's true. Josephine said, after Swallow, she thought Rowan'd never get it together. And now she has. That's not rude.'

'It's Birdie,' said Rowan. 'Not me.'

'It must be a bit you,' Matty said.

'Oh, Rowan always thinks she's no good,' Lizzie said.

'She was right once,' Shrimp said. 'But not now,' she added hastily.

'Has your ma said anything about you riding again?' Lizzie asked Matty.

'Oh, yes, she's forever talking about it. I don't say anything. She's looked at a couple of ponies but I refused to go. She says it'll do me good. Take me out of myself, she says. But I say, look what it did in the first place. I wouldn't need taking out of myself it I hadn't been half killed already.'

Rowan's heart sank into her best shoes. Mrs Prebble was looking now! And Matty didn't want one anyway.

'Isn't there any sort of pony you'd like?' she asked desperately.

'I wouldn't mind one – the sort that doesn't exist!' Matty laughed. 'Like a car. You know. Turn the key and it starts. Put the brake on and it stops.'

Rowan felt her evening was ruined at the turn the conversation had taken. Mrs Prebble was looking already! It was only July and there were still two months to go before her lease on Birdie was up.

When they got to the circus car park Mrs Hawes said it looked like a hospital outing, with Matty on her crutches and Charlie with his arm in a sling, and they all got the giggles. Shrimp tied a white scarf round her head like a bandage and Hugh affected a worse limp than Matty's. Rowan tried to pretend it was all very funny but she was so cast down by Matty's remarks that she couldn't join in. It was pretty feeble anyway; she bit her lip and hung back.

There were horses, thank goodness, she noticed.

A poster showed an Appaloosa (a spotted horse) standing on its hindlegs with a bespangled ring-mistress brandishing a whip. The same lady appeared to be selling the tickets, with her spangles on underneath a tracksuit – 'You can see,' Hugh remarked. 'In circuses, they all do everything.'

In spite of the several local councils who wouldn't have the circus on their land, the show seemed to be attracting a good crowd on the hot summer evening. Even Rowan forgot her woes when the clowns came on and the canned music started blaring. There were no tigers or elephants, but a very funny goat which butted the clowns, four poodles, a horse just like the Armchair that cantered round and round for a couple of acrobats to leap on and off, and a troop of six Shetlands which did a display, circling, rearing and bowing to the crowd. Hugh said he bet he could teach Cascade to do a few things like that and Shrimp said Cascade reared and bucked already, what was so special? And Hugh said, 'You could sell them Bonzo. Just what he's fit for,' so Shrimp hit him and Joan Hawes had to call them to order.

Near the end, before the flying trapeze, the bespangled lady brought on two liberty horses, a matching pair of Appaloosas, and they did a high-school act. At one point one of them lay down and she got on its back. It then got up and she twirled about a bit before jumping off.

Lizzie said to Matty, 'That's what you want, one that'll lie down for you to get on.'

Matty laughed. 'My mother would die – all those spots!'

The idea slipped into Rowan's head, hearing the exchange – a circus horse! They seemed to do it by word of mouth. No legs to make them go: they were totally obedient to the lady in spangles. She twirled her whip and pointed with it, but never touched them. She spoke to them a lot, quite quietly, and gave them something when they had reared up and walked a few steps on their hindlegs. They watched her all the time and seemed to be very attached to her. They were in beautiful condition, with shining coats.

'I'm sure I could do that,' Hugh said when they went out.

'You'd look lovely in spangles,' Lizzie jeered.

'Your legs in tights! They'd all pay to come and look!' Shrimp said.

After the flying trapeze act Charlie said, 'Think you could do that too, Hugh?' and Hugh grinned rather sheepishly and shook his head. At last, they all thought, something he couldn't do!

When Rowan got home her mother remarked that she seemed a bit glum and Rowan told her why.

'I can't bear to lose Birdie! Not now!'

'I thought you were going to do some part exchange—?'

'Oh, Mum, I've got to find it first! I was thinking tonight, when that horse lay down, a circus horse might be just the thing. Save they're all spotted or piebald – Mrs Prebble hates coloured horses. You'd think, circus horses must retire after a bit, and need a good home – the Prebbles would be a very good home . . . but it's got to be a decent colour . . . how can I find out? That circus didn't have an address – I looked on their posters, but there was nothing. I suppose they are always travelling on.'

'They have winter quarters, I think.'

'If I could talk to that lady – she might help—'

'Surely if it was the right horse, Mrs Prebble wouldn't mind a funny colour?'

'No one in their right mind would, but Mrs Prebble—!'

'Yes, she's not very understanding, is she? I could try and find out for you, if you like – go and talk to that circus woman. What do I have to ask for?'

'Oh, Mum – tell her what it's for: Matty having a useless leg, and not even wanting to – it's got to be a kind, darling horse, and beautiful to suit Mrs Prebble, and darling for Matty to want it – and cheap, cheap enough so that we can afford it, to give to Mrs Prebble in exchange—'

'Part exchange, I thought you said.'

'Oh, *Mum*!' Rowan wailed.

'Oh, stop being neurotic, you're as bad as Mrs Prebble herself!' her mother said briskly. 'If we were to find this paragon of a horse, the thing to do would be send Mrs Prebble to see it, surely? Not buy it ourselves.'

'Yes!'

'And Matty too, I dare say. From what I've heard, she has more idea of what she wants than her mother does.'

'Yes, take Matty to see it! Not Mrs Prebble at all. Then she can tell her mother she wants it!'

Rowan's mother laughed. 'She might do it for you, Rowan, if you ask her nicely. She seems quite a sensible girl, not a bit like her mother.'

'Oh, Mum, yes!'

Rowan could see the idea taking shape. It only needed the right horse.

'When you're at school tomorrow I'll go and find that woman then, and ask questions. It's worth a chance. But don't bank on it, darling. I really think you're getting a bit obsessed with this pony business – it's not the whole world, you know.'

'Oh, but it is!' Rowan wanted to shout out. But she bit her tongue and kept the words to herself.

Chapter Eight

The team for the Barnfield Hill competition had to consist of four riders under fourteen. Auntie Millie chose Hugh and Rowan and two formidable sisters called Harriet and Fiona Brown. Harriet and Fiona rode a pair of ugly home-bred full-brothers called Bill Flowerpot and Ben Flowerpot. Both were good jumpers. None of them was brilliant at dressage and Josephine gave them some schooling in the test. Bill and Ben powered round the manège, lifting up their knees and tucking in their heads, and finished the test in half the time it should have taken; Hugh kept forgetting the way, and Rowan could never quite make out whether Birdie was on the right leg or not without looking down which Josephine told her was bad.

'I just hope you can all jump better than you can canter a circle,' she despaired.

Rowan had never jumped in a team competition

before and discovered that it was much more harrowing than competing for oneself. If she made a hash of it, she would let the others down. They were supposed to be sporting and nice to each other in adversity, but Rowan couldn't see Hugh being nice to her if she boobed and stopped them winning.

'It's character building,' Charlie said happily. 'If, for example, you fall off and break your collar bone, you smile and jump back on and finish the course because if you withdraw your team will be eliminated.'

Rowan wasn't too sure if he was joking or not. But it did seem rather like it. Josephine said it wasn't as bad as that these days because now when you fell off they made you lie still until they decided you weren't fatally injured, which sometimes took ages – 'Not like when we were little; Auntie Millie would push you back in the saddle and clap your pony on the backside before you knew what had happened. But in a team, you do feel dreadful if you let the others down, it's quite true.'

None of this inspired Rowan with confidence.

Josephine said, 'Just get it in perspective, Rowan. It's only a fun thing, when all's said and done. *Enjoy* it! Charlie's not saying anything, but when he rides Out of the West in his first proper event in September, if he doesn't do well it could mean we're all out of a living

510

here! Mr Hicks is such an impatient man, and doesn't really understand the business at all. It makes it so difficult. Think of all that when you worry about Birdie.'

'Oh, I will! I'm sorry!'

'Don't expect to win anything. Just do your best and remember it's fun!'

'Yes!'

The worse she did, of course, the better it would be for selling Birdie – no one would want her. Rowan tried to remember this.

Her mother hadn't got very far with the circus lady. When she went to find her, she discovered the circus had moved on, and nobody seemed to know where to. She found out its itinerary eventually by contacting a theatre ticket agency, and drove to one of its most con-venient sites, which even then was fifty miles away. The circus lady hadn't got any old horses but gave her the name of a farm in Surrey where she thought a retired acrobat had a few 'resting' horses. She wasn't sure if she remembered the man's name correctly, and the address had no telephone number that she knew of.

'We can't get in touch without a name, not without actually going there, can we?'

'We can go there! On Sunday!'

Pauline Watkins was dubious. 'I suppose it's not too far . . . the motorway . . . I'm sure it's a wild-goose chase, but—'

'Oh, please!'

They went. It was very hot and there was a tail back on the motorway, and they couldn't find the village and Pauline Watkins was nervous about what on earth they were going to say when they got there . . . if they ever got there . . .

'I'll do the saying,' Rowan said firmly.

When they eventually found the farm they were somewhat alarmed to see that it was a very smart and beautiful place obviously owned by a Surrey stock-broker. They drove up a long avenue to an elegant house set about with manicured lawns and rose beds. In a field beside the avenue some horses were grazing, but none of them looked like circus horses, more like hunters and children's ponies.

'You go and ask. They're probably all having sherry before lunch.'

Pauline parked beside several smart estate cars and a Rolls-Royce.

Rowan got out and knocked at the front door. A manservant answered and looked at her kindly. Rowan scrambled out her bit of paper from the circus lady.

'I'm looking for Mr – Mr—' The name was impossible to pronounce so she shoved the paper under the man's nose. 'We were given this address.'

The man took it.

'Oh, yes, Bob. He's round the back, dear. In a caravan. That way.' He pointed across the expanse of gravel which wound away behind a treble-doored garage.

Rowan thanked him and rushed back to the car. They drove round the garage and followed the gravel into a stable yard. At the back of the yard was a five-barred gate into a field, and at the gate stood two chestnut Arabs with long flaxen manes.

'They look like circus horses!'

The caravan, lodged beside a haybarn, had diamond-glitter embellishments and windows with flowers engraved on them but it had a forlorn air in its retirement, and flat tyres. Its travelling days were over, as – it appeared – were Bob's. Bob was elderly, lame and garrulous. He offered them a cup of tea and told them the story of his life before they got around to the object of the visit. He was – had been – an acrobat before he fell fifty feet and missed the safety net . . . yes, the two chestnuts were retired liberty horses.

'Never been separated in their lives. And never will be, m'dear.'

Rowan knew Mrs Prebble hated Arabs and they certainly didn't want two. She put her case as clearly as possible. Retired, gentle, obedient . . . fantastic home . . . no spots . . .

'Mostly we put 'em down when they can't work no longer. It's kinder.'

'There must be one somewhere!'

'There ain't nothing here, m'dear.'

As Rowan looked about to burst into tears, Bob had a rapid rethink and said, 'There's an address I can give you – woman who has Andalusians. The circus had a few off her; they're very easy to train. No spots. Very kind. Very nice horses. She always said she'd want 'em back if we finished with 'em. Particular sort of lady.'

Rowan had never heard of Andalusians, but took the address eagerly. It was in Norfolk, miles away. Pauline Watkins thanked the old man and they departed.

'I suppose you want me to drive to Norfolk now?'

'We could ring her.'

'Ask her for a free horse, on the phone?'

'Oh, Mum!'

Rowan was in despair again. Her mother got cross and told her to stop wanting the impossible and they had a row. A bad day, Rowan thought gloomily – all because of her good intentions. She asked Josephine what an Andalusian was.

'Very old Spanish breed, very nice horse. It's not a breed that's taken off in England, not in a big way. Not tall enough perhaps, or overshadowed by the Arab.'

'How big?'

'Fifteen two-ish.'

Later Rowan looked it up in a book and it said, '. . . It has enormous presence and an appearance of great elegance . . . though courageous and spirited, few breeds are more docile and gentle.' The very thing!

Her mother refused to go to Norfolk. 'It's a wild-goose chase, Rowan,' she said severely.

Rowan daren't ask Charlie, and didn't want to talk to Lizzie about it in case Hugh got to know. It was such a long shot and her mother had lost patience, so she knew she was being a bit stupid about the whole thing.

'Once you get an idea into your head, you can't leave it alone,' her mother said crossly. 'You're like a dog with an old bone. You bury it somewhere and then keep going back to it. You can't arrange other people's lives, Rowan. You should know that by now.'

'It's mine I'm trying to arrange.'

'Well, it seems to involve a lot of other people.'

Her mother refused to ring up the woman in Norfolk, so Rowan decided she would ring the woman herself. She had to wait till her mother was out, and then she dithered for half an hour before she dared to dial the number. Even she could see it was a bit of a cheek to ask a perfect stranger for a free, or very cheap horse. Perhaps she could—

'Arbuthnot speaking.' The voice was like a bark. Rowan jumped.

'Um—'

'Who's that? Speak up!'

Rowan was so frightened she put the phone down. Then she cried. She wanted to ring back but didn't dare. Then she cried because she was so *feeble*. She couldn't just leave it now. The sense of failure would be too awful. In the end she wrote down what she wanted to say on a piece of paper and held it in front of her as she dialled the Norfolk number. It trembled in her hand so she could scarcely see what she had written.

'Arbuthnot speaking!'

'I understand you have Andalusian horses?' She tried to sound like Mrs Prebble, tough and confident.

'Yes.' Another bark.

'I am looking for a retired Andalusian horse to go to an excellent home to be ridden by a girl who was severely injured in a riding accident. She wants a suitable horse to get rehabilitated.' (The last sentence didn't sound so good said as it looked written down, and she stumbled over rehabilitated – six syllables!) She pressed on, 'It needs to be perfectly quiet but willing and good looking and preferably bay.' Her voice got progressively less like Mrs Prebble's and more like Rowan Watkins's with every word.

'You don't want much, do you? Who are you?'

'I'm Rowan Watkins.' With a burst of inspiration (not written down) she added, 'Bob somebody gave me your address. He's an old circus man in Surrey, an acrobat – he fell off – he has two retired Arabs and he told me about you. He said to go and see you, but you're rather far away.'

'Are you a child?' asked Ms Arbuthnot suspiciously.

'I'm just twelve.'

'The horse is for you?'

'No, my friend. She's fourteen, and a very good rider, but her legs don't work now, so we thought – perhaps – a retired circus horse, that does things if you tell it . . .' Rowan, listening to herself, had never heard such a load of rubbish. She added valiantly, 'It's a very experienced home. Her mother's a Pony Club instructor.'

'Why isn't her mother ringing me up then?'

Rowan groaned. It would take all night to explain.

There was a long silence.

Then, 'Listen, child. I have a horse that might suit you, a pensioned off *haute école* horse, not old, but with some hindleg trouble that means he can't perform any more. I would let him go for nothing to a very good home, for hacking. But you would have to come and see me and I would have to come and see the home and all sorts of things like that which I think an adult would have to arrange. So if you are still interested sort it out with some responsible person and call me back.'

With which she put the phone down.

Rowan sat stunned. Having expected nothing, in seconds she had cracked the whole conundrum. She found it hard to believe, and was even tremblier now than when she had started. She lay back in the arm-chair, staring at the cracked ceiling, taking long, calming breaths. The ceiling whirled. The magic horse existed! What next?

What next seemed to be team practice for the

competition – nobody wanted to know about Rowan's circus horse.

'Count me out,' said Charlie. 'I've told you – I won't do another deal with Mrs P for all the tea in China.'

Josephine, rather more reluctantly, agreed. 'We can do nothing right for that woman. We really can't get involved with her again, Rowan. Anything we find for Matty is bound to be wrong.'

Pauline Watkins said it was no good going all that way with Rowan – neither of them knew enough about horses.

'Just tell Mrs Prebble you've found her a horse. Won't that do?'

'She won't take it from me! She'd take it from Charlie or Josephine, but not me. Especially if she knows it's a circus horse. She's a terrible snob about horses.'

'Well, honestly, Rowan, you do get crazy ideas. It seems you want you and me to go to Norfolk and bring back this horse on the off chance Mrs Prebble might find it suitable for Matty. Just a chance! For goodness' sake tell Mrs Prebble what you've found and leave it to her. Or tell Matty. It's for Matty, after all.'

But Rowan knew Mrs Prebble wouldn't go all the way to Norfolk to look at a horse that she, Rowan, recommended. If she took Matty and Matty liked it, she might persuade her mother. But how could they get there? Worrying about the Andalusian horse made Rowan almost forget the competition, so that when there was a last dressage practice at High Hawes with Josephine in charge and Auntie Millie turned up to give them a sort of Before Agincourt lecture she had to bring her mind back to the problem in hand – which suddenly seemed a larger problem than Matty's horse. Auntie Millie took her on one side.

'I'm rather throwing you in at the deep end, Rowan. Just do your best, that's all I'm asking. It will be splendid practice for you to ride in this sort of competition.'

Rowan recognized this as a sort of let-out if she did badly, and as a sign that great things were not expected of her. Instead of comforting her, it spiked her pride. Auntie Millie hadn't seen her giving Out of the West a lead over the water! She glowered.

'Why, you look just like Hugh!' Auntie Millie said, and laughed. She had a laugh like a hyena. She patted Rowan on the knee and said, 'You're my girl, Rowan!' and wandered off.

What this meant, Rowan had no idea.

* * *

The day of the Barnfield competition was the same day as Charlie had to take Out of the West to his first big event. Josephine was going with him and Priscilla was going to ride Wilfred in the Novice competition. They commandeered the big horsebox and left the trailer for Hugh and Rowan. Joan Hawes was going to drive the ponies.

'I'm really sorry I can't come with you,' Josephine said to Rowan. 'You're on your own today, but just remember, keep cool, think of it as good practice, not something you've got to win. Just do your own thing, enjoy it!'

Is that what she was going to say to Charlie, Rowan wondered? Charlie seemed to be giving Hugh a big talking-to, very stern, and Hugh was looking wriggly and cross, but afterwards Charlie came across to Rowan and said, 'Good luck, Rowan.'

'And you!'

If only she could go with him and watch him on Out of the West! She knew it would be spectacular and that, in his way, he was as nervous as she was, because of Mr Hicks. If Out of the West had been his own horse . . . But if he had been, she knew he wouldn't be going. Charlie thought it was too soon. His shoulder still hurt him because he hadn't rested it enough, and he looked drawn and serious.

After they had departed, Rowan and Hugh loaded their ponies into the trailer and Lizzie and Shrimp came out with a huge picnic basket. Mrs Prebble called in to drop Matty, who wanted to travel with them in the Land Rover instead of with her mother, and Mrs Prebble said to Rowan, 'Don't let the pony down, my girl.'

Lizzie, overhearing, put her tongue out and as Mrs Prebble flounced round she saw her. Lizzie, very quickly, said to Rowan, 'I've got an ulcer on my tongue. Can you see it?'

They then got the giggles, and Lizzie kept saying, 'Don't let the pony down, my girl!' in her Mrs Prebble voice, and Hugh was let in on the joke and joined in. They then noticed that Matty was looking horribly miserable and stopped, because she had to live with the woman, poor girl.

'She can't help it,' Matty said miserably.

'Come on, squash up,' Joan Hawes said cheerfully, to change the subject. 'Give Matty some room, Hugh. Or get in the front with me – that would be best.'

They checked that they hadn't forgotten anything. It was going to be tough without Josephine or Charlie to mastermind them – even Hugh was used to having their back-up. But when they got on the road Rowan found that her excitement rather over-rode everything else, and little fountains of fear and joy and terror and anticipation kept bursting up in her stomach. Surely she was practised enough now to take it all more calmly? But being in a team was different. It mattered terribly, doing well.

The Barnfield Hill event was set in old-fashioned farmland, with hedges. There was a huge field to collect in, edged on one side by a large wood. A jump ominously called the Leaf Slide led into the wood, and down a winding path to a coffin jump over a track, then up and out into a big park where there was a long uphill gallop with fallen trees to jump. On the way back, downhill, there were some island jumps, then some rails back into the wood and another winding path leading steeply down to a stream which you had to jump, across banks strengthened with railway sleepers.

'Lots of 'em refuse here,' Hugh said casually, as they walked around.

Lizzie said, being Josephine, 'You've got to get her back well in control, coming home into the wood, Rowan, because the long gallop through the park makes them all tizzed up. If you come too fast down to the stream you'll hit a tree, or miss the right line to the jump.'

'And lots of spectators stand there to watch the fun,' Hugh said, 'and they get in the way.'

'No, they don't,' Lizzie said. 'Not if the fence-judge is any good. But Birdie might be spooked by them. She's not done much of this before.' Then, seeing Rowan's look, she added soothingly, 'But she'll be heading for home and loving it, don't worry.' Then she couldn't help adding, 'But don't come too fast!'

Rowan missed Josephine, who would have walked the course with her sternly and helpfully. Hugh had done the course several times before and threw out what he thought was useful information, but in a really scaring way. Rowan knew that it was harder for her, on a pony strange to the course. The Flowerpots had both ridden the course before, too. She would be the discard, she was convinced. (Only the best three in the team of four were counted for the results.) But Fiona Flowerpot said, 'Don't be bothered – it's nice. I bet your dressage is better than Hugh's.'

Rowan didn't think so, as she had seen Hugh really trying at home, and he was good. Anyway, Hugh was on her side. It wasn't Hugh she had to beat, but her erstwhile Swallow, who was in the home team. He was being unboxed across the field by Tom Thug, and Rowan went to see him. Tom Thug let her hold him while he fetched his tack. Swallow nuzzled her in a friendly way and Rowan was sure he remembered her. He looked very well and fit, and Rowan was comforted by the fact that he was doing what he wanted to do with his proper owner, not having to go slowly like he had with her.

'You were too clever for me, Swallow,' Rowan whispered.

She gave him a Polo mint and he licked her hand. He had old sores at the corners of his mouth, she noticed, from his severe bit. But he had only himself to blame, as Hugh would have said. She walked back to Birdie, confused with her allegiances.

Auntie Millie arrived and boomed encouragement at them. Although she said things about enjoying it and just doing your best and made out it was fun, Rowan thought that in her heart Auntie Millie was as keen on winning as Mrs Prebble. She had a sort of glint in her eye. She hadn't really ridden in all those point-to-points just for fun, Rowan guessed. Her house was said to be full of tarnished silver cups from the glory days of her past.

They had to ride the dressage test first, then go cross country, and show-jump last. It helped a lot with one's score to do a good dressage test, and Rowan had practised diligently with Josephine and hoped to get off to a good start. Birdie was the right shape for it and was naturally balanced, which was a great help. Bill and Ben the Flowerpot Men powered round as usual, fast but accurate, with their noses tucked in and their large hooves hammering out perfect circles. They were Welsh cobs, and almost indistinguishable, bright bays with heavy black tails. Of their team, Birdie was the only elegant member but, as Auntie Millie was fond of saying, handsome is as handsome does.

Hugh went in and Rowan stood waiting, her heart beginning to pound uncomfortably. Lizzie stood by her in her Josephine role, and they watched Hugh get halfway through the test then forget what came next. Luckily he was quite near them and Lizzie saw him pull up and shouted at him quickly, 'Change rein at K, sitting trot!' The judge, about to give him the hooter, desisted.

'Idiot,' Lizzie said.

His free walk turned into a trot and his canter circles were wild, and Rowan thought with a certain satisfaction that she might, if she was lucky, get a better score than Cascade.

It was the first test she had ever attempted in proper competition. Hugh had thought he could do it standing on his head, but Rowan's intense, nervous concentration made Birdie prick up her ears and gather herself together in her best Josephine-drilled manner, wondering what the tension was for. She bent her long neck softly to the bit and streamers of foam flew from her mouth as she circled elegantly on the proper leg, to left and to right. Rowan remembered not to look down, not quite sure if she was on the proper leg save that it felt like it, and Lizzie would have hissed at her if she wasn't – she was close enough. Hugh sat watching, scowling. Birdie felt pliable and sweet as a willow twig in the breeze: Rowan could not believe her luck. She pulled her back for the free walk . . . a bit too free . . . Birdie looked up, saw Cascade and whinnied – horrors! Rowan gave her a sharp kick and she gave a prance and a skitter, then relaxed again. About two out of ten for free walk, Rowan thought crossly. All Hugh's fault! After that not too much went wrong, apart from not making her transitions in quite the right places, and the usual trouble with standing square for the halt – squarish, but not perfect. And Birdie bit at a fly on her leg before moving off.

'That was good!' Lizzie said.

'Well done, my gel!' said Auntie Millie. 'You seem to get on well with that pony. Better than that little hellcat Hugh had at camp last year. I thought that was yours?'

'It's Tom Thug's now. Tom Trugg, I mean.'

'Hotspur? Is that the same pony?'

'Yes.'

'Well, blow me. We had it in camp and I never recognized it!'

They stayed to watch Swallow/Hotspur do his dressage test, for which Rowan didn't envy Tom Thug. The pony, knowing that the day was for jumping, was in his most excitable mood, and put in several bucks when cantering. How Tom Thug managed to get him to walk at all Rowan found incredible, and standing still after the halt . . . the pony sort of bounced on the spot, every muscle quivering with the effort of restraining himself.

'Damned good riding, to get any sort of a score on that animal,' Auntie Millie exclaimed.

'He'll make up for it the rest of the day though,' Matty said.

She was bounding about on her crutches, not noticeably upset not to be competing. The grass was too rough for her wheelchair. Rowan thought of the perfect, gentle horse . . . but no, not to worry about that now! The cross country was already under way and her number was coming up fast.

Now she felt the panic rising.

Lizzie, seeing her face, said, 'Don't be daft. Birdie will fly over everything.' She put her arms round Birdie's neck and laid her cheek against the gleaming coat. 'I wonder how Charlie's doing?'

Rowan thought of Charlie's strained face, and thought of Mr Hicks watching him, his tight, money-maker's lips pursed up. If Prissy made a hash of it on Wilfred, her father would be in a terrible mood. Charlie had to bear the brunt of it, for both Prissy and himself, and mustn't answer back. It made her feel a lot better, that her day was quite simple compared with Charlie's.

The first teams were already on the cross-country course and messages came back that nobody was going clear so far. The water was causing trouble as usual and a jump in the park near the pond, where you approached round quite a sharp bend under the trees, was getting quite a lot of run-outs. Mrs Prebble was out scouting for them and sent a message back: 'Approach it at a trot!'

'Yes*sir*!' said Hugh crossly. 'What an old bosscat your mother is,' he said to Matty. But Matty only laughed. She seemed to enjoy not doing it, only watching.

But Rowan thought what a waste it was, when she was such a brilliant rider. Life was very unfair.

Matty said, 'I'm going out to the wood to watch you go round. You can see more from the edge. Are you coming, Lizzie?'

'All right.'

Lizzie wasn't sure if it was fair to leave Rowan before the off, but she had Hugh and Harriet and Fiona with her, so she set off with the swinging Matty. Someone in a car quite soon gave them a lift, Rowan was pleased to see. Matty was a real goer on her crutches, just like on her ponies. Without Lizzie, she got the trembles again. But then Auntie Millie came over and made them all laugh. 'It's chaos out there. You've just got to go very steadily and *think*. The trouble is all being caused by witless riding. I know you will have no problems.' There was no reply to that.

They rode down to the collecting ring. As all their ponies were goers they were more concerned with keeping them calm than riding them in, so they walked round together in big circles. Tom Thug set off on Swallow, obviously without anyone having told him to approach the jumps at a trot. Watching him, Rowan was filled with relief at the way things had turned out – she could never have done that! Swallow flew into the wood, and came home in very short time, the first clear.

'No one will beat Hotspur,' Rowan heard someone say.

Tom Thug got off and loosened his girths and, still on his feet, walked Swallow round to cool him off. It was apparent now that he was getting rather large for the pony, and was resting him as much as possible. Hugh watched him thoughtfully. Hugh was quite small for his age, much lighter than Tom Thug.

Hugh was going to go first, then Harriet on Bill Flowerpot, Fiona on Ben and Rowan last. Hugh set off fast, but did not appear again for a long time, and Harriet was not allowed to go as the All Clear signal did not come from the wood.

'Something's gone wrong,' Harriet said. 'It must be a fall, to be so long.'

'That means Hugh will be our discard score,' Fiona said. 'His dressage was pretty dire as well.'

Rowan listened to these seasoned campaigners making their calm assessments, and realized that if Hugh's was the discard score, hers was going to have to count. Not only did this thought scare her rigid, but she seemed to be the only one wondering if Hugh or Cascade were hurt. Harriet and Fiona were only thinking about winning.

But soon Harriet was given the flag to go, and Hugh appeared again leading Cascade out of the wood, with Lizzie running some way behind and Matty hopping in their wake. Cascade's white front was caked with mud, and Hugh had twigs in his collar and blood trickling out of his nose.

'What happened?' Fiona squeaked.

'He slipped going into the water – completely lost his legs and hit the sleepers. We all went flying. I landed right up the far side and hit the tree, and he got wedged in the ditch and we had a devil of a job to get him out. I hope he's all right.'

He slipped off, undid the girths and started to examine Cascade's legs.

Rowan thought he did seem to get into a lot of trouble, in spite of being such a good rider – no doubt Auntie Millie's exhortations to trot had fallen on deaf ears. Perhaps someone like herself, only too anxious to trot instead of gallop, might do better? It then occurred to her that she had to, if Hugh was now their discard member. That gave her several refusals in hand (twenty faults for the first, forty for second) before she topped his score. Awful butterflies started to dance in her stomach. If Hugh couldn't jump the water . . .

'Oh, Hugh! Poor Cascade! Is he all right?'

Lizzie came running up, and Auntie Millie appeared in a Land Rover shouting, 'You idiot boy! Too fast! Too fast!'

'I couldn't help it. I couldn't stop him.'

'Pony all right?'

Rowan decided the excitement was not doing Birdie any good and rode away from them trying not to think disaster. Harriet came back in one piece but said she had had a stop, and Fiona cantered off with her jaw set looking like Winston Churchill. Rowan rode down to the start and they all shouted good luck at her, and the starter took her number.

'Twenty seconds.'

Rowan trotted two small circles and the starter shouted, 'Off you go!' and set the stopwatch. Rowan was cantering without being aware of having done anything to tell Birdie – Birdie was obviously delighted to be away, and was taking a strong hold and the Leaf Slide was coming up fast. This was one of the trot-at jumps, because it had a drop that the pony didn't see until the last minute, and if it was going fast and put the brakes on suddenly you were bound to jump it alone. Or so Rowan thought. She slowed down, Birdie boggled, stopped, and jumped. Rowan shot up in the air and bit her tongue but landed back in the right place on the way down. Slither and snort . . . Birdie scrambled clear, shook her head, and trotted fast along the winding path – not a fast place, as it twisted so. She was all eyes to see what was coming next.

Rowan saw a knot of spectators and a jump judge sitting on a shooting stick looking expectantly her way. The jump was over a telegraph pole into a slightly sunken lane, two strides across and up the other side. Josephine would have been shouting, 'Legs!' Rowan thought, so she drove on as she felt Birdie looking at everything except the jump. She came to the bar, boggled again and did the same cat-hop over as she had done at the Leaf Slide. But clear. She leaped out with great enthusiasm and tore away up the wide ride on the other side to the jump that led out of the wood. Horses always jumped well out of a wood, out into the open away from imagined lions and tigers. Birdie flew it and went tearing out into the park with her glorious long thoroughbred stride. This is where the going-steady advice got thrown to the winds and the ponies got into their galloping mode, loving the great open expanse ahead of them and the excitement of the jumps. Rowan began to understand only too well why there had been disasters out here, for the going-slow advice was almost impossible to heed. And going fast was gorgeous! She felt like singing as they flew a fallen log so fast it hardly felt like a jump, just a longer stride. How she trusted Birdie! She would never have done this on Swallow, just been simply bolted with and scared stiff. But when she took a pull at Birdie, at the top of the hill, Birdie dropped her head and came back to her. Just as well, for she remembered that the next jump was the one causing trouble. There was a pond in the middle of the park with trees round it, and you had to ride round the pond, between markers, ducking under the trees, and jump a sort of garden seat with straw bales sitting in it which one couldn't see until the last minute because of the trees.

'Trot,' Rowan remembered, and trotted. No wonder most ponies had run out! Even scrupulously doing what she was told, Rowan came to the seat very suddenly. Birdie stopped with a jolt, but at least it was from a trot and not a fast canter and Rowan didn't go flying over her head. She sat down hard, kicked like crazy and Birdie leaped forward, clearing it in one enormous bound. Miraculously, Rowan stayed with her and they belted down the long hill. There was a jump of heavy poles in the way which they took in their stride – good steering. Rowan congratulated herself! –

then it was panic stations: the jump back into the wood coming up fast and darkness beyond.

However had Tom Thug managed to stop Swallow here, Rowan wondered? She came on it too fast and jumped it luckily. Birdie skewed and her back legs rattled on the top. Rowan lost her seat and a stirrup and hauled on the reins in a sweat. The path ahead was twisting and steeply downhill and no place to be going fast. Birdie came almost to a halt, rather cross, and Rowan got her stirrup and her breath back.

Clear so far! Now the nasty water-jump where Cascade had come to grief. The path twisted steeply down between the trees, and Birdie slithered on her hocks, following the gruesome score marks of those that had gone before. The ditch yawned black below. It wasn't big, but looked formidable in the dark shadow of the trees. Rowan felt Birdie quail beneath her. Don't stop now! – twenty faults they couldn't afford! Spectators crowded the far bank, tucked back into the undergrowth. How they must have enjoyed poor Cascade getting stuck and Hugh flying through the air, Rowan thought angrily, and gave Birdie such a determined clap with her legs that the mare stopped boggling and hopped over it with an air of amazement.

After that it was uphill to a lovely jump out into the

field and back to the finish over a water trough which Birdie jumped with about a metre to spare.

'Well done!' Auntie Millie was shouting as Rowan pulled up.

'I went clear!' Rowan squeaked.

'Fantastic!'

'Wonderful! Fiona went clear too, so we're in with a chance.'

Auntie Millie's eyes gleamed and the hairs on her chin bristled with triumph. Hugh stood scowling, not a good loser.

'It will all depend on the show jumping,' Auntie Millie said. 'We have two clears and a twenty for the cross country, the same as Barnfield Hill. Our dressage scores are better than theirs – Swallow was a disaster there, but he'll go clear jumping, that's for sure. It won't be decided until the very end, by the look of it.'

Mrs Prebble came toiling up the hill with Matty swinging along beside her. She was beaming for once.

'Our little mare went very well,' she enthused.

Our, thought Rowan! The remark went over her like a douse of cold water. She wanted to shout, 'MY little mare!' but was too cowardly.

'Rowan's riding got her round,' Auntie Millie said tartly.

Mrs Prebble did not reply, but her smug look did not disappear.

'There's great potential there.'

'As a pair,' said Auntie Millie. 'They understand each other. Birdie's not done well with anyone else.'

'She's young. Still learning,' said Mrs Prebble.

She still owned her, after all, and her enthusiasm was valid enough. Rowan, through a sudden blur of tears, saw Auntie Millie's lovely chin jutting aggressively, and thought – like a flash – Auntie Millie will sort out the circus horse for me! Why ever hadn't she thought of it before? Of course Mrs Prebble would take Auntie Millie's word that the horse was the right horse – if it was, of course. Thrown by all these conflicting emotions, she slipped down from Birdie and laid her cheek against the sweaty neck, hiding her face. It *must* come right, she vowed.

She saw then how it was for Hugh, wanting Swallow and not getting him, and being so ambitious, and she was nice to him and he told her how he had made such a bad mistake at the ditch. He owned up to it, responding to her sympathy. He was worried about Cascade, having got stuck, and wondered whether he had strained anything. But there was no evidence of anything being wrong.

Their mothers opened up the picnic basket and they scoffed eagerly. Rowan's head was in a whirl. She found it hard to believe how well it had gone for her so far – failure had become so engrained. At last she saw, like everybody else, that losing Swallow had been a blessing in disguise.

Auntie Millie went to study the score sheets which were being pinned on the side of the secretary's caravan. The fewest penalties, for dressage and cross country, were scored by themselves and Barnfield Hill. They led Barnfield Hill by four marks.

'That's one knock-down in the show jumping.' She shook her head. 'Very close.'

Rowan did not want to think about it. Doing what Josephine said, just going for a sensible ride, not thinking about winning, was going to be very hard. With her new idea about the circus horse, and horrible Mrs Prebble's threats, her head was whirling and beginning to ache. Lizzie told her to calm down.

'It's only a potty competition. As if it matters!'

It didn't, but seemed to, terribly. To make it worse, she saw Mrs Prebble talking to the man who had enquired whether Birdie was for sale at Otty's show. She turned away, sick with anxiety. The better she did, the more the man would offer!

The show jumping had started and Auntie Millie took them off to walk the course. It was rider demanding, all twists and turns, but only two really formidable jumps, a double and a high set of upright rails. There was a time to get round in, but generous enough. It wasn't against the clock. The advice Auntie Millie was shouting out went right past Rowan's ears. She couldn't take any more of it. She knew she just had to go very carefully and not get lost. She studied the course plan and forgot about the actual jumps. Losing one's way was going to be very easy. Lizzie said she'd stand on the ropes and shout at her if she looked like going wrong. Hugh said she'd be eliminated for outside advice.

'I'll shout quietly,' Lizzie said.

'I won't go wrong,' Rowan said stonily.

She seemed to have no heart left. She felt drained and empty. Lizzie looked at her anxiously and said, 'I don't know why anybody does this. Hugh's as sick as a parrot and you look as if you're going to throw up any minute.'

'It's Mrs Prebble,' Rowan muttered.

'Oh, her – enough to make anyone throw up.' Then she added, 'Get on. It's better when you've started.'

Luckily their time to jump was after Barnfield Hill's

540

so they would know exactly how much effort was needed. The third-placed team was not much below them and they could blow it completely if things didn't go right for them. But so could the others. They circled the collecting ring, the four of them together. The Flowerpot Men were eager but not always accurate jumpers, Cascade would go clear but what good was that now he had made a cricket score in the cross-country? And Birdie . . . Birdie was as good as her rider, Rowan thought, quailing.

The first Barnfield Hill rider went in, the high powered Melinda Bottomly. She was smooth and stony faced and, although presumably only fourteen, looked seventeen and rode a fifteen-two horse.

'Her parents run a training centre for eventers,' Fiona Flowerpot said to Rowan. 'Not fair, is it?'

About to agree, it struck Rowan that, hopeless as she was, she was trained by fairly professional people herself. How could she say it wasn't fair? Melinda did a copybook round. She had gone clear in cross country and had the lowest dressage score of the day.

'Yuk,' said Hugh.

Now that he was the discard score and didn't care, they all knew he would do a super clear. It just worked that way. Rowan thought if she knocked everything down and fell off or was eliminated, Hugh's score would count after all. The way she felt she thought that was what would happen.

The next two Barnfield riders also went clear. The crowd cheered and clapped. Their boss lady was looking pleased, as well she might, with only brilliant Swallow to go.

'If he's clear, you've all got to go clear as well to win,' Auntie Millie said. 'No room for any knock-downs at all.'

They had worked that out already and didn't think it was possible.

Swallow, after cross country, was a double handful for Tom Thug, prancing into the ring and crabwising to the first jump as his rider tried to contain him. Rowan heard someone say what a dangerous pony Hotspur was and shouldn't be allowed in the Pony Club but the person standing next to her said he was brilliant and brilliance was rare. 'A rider for that sort of brilliance is rarer,' said the critic, and Rowan could not quite believe that this was the pony she had tried to learn to ride on – no wonder she had felt in a permanent panic about the whole thing!

If Swallow was brilliant, so was Tom Thug, she realized, letting him go on and trusting the pony's own judgement, but turning him with rare skill round the tight turns. But as he came in to the nasty double he turned too quickly and got Swallow wrong. Swallow, unbalanced and off his stride, made a valiant leap over the first bar which stayed put, but then was all wrong for the second bar and was forced to refuse. It was patently a rider fault. Tom Thug's poker face remained stony. He turned back and jumped the obstacle perfectly and finished without a fault, but that made Barnfield Hill seven faults down (three for a refusal).

It was terribly hard not to cheer at Swallow's mistake. It was magic luck for them, they all acknowledged what a clever rider Tom Thug was. Rowan could see from his thoughtful expression that Hugh was actually wondering if Tom Thug might ride better than he did. He was silent, and almost jumped when Auntie Millie bawled, 'You're in first, Hugh – wake up!'

As he rode into the ring she said to the girls, 'Two down and you've lost it, remember. By one point. One down we can allow. Or two refusals. No more.'

The mathematics amazed Rowan.

Hugh rode a perfect clear, a copybook round, and came out looking almost tearful. Auntie Millie said, 'Well done, Hugh! Beautifully ridden.' She patted his knee in her grandmotherly fashion, knowing exactly how he felt – worse than ever to do so well after making such a hash of the cross country. Her opposite number of the Barnfield Hill tribe, standing by the entrance to the ring, was white with tension. Rowan's mother was standing with Joan Hawes at the ringside – they were actually laughing and eating ice creams! How could they? Rowan wondered, aghast. Already, although she was the last to go, her heart was hammering with nervousness. It was agony to watch the Flowerpot Men. They were eager and bold but rather clumsy and both rapped several jumps without actually dislodging anything. But just when they all felt it safe to let out their breath, Ben Flowerpot knocked the last jump hard. The pole leaped up in its cups, came down, bounced, and fell. A huge groan went up from the crowd. Rowan's heart went from hammering to plunging. She gathered up her reins.

Auntie Millie's chin bristled militantly. 'A clear, Rowan,' she boomed. 'Or we're lost.'

They led by three points. One knock-down and they would lose by one. A refusal and it would be a tie. No one wanted a tie.

'Birdie, save me!' Rowan whispered to her.

She no longer felt afraid of losing her way, having

watched seven go round, and had learned a little from watching – certainly to get a good straight line at the tricky double. The rest was in the lap of the gods or, rather, in Birdie's dear heart. She would do everything in her power not to mess her up.

Birdie felt so lovely, keen but not silly. Just as she faced the first jump, Rowan thought of dear Charlie and Josephine, and all her stupid irresolution melted away. As if she had anything to be frightened of, when she had sailed over that water-jump! They knew she could do it.

And I will, she said.

Birdie was no Swallow, fighting and plunging, but came to her hand every time she asked her to steady. Get her straight and right, and then legs and confidence, and over she flew. She was a natural jumper and needed only steering and her pace to be monitored. But Rowan knew that her seat was far less certain than Hugh's and Tom Thug's and Melinda Bottomly's – they had been riding all their lives and she only a year. It was much harder for her to land and be ready instantly to turn for the next jump which never seemed to be straight ahead, but always round a corner or skew on. Her heart was in her mouth, keeping her stirrups and her cool. She came to the double straight as planned, but Birdie jumped so big that the two strides in the middle were too short for her. She changed them into one and took off while Rowan was still landing – or so it felt to Rowan, flying through the air again before she was ready for it and getting left behind. She had the sense to let the reins slip, but then was tearing down on to the last jump with no control at all. She could sense the whole crowd holding its breath and Auntie Millie's anguish was as nothing to her own, seeing the round about to be blown apart at the very end.

But Birdie, galloping with joy, lifted and flew and the poles were miles below and Rowan was in heaven, hearing the great cheer that went up, carrying them on round the ring at forty miles an hour.

'Pull up, girl!' she heard the furious Barnfield lady shout, standing at the entrance to the ring, and Rowan pulled and Birdie saw that there was nothing left to jump and cantered politely out of the ring into the waiting arms of her fellows.

'They were all shrieking with joy, but quietly, so as not to be rude – squeaking more, eyes glittering with triumph.

'No one can beat us now,' Auntie Millie said. 'Well done, my dear, that was a splendid round.'

Mrs Prebble came marching up, beaming again.

'Splendid!' she said to Birdie, and patted her neck. She did not look at Rowan.

Rowan slipped out of her saddle to loosen the girths, burying her head under the saddle flap. She had to talk to Auntie Millie about the circus horse – there was no time to be lost. With every success Mrs Prebble's hold over Birdie was growing.

'Don't look so miserable – you're our heroine!' Auntie Millie was laughing. 'You've all done splendidly – and you too, Hugh – you can't win every time. Give the others a chance sometimes.'

She gave him an affectionate hug. How lucky they were to have such an encouraging boss; even if they had lost she would have encouraged them, Rowan knew, not like the awful Barnfield Hill lady who was spitting blood at the ringside and – no doubt – trying to work out if she could query the score in the cross country to make a few more points. She only had to find four to win. She could still object.

Auntie Millie went off talking to Mrs Prebble and Matty hopped up and stood looking quizzically at Birdie.

She said to Rowan, 'I really hated that mare. You've done wonders with her.'

Rowan said, 'It's not me. It's Josephine mostly.'

Hugh said, 'Your ma hypes them up too much, Charlie says.'

'Oh, Charlie says,' Matty repeated mockingly. 'We haven't all got a Charlie and Josephine, have we? Some of us have got a Mummy Prebble.' She laughed.

Rowan and Hugh didn't know how to take this remark. It was her own mother she was talking about.

'Well—' Hugh started, and then thought he shouldn't say it.

Rowan said, 'You could keep a horse with them, like me.'

'What horse?'

'The right one.'

'This myth,' said Matty.

'You do want—?' Rowan's voice shook.

Matty looked bleak suddenly. 'What's the use? I can't.'

'It's wanting that matters.' It mattered to Rowan, anyway.

'It's only days like now, watching you, makes me think I – well – oh, don't talk about it! We don't talk about it, it's too embarrassing. Nobody does, haven't you noticed?'

Rowan thought it was true, what she said; they none

of them asked Matty what it was like not being able to run about any more. They studiously avoided any talk of her disability, although they all thought about it quite a lot, and said poor Matty a lot to each other. To her, they pretended she was just the same as they were. It was a way of not getting embarrassed. It was perfectly obvious, on a day like this, that she would feel her loss keenly. She had been a brilliant rider, not just good. She had been in every Pony Club team going. Except with Birdie.

'Well, Ma's not going to leave the subject alone, that's for sure. Riding again. But she can't make me.'

They led their ponies back to the trailers. Rowan saw that the others thought the day was over, but she felt that for her it was only just starting.

Chapter Nine

Going home, Rowan asked Auntie Millie to give her a lift in her Land Rover.

'I want to talk to you. It's very important.'

Looking at the white, set face, Auntie Millie could see it was.

'Very well, but I'll have to shift a few things first.'

The few things on the passenger seat turned out to be a bag of barley, a saddle needing stuffing, a box of eggs, an overflowing handbag and a bundle of binder twine. Rowan helped to stow it in the back, leaving the eggs and the handbag at her feet. Her mother and Joan Hawes made no comment and Rowan guessed they had asked Lizzie why, but Lizzie didn't know either. She appreciated being left alone. Interfering mothers were a pain.

'So what's this all about?'

The day was over, the prizes and rosettes had been

distributed, the Barnfield Hill objection over-ruled. Horseboxes and trailers were all trundled away over the field. Auntie Millie crashed her gears into first.

Rowan poured out her story, how her lease on Birdie was up in October and people wanted to buy her. But Mrs Prebble had promised – if they found the right horse for Matty . . . It went on and on, her story. The circus . . . the old acrobat . . . Mrs Arbuthnot . . .

'Amelia Arbuthnot, you mean? Our husbands used to shoot together. Funny old gel. You rang her up? How brave. Did she bark at you?'

'Yes. But she said . . .'

Rowan's spirits bounded at the thought of old Millie knowing Mrs Arbuthnot. But why not? Old horsey people knew each other, after all those years hunting and showing and breeding and milling around – it was natural. Encouraged, she rounded out her tale: 'She's got the right horse. But it's in Norfolk, and Charlie refuses to go and see it.'

She explained why.

'Well, I don't blame him. Lucy Prebble can be very difficult. But underneath, you know, if you dig deep down, she's not a bad stick. Thwarted in this life – same old story – makes her child do what she can't do herself. She was a brilliant show jumper in her youth, as a child, you know. Quite famous. Very competitive.'

Auntie Millie overtook two horse boxes, the ancient Land Rover rattling so loudly that conversation was impossible for a while. When she slowed down again Rowan said, 'Would you go up to Norfolk and see if this horse is suitable for Matty? And if it is, tell Mrs Prebble that we've found the right horse?'

It was a terrible cheek, asking that. She countered. 'You could ring her first, perhaps, and ask about this horse. It's a pensioned-off *haute école* Andalusian.'

Auntie Millie didn't say anything. She passed a car and trailer, waving at the driver, and turned onto the road over the top of the downs that led to High Hawes.

Rowan remembered this was where Swallow, running loose, had caused Mrs Prebble to crash her car. It seemed a century ago! What was she doing, sitting in the famous Mrs Mildmay's car asking her to do this thing?'

'Why not?' said Auntie Millie. 'I wouldn't mind see- ing Amelia again.'

'You mean it?! And take me?'

'Yes, dear, why not? We can have a nice day out. Amelia knows a half-decent horse when she sees it. I'll have a chat with her on the phone.'

'Oh, yes, *please!* She said an adult. To talk to an adult.'

Rowan couldn't believe it. She wanted to throw her arms round Millie Mildmay and hug her, whiskers and all.

'Of course, it's crazy. To interfere, I mean. But it's true Lucy Prebble is still looking at show jumpers for Matty. She's got tunnel vision. Quite unsuitable.'

'It can lie down, for her to mount,' Rowan breathed.

'How sweet! How nice. I'd like one like that. If Lucy turns it down, it might suit me.'

Rowan was now almost sobbing with joy. Why on earth couldn't she be cool? she wondered. Everything mattered so! She couldn't believe it when something went right for a change.

Millie Mildmay, very perceptive, said, 'Is it a secret, you finding this horse?'

'My mother knows and won't have anything to do with it. Nor will Charlie or Josephine. If we go, I'd rather they didn't know.'

'Fine. We'll keep it under our hat, eh? I'll ring Amelia tonight and have a chat.'

'Oh, thank you!'

Rowan found that her day had turned into a red letter day with gold stars and cannons exploding. All her worries suddenly seemed over. And Birdie had been fabulous and so had she, not falling off or in any way making a fool of herself.

When Auntie Millie put her down and drove away the others had not yet arrived, but Charlie and Josephine were unboxing.

'How did you do?' Rowan shouted.

They laughed. They could see by her face that she had done very well.

'We won! We won!' she shouted. 'And Birdie was clear all the way, and show jumping as well!'

They both hugged her, and said all the right things, and then told her that Wilfred had gone beautifully for Priscilla and they came fourth in the Novice and Mr Hicks was so pleased that he hadn't minded that Out of the West had done a bad dressage and knocked down three show-jumps – 'But he did a superb cross country inside the time!' Mr Hicks had taken Priscilla home in glory and, before he departed, tipped Charlie ten pounds. 'Like I was a stable lad. I couldn't believe it!'

When the others came back they were all so excited that no one thought to ask Rowan why she had travelled home with Auntie Millie. Even her mother never remarked on it, and when Auntie Millie rang later in the evening to talk to Rowan, she assumed it was to congratulate her on the day.

Mrs Mildmay told Rowan she had made an appointment for Sunday. 'Amelia has asked us both to lunch. How very nice! We'll have a good day out, however the horse turns out. I'll pick you up at ten o'clock, dear.'

Rowan didn't tell anyone, not even her mother, hugging the possibility to herself. Every day of the week seemed twice as long as usual. When Auntie Millie's old rattle-trap pulled up outside their cottage on Sunday morning, Pauline Watkins was at the top of a ladder upstairs decorating her bedroom. Rowan shouted up the stairs, 'I'll be back this evening!'

And the journey was under way, the battered Land Rover tearing across the countryside as once the old lady's point-to-pointers had been driven over the jumps. Rowan, used to being driven too fast by her father, at least had never felt in his car that it might fly to bits at any minute, which made the journey with Millie a good deal more hair-raising. Rowan had to keep a hold on her hopes – she couldn't remember what Mrs Arbuthnot had said about her old circus horse . . . it was bound to be a crock, unacceptable to Lucy Prebble. She thought – too late – she should have got Matty on her side, telling her in advance of the plan. Sensing her anxiety, Auntie Millie patted her on the knee and said, 'You've a very nervous temperament, my child. It's bad for the horses.'

They found the Arbuthnot establishment after several false alarms – 'Yes, I remember, this is her lane. Her house is at the bottom' four times before the right house appeared. ('My memory is not what it was.') The lane was the worst yet, and the house a dilapidated bungalow set before an equally dilapidated stableyard – once a beautiful brick-built set of barns but now reinforced with breeze blocks and corrugated iron in necessary places, giving the whole place a decidedly one-eyed look.

'Poor old Amelia,' said Auntie Millie. 'She's not been the same since Archie died.'

Amelia Arbuthnot turned out to be another Auntie Millie as far as Rowan could see, the same weather-beaten look and hip-unhappy walk, but she greeted them warmly. She largely ignored Rowan, and Rowan could see that there was to be a lot of reminiscing and irrelevant talk before they got down to business. She had to reconcile herself as they sat down in the untidy kitchen while Amelia set out ham and baked potatoes and packet bread. At any other time she would have found the horsey conversation interesting, but she was too sweaty with anticipation now to appreciate it. It seemed an age before the talk got around to the purpose of the visit.

Auntie Millie gave a graphic account of Lucy Prebble's tunnel vision and poor Matty's disability, and of how Rowan so desperately wanted to buy Birdie.

'You're the gel that rang me up?' Mrs Arbuthnot at last noticed that Rowan was there.

'Yes. You said you had an Andalusian circus horse that needed a good home. The Prebbles would be a terribly good home.'

'Hmm.'

'I thought it would be worth having a look at him,' Auntie Millie said.

At last they got up from the table. The two old girls were talking about somebody called the Galloping Golightly as they tottered out into the stable yard and stood for another five minutes outside the barn door remembering a hunt with the Beaufort which had ended in disaster – hilarious, by their squawks of laughter – then at last Amelia opened the door and they went inside. There was a row of six looseboxes, two of which were occupied.

'The end one,' said Amelia.

Rowan ran forward and peered over the door.

Somehow, because it was a circus horse, in spite of being told it was a bay, she had still expected spots or stripes or something ridiculous. But the horse was a bay, not commanding, but with a presence of great dignity and kindness. Looking at him, Rowan could sense it. He had large gentle eyes which surveyed her with the same curiosity as she bent on him. A beautiful head, a crested neck with a long mane, and a strong compact body. Clean black legs.

'Oh, he's beautiful.'

Auntie Millie snorted up behind her.

'Hmm.' After a long consideration, she said, 'Nice.'

'I can assure you,' Amelia said, 'as far as anything in this world is a certainty, this horse is safe, kind and honest. He would not harm a hair of your little girl's head.'

'Does he go on? She's no legs to use, remember.'

'Yes. He walks out. He obeys the word. If you want to trot you just say so.'

Rowan thought this was a frightfully good idea. Why weren't all horses trained like that?

'What's wrong with him?'

'He's getting on. He's fifteen. His tendons wouldn't stand a day's hunting and jumping wouldn't be wise. But hacking around – fine.'

'It would get her going,' Auntie Millie said.

'Do you want to try him?'

'Why not?' said Auntie Millie.

Rowan had never thought to see Auntie Millie ride. Amelia fetched her a pair of steps from the tack room and she climbed into the saddle and rode out into the paddock. The horse went with his neck arched, delicately mouthing his bit, and the old lady sat perfectly in the saddle, smiling. When she said, 'Trot', the horse trotted, smooth as silk, and Auntie Millie sat without rising, like one piece with the horse. Rowan watched, entranced. The funny old bundle of clothes in the saddle rode like Charlie, like Josephine. When she cantered, she was as graceful as a girl, all in one with the perfectly collected horse.

When she came back to the gate, she said, 'I don't know about Matty, but I'll take this horse off your hands, Amelia.'

'Done,' said Amelia.

'How much are you asking?'

'A gift to you, my dear. He needs a home.'

'Great.'

'You can borrow my trailer and take him with you. You've got the Land Rover, I see. I don't need the trailer for a month or so.'

'Why not?' said Auntie Millie.

The two old ladies set about connecting the Land Rover to a decrepit trailer that was parked in a barn, while Rowan was told to untack the horse. She did so, bemused. She was wondering if her plan had gone haywire – it hadn't been her idea for Auntie Millie to have the horse, for goodness' sake! But the fact they were taking it back with them . . . she didn't know what to think. It was hopeless to ask. She might have been invisible for all the notice they took of her. They put straw in the trailer and a haynet, and Amelia led the bay horse inside while Auntie Millie put up the back ramp. Then they kissed affectionately and Auntie Millie got into the driving seat.

'Oh, by the way, Rowan said he lies down for mounting. That could be very useful out in the country.'

'He stretches down, straddles his legs out and his back goes down about four inches. Just tap him behind the knees with your whip and say "Down".'

'Brilliant!'

Rowan hopped up. Auntie Millie started the engine. Rowan shouted at Amelia, 'What's his name?'

'Matador,' she shouted back.

Matador for Matty, Rowan registered. But was he?

560

'Are you going to keep him?' she asked after they had bumped down the long drive and were out on the road.

Auntie Millie brayed with laughter.

'Poor Rowan! You've done a great job, dear, finding a horse like that. Now you're frightened I'm going to keep him! Well, I certainly will if Lucy Prebble is stupid enough to turn him down. We'll say he's *ours* just for now, see how it goes. You must have found out by now that you can't tell Lucy Prebble what's good for her. She has to be tricked.'

'How do you mean?'

'She has to make up her own mind. If you tell her, she'll jib. If she was a horse, she'd have been shot by now.'

Rowan wasn't sure what to make of this. Her plan had gone swimmingly but now seemed out of her control.

'Work on Matty,' Auntie Millie said.

Rowan was no wiser when they got home. It transpired that Auntie Millie had no stable to put the horse in, and Rowan hadn't the nerve to take him to the Hawes. Perhaps Babar would have him – then she remembered.

'We've got a loosebox at home! We can put him there tonight.'

'Good thinking!'

In the now fading light they coasted down the long hill into the village and Auntie Millie pulled up outside the gate into Rowan's back garden. The lights were on in the cottage and there was a faint smell of baking in the air. Rowan had already cleaned out the loosebox and scrubbed the old manger; the roof was sound and the doors oiled.

'We'll unload him and put him in, then I'll go and fetch some hay and straw from Mr Bailey down the road.'

Rowan's mother, hearing their voices, came out to see what was going on.

'I'm borrowing your loosebox for a night or two, my dear, for a horse I've acquired. I'm sure you don't mind?'

Without waiting for an answer she bobbed back to the Land Rover and drove away, leaving Pauline Watkins peering suspiciously over the half-door.

'Just tell me what you're up to, my girl!'

It had been a long day, and Rowan was no longer sure of herself. She felt exhausted with all her conflicting emotions.

She said, 'It's that horse in Norfolk I told you about. Mrs Mildmay took me to look and liked him. He's hers now. That woman gave him to her.'

'I thought he was for Matty.'

Rowan didn't know any longer. She realized she felt very tired, shattered by the long, bone-shaking drive and the eternal doubts. Auntie Millie came back with feed and bedding and they made the horse comfortable and gave him a tin bath full of water. He seemed quite unfazed by his new quarters and fell to munching his hay. Rowan supposed his circus life had made him used to new quarters all the time.

'You can look after him for a few days,' Auntie Millie said when they were finished. 'Ride him out and let everyone see him. Tell them he belongs to me and you're keeping him for me until I get my stable mended. Let the gossip flow, my dear. You'll find Lucy Prebble will be along in no time.'

'But will you – do you want him – for your own?'

'Oh my dear, if only–! But those days are gone, I'm afraid. He's for Matty, like you said.'

At last, Rowan thought – she could sleep happily! Her plan was working out. Auntie Millie was a darling. Her mother was looking confused, as well she might, but Auntie Millie gave her a quick hug and said, 'You've got a very determined daughter, my dear. You should be proud of her.'

She drove away.

'Should I?' asked Pauline Watkins dubiously.

But Rowan had no answer.

Rowan had a lesson the next evening after school with Josephine. When she went up to High Hawes she collected Birdie's saddle and bridle and, instead of catching her out of the field, she whizzed home on her bicycle and tacked up Matador. She had to let out the bridle which was a muddle and the bit was rather small and the saddle girth only met up with a colossal amount of tugging but eventually, flushed and anxious, she led Matador out of his stable into the lane and mounted him. She was trembling with anxiety. He felt enormous after Birdie but, somehow, kindness seemed to exude from him. She turned his head up the hill and he strode out happily, mouthing his bit, as light on her hand as Birdie and every bit as lovely.

By the time she turned into the yard at High Hawes she was alight with excitement. Nobody – but nobody – could fault this horse!

'What on earth—?'

First to see her was Lizzie. She let out a shriek. Hugh

looked out of Cascade's box. His eyes came out on stalks.

'Whatever's that?'

Charlie came out of the feed shed with a haynet over his shoulder, stopped in his tracks and said, 'Birdie's grown in the night! Whatever have you got there?'

'I've come for my lesson.'

'On what, might I enquire?'

'Matador.'

'And where did Matador come from?'

'He's Mrs Mildmay's.'

They positively reeled in their tracks.

'Auntie Millie's?'

'She put him in my loosebox till she's mended her own and she told me to exercise him. So I am.'

She touched Matador with her heels and he walked on to the gate of the school. The Hawes stood in a row and watched, speechless. Charlie opened it for her. She went through and started walking round, feeling herself flushing up as Charlie, Lizzie, Hugh and Shrimp leaned over the rails to watch. After two circuits, when no one had said anything, she said softly, 'Trot', and Matador trotted. He tucked in his nose and went into a perfect dressage medium trot, as if she were a brilliant rider. But she only had to sit there. He felt as if he moved on springs, and to sit to his trot was as easy as sitting to his walk. And when he cantered it was like sitting in an armchair, gently floating round the school, riding on a cloud. She circled to the left and to the right, and came back to the gate to halt. He stood foursquare, like a statue.

Josephine had joined the silent row of spectators. They all stared, and Rowan smiled. She leaned forward and patted Matador's neck.

'Nice, isn't he?'

Charlie smiled. 'He's for Matty?'

They all started to scream at her, 'Where did you get him?' 'Did you buy him?' 'Is he really Auntie Millie's?' 'How did you find out about him?'

Charlie said, 'You are a clever little twit, Rowan, aren't you?' But he was still smiling. 'I think you might have got it right this time.'

Josephine wanted to try him, so did all the others. But Josephine said only her, and mounted him and Rowan watched this dream horse drifting round the school. With every stride he took her pride and happiness expanded, until she thought she would burst. The others were all leaping about shouting, 'Fantastic!' and 'Brill!' and 'Magic!'

Rowan tried to remember the drawbacks. 'He's fifteen and his tendons aren't very good. Light hacking only, she said.'

'He's perfect, Rowan.' Josephine brought him back to the gate. Charlie gave him a Polo mint out of his pocket and the horse bent his head and lifted it delicately between his lips. 'You're a great fellow.' Charlie patted his neck.

'What's the plan?'

'Gossip, Auntie Millie said. Mrs Prebble will hear the gossip and come and look.'

'Of course she will! Everyone who hears that Auntie Millie has got herself a horse will want to have a look.'

'If Mrs Mildmay is in charge, you can't go wrong,' Josephine said.

'You are clever, Rowan,' Lizzie breathed. 'We couldn't work out what you were up to, going home with Auntie Millie.'

'I said it was a plot,' Hugh shouted. 'I was right!'

Charlie laughed. 'Is she paying you livery, Rowan?'

Rowan was flooded with relief, that all her beloved Hawes were so approving. Josephine said she should forgo the lesson, and just hack out with Lizzie to give the horse an easy exercise before it got dark. So Rowan and Lizzie rode across the dusking downs and

Rowan, at last, thought everything might turn out all right.

Rowan loved having a horse in her own loosebox. Going down in the morning, pulling on her anorak and smelling the first hint of autumn, seeing the last star fading over the top of the downs above as she went down the garden and hearing Matador's soft whicker of welcome as he heard her step, made getting up quite different. No snuggling back under the blankets when the alarm clock went off. If she was extra early she had time to take him out to graze on what was supposed to be their lawn for ten minutes after he had had his feed. And every evening she rode him out with Lizzie. Coming home, putting his bed right and filling his haynet, she loved to lean over the door before she went in to watch him eating, clean and snug in the old box. Birdie might miss her, but Rowan was no longer anxious. She had done all that was possible to do and perhaps, if it all went wrong, she would still have Matador. It was too soon to count her chickens and Rowan had – at last – learned to be philosophical.

The gossip travelled. Jerry Patterson rang up to find out if he was hearing things – Auntie Millie had bought a horse? Otty rang up, and Babar came round to see and have a ride. 'Oh, what a dream!'

Four nights later Matty came down. She was on her own, having swung all the way on her crutches. Rowan was in the stable, mucking out.

'I had to see this! Auntie Millie buying a horse! Why is he with you?'

'Just until her stable's mended,' Rowan said, trying to sound nonchalant.

'But she's all crocked up. She can't ride any more.'

'She thought he was suitable. That's the point.'

'Holy cow, Auntie Millie riding!'

Mattie laid her arms on the loosebox door and peered in. Matador turned round and came to see if there were any Polo mints.

'Well, you're a nice man, I must say.' Matty laughed. 'Someone said he was a circus horse. I thought he'd be one of those spotted wonders.'

'He's brilliant. You just have to say, and he does it.'

'Like what?'

'Look.'

Rowan sent up a prayer. She touched Matador behind the knees with the broom handle and said, 'Down.'

Matador turned his head and looked at her, as if in surprise. He scraped his hindlegs out behind him like a

569

dog stretching, and slid his forelegs out in front of him and went down so that his belly was not far off floor level. Rowan slipped onto his back, and Matador slithered his feet back underneath him. He then turned to Matty for another titbit.

Matty was impressed. 'That's great. It's all right getting on with a chair in the stableyard, but not much good if you have to get off in the country and there's not a gate or a bank for miles. Great for Auntie Millie.'

'That's what she said. But I don't know if she's going to keep him. A friend gave him to her. She told me she didn't really think she could ride again, but he was too lovely to refuse.'

'Might you have him?'

'I don't know. He's fantastic to ride.'

Matty opened the loosebox door. 'Tell him to go down again.'

Rowan gave the aids, and Matador straddled himself out again. Matty hopped forward and was on his back in one quick movement. Matador gathered himself up again and turned back to his haynet, snatching a mouthful.

'Hey, that's great!' Matty laughed.

Her head was nearly touching the rafters. She

said, 'Go and get his bridle and I'll ride him out.'

Rowan fetched the bridle, feeling really scared. She knew she shouldn't do it, but she also knew she must. She put the bridle on and passed the reins back to Matty.

'It feels fantastic!'

Matty was as white as a sheet, and more scared than Rowan.

'You only have to tell him,' said Rowan. 'Walk.'

'Open the door.'

Rowan opened it. Matty said, 'Walk on,' and rode out into the garden. The gate into the lane was open where Rowan had come in on her bike, and Matty rode out of the gate and turned up the lane. She was bareback and had no hat on. Rowan ran after her.

'I say, Matty!'

But Matty didn't stop or even turn round. Matador was walking out with his eager springy pace, disappearing up the lane in the beginning of the evening dusk. Rowan watched her, feeling sick with responsibility – was it all her fault, or a bit Matty's? All hers, she suspected.

She supposed she ought to go with her. But then she assumed Matty would be back in a minute. She finished off the mucking out, only a matter of a couple of minutes and then, worried, went to look up the lane. But there was no sign of Matty coming back. Rowan went and fetched her bike. She's gone to call on the Hawes, she thought. It was obvious – see their faces!

Excited, Rowan pedalled up the hill, head down. It was just starting to go dusk and the sort of evening that smelled amazing and promised all sorts of exciting things ahead. Or so Rowan always thought. She was half laughing, half frightened, at the success of her plan. Matty riding into the yard at High Hawes ... they would all die, seeing her! Rowan couldn't wait.

She pedalled into the yard, but it was all quiet. She went round the back, and found only Shrimp bringing Bonzo in from the field.

'Hi! Have you seen her?'

'Seen who?' asked Shrimp.

'Matty. Matty riding!'

'Matty riding? Never! Who on – you mean—?'

'Isn't she here?'

'I haven't seen her.'

'What about the others?'

'They're having tea. Matty hasn't been here. Nobody's seen her that I know of.'

'But she came up here, riding Matador.'

'She must have gone past.'

'Did you hear her? Did you hear hooves on the road?'

'Now you come to think of it, yes. Bonzo whinnied. I thought it was you. About five minutes ago.'

'Where's she gone?'

Rowan, thinking of Matty bareback, hatless . . . what was she thinking of, to have ridden away? Matty all alone, not even her crutch . . . the plan was working so well it was terrifying.

'She must have gone on the downs,' Shrimp said. 'Where else?'

'Oh, I don't believe it!'

There was no denying her flooding guilt now. Was Matty mad? Rowan ran towards the house and the rock that was Joan Hawes. She would know what to do. They were all sitting round the table eating and were startled by her hysterical arrival. 'Matty's gone!' she wailed.

Hugh thought it was terribly funny – 'What you wanted, wasn't it?' – Charlie and Josephine looked serious and Joan Hawes said, 'But it's nearly dark! Are you sure she's gone on the downs?'

'Where else could she go? She didn't come back.'

'It's the most likely place,' Charlie said.

'She's got no saddle!'

'But if that horse is the magic horse he appears to be, no harm will come to her,' Josephine said sensibly.

'It's strange ground to him,' Charlie said.

'And it's dark. The child is mad,' Joan Hawes said abruptly. 'Really – you children! We'll have to go and look for her.'

'Josephine and I can ride up – we'll find her,' Charlie said. 'Don't worry. She won't have gone far.'

'I don't want Lucy Prebble up here, for goodness' sake! Demanding to know where she is. Off you go, and hurry up. Rowan, you are a lunatic.'

'I thought she was just going up a bit and back! I didn't know she'd just go!'

'You stay with me. We'll go in the Land Rover. Lizzie and Hugh, you stay here. You can deal with Mrs Prebble if she rings up. Or no, on second thoughts, don't answer the phone. We want Matty back first – if we're lucky, Lucy won't find out.'

They scattered. As Rowan ran out, Josephine caught her arm and whispered, 'Cheer up, Rowan, he won't hurt her. Remember, the girl's a great rider.'

And Rowan, running for the Land-Rover, held onto that thought.

Matty, coming out through the trees, saw a new moon,

a thin sliver of light, shivering over the shoulder of the far down. She knew that you wished on a new moon. The wish was easy: 'I want – oh, I want – to do all this again, to be able – to ride. To run. Not to be hopping like a frog.' The horse's soft coat, just darkening with winter, was warm under her thighs and the intelligent ears were pricked up ahead, watching the chalky path in the dusk. Matty turned him onto the grass. She knew this way so well. It was like coming home, passing the sarsen stone, turning uphill where the way divided, following the footprints where the Hawes exercised. The horse strode out, kind and willing.

She had only meant, after all, to go up the lane and back. But Matty had forgotten that now, revelling in the excitement that flooded her. She hadn't even thought that she wanted to ride again – not all that aggro with her mother again! But this was something else, this feeling of total trust in the horse moving quietly up towards the stars that glittered over the black crest of the down. Matty felt she could touch them. When she gained the summit she could see in every direction, across the dark horizons of the downs beyond and back to the lights of the village in the valley directly below. She felt like God.

She only had to say to him, 'Trot', and then, 'Canter',

and then she was floating along between the earth and the sky, the muffled thud of hooves the only sound, the cold air flying past her cheeks, the long mane streaming out between her hands. Everything had come right at last and she knew she could ride for ever.

When Matty didn't come home and it was dark, Mrs Prebble rang the Hawes household. Lizzie and Hugh heard the phone ringing but, acting on instructions, didn't answer it. Mrs Prebble then rang Pauline Watkins.

'Is Matty with you?'

'Not that I know of. Rowan's out in the stable. I'll go and ask her.'

Pauline Watkins went down the garden to find an empty stable, no sign of either Rowan or Matty, and a pair of crutches lying in the grass. 'Don't panic,' she said to herself. She wasn't sure what she was most frightened of: what Rowan and Matty were getting up to, or what Mrs Prebble was going to say about it.

'Gone out on a *horse?*' bawled Lucy Prebble. 'What horse?'

'It belongs to Mrs Mildmay.'

'*Mrs Mildmay!* What sort of a horse?'

'Don't ask me. Big and brown. You'd better ask her yourself.'

'I most certainly will! I shall be over directly.'

Pauline Watkins groaned. She had no idea, when it all got technical. Was Rowan to blame? It was part of the ploy to get Mrs Prebble to let them have Birdie, she remembered, but Mrs Prebble had sounded far from happy. The more she thought about her, the less Pauline Watkins wanted to face Mrs Prebble. After a few minutes' thought, she got out her car and drove up to High Hawes. She had thought to find it buzzing, but when she drove into the yard everything was silent and in darkness. She turned off her engine and sat there, feeling annoyed.

Lizzie and Hugh, hiding in the feed shed, realized who it was and came out reluctantly. They told her what had happened.

Then Mrs Prebble arrived.

Then Auntie Millie.

Then Joan Hawes and Rowan.

They all stood talking nineteen to the dozen in the stableyard. Rowan crept out with Lizzie. They ran out through the wood and to the gate that led out on to the downs. Rowan was in tears again, and Lizzie white faced.

'They're going to ring the police!'

'Auntie Millie won't let them,' Lizzie said stoutly.

'Don't be stupid. If she's out there, it's because she's enjoying it. Isn't that what you wanted?'

'Yes!'

'Well then. Charlie and Josephine will bring her back, don't worry. There's nothing wrong.'

'Yet! Mrs Prebble's furious!'

'She's always like that – you know that. Mum will cool her down. And Auntie Millie will shut her up. And everything will be all right.'

'Suppose—'

'Oh, shut up! She'll be all right!'

They leaned on the gate looking up at the dark crest of the downs. The new moon hung there, bright and consoling.

'Have you ever ridden in the dark?' Lizzie asked. 'It's lovely.'

'Like the night you rode Birdie at camp? It was like this, wasn't it?'

'Yes. And it turned out all right. So will this.'

Rowan was shivering. They neither of them wanted to go back.

'Auntie Millie will have sorted it all out now. They'll be boozing in the kitchen. They'll be buttering up Mrs Prebble.'

'I hope so.'

They sat on the gate, waiting. After what seemed a very long time, they thought they heard the sound of voices, the chink of a hoof on the chalk.

'Listen!'

Somebody laughed.

'It's Matty,' Lizzie whispered.

They opened the gate, and in the darkness saw the gleam of moonlight on three dark horses moving slowly down the hill towards them. Charlie was in front on Out of the West, Matty next, and Josephine bringing up the rear on Wilfred.

'It's us!' Lizzie shouted. 'Everyone's waiting for you!'

'Who's everyone?' Charlie asked.

They pulled up and heard the story. 'All of them, all waiting,' Lizzie said. 'We couldn't bear it.'

'No harm's done,' said Charlie.

Matty, riding past, leaned down to Rowan and said, 'He's wonderful.'

They rode on and Lizzie and Rowan followed. When they got to the yard Rowan went up to Matty and said, 'I'll take him home.'

'You can put him in a box and come indoors,' Charlie said. 'If everyone's there, you should—'

'No! I'll take him.'

Before he could say any more she snatched the reins

out of Matty's hands and led him away out of the yard. He came kindly. Rowan walked on dumbly down the long hill to home, seeing their long shadows bobbing across the lane. The horse had looked after her. Matty's eyes had been shining under the dark swing of her black hair. She was like a new person.

'Dear Matador,' Rowan said.

His haynet was hanging up and the bed forked out. Rowan slipped off his bridle and shut the door behind him. She stayed there, watching him. It was cold now, with the smell of autumn and the dew heavy in the trampled grass, the smell of cows coming up from the river. If she went to the gate she could hear the soft cropping of the ponies on the far bank, see the white ghost of Cascade and the shadow that was Birdie. *Her* Birdie. When would her mother come?

But it was Charlie who came.

He found her sitting outside the stable door, her head buried in her arms.

'They're all celebrating up there,' he said. 'Laughing and shouting. Why don't you come?'

'Is it all right?'

'Yes, she's like a cat purring. She's given you Birdie. She wants to see you. I think she wants to give you a kiss.' He laughed.

'You're joking!'

'No, truly. Would I, about you and Birdie?'

'You mean, it's all right?'

'I've told you, it's all right.'

And Rowan burst into tears again, and went back to High Hawes with Charlie.